# SWORD AND SORCERESS

## AN ANTHOLOGY OF HEROIC FANTASY

*Edited by*
*Marion Zimmer Bradley*

**DAW BOOKS, INC.**
DONALD A. WOLLHEIM, PUBLISHER

1633 Broadway, New York, NY 10019

First Printing, May 1984

1  2  3  4  5  6  7  8  9

  DAW TRADEMARK REGISTERED
U.S. PAT. OFF. MARCA
REGISTRADA. HECHO EN U.S.A.

PRINTED IN U.S.A.

# CONTENTS

# THE HEROIC IMAGE OF WOMEN: WOMAN AS WIZARD AND WARRIOR

*An Introduction by Marion Zimmer Bradley*

The special sub-genre of fantasy known as "sword and sorcery" has been the last to be integrated between man and woman. Until recently, this bastion of male-dominated adventure fiction was the last stronghold of the brawny male hero; women were the reward or the incitement for his adventures, but never shared them. Woman, in sword-and-sorcery fiction, when not a mere "screaming maiden" to be rescued from dragons, dangers and doom-laden Evil Wizards, remained strictly offstage, emerging now and again to reward the hero with her dower kingdom and a chaste kiss.

But women read fantasy too, and we get tired of identifying with male heroes. Many of us wanted our own adventures, in the manner of Jirel of Joiry, creation of old-time fantasy writer C.L. Moore.

There were occasional women characters who stood out as independent. Robert E. Howard, creator of "Conan the barbarian" created also Red Sonya, who, having seen her mother raped and murdered, refused to give herself to any man who could not best her with the sword. Elric of Melnibone, in the series created by Michael Moorcock, encountered the occasional woman warrior or Evil Sorceress.

When I first began writing, and later editing anthologies featuring women in heroic fiction, I quickly discovered that I could not write the usual story, substituting a mighty Amazon warrior for the hearty hero. Women, in general, do not go on quests in the manner of male heroes. (We will here skip about four paragraphs of Freudian psychology, explaining the desires of women warriors in terms of sexual envy or desire for male appurtenances; it just doesn't happen that way.)

It has been pointed out by more than one authority that Amazons, a constantly recurring legend in almost every culture, were not invented by women. Some authorities, on what seems to be very shaky scholarship, have tagged this universal appearance of Amazon figures as "evidence" of a pre-existing, primordial "matriarchal society" in which women ruled and men were subservient. I find no hard evidence whatever for the existence of this culture, and I tend to get a little annoyed when feminists blithely speak of "the old days of the matriarchy" as if it were a proven fact. I like to distinguish carefully between history and fantasy. If feminist theory feels that "if Amazons did not exist, we will have to invent them," so much the worse for feminist theory. If we cannot live with the truth, so much the worse for *us*.

Yet the concept of Amazons has been with us for a good long time. In an excellent book, Abby Kleinbaum points out that "neither in the Greek nor Roman classical tradition did the Amazon image serve to glorify women. Instead it was used by male authors, artists and political leaders," and, as she points out, in these recurring tales, the Amazon exists to be defeated by men, and usually raped or humbled sexually as well. "The Amazon image," Kleinbaum points out again, "is always on the verge of breeding out or fading away." The Amazon is invented to be defeated, again and again, converted into a servile wife, conquered or killed. "But, dead or alive in the end, the Amazon in her never survives." Kleinbaum points out "What everyone wants to hear is the story of that splendid Amazon queen whose hatred of men melted away before the military and sexual prowess of a true hero." The Greeks had to invent Amazons, she seems to be saying, to prove that they could conquer women; not only the semi-idiots in virtual purdah whom they actually married, but the theoretical "strong woman" as well.

This image is very magnetic, but very threatening, both to men and women. When, in the course of the Darkover stories, I began writing of Free Amazons/Renunciates, many women felt threatened and defensive about them, and felt compelled to write and tell me, a stranger, how truly liberated they were in their own marriages, and how little they wanted to be associated with any idea of free women. Even though most feminists considered my realistic and relatively tame Free Amazons as "a sellout to men, a copout from the challenge of creating a truly feminist society," many men and women felt I had gone further with the Free Amazons than was safe or seemly. Many women found role models and freedom in the Darkovan Free Amazons; yet to many more they were, like all Amazons, an intolerable threat and a menace. Some called my first novel of the Free Amazons "the mandatory femlib book which must be written by every woman writer."

Yet it was not all men who wrote the classic story proving that men could comfortably defeat the Amazon image; not only men who invented the Amazon in order to prove that she could be defeated. Women, too, wrote of Amazons to prove that they could defeat the Amazon in *themselves*. When I was editing two volumes of Free Amazon stories—for we received two or three Free Amazon stories for every Darkover story on any other subject—I actually classified the usual Amazon story as what we called "Subject A." In general, this story was as follows: "Free Amazon finds a man she can love and trust."

In the process of discovering whether sword-and-socery fiction could *truly* show the woman as wizard and warrior, I discovered that the field had already developed its own cliché situations. As I said just above, the first was the story which defused the woman's anxiety about competing with men: the "Subject A" story in which a Free Amazon, lonely and unhappy among women, found a man she could love and trust, and all too often, alas, a man to whom she felt compelled to give up her unwanted freedom. I have a certain revulsion, personally, against this story. Yet it evidently has its own power, or it would not be written by so many women.

The second classic theme—or perhaps even the first—is the story of rape and revenge. Red Sonya, mentioned above, is a character embodying this classic image. Still another is Jirel of Joiry's first adventure, *The Black God's Kiss*. Written fifty years ago this summer, Catherine Moore tells the story of Jirel of Joiry, made captive and humiliated by Guillaume, who goes into a terrifying world of alien wizardry to seek revenge—revenge she cherishes even more than an offered escape. After many terrors in the underworld, Jirel finds her revenge in the "Black God's Kiss"—which, when brought out into the light and bestowed on her conqueror, instantly kills Guillaume—and makes Jirel aware that she loved the man who had conquered her, that his death had extinguished all the light in the world for her. The classic women's story, then—that a woman's pride only stood in the way of true happiness—interpreted as surrender to a man.

But very few of us, woman readers who grew up in the early days of sword-and-sorcery fiction, interpreted it that way. We all grew up excited by the possibility of being free and independent swordswomen in our own right. Many of us even managed to conceal from ourselves the subtext that this revenge would harm us more than our conquerors, or that our true happiness should lie in surrender. And many of us went on to create women who were genuinely autonomous. Unlike Jirel, today's Amazon warriors do not love and defer to their conquerors.

In creating this anthology, I tried to avoid stories which simply turned the old cliché upside down, and made the women dominate the men. I avoided stories which showed women simply as the obedient "sidekick" or "faithful Indian companion" of the Mighty Hero, but I also avoided stories where the women dominated the simple-minded men. I think all of these stories deal with men and women simply as people, as fellow human beings who can work side by side without the need for one or the other to dominate or conquer.

I had hoped at first to avoid the story of "rape and revenge," but I soon realized that this is a very real archetype and image in heroic fiction. I once commented that in the sword-and-sorcery story, the seamy underside is always rape; that where men seek adventure, one of the things they seem to seek is women to be distributed as prizes and objects. The story of revenge is common enough in fiction; the man who, deprived of home, kinsfolk or property, goes after reprisal. One of the commonest themes in fiction about, or even *by* women, from Jirel of Joiry to the present day, is the woman who demands honorable revenge for her own rape or dishonor. The theme of the woman who defends or avenges herself, then, is an honorable theme, and I bought three stories on that theme. In "Severed Heads," Glen Cook's young heroine undertakes a quest to avenge her honor—but with an extra twist; the rapist had added injury to insult by kidnapping the young son she had borne to her ravager, and while she could live with the first assault, she refused to endure the second. In Jennifer Roberson's "Blood of Sorcery," the imprisoned shapechanger must fight her way free, or live with the burden of the sorcerer's taint. And in "Sword of Yraine," young Shanna sees her priestesses and her young friends attacked and raped before her eyes; shall she submit likewise, or shall she take up the sword in her own defense? None of these are cliché situations, but all demand serious moral choice and personal accountability.

There are other kinds of stories. Phyllis Ann Karr's Frostflower and Thorn story, as well as Emma Bull's "The Rending Dark" show a woman warrior and a more peaceful woman traveling together, the two sides of womanhood. Aynber in Charles de Lint's "Valley of the Troll" travels with her wizard friend Thorn Hawkwood in an equal partnership, as does Skorpia in Janet Fox's "Gate of the Damned." The Dahomey woman warrior Dossouye, in Charles Saunders' "Gimmile's Songs" is vulnerable to the musician in Gimmile. Why do women become warriors or wizards? The answers are as many as the stories.

As in all good fiction, though these stories range from heart-rending seriousness to the heights of farce—as in the delightful thief-outwits-thief foolery of "Taking Heart" or "Valley of the Troll"—the characters face adventures which force them to decide for themselves what they are and what they will be. This is, I think, the value of heroic fiction—that it forces us to confront the heroic within ourselves—and to face our own nightmares and self-images. I don't think this need is limited to men, or to women. Stories limited to men's affairs are only half the story. Stories limited to women's affairs are, equally, only half of the human truth. There is male and female within each of us, and I think both men and women can read these stories and find both the good and the bad within ourselves. Valor has neither race nor color—nor does it have gender. That I have chosen stories mostly about women is a personal preference—not a prejudice. That I have chosen stories about both men and women, and written by both men and women, is, I hope, a sign of the times, and a hopeful outlook for the future of heroic fiction. And, since life always imitates art, it may be a heroic sign for the future of both women and men. Anyone can write male sexist fiction: anyone can write feminist propaganda. I hope to avoid both, and to entertain you while I'm doing it. From first-timers to old favorites, I think this anthology has done it. I'm proud of it, and I hope you agree with me.

Because, whatever the philosophical bias for choosing the stories, there is only one purpose in fiction, and that is to entertain the reader, and to make her—or him—think.

MARION ZIMMER BRADLEY

# SWORD
# AND
# SORCERESS

Among the finest of modern sword-and-sorcery writers one must rank Phyllis Ann Karr; her two novels *Frostflower and Thorn* and the sequel *Frostflower and Windbourne* have added enormously to the literature of women warriors and wizards, without resorting to the "naked Amazon in a tin brassiere" variety of story. She has also written an excellent Arthurian novel, *Idylls of the Queen,* but I did not know until I requested biographical and bibliographical details for this biography that she was also a devotee and writer of mystery stories and whodunits, having appeared in such a high-prestige example of that genre as *Ellery Queen's Mystery Magazine.*

Phyllis Ann Karr lives in the American Midwest, a native of Indiana, currently living in Wisconsin. She describes herself as "unmarried and contentedly celibate" stating that this handicaps her only in the writing of modern romances. This hardly seems a loss to the literary world while she goes on writing her excellent stories of Frostflower and Thorn, the sorceress and swordswoman who travel together and frequently find themselves fighting against menaces both mundane and sorcerous; as in this new adventure.
—MZB

# THE GARNET AND THE GLORY
## by Phyllis Ann Karr

The Oldhill men told Frostflower that such a fog as this always meant that Dathru the Terrible had summoned folk to him from strange places, places no one could reach when the fogs lifted.

These two Oldhill men were called Firstson and Thirdson. In spite of their sex, they appeared to be warriors, although more gentle in their manner than most of the female warriors of the Tanglelands. They explained that they were posted here to watch for those whom Dathru summoned to his "Great Chambers." Sometimes these strangers seemed fierce, almost as evil as Dathru himself, and then the watchers in the fog stayed hidden. More often the newcomers seemed simple honest folk, like Frostflower and her companion, unaware why they had been summoned. Then the watchers would come forward and warn them to turn away while they could.

17

Some of the strangers did turn back. Others insisted on continuing the way that would guide them mysteriously to Dathru's Great Chambers. Sometimes loud shrieks came from the direction of the Great Chambers, sometimes laughter, sometimes soft music or other sounds.

Frostflower would have followed whatever unfelt guidance Dathru used to bring his guests to his dwelling. No sorceron could use power for evil purposes and retain it afterwards: therfore, the common folk of the Oldhills, like those of the Tanglelands, were simply seeing evil where none existed. And another sorceron might learn many secrets from one who had mastered such an undreamed skill as bringing visitors bodily from far places, as Dathru had brought the young sorceress and her warrior friend Thorn, somehow, in the fog that dropped down a few hours ago on the sluggish old Glant river . . . and when Frostflower had pushed back the mist, the river banks had no longer been the familiar rolling, weed-matted shores, but the rocky edges of a river the Oldhillers called Down-to-Peace.

Thorn, however. remained cautious of strange sorceri. A year's friendship with Frostflower had not completely quieted her lifelong fears and hatreds of sorcer-folk. "Hellstink, Frost," the warrior insisted, "you don't even know all the sorceri in the Tanglelands. How the demon's toenails can you be sure none of them have ever found some way around your ban on hurting anyone? You've said yourself you can't be sure anymore how your own rules work. And if this Dathru means us well and happy and a cozy, comfortable little discussion over soft curds and cider, why let only you speak the language of this blasted place? Gods, I would have speared these bastards—Firstson and Thirdson—for robbers if you hadn't started telling me what they were shouting at us."

"Perhaps," said Frostflower gently, "Dahtru could touch only my tongue because I am another sorceron. His power can hardly be perfect in this, or he would have touched my mind as well as my tongue, so that I could hear the difference between the two languages as I speak and listen to them."

Thorn grunted. "Demonstink, you can't just say, 'He means well because he's a sorcerer,' and ignore what our friends Firstson and his brother here are trying to tell us."

Frostflower was sure, although her friend had tried to hide it under a bit of swagger, that at first Thorn had been convinced all three of them—she, Frostflower, and the dog Dowl—had been drowned without knowing it and were wandering in the Hellbog of the farmers' creed or the afterdeath world of the One God, or maybe somewhere in between.

"We may be dead, after all," said the sorceress, feeling mischievous. "Dathru—it sounds rather like the name of one of your own gods, does it not? Jehandru, Alrandru—"

"It doesn't translate," said Thorn.

"What?"

"Everything else—Firstson, Oldhills, Down-to-Peace—when you say it, it comes out as good, ordinary words. But Dathru—that one I hear the same when they say it as when you say it. So it doesn't mean anything but 'Dathru'—whatever that means."

"Perhaps it has some meaning in an older tongue, like the names of your gods," Frostflower suggested.

"Yes. And perhaps he didn't put that older language into your head because whatever 'Dathru' means is so ugly it'd frighten even you away. Come on, Frost, let's go back to the boat and get out while we can."

"If Dathru is as evil as you wish to believe," replied the sorceress, "may we not end by rowing forever in the fog on a river that is not our Giant? We must at least have a little rest before we undertake that, Thorn!"

So, in the end, they went with Firstson and Thirdson to the Outpost, to rest until the fog had lifted.

Firstson and Secondson both had wives, Firstdaughter (apparently of another family) and Likely. These women were brave enough to live here with their husbands while the Three-Sons shared the duty of watching and warning strangers who came in the fog, but they were not warriors themselves, and all five of the Oldhill folk seemed to find it incredibly strange that Thorn should follow that calling.

This, however, was nothing to their reaction on getting their first clear look at her knife, Stabber, when she swung off her fog-dampened cloak and they saw the handle showing above the old leather sheath. Secondson, Firstson, and Likely all closed in at once, snatching for the weapon. Firstson caught it from Thorn's sheath and bent to examine it in the firelight, the others clustering noisily round him. Firstdaughter, meanwhile, seemed to take fright at the stranger's knife, and kept as far from it as possible, rubbing her fingers on the sooty, clay-daubed beams above the fire and drawing black marks on her cheeks and forehead as if to protect herself, while Thirdson stood in everybody's way, trying to help Frostflower calm Thorn.

As it proved, the Oldhillers were simply awed and delighted

with the large garnet in the hilt of Thorn's knife. They had never seen this sort of gem, large or small; and, while agreeing that the sheen-amber in the sword's handle, of which Thorn herself was actually prouder, was also a pleasing stone, it was the garnet that most fascinated them. They thought it might have value as a charm, and Firstdaughter, wiping the soot from her face, proposed tying bark around the gem, setting the bark afire, and holding it under water to see whether it would continue to burn. Refusing to try any such experiment, Thorn tied Stabber into its sheath with a length of old trouser-lacing to discourage another snatch for it.

Thorn ate more fully than Frostflower that evening. The Oldhillers had plenty of meat in their small storeroom, but only a small amount of vegetable food and no milk or milk products. Choosing not to risk startling them by growing new vegetables in their sight, Frostflower contented herself with a bowl of fibrous, badly ground porridge and a mug of water.

Thorn never drank wine, but she was not on her guard against the brown beverage made somehow from animals' blood. It must have been fermented, because she relaxed noticeably after drinking a mugful. When Frostflower went to sleep in a kind of trough filled with herbs, Thorn was dicing with the Oldhillers, having succeeded, without spoken language, in teaching them a few Tanglelands games of rolling and counting.

The dice game was loud, the room smoky and bright with the fire, and the sorceress overtired and rather hungry; but at least the herbs in her bedding smelled sweet enough to filter out the worst of the room's other odors. She closed her eyes, concentrated on a simple exercise for sleep, and soon drowsed off.

When she awoke, the fire was faintly glowing embers, the room almost completely dark and filled with snores. One patch of light, like a white shadow in a black landscape, fell on Thorn through the smoke-hole in the roof and showed her breathing smoothly, wearing her belt and dagger even in sleep.

Frostflower smiled, rose softly, and groped her way to the door. Only Dowl woke, his whine blending with the soft squeak of the doorpegs. She took a moment to fondle his shaggy head. He thumped his tail a few times against the floor, sighed, and settled back down to sleep. She slipped outside.

The mist had cleared, and the landscape spread out dark gray in a long, gradual cupping between the Outpost and a distant ridge of low but sharpish hills. Trees and boulders seemed to cast two shadows, in opposite directions. Looking up, Frostflower saw three moons, all full, two on opposite sides of the sky, and one almost directly overhead. None of them was as bright as the moon she knew, but together they shed enough light to dim out all but the brightest stars.

The sorceress hesitated a moment. Then, closing her eyes, she walked forward at random until her feet seemed sure of one direction. How the sorcerer was guiding her she could not say, but what seemed a lingering, beckoning trace of hope left in the air gathered strength again as she walked.

One of the moons was setting by the time Frostflower saw that part of the ridge's outline was made up of nine even, cylindrical shapes, like massive watchtowers, Dathru's Great Chambers.

The atmosphere refracted the setting moon into a huge oblong, rather like a purplish, moss-green egg on its side, to shine behind the Great Chambers. They seemed melancholy, lonely despite their number and closeness, but hardly foreboding. No shrieks issued from them. Frostflower approached.

The middle tower stood on a semi-circular wall and four thick pillars. At first there was just enough light within the base for Frostflower to see the pillars and arches, but as she came closer the interior light brightened until its radiance lay over the ground in five thick streaks, showing the green of the grass.

When she had passed beneath the middle arch the light vanished, leaving only one fine, brilliant line lying like a hair across the smooth stone floor. At its far end, the line broke into short lengths where it fell on a flight of stairs. Dathru must have the same control over light that the sorceri of the Tanglelands had over weather, and he was playing with it for the amusement of his guest and himself. Smiling, Frostflower followed the line and mounted the stairs. At the top was a doorway, covered with a curtain that seemed to be woven from some stuff like softened fish scales spun out into fine, lustrous strands. Frostflower drew the curtain back gingerly.

The light within almost stunned her at first. Then she saw Dathru. His robe was deep crimson and he wore a pendant of several kinds of inlaid wood on a heavy gold chain around his neck. His face, like his body, was neither thin nor fat. The crease across his forehead was deep, and he had wrinkles at the corners of his eyes. His hair, thick, brown, and silvering at the temples, flowed gracefully along his shoulders, some locks mingling in front with the lustrous brown beard that reached halfway to the pendant. Her first sight of him affected her almost as Wonderhope had affected her ten years ago, when they had considered for a time sacrificing their sorcerous power for the sake of lying in one another's arms.

The moment passed, and she saw Dathru as merely another sorcerer, wise, scholarly, and benevolent, although in a far richer home than any sorceri of the Tanglelands could enjoy. The light that had dazzled her came from five glowing glass cubes, each a different color, suspended by silver chains from the painted ceiling. The walls of the room were either formed of or covered by huge panels with pictures worked in copper, gold, and silver filigree. The floor was a geometrical mosaic of black, white, and red marble, laid in large unbroken slabs, perfectly smooth and polished to an almost metallic sheen. Dathru sat in a high-backed armchair of water-clear glass and wore belt, rings, and sandals set with faceted chunks of metal so brightly polished that for a moment Frostflower mistook them for gemstones.

Smiling, he rose and came toward her, arms extended. "Welcome, sister, and forgive me. I had not realized, at first, that yours is one of those rare worlds in which Power depends on virginity. It was an inexcusable oversight, but allow me to say that, looking at you, I could regret very much that you had not come from one of the many worlds where the opposite law holds."

Something in his words seemed at variance with his manner and appearance. "How did I know," said Frostflower, "that you were indeed Dathru, and not a companion of his?"

"Dathru has no companions." His smile widened. "A few servants, yes, but only at my need."

"I think," Frostflower said slowly, "that this other law of power, the . . . opposite to virginity, is not the only difference between your customs and ours."

He nodded. "Not all my guests are quite so ready of understanding. But I would not despise a permanent companion, could I find the right one."

He put his hands around hers. Something in his touch made her pull free again with a shudder. He smiled and touched her arm, this time like a father or teacher. "Do not fear, sweet sorceress. I would do nothing to rob you of your power. How are you called in your world?"

"Frostflower." She was surprised. "You've put the language of your Oldhills into my tongue, and you do not know my name?"

"The language—it's a simple skill. I learned it from one of my first guests, Eriside of the world of two suns. I merely cast the charm like a great net, and it works upon almost all sorcering folk, from whatever world, whose power is near enough akin to mine that it can be adapted to this, my world. But your name I did not know. It must be a beautiful name in your own language, as it is in mine."

"How did you choose me, then, to bring me here? Or do you throw out a net into all these worlds you speak of, and draw in the first creatures you catch?"

"The 'other worlds I speak of?' " he said. "Have you indeed come from so provincial a place as that?" He laughed. "No—I have seen your world, or the very small part of your world which your people inhabit; and I know what skills—what pitifully few skills—you can practice with the power. But I had not hoped to be so fortunate in my 'catch' of your sorcering folk."

He tapped one of the pieces of wood in his pendant. A glass pedestal appeared before his chair. On the pedestal was a thin ring of white gold, about a hand's-breadth in diameter, standing upright on a base of polished wood.

Dathru led Frostflower to the chair. It had a blue velvet cushion on the seat. No Tanglelands sorceri used silk or velvet, since such cloth could only be made at the cost of killing the worms; Frostflower removed the cushion, her fingers tingling with involuntary disgust, before she sat.

Dathru stood on the other side of the pedestal, looking at her through the ring. "Concentrate on the wooden base."

She obeyed, desire for knowledge overcoming the slight suspicion she had begun to feel toward him. Soon she became unaware of his face peering at her through the ring. A pearly fog began to grow up from the wooden base. She let her gaze move upward, following the fog until it filled the ring.

The fog dissolved and left the space inside the ring filled with an image of some small part of the Tanglelands. She saw two sorceri preparing their midday meal. One was growing corn, getting from knees to feet in order to keep one hand on the stalk as it reached maturity. The other remained kneeling, a large purple eggplant ripening between her hands.

"I have watched your people grow plants and heal sicknesses by what I take to be the manipulation of time," said Dathru, "and I have watched them direct winds, clouds, and lightning bolts. Your puny manipulation of the weather does not interest me. I need not wait until storms arise of themselves; I can bring them out of a clear sky."

For the first time in her life, Frostflower felt what the layfolk of the Tanglelands must feel at sight of the skills that she herself had lived with and studied since childhood.

The space within the ring grew misty again, clearing this time to show a different landscape, a forest denser than any she had ever seen before, where strange plants with immense, moist-shiny leaves jostled each other, wildly colored birds and huge insects flew, and a nearly naked man with gleaming skin and a mask of carved wood cooked something smoky on a small, green fire. The third world Dathru showed her seemed to be filled with an immense town, where buildings shaped like elongated drinking cups stood thick as sheep from horizon to horizon, while roads, raised on tall trestles, moved of themselves between the buildings. A fourth scene showed black sand beneath a hazed sky, with two suns shining redly through the haze and a being who looked human, except for the membranes growing from arm to knee, swooping like a bat from a red-leafed tree to a spring that sent up a tall spray of water now and again. And so Dathru went on, showing Frostflower world after world, all silent—for the ring did not carry sound—but all in tiny, exquisite detail, until she ached with jealousy for such power as his. Among the wisdoms and skills of so many worlds, the uses and interpretations of power developed by so many minds, there must surely be such answers as Frostflower sought.

"Could I learn these skills?" she whispered, not quite daring to touch the ring. "To use such a ring, to summon fellow sorceri from all these worlds?"

The last image faded, and once again it was Dathru's face she saw. "You could learn easily enough," he said, "but I have only the one Circle."

"Others could be made?"

"Perhaps. This power is native to my world, little sister Frostflower, but it might possibly be adapted to the skills and materials of yours."

"I will learn! Willingly, eagerly, if I have the power for it . . ."

"And what will you give me in return?" said Dathru.

She was taken aback for a moment. She had never heard of a sorceron asking payment for the sharing of knowledge. Yet other things were bought and sold, so why not teaching? "What do I have," she asked, "that would be a fair price for such a skill?"

"Your technique of manipulating time. For that I would have some use."

"Time?" It was the first skill children were taught, after the basic exercises, in most Tanglelands retreats. "I had not thought that a sorcerer who could do what you can do would be ignorant of such simple skills with time as those we practice."

Dathru shook his handsome head. "What is elemental in one world may be undreamed of in another. Your folk, Frostflower, have perfected the control of time to a degree rare in any world.

To be able to wither an enemy from youth into senility at a touch!''

She shivered. Of all the uses of time manipulation, Dathru had chosen to speak of the sad, desperate, destructive use—and with so much apparent enthusiasm! "I fear you may have seen less of our skills than you believe," she said. "No sorceron can use the skill in that way more than once without losing all power. Nor could we restore youth. We can only spread or slow onward progress, not cause development to turn backwards, the sprout to curl back into the seed."

"In your world, perhaps," said Dathru, "you can destroy your enemy only once. But in another world, who knows what adaptations might be wrought?"

She tried to put herself on guard against seeing malice in Dathru where none might exist. "Perhaps," she said, "if my skill with time is so rare in your world, I should demand more in exchange for it."

"You will have more." He stroked her arm, and she tried to suppress a shudder. "You will live with me here," he went on, "or we may settle in some even more congenial world. We will find the place and the way to free you from the rule of virginity—a perverted exception of law in the universe—and I will teach you the joys of the other, the common and natural, law of power. We will be the rulers of our world, you and I—ever served, ever feared, remaining young for eons to enjoy our power and wealth. . . ."

She tried to rise from the chair. He put out both hands, reaching around the pedestal with its Circle, and touched the arms of the chair, fencing her in.

"I will teach you nothing, Dathru," she said. "Not unless you can persuade me that what the common folk of these Oldhills say of you is as false as what the farmers' folk of the Tanglelands say of us."

He smiled. "So you are all silly, innocent sorcer-folk in your world, little sister? Power is to be enjoyed to the fullest, used to one's own advantage, not wasted in silly, harmless trifles." He touched her again.

Thank God the glass pedestal was still between them! At least Dathru could not touch her with more than his hands. She seized the Circle with one hand, the pedestal with the other. "Let me leave, Dathru! Let me leave or—"

He laughed and gripped both her arms above the elbow. Lifting the Circle, she pushed and kicked the pedestal, trying to knock him off balance. He laughed again and fell forward on top of her. The pedestal was no longer between them. As he had made it appear, so he must now have made it vanish again. She tried to throw the Circle into his face before it, too, vanished—but it was already gone. He was lying on her, laughing into her throat. She shuddered and stiffened.

"Let me go, sorcerer," she said, "or, by the farmers' great God Jehandru, I will blast you into senility though I lost my power for it."

He rose at once. But as he rose he pressed one thumb against his wooden pendant. A burning weight settled on Frostflower's breast, invisible and intangible but so heavy that for a moment she could neither move nor breathe. She could only watch helplessly as he caused a supple copper chain to writhe up like a snake through the marble floor and coil itself round and round her. When the chain had tightened and hardened to hold her fast, Dathru took his thumb from the pendant and she could breathe again, though she still felt a wide bruise aching above her sternum.

"My bit of wood had touched you there," said the sorcerer. "Thus, I am able to use it to give you pain. Ingenious, is it not? A tool I adapted from the skills Jitasa the scaled-woman of the Swampy Places taught me. Had this touched another part of your body. . . ."

He walked slowly around her. She closed her eyes, feeling his tread vibrate through the marble floor. Then she felt the thicknesses of cloth beneath her, fluffing up into cushions—velvet cushions! Dathru was causing a bed to grow up beneath her. She would have tried to roll off, but, opening her eyes, she saw copper bars and stiff copper latticework rising above the edge of the bed.

"I have watched enough," said Dathru, "to know that even the sorcerers of your world, with all their power over time, cannot affect a person they are not touching. Someday, perhaps, you will learn to aim your control of time through the air toward some creature with whom you are not in physical contact. If you will teach me and accept my teaching, fair Frostflower, we may be able to perfect such a technique here together. But for now, you cannot harm me."

Frostflower closed her eyes again. If she could go deeply enough into trance before he started to do whatever he meant, perhaps. . . .

She felt a puff of his breath strike her forehead. He spoke her name.

* * *

Thorn awoke with a snort, a headache, and a pressing need to empty her bladder. "Damn brown footwash," she muttered, thinking of the beverage of which she had drunk almost two mugsful over dinner and dice. It must have been some kind of bloody wine, and she cursed herself for not realizing it and sticking to water, like Frost.

Feeling for Stabber, making sure he was still in his sheath at her waist, with his garnet in place, she got up and groped her way outside. Blinking at the sight of three full moons, one half below the . . . western horizon? eastern? . . . she located the hole where her hosts took care of their emptying needs.

The fog had cleared. If it was still clear in the morning, they would leave at dawn to find the boat and the river. Gods, it was bright enough to start out tonight . . . but probably Frost and the mongrel needed their sleep. Thorn knew she could use a little more rest herself, though reawakening in this demon-twisted land had keyed up her senses to a nervous pitch all over again.

She returned to the stable for humans that the Oldhillers lived in. At the door she hesitated. Thorn could hardly blame the Oldhillers for closing up their sleeping-place to keep out the moonlight . . . but it also kept out the air. She decided to stand in the open doorway until she felt sleepy again. Leaning against the jamb, she moved her gaze around the room. As her eyes adjusted, she saw that the bed where Frostflower had gone to sleep was now empty.

Frostflower was wandering in a place of gray sky and black grass. Black trees thrust up here and there from the flat plain—bare trees, crooked and angular, with large, stark limbs that stuck out randomly from each trunk, like knives thrust from all directions at once into a joint of farmers' meat. Yet somehow these trees exuded a sense that they were not only alive, despite their lack of tiny twigs and branches, but growing without the need of leaves or sunlight.

The only light in this land came from a double moon, like two unshelled eggs melted together in the cooking-pot. It even seemed to have two yolks—two roundish blotches of darker brown in the buff circles. This moon cast no shadows. Far in the distance were mountains—scrawny mountains, mere gaping pinnacles of rock. On all other sides, she could see nothing but flat plain punctuated with trees. Long red garlands were draped across some of the branches.

Frostflower started walking toward the mountains. The grass was slippery underfoot, and at the same time slightly boggy, as if saturated. An unpleasant smell, like an excess of salt, pepper, and preserving spices mixed with the air from a farmer's slaughterhouse, made breathing difficult. No living thing except Frostflower moved in the land.

Once she came to a stream, but it flowed so thickly, with such a sweetish, brackish smell, that she did not drink, although she was incredibly thirsty. When she looked up from the stream, trees blocked her way wherever she turned. She had somehow lost herself and wandered into a clearing in a forest of the black trees. She saw great, dripping lumps now, as well as the crimson ropes, wedged in their limbs.

She forced herself to step between two trees, and it became obvious that the lumps were carcasses of freshly slaughtered animals.

The sorceress turned quickly to flee back to the clearing. It was no longer there. She was in the midst of the woods where some unknown flesh-eaters stored their meat. Turning yet again in the direction she could now only hope led to the mountains, she closed her eyes, stretched out her arms, and took a few steps forward.

Her hand touched a lump of wet flesh and she drew back with a gasp, opening her eyes. It was better to see than to touch. Her hand had met a small corpse that seemed to be a dog . . . or a human infant.

She began to run, keeping just enough presence of mind to continue as straight as possible toward the mountains. She misjudged her speed and distance, and struck up against a tree. Against the burden of flesh on the tree. Drawing back, she saw that it was a torso—headless, legless, lacking one arm, pinned to the tree by a dagger through the wrist of the other arm, unmistakably the naked body of a human woman.

Then Frostflower began to run wildly. She splashed through a crimson stream and hove up panting against a tree that at first seemed to be blessedly bare. But she looked down and saw the head of the infant Starwind—the child she had left in safety at Windslope Retreat—and she looked up and saw Thorn's head, impaled on a branch above her.

Then, at last, she screamed aloud. The scream brought her back to consciousness.

"I do not know what the dream was," said Dathru, "but I know it was evil and unpleasant. And I can continue giving you such dreams indefinitely without wasting your flesh, until you teach me what I wish to know."

*       *       *

Thorn gave Dowl a fist in the ribs. The dog awoke whining and thumping his tail. "You fool mongrel," the warrior muttered, "she's gone off to find that turd of a sorcerer. Why the Hellbog didn't you wake up and stop her—at least bark?" Dowl whined again and got to his feet.

Any help the Oldhillers might give would not be worth the confusion of shouting at them. Thorn set out alone, just herself, sword Slicer, knife Stabber, and her new spear Skythrust that she could now throw well enough to skewer a squirrel on the run. And Dowl trotted along beside, sniffing for Frostflower.

The sorceress knew she could not endure many more such dreams. Nor could she escape the dreams by simple trance. Perhaps free-travel? It was dangerous. When Dathru realized she was not in her body, he might destroy the body. Yet that would be preferable to aiding him in his wickedness. And perhaps he would want her teaching too much.

Three nightmares she had undergone, finding the heads and dismembered bodies of those she loved—Starwind, old Moonscar, Wonderhope, Thorn . . . sometimes she witnessed their deaths, as when she had seen her own mother and the priestess Inmara disembowling each other in a place where steam rose from gaping cracks in a metal floor. Her flesh was undamaged, but Dathru was allowing her a brief respite to guard against her mind giving way. Pretending to sleep, she concentrated. It was not easy, and she came raggedly out of her flesh at last.

Even while the conscious essence was free of it, the body continued to breathe, the heart to beat. Dathru did not seem to realize that his victim's essence was no longer bound by his copper chain.

Or was she free of him, even now? He stopped and blew on her forehead, then spoke her name. She wavered. This time it was a red swamp she was going into, a place where snakes and insects scratched up her legs as she sank to the knees in acidic slime. But this time, at least, she remained conscious that it was an illusion. Fighting it, she watched the sorcerer bend over her form, studying her greedily. Perhaps—thank God—Dathru truly knew nothing of the skill of free-travel; he seemed not to notice anything amiss.

He must eventually realize his victim was no longer wholly in his power. Meanwhile, she hurried from the room and from the Great Chambers before he could suck her consciousness deeper into the dream, after all.

The nightmare faded as she got farther from Dathru, but the

last vestiges of horror did not recede until she was fully a
hundred paces from the sorcerer's dwelling. There she paused,
unwilling to go farther from her body than necessary.

As she waited, she saw Thorn and Dowl coming toward her in
the moonlight.

Thorn did not like the look of what Frost had said the Oldhillers
called Dathru's "Great Chambers." Well, this rotten-stalk Dathru
seemed to have enough enemies; maybe he did need strong walls
as well as sorcery to protect himself. But anyone who needed
that much stone to wall himself in could not be totally immune to
injury from plain, honest steel.

Dowl did not seem to like the place any better than Thorn did.
He stopped about a hundred paces away from it, whined, and
began snuffing around in a circle.

"No, she's not out here, you damn dog," said Thorn. "Stop
acting like a bloody quarterwit."

Dowl looked up at the sound of Thorn's voice, whined, and
continued going around in his circle. "All right," said the
warrior, "stay here and cool your paws. I don't need you any
more. Frostflower's obviously gone inside that bloody tower-
place, so you just keep out of my way."

The warrior strode on toward the middle tower, wondering if
its arched base was really so open as it looked. After a moment,
Dowl came padding after her.

Animals could not sense free-travellers in the Tanglelands, yet
Frostflower was sure Dowl had sensed her presence here. He had
not responded to her attempted touch, but he had snuffed the
ground in nearly the place she "occupied." It must be some very
subtle modification of her powers in this world.

She tried—God! how she tried—to touch Thorn's consciousness somehow as she had, all unexpected, touched Dowl's. But
with other humans it seemed exactly as in the Tanglelands. And
Frostflower could not warn her friend against going into Dathru's
stronghold. She could only follow. But to what purpose? Not
only was she unable to help Thorn, but as she came back toward
Dathru, the shapes of nightmare began superimposing themselves once again on reality. Yet the sorceress returned, unseen,
unfelt, and helpless, beside her friend.

It seemed too easy. Half the ground floor of the tower was an
open, semi-circular yard, enclosed only by four pillars with wide
archways between. At the top of a short flight of stairs was a

doorway guarded only by a curtain, and enough light came through the curtain to guide Thorn safely and quietly to the stairs.

She hoped Dowl would keep still. She slipped Skythrust into his narrow spear-sheath across her back. For honest, hand-to-hand work she preferred her first weapons, sword and knife.

The curtain was some lustrous material like nothing Thorn had ever seen before. She hesitated a moment, but if she did not act quickly Dowl might bark or whine and cost her the element of surprise. Using her dagger hand, she thrust back the curtain.

Through a blood-red mist filled with vague, lumbering shapes which half obscured the fine metal filigree of the chamber, Frostflower saw that Dathru had not yet, to all appearances, realized she was elsewhere than in her body, suffering the full grip of the nightmare. She could not, however, see her own body clearly; it was a mere dark shape hidden from full view by the high copper mesh border of the bed. Thorn would not be able to recognize her either.

A wave of shock seemed to go through the chamber as Dathru looked up at Thorn. It was replaced almost at once by an effusion that the sorceress could now recognize as bait thrown by one sex to the other. A bait Thorn, unlike Frostflower, was never slow to take.

"Well, well," said the man in crimson, "a visitor. Welcome, my dear friend from another world."

He stroked his silky brown beard, and Thorn could almost feel the pleasure of his hands stroking her own hair, back, sides . . . but she also remained sufficiently on guard to notice the greedy way he glanced at her knife.

"So now you can talk to me in my own language," she said. "Why didn't you fix things so that I would understand those people out there?"

"You have not come alone? Ah, yes, you must have come alone. None of the fools of this land come near me. They fear me, you see, and they may have reason . . . but with a woman like you at my side, to share my power. . . ."

Thorn tried to ignore the twitching of her flesh. She tightened her hands on her weapons. "I'm no bloody sorceron, Dathru, and I'm not going to settle down with one. A few hours, maybe . . . Why the Hellbog are you looking at my knife like that? Which do you want, me or Stabber?"

"No sorceress in your own world, perhaps," said Dathru,

"but you have the power here. Were you not able to push aside my curtain? Yes, a woman like you, dressed in fine velvets and silks next your skin . . . when you choose to dress at all. . . ."

Thorn was wavering—Frostflower could see it.

Dowl, torn between the sense of Frostflower near him and the scent of her body across the room, trotted halfway to the bed, whined, and circled back to crouch in front of Thorn. She half kicked him out of the way and took a step toward Dathru. The sorcerer came a few steps forward, as if to meet her in the middle of the room, before she saw her friend's body in the bed.

There was only one chance of alerting Thorn. The nightmare had, apparently, been progressing at its usual pace in Frostflower's brain. She sensed that it was nearing its climax. If she were back in her body in the full grip of nightmare, with a fleshly throat to scream, and if it climaxed quickly enough. . . .

It would be as difficult as walking slowly into a blazing fire. But Thorn had taken another step toward Dathru, and he toward her, holding out his hands as if eager to receive her sword and knife by their handles.

. . . The only way out of the mud that had closed over her head was by climbing up a scaly thing that writhed in her groping hands. Her mouth and nose filled with rot-tasting slime, her lungs starving, she felt her way up, her nails tearing on the spiny, twitching scales. Her head above the surface at last, she coughed and spit until she got enough mud out of her air passages to breathe. She opened her eyes, blinking away the acidic slime, and saw a huge, scaled head plunging down at her. Impaled in its lower teeth was Thorn's mangled body.

Frostflower screamed.

The scream broke Thorn's fascination. Suddenly she realized what the black bundle was that lay in that dainty copper trough of a bed, and why Dowl had jumped up and begun licking it. And in the moment of her disillusion, Thorn saw it was not her body Dathru desired, but her weapons.

He was a male, but he was also an outlaw and a sorcerer, and she had to act before he could appeal to her lust again. "You want Stabber so much," she shouted, "take him!" and hurled the blade straight to its target, right above the wood pendant on Dathru's breast.

\*       \*       \*

Frostflower's own scream had wakened her from the nightmare. As Dathru fell to the floor, his copper chain fell from her body and the bed with its velvet cushions melted into nothingness, leaving her on the floor, weeping into Dowl's fur.

Thorn kicked the sorcerer's body over with one foot and retrieved Stabber. "So bloody powerful," said the swordswoman. "He could bring us here, put the language into your head—gods know what else—and one good knife to the heart ended him like anyone else."

"The garnet," said Frostflower. "The garnet in Stabber's handle. They have no jewels like it here, Thorn . . . it must have great power here."

Dathru's glass chair had vanished, like the bed, but the white-gold Circle had reappeared, lying on the floor beyond Dathru's body. The bed and chair must have been delusions, while the Circle was real and he had only made it seem to vanish. Frostflower crawled across the marble floor to it, avoiding Dathru's body by a good distance. Then, cradling the metal ring in one arm and with the other arm around Dowl, she rocked back and forth, weeping softly, until Thorn came and held her close, like a mother.

"You're a better sorceress than that dead pricker ever was," said Thorn. "You can get us back to the Tanglelands again."

"How?"

"If he got us here," said Thorn, "you can find the way he did it. You're good, Frost, you're good."

Frostflower smiled. Her friend was so sublimely confident. But she might be able to learn from Dathru's sorcery after all, though she must experiment with care. "Thorn," she said, setting the Circle carefully on the floor beside her and fondling Dowl with both hands, "will you bring me the pendant—the wooden pendant he wore around his neck?"

Glen Cook, whose "Severed Heads" is one of the three tales of "rape and revenge" which I mentioned in the introduction to this volume, has here told an unusual and moving story of this universal theme. When I began reading for this anthology, I admit to being prejudiced against male authors writing heroic fantasy; I felt I had read too many mindless stories of the old-style heroic fiction, and my attitude was quite simply:

"Blood and thunder, guts and gore;
Hero tales are such a bore."

But such writers as Charles Saunders, Charles de Lint, Steve Burns and Robin Bailey—to name only men represented in this anthology—quickly changed my mind.

When first I read "Severed Heads" I thought Cook a new writer; a query to his agent informed me that he is an unusually prolific newcomer, having written and sold eleven novels in the last three or four years, as well as a couple of dozen stories to virtually every magazine in existence, including *F&SF*, *Asimov's*, *Whispers*, *Night Voyages*, and many others.

Narriman, perhaps the youngest heroine in this anthology, lives the truth mentioned in the story; that without our fellow man, we are no more than severed heads which roll alone through the desert. Can it be that one reason for the mindless bias to uninvolved, blood-and-thunder old-time sword and sorcery fiction—which gave it such a bad name—was that the early writers, writing only of their fellow *man*, fell into the trap of using the women in the story only as narrative devices, objects, cardboard figures without even such small dimensions of emotional existence as were granted to the men? Thus the male characters, too, were only "severed heads" rolling around in the desert of "thud and blunder" fiction, with plenty of blood and guts but no emotional reality. Glen Cook does not fall into that trap. Not once.—MZB

# SEVERED HEADS

## by Glen Cook

### I

Narriman was ten when the black rider came to Wadi al Hamamah. He rode tall and arrogant upon a courser as white as his djellaba was black. He looked neither right nor left as he passed among the tents. Old men spat at his horse's hooves. Old women made warding signs. Children and dogs whined and fled. Makram's ass set up a horrible braying.

Narriman was not frightened, just confused. Who was this stranger? Why were her people frightened? Because he wore black? No tribe she knew wore black. Black was the color of ifrits and djinn, of the Masters of Jebal al Alf Dhulquarneni, the high, dark mountains brooding over Wadi al Hamamah and the holy place of the al Muburak.

Narriman was a bold one. Her elders warned her often, but she would not behave as fit her sex. The old ones shook their heads and said that brat of Mowfik's would be no good. Mowfik himself was suspect enough, what with having gone to the great wars of the north. What business were those of the al Muburak?

Narriman stayed and watched the rider.

He reined in before her father's tent, which stood apart, drew a black rod from his javelin case, breathed upon it. Its tips glowed. He set that glow against the tent, sketched a symbol, ⵜ . The old folks muttered and cursed and told one another they'd known despair would haunt Mowfik's tent.

Narriman ran after the stranger, who rode down the valley toward the shrine. Old Farida shouted after her. She pretended not to hear. She dodged from shadow to shadow, rock to rock, to the hiding place from which she spied on the rites of her elders.

She watched the rider pass through the Circle with arrogance unconquered. He did not glance at Karkur, let alone make obeisance and offerings. She expected the Great Death to strike him ere he left the Circle, but he rode on, untouched. She watched him out of sight.

35

Narriman stared at the god. Was Karkur, too, a frightened antique? She was shaken. Karkur's anger was a constant. Each task, each pleasure, had to be integrated with his desires. He was an angry god. But he had sat there like a red stone lump while a heathen defiled his Circle.

The sun was in the west when she returned to camp. Old Farida called for her immediately. She related what she had seen. The old folks muttered and whispered and made their signs.

"Who was he, Farida? What was he? Why were you afraid?"

Farida spat through the gap in her teeth. "The Evil One's messenger. A shaghûn out of the Jebal." Farida turned her old eyes on the Mountains of A Thousand Sorcerers. She made her magic sign. "It's a mercy your mother didn't live to see this."

"Why?"

But just then the guard horn sounded, ending on a triumphant note. The hunters had returned. Karkur had favored the tribe. Narriman ran to tell her father about the stranger.

## II

Mowfik had an antelope behind his saddle, a string of quail, a brace of hares, and even a box terrapin. "A great hunt, Little Fox. Never was it so fine. Even Shukri took his game." Shukri could do nothing right. He was, probably, the man Narriman would wed, because she was her mother's daughter.

Her father was so pleased she did not mention the stranger. The other hunters heard from the old ones. Dour eyes turned Mowfik's way. Narriman was afraid for him till she sensed that they felt pity. There was a lot of nodding. The stranger's visit had confirmed their prejudices.

Mowfik stopped outside their tent. "Little Fox, we won't sleep much tonight. I hope you've gathered plenty of wood."

She heard the weariness in his voice. He had worked harder than the others. He had no woman to ride behind and clean game, no woman to help here at home. Only old Farida, his mother's sister, bothered to offer.

Marriman took the quail and hares, arranged them on a mat. She collected her tools, stoked up the fire, settled down to work.

The sun settled westward and slightly south. A finger of fire broke between peaks and stabbed into the wadi, dispelling shadows. Mowfik glanced up.

He turned pale. His mouth opened and closed. Finally, he gurgled, "What?"

She told him about the rider.

He sat with head bent low. "Ah, no. Not my Little Fox." And, in response to an earlier question, "There are those even Karkur dares not offend. The rider serves one greater than he." Then, thoughtfully, "But perhaps he's shown the way. There must be a greater reason than a feast when game runs to the hunter's bow." He rose, walked into the shadows, stared at those dread mountains that no tribe dared invade. Then he said, "Cook only meat that might spoil before we get it smoked."

"Tell me what it means, Father."

"I suppose you're old enough. You've been Chosen. The Masters sent him to set their mark, that all might know. It's been a long time since a shaghûn came. The last was in my mother's time."

## III

Mowfik had been north and had bathed in alien waters. He could think the unthinkable. He could consider defying the Masters. He dug into his war booty to buy Makram's ass. He loaded all he possessed on two animals and walked away. He looked back only once. "I should never have come back."

They went north over game trails, through the high, rocky places, avoiding other tribes. They spent twelve days in the hills before descending to a large oasis. For the first time Narriman saw people who lived in houses. She remained close to Mowfik. They were strange.

"There. In the east. That is el Aswad, the Wahlig's fortress." Narriman saw a great stone tent crowning a barren hill. "And there, four days' ride, lies Sebil el Selib, the pass to the sea." He pointed northeast. His arm swung to encompass the west. "Out there lies the great erg called Hammad al Nakir."

Heat shimmered over the Desert of Death. For a moment she thought she saw the fairy towers of fallen Ilkazar, but that was imagination born of stories Mowfik had brought home from his adventures. Ilkazar had been a ruin for four centuries.

"We'll water here, cross the erg, and settle over there. The shaghûn will never find us."

It took eight days, several spent lost, to reach Wadi el Kuf, the only oasis in the erg. It took fourteen more to finish and find a place to settle.

The new life was bewildering. The people spoke the same language, but their preoccupations were different. Narriman thought she would go mad before she learned their ways. But learn she did. She was the bold one, Mowfik's daughter, who could question everything and believe only that which suited her. She and her father remained outsiders, but less so than among their own people. Narriman liked the settled people better. She missed only old Farida and Karkur. Mowfik insisted that Karkur was with them in spirit.

## IV

Narriman was twelve when the rider reappeared.

She was in the fields with her friends Ferial and Feras. It was a stony, tired field. Ferial's father had bought it cheap, offering Mowfik a quarter interest if he would help prove it up. That morning, while the children dug stones and piled them into a wall, Mowfik and his partner were elsewhere. Feras had been malingering all morning, and was the scorn of Narriman and his sister. He saw the rider first.

He was barely visible against a background of dark rocks and shadow. He was behind a boulder which masked all but his horse's head. But he was there. Just watching. Narriman shuddered. How had he found them?

He served the Masters. Their necromancy was great. Mowfik had been foolish to think they could escape.

"Who is he?" Ferial asked. "Why are you afraid?"

"I'm not afraid," Narriman lied. "He's a shaghûn." Here in the north some lords had shaghûns of their own. She had to add, "He rides for the Masters of the Jebal."

Ferial laughed.

Narriman said, "You'd believe if you had lived in the shadow of the Jebal."

Feras said, "The Little Fox is a bigger liar than her namesake."

Narriman spit at his feet. "You're so brave, huh?"

"He doesn't scare me."

"Then come with me to ask what he wants."

Feras looked at Narriman, at Ferial, and at Narriman again. Male pride would not let him back down.

Narriman had her pride too. I'll go just a little way, she told herself. Just far enough to make Feras turn tail. I won't go near him.

Her heart fluttered. Feras gasped, ran to catch up. Ferial called, "Come back. Feras. I'll tell Father."

Feras groaned. Narriman would have laughed had she not been so frightened. Feras was trapped between pride and punishment.

The certainty of punishment made him stick. He meant to make the whipping worth the trouble. No girl would outbrave him.

They were seventy yards away when Feras ran. Narriman felt the hard touch of the shaghûn's eyes. A few steps more, just to prove Feras was bested.

She took five long, deliberate steps, stopped, looked up. The shaghûn remained immobile. His horse tossed its head, shaking off flies. A different horse, but the same man. . . . She met his eyes.

Something threw a bridle upon her soul. The shaghûn beckoned, a gentle come hither. Her feet moved. Fifty yards. Twenty-five. Ten. Her fear mounted. The shaghûn dismounted, eyes never leaving hers. He took her arm, drew her into the shadow of the boulder. Gently, he pushed her back against the rock.

"What do you want?"

He removed the cloth across his face.

He was just a man! A young man, no more than twenty. He wore the ghost of a smile, and was not unhandsome, but his eyes were cold, without mercy.

His hand came to her, removed the veil she had begun wearing only months ago. She shivered like a captive bird.

"Yes," he whispered. "As beautiful as they promised." He touched her cheek.

She could not escape his eyes. Gently, gently, he tugged here, untied there, lifted another place, and she was more naked than at any moment since birth.

In her heart she called to Karkur. Karkur had ears of stone. She shivered as she recalled Mowfik saying that there were powers before whom Karkur must nod.

The shaghûn piled their clothing into a narrow pallet. She gasped when he stood up, and tried to break his spell by sealing her eyes. It did no good. His hands took her naked flesh and gently forced her down.

He drove a burning brand into her, punishing her for having dared flee. Despite her determination, she whimpered, begged him to stop. There was no mercy in him.

The second time there was less pain. She was numb. She ground her eyelids together and endured. She did not give him the pleasure of begging.

The third time she opened her eyes as he entered her. His gaze caught hers.

The effect was a hundred times what it had been when he had called her. Her soul locked with his. She became part of him.

Her pleasure was as great, as all-devouring, as her pain the first time. She begged, but not for mercy.

Then he rose, snatched his clothing, and she cried again, shame redoubled because he had made her enjoy what he was doing.

His movements were no longer languid and assured. He dressed hastily and sloppily. There was fear in his eyes. He leaped onto his mount and dug in his heels.

Narriman rolled into a tight ball of degradation and pain, and wept.

## V

Men shouted. Horses whinnied. "He went that way!"

"There he goes! After him!"

Mowfik swung down and cast his cloak over Narriman. She buried her face in his clothing.

The thunder of hooves, the cries of outrage and the clang of weapons on shields, receded. Mowfik touched her. "Little Fox?"

"Go away. Let me die."

"No. This will pass. This will be forgotten. There's no forgetting death." His voice choked on rage. "They'll catch him. They'll bring him back. I'll give you my own knife."

"They won't catch him. He has the Power. I couldn't fight him. He made me *want* him. Go away. Let me die."

"No." Mowfik had been to the wars in the north. He had seen rape. Women survived. The impact was more savage when the victim was one of one's own, but that part of him that was Man and not outraged father knew this was not the end.

"You know what they'll say." Narriman wrapped his cloak about her. "Ferial and Feras will tell what they saw. People will think I went willingly. They'll call me whore. And what they call me I'll have to be. What man would have me now?"

Mowfik sighed. He heard truth. When the hunters returned, chastened by losing the man in their own territory, they would seek excuses for failing, would see in a less righteous light. "Get dressed."

"Let me die, Father. Let me take my shame off your shoulders."

"Stop that. Get dressed. We have things to do. We'll sell while people are sympathetic. We started over here. We can start again somewhere else. Up. Into your clothes. Do you want them to see you like this? Time to make the brave show."

All her life he had said that, whenever people hurt her. "Time to make the brave show."

Tears streaming, she dressed. "Did you say that to Mother, too?" Her mother had been brave, a northern girl who had come south out of love. She had been more outsider than Mowfik.

"Yes. Many times. And I should've held my tongue. I should've stayed in the north. None of this would have happened had we stayed with her people."

Mowfik's partner did not try to profit from his distress. He paid generously. Mowfik did not have to waste war booty to get away.

## VI

A Captain Al Jahez, whom Mowfik had served in the wars, gave him a position as huntsman. He and Narriman had now fled eight hundred miles from Wadi al Hamamah.

Narriman began to suspect the worst soon after their arrival. She remained silent till it became impossible to fool herself. She went to Mowfik because there was nowhere else to go.

"Father, I'm with child."

He did not react in the traditional way. "Yes. His purpose was to breed another of his kind."

"What will we do?" She was terrified. Her tribe had been unforgiving. The settled peoples were only slightly less so in these matters.

"There's no need to panic. I discussed this with Al Jahez when we arrived. He's a hard and religious man, but from el Aswad originally. He knows what comes out of the Jebal. His goatherd is old. He'll send us into the hills to replace him. We'll stay away a few years while he stamps your widowhood into everyone's mind. You'll come back looking young for your age. Men will do battle for such a widow."

"Why are you so kind? I've been nothing but trouble since that rider came down the wadi."

"You're my family. All I have. I live the way of the Disciple, unlike so many who profess his creed because it's politic."

"And yet you bow to Karkur."

He smiled. "One shouldn't overlook any possibility. I'll speak with Al Jahez. We'll go within the week."

Life in the hills, goatherding, was not unpleasant. The land was hard, reminding Narriman of home. But this was tamer country. Wolves and lions were few. The kids were not often threatened.

As her belly swelled and the inevitable drew nearer, she grew ever more frightened. "Father, I'm not old enough for this. I'm going to die. I know it."

"No, you won't." He told her that her mother, too, had grown frightened. That all women were afraid. He did not try to convince her that her fears were groundless, only that fear was more dangerous than giving birth. "I'll be with you, I won't let anything happen. And Al Jahez promises he'll send his finest midwife."

"Father, I don't understand why you're so good to me. And I'm baffled as to why he's so good to you. He can't care that much because you rode in his company."

Mowfik shrugged. "Perhaps because I saved his life at the Battle of the Circles. Also, there are more just men than you believe."

"You never talk about the wars. Except about places you saw."

"Those aren't happy memories, Little Fox. Dying and killing and dying. And in the end, nothing gained, either for myself or the glory of the Lord. Will you tell the young ones about these days when you're old? Those days weren't happy, but I saw more than any al Muburak before or since."

He was the only one of a dozen volunteers who survived. And maybe that, instead of the foreign wife, was why he had become an outcast. The old folks resented him for living when their sons were dead.

"What will we do with a baby, Father?"

"What? What people always do. Raise him to be a man."

"It'll be a boy, will it?"

"I doubt me not it will, but a girl will be as welcome." He chuckled.

"Will you hate him?"

"Hate him? We are talking about my daughter's child. I can hate the father, but not the infant. The child is innocent."

"You did travel in strange lands. No wonder the old ones didn't like you."

"Old ones pass on. Ideas are immortal. So says the Disciple."

She felt better afterward, but her fear never evaporated.

## VII

"A fine son," the old woman said with a toothless smile. "A fine son. I foretell you now, little mistress, he'll be a great one. See it here, in his hands." She held the tiny, purplish, wrinkled, squalling thing high. "And he came forth with the cap. Only the truly destined, the chosen ones, come forth with that. Aye, you've mothered a mighty one.''

Narriman smiled though she heard not a tenth of the babble. She cared only that the struggle was over, that the pain had receded. There was a great warmth in her for the child, but she hadn't the strength to express it.

Mowfik ducked into the tent. "Sadhra. Is everything all right?" His face was pale. Dimly, Narriman realized he had been frightened too.

"Both came through perfectly. Al Jahez has a godson of whom he can be proud." She repeated her predictions.

"Old Mother, you'd better not tell him that. That smacks of superstition. He's strict about religious deviation."

"The decrees of men, be they mere men or Chosen of the Lord, can't change natural law. Omens are omens."

"May be. May be. Shouldn't you give her the child?"

"Aye. So I should. I'm hogging him because one day I'll be able to say I held such a one." She dropped the infant to Narriman's breast. He took the nipple, but without enthusiasm. "Don't worry, little mistress. Soon he'll suckle hearty."

"Thank you, Sadhra," Mowfik said. "Al Jahez chose well. I'm in both your debts."

"It was my honor, sir." She left the tent.

"Such a one, eh, Little Fox? Making him the Hammer of God before he draws his first breath."

Narriman stared up at him. He wasn't just tired. He was disturbed. "The rider?"

"He's out there."

"I thought so. I felt him."

"I stalked him, but he eluded me. I didn't dare go far."

"Perhaps tomorrow." As she drifted into sleep, though, she thought, You'll never catch him. He'll deceive you with the Power. No warrior will catch him. Time or trickery will be his death.

She slept. And she dreamed of the rider and the way it had been for her the third time.

She dreamed that often. It was one thing she kept from Mowfik. He would not understand. She did not understand herself.

Maybe she *was* a whore at heart.

## VIII

Narriman called the child Misr Sayed bin Hammad al Muburak, meaning he was Misr Sayed, son of the desert, of the al Muburak tribe. Hammad could be a man's name also, so it became that of her missing husband. Misr's grandfather, however, called him Towfik el-Masiri, or Camel's Feet, for reasons only he found amusing.

Misr grew quickly, learned rapidly, and was startlingly healthy. Seldom was he colicky or cranky, even when cutting teeth. He was happy most of the time, and always had a big hug for his grandfather. Narriman remained perpetually amazed that she could feel so much love for one person. "How do women love more than one child?" she asked.

Mowfik shrugged. "It's a mystery to me. I was my mother's only. You're your mother's only."

The first two years were idyllic. The baby and goats kept them too busy to worry. In the third year, though, Mowfik grew sour. His heart was not in his play with Misr. One day Narriman found him honing his war sword and watching the hills. Then she understood. He expected the rider.

The prospect fired her fantasies. She ached for the shaghûn. She held her left hand near the fire till pain burned the lust away.

Shortly after Misr's third birthday Mowfik said, "I'm going to see Al Jahez. It's time you became Hammad's widow."

"Will we be safer there? Won't the shaghûn just ride in like he did before?"

"Al Jahez thinks not. He thinks the priests can drive him away."

Narriman went to the tent flap, surveyed the unfriendly hills. "Go see him. I'm afraid to go back where people might cry shame, but I'm more scared of the shaghûn."

"I'd hoped you'd feel that way."

She had begun to relax. The night had passed without incident. Mowfik should be back by noon. If she could stay too busy to worry. . . .

It was almost noon when Misr called, "Mama, Grandpa coming." She sighed, put her mending aside, and went to meet him.

"Oh, no. Karkur defend us." Misr could not be blamed for his mistake. He'd seldom seen anyone but Mowfik on horseback.

The shaghûn was far down the valley, coming toward her. He seemed larger than life, like a far city seen through the shimmer over the great erg. He came at an unhurried walk. The rise and fall of his animal's legs was hypnotic. He did not seem to draw any closer.

"Go into the tent, Misr."

"Mama?"

"Do it. And don't come out till I tell you. No matter what."

"Mama, what's wrong?"

"Misr! Go!"

"Mama, you're scaring me."

She gave him her fiercest look. He scooted inside. "And close the flap." She turned. The rider looked twice as big but no nearer. His pace was no faster. The shame in her heart grew with the heat in her loins. She knew he would take her, and her evil side called to him eagerly.

He came closer. She thought of running into the hills. But what good that? He would hunt her down. And Misr would be left alone.

She snatched the bow Mowfik used for hunting, sped an arrow toward the rider. She missed.

She was good with that weapon. Better than her father, who remained perpetually amazed that a woman could do anything better than a man. She should not have missed. She sped a second and third arrow.

Each missed. The fourth plucked at his djellaba, but only because he was so close. There was no fifth. She had seen his eyes.

The bow fell from her hand. He dismounted and walked toward her, reaching.

Only one moment from the next hour stuck with her. Misr came outside, saw the rider thrusting into her, ran over and bit him on the buttocks. That would remain with her forever, in that mixture of amusement and pain such a thing could recall.

Afterward he stared into her eyes. His will beat against her. She dwindled into sleep.

Cursing wakened her. It was the violent cursing of savagery and hatred. She felt too lazy to open her eyes.

She recalled the inexorable approach of the man in black coming up the valley on a line as straight as the arrow of time. She recalled his touch, her fevered response. She felt the sun on her naked shame. She flew up, wrapped herself in discarded clothing.

Mowfik belabored a fallen tree with his axe, cursing steadily.

He blasphemed both Karkur and the Lord of the Disciple. She scrambled into her clothing, frightened.

Exhaustion stopped Mowfik. He settled on the tree trunk and wept. Narriman went to comfort him.

"It's all right, Father. He didn't hurt me. He shamed me again, but he didn't hurt me." She put her arms around him. "It'll be all right, Father."

"Little Fox, he took Misr. It wasn't you this time."

## IX

Narriman changed, hardened, saddened. The Narriman of Wadi al Hamamah would not have recognized her. That Narriman would have been terrified by her.

Mowfik took her to see Al Jahez. The captain was properly outraged. He set his men to scouring the country. He sent an alarm across the kingdom. He appealed to the Most Holy Mrazkim Shrines for a Writ of Anathema, and for prayers for the Lord's intervention.

"And that is all I can do. And it's pointless. He won't be seen. Those who serve the Masters come and go as they please."

"Can't somebody do something?" Narriman demanded. "How long has this been going on? How many women have had to suffer this?"

"It's gone on forever," Al Jahez said. "It went on throughout the age of Empire. It went on before the Empire was born. It'll go on tomorrow, too."

"Why isn't it stopped?"

"Because no one can stop it. One of the Emperors tried. He sent an army into the Jebal. Not one man returned."

She was venting frustration. She knew the futility of battling the Masters. No, this was personal. This was between herself and one shaghûn. The Masters were but shadows beyond the horizon, too nebulous to factor into the emotional equation.

"That man took my son. *My* son. I don't recognize his claim. He did nothing but force me onto my back."

"Narriman?" Mowfik said, baffled.

"I want my son back."

"We can't do anything about that," Al Jahez said. "The shaghûn is who he is, and we're who we are."

"No."

"Narriman?" Again Mowfik was puzzled.

"I thought about this all day, Father. I'm going after Misr."

Al Jahez said, "But you're a child. And a woman."

"I've grown up the past few years. I'm small, but I'm no child. As to my sex, say what you will. It won't change my mind."

"Narriman!"

"Father, will you stop saying that? You stood by me when I begged you not to. You drowned me in love I did not deserve. Stand by me now. Give me what I need to get Misr back. Teach me what I need to know."

Al Jahez shook his head. "Mowfik, you were right. She *is* remarkable."

"Little Fox. . . . It would take so long. And I'm not rich. I can't afford weapons and mounts and. . . ."

"We have a horse. We have a sword. You were a soldier. I can survive in the wilderness. I was of the al Muburak."

Mowfik sighed. "The sword is too heavy, girl."

Narriman glanced at Al Jahez. The captain tried to disappear among his cushions.

"Little Fox, I don't want to lose you too. I couldn't bear that." Mowfik's voice cracked. Narriman glimpsed a tear in the corner of one eye. This would cost him dearly from his beggared emotional purse.

He did not want to see her ride away. His heart said he would not see her again.

That dark rider had stolen her from him as surely as he had stolen Misr. She threw her arms around Mowfik. "Father, I have to do this. Wouldn't you come after me?"

"Yes. Yes, I would. I understand that."

Al Jahez said, "This isn't wise. The impossibility of dealing with the shaghûn and the Jebal aside, what would happen to a young woman alone? Even honest men would consider her fair for a moment's sport. Not to mention slavers and bandits. The Disciple instituted a rule of law, little one, but the Evil One, as ever, rules most of the land."

"Those are problems to face when they arise." What he said was true. She could not deny that. Women had no legal status or protection. When the shaghûn forced her onto her back he injured her father, not her. An unattached woman was not a person.

Her resolve was not shaken. Damned be the problems, and anyone who stood in her way.

## X

When she wanted something badly Narriman got her way. Mowfik surrendered in the end. Once he gave in, Al Jahez grudgingly endorsed her training.

Narriman pursued it with a dogged determination that, in time, compelled the respect of Al Jahez's men. She arrived early and left late, and worked harder than any boy.

She was hard. She ignored bruises and aches. Her instructors called her Vixen and backed away when the deadly fire rose in her eyes.

One day she browbeat Mowfik into taking her to the captain. She told Al Jahez, "I'm ready. I leave tomorrow."

Al Jahez addressed her father. "Will you permit this, Mowfik? A woman under arms. It's against nature."

Mowfik shrugged.

Narriman said, "Don't stall me. Father's done that for weeks. I'll go with or without your blessing."

"Mowfik, forbid this madness."

"Captain, you heard her. Shall I put her in irons?"

Al Jahez looked at her as if he would cage her for her own protection. "Then marry her to me, Mowfik."

Though struck speechless, Narriman understood. Al Jahez wanted the legal rights of marriage. So he could forbid, so he could call upon the law if she persisted. If she rebelled they could hunt her like a runaway slave.

Pure terror gripped her. She stared at her father, saw him tempted.

"Captain, heart and soul cry for me to accept. But I can't. A stronger voice bids me let her go. No matter how it hurts me."

Al Jahez sighed, defeated. "As you will. Child. Bring your father no sorrow or shame." He scowled at her expression. "No sorrow or shame of your own doing. That which is done by a shaghûn isn't of your doing. They're like the great storms in the erg. A man—or woman—can but bow his head till they pass. Come. The priests will bless your quest."

They waited in their fine ceremonial raiment. Al Jahez's eyes twinkled. "You see? Even the old captain begins to know you."

"Perhaps." She wondered if she was too predictable.

The ceremony was less important to her than to Mowfik and Al Jahez. She endured it for their sakes. She would ride with Karkur.

"Now then," Al Jahez said. "One more thing and I'll harass you no more. Gamel. The box."

A priest presented a sandalwood box. Al Jahez opened it. Within, on white silk, lay a pendant. It was a small, pale green stone not unlike many she had seen on the ground. Al Jahez said, "Perhaps this will be gift enough to repay you, Mowfik." And to Narriman, "Child, the Disciple teaches that even the acquiescence to sorcery is a sin, but men have to be practical. The Disciple himself has shaghûn advisers.

"The stone is an amulet. It will warn you if you are near one with the Power. It will begin to grow cooler when you're a mile away. When you're very near it will shed a green light. It's the best weapon I can give you."

Narriman tried to control the shakes. She failed. Tears broke loose. She hugged the captain. He was so startled he jumped away, but his face betrayed his pleasure.

"Go with the Lord, Little Fox. And Karkur if it pleases you."

"Thank you," she said. "For everything. Especially for being Father's friend."

Al Jahez snorted. "Ah, child. What are we without friends? Just severed heads rolling across the sands."

## XI

Narriman looked back just before Al Jahez's fortress passed out of sight. "That's yesterday." She looked southward, toward the great erg. "There lies tomorrow. Eight hundred miles." She gripped her reins, touched the amulet between her breasts, her weapons, the bag that Mowfik had filled with war booty when he thought she was not looking. He had done everything to dissuade her, and everything to help her.

She looked back again, wondering if their concepts of manhood and womanhood would compel them to send guardians.

"Go, Faithful," she told her mare. The fortress disappeared. Her heart fluttered. She was going. Alone. A severed head, rolling across the sand, cut off from her body—with a little help from the rider.

She pictured him as he had been the day he had taken Misr. She got that warm, moist feeling, but not as powerfully. Hatred had begun to quench that fire.

She wished there was a way a woman could do to a man what he had done to her.

The wilderness was all that she had been warned. It was bitter, unforgiving, and those who dwelt there reflected its harshness. Twice she encountered men who thought her a gift from heaven.

The first time she outrode them. The second, cornered, she fought. And was surprised to find herself the victor.

Though she had told herself she was the equal of any man, she'd never believed it in her heart. Could the wisdom of centuries be wrong? She rode away more mature, more confident.

The great erg was more vast than she remembered. It was hotter and more harrowing. She had no one and nothing to distract her.

"The severed head has to roll without its body." She put her thoughts into words often. Who was to hear?

She had no choice but to enter Wadi el Kuf. They were shocked to see her, a woman in man's wear, hung about with weapons, talking as tough as any wandering freesword. Even the whores were scandalized. Nobody knew what to make of her. She bought water, asked questions, and rode on before they regained their balance.

Someone came after her, but one arrow altered his ambitions.

She rode with dust devils as companions. The al Muburak believed dust devils were ifrits dancing. She called out, but they did not respond. After a few days she began to think oddly, to suspect them of being spies for the Masters. She mocked and taunted them. They ignored her.

Finally, she checked the amulet. Not only did it not shed light, it was not cool. "So much for old stories."

She rode out of the erg and paused at the oasis she had visited coming north. There, as at Wadi el Kuf, she asked about a man in black traveling with a child. There, too, no one had seen such a traveler.

"Of course," she muttered. "And maybe they're telling the truth. But he's human. He *had* to stop at Wadi el Kuf." But he need not have appeared as a shaghûn out of the Jebal, need he?

No matter. She knew his destination.

Fourteen days passed. She rode into Wadi al Hamamah.

The al Muburak were not there. It was the wrong time of year. They were farther west, stalking wild camels in hopes of adding to their herd.

She camped in the usual place, and when night fell she went to Karkur.

After the proper greetings and obeisances, she told her story in case Mowfik was wrong about his being able to follow an al Muburak anywhere. Karkur sat and listened, firelight sending shadows dancing across his ugly face.

She said, "Father says you aren't as great as I thought. That others are more powerful so sometimes you don't dare help. But if there's a way you can, help do what I have to do.''

She stared at the image. The image stared back. Time passed. The fire died. The moon rose, filled the Circle with shifting shadows.

"Karkur, there's a man named Al Jahez. He follows the Disciple, but he's a good man. Could you reward him? Could you tell Father I've come here safely?''

She thought, I'm talking to a lump of rock as though it really could do something. "Tell Al Jahez the severed head goes daft after it's separated.''

The moon was great, full thing that inundated the wadi with silver light. She leaned back and stared.

Something startled her. Fool, she thought. You fell asleep. Her dagger filled her hand. She searched the shadows, saw nothing. She listened. Nothing. She sniffed the air. Again nothing.

She shivered. It was getting cold. Colder than she remembered the nights this time of year. She pulled her cloak tighter.

And realized that the cold radiated from one point. The amulet!

She snatched it out. Green! Glowing green. She searched the shadows. Had the shaghûn come out to meet her?

The stone flared. It crackled. An emerald snake writhed between it and Karkur. A cold wind swirled around the Circle. Dead leaves pattered against her. She glanced up. No. The sky was clear. Stars winked in their myriads. The moon shone benevolently.

The emerald snake turned amber shot with veins of blood. Narriman gasped. That was the combination they mentioned when they talked about the Great Death.

The snake died. The stone grew less cold, became just a small, pale green piece of rock lying in her hand. She stared at Karkur.

"What have you done? What have you given me? Not the power of the Great Death?''

The image stared back, as silent as ever. She was tempted to rant. But Karkur gave short shift to ingrates. He was more a punitive than a helpful god. "But loyal to his people," she said. "Thank you, Karkur.''

She hurried through the parting rituals and returned to camp. She fell asleep still astonished that Karkur had responded.

There were dreams. Vivid dreams. She rode into the Jebal, moving with an absolute certainty of her way. She knew exactly when to expect the first challenge.

The dream ended. The sun had wakened her. She felt fit and

rested. She recalled every detail of the dream. She looked down the wadi. A dumb stone god? She examined Al Jahez's stone. It looked no less ordinary this morning.

## XII

The trails were faint, but she followed them confidently. Once she noted an overturned stone, darker on the exposed side. Someone had been this way recently. She shrugged. The amulet would warn her.

The mountains were silent. All the world was silent when you rode alone. The great erg had been filled with a stillness as vast as that of death. Here it seemed there should be some sound, if only the call of the red-tailed hawk on the wing. But the only sounds were those of a breeze in scrubby oaks, of water chuckling in one small stream.

She moved higher and higher. Sometimes she looked back across the hills where the wadi lay, to the plain beyond, a distance frosted with haze. The al Muburak might profit from such a view.

Night fell. She made a fireless camp. She drank water, ate smoked meat, turned in as the stars came out.

She wakened once, frightened, but her stone betrayed no danger. The mountains remained still, though the wind made an unfamiliar soughing through nearby pines. She counted more than a dozen meteors before drifting off.

Her dreams were vivid. In one her father told Al Jahez he was sure she had reached Wadi al Hamamah safely.

The mountains continued their rise. She rested more often. Come midday she entered terrain scoured by fire. That stark, black expanse was an alien landscape.

The trees changed. Oaks became scarcer, pines more numerous. The mountains became like nothing in her experience. Great looms of rock thrust out of their hips, the layering on end instead of horizontal. Even where soil and grass covered them she could discern the striations. Distant mountainsides looked zebra-striped in the right light.

Higher still. The oaks vanished. And then, in the bottom of one canyon, she encountered trees so huge a half dozen men could not have joined hands around their trunks. Narriman felt insignificant in their shadows.

She spent her fourth day riding up that canyon. Evening came early. She almost missed the landmarks warning her she was approaching the first guardian. She considered the failing light. This was no time to hurry. She retreated and camped.

Something wakened her. She listened, sniffed, realized the alarming agent was no external. She had dreamed that she should circle the watchpost.

"Come, Faithful," she whispered. She wrapped the reins in her hand and led away.

She knew exactly where to go, and still it was bad. That mountainside was not meant for climbing. The brush was dense and the slope was steep. She advanced a few yards and listened.

The brush gave way to a barren area. The soil was loose and dry. She slipped several times. Then her mare went down, screaming and sliding. She held on stubbornly.

The slide ended. "Easy, girl. Easy. Stay still."

A glow appeared below. She was surprised. She had climbed higher than she had thought. The glow drifted along the canyon.

"I can't fail now. Not at the first hurdle."

Her heart hammered. She felt like screaming against clumsiness, stupidity, and the whim of fate.

The glow drifted down the canyon, climbed the far slope, came back. It crossed to Narriman's side and went down again. It repeated the patrol but never climbed far from the canyon floor. It never came close enough to make her amulet glow. It finally gave up. But Narriman did not trust it because it had disappeared. She waited fifteen minutes.

The sky was lightening before she felt comfortably past. She was exhausted. "Good girl, Faithful. Let's camp."

## XIII

A horse's whinny wakened her. She darted to Faithful, clamped her hands over the mare's nostrils.

The sound of hooves on brookside stone came nearer. The amulet became a lump of ice. She saw flickers of black rider through the trees.

This one was stockier than her shaghûn.

*Her* shaghûn? Had he touched her that deeply? She looked inward, seeking the hatred of rider and love of son that had brought her to the Jebal. And it was there, the hatred untarnished by any positive feeling.

Then the rider was gone, headed down the canyon. Was he going to the guardian?

She had no dream memories of the canyon above the guardian. Why not? Couldn't Karkur reach into the realm of the Masters?

The uncertainty became too much. She dismounted and walked. No need to rush into trouble.

Minutes later she heard a rhythmic thumping ahead. Something rumbled and crashed and sent echoes tumbling down the canyon. She advanced more carefully, sliding from cover to cover.

She did not know where they came from. Suddenly, they were there, across the brook. They walked like men but were shaggy and dark and tall. There were four of them. The biggest growled.

"Damn!" She strung her bow as one giant bellowed and charged.

Her arrow split its breastbone. It halted, plucked at the dart. The others boomed and rushed. She sped two quick arrows, missed once, then drew her saber and scampered toward a boulder. If she got on top. . . .

Neither wounded monster went down. Both went for the mare. The others came for her.

Faithful tried to run, stumbled, screamed. The beasts piled on her.

Narriman drew her razor-edged blade across a wide belly. The brute stumbled a few steps, looked down at its wound, began tucking entrails back inside.

Narriman glanced at the mare as she dodged the other beast. The wounded creatures were pounding her with huge stones.

A fist slammed into Narriman's side. She staggered, gasped. Her attacker bellowed and closed in. She tried to raise her saber. It slipped from her hand. She hadn't the strength to grip it.

The thing shook her half senseless. Then it sniffed her and grunted.

It was something out of nightmare. The thing settled with Narriman in its lap, pawed between her thighs. She felt its sex swell against her back.

Was the whole Jebal rape-crazy? "Karkur!"

The thing ripped her clothing. Another grunted and tried to touch. The beast holding Narriman swung at it.

She was free for an instant. She scrambled away. The beast roared and dove after her.

She closed her hands on her amulet. "Karkur, give me the strength to survive this."

The beast snorted weirdly, uttered an odd shriek that tortured the canyon walls. It stumbled away, enveloped by an amber light laced with bloody threads.

Another beast came for her. Its cries joined those of the other. Narriman scrambled after her saber. The last beast, with an arrow in its chest, watched her with glazed eyes, backed away. She arranged her clothing, ran to Faithful.

"Poor Faithful." What would she do now? How would she escape the Jebal without a horse for Misr?

The beasts in amber kept screaming. The Great Death was a hard death. It twisted their muscles till bones broke.

The screaming finally stopped.

She heard distant voices.

Hurriedly, she made a pack of her possessions, then climbed the canyon wall. She found an outcrop from which she could watch the mess she had fled.

Those things! She recalled their size and smell and was sick.

The investigators were ordinary men armed with tools. They became excited and cautious when they found the beasts. Narriman heard the word shaghûn several times. "Keep thinking that," she murmured. "Don't get the idea there's a stranger in the Jebal."

Her shakes faded. She offered thanks to Karkur and started across the mountainside.

What were those beasts? Those men feared them. She moved with saber in hand.

The investigators had come from a lumbering camp. She watched men drag a log up a road, toward the head of the canyon. Why? She shrugged. The Masters must want it done.

She took to that road once she passed the camp.

That afternoon she heard hoofbeats. She slipped into the underbrush. "Oh, damn!" The horseman carried two of her arrows and Faithful's saddle. She strung her bow, jumped into the road, shouted, "Hey! Wait a minute!"

The rider reined in, looked back. She waved. He turned.

Her arrow flew true. He sagged backward. His horse surged forward. Narriman caught it as it passed. She dragged the body into the brush, mounted up wondering how soon he would be missed.

The canyon walls closed in. The brook faded away. She reached the summit. The road wound downhill, toward a far haze of smoke. There were a lot of hearthfires down there.

## XIV

She traveled for two days. The only people she saw were men working logs down the road. She avoided them. She topped a piney ridge the second evening and saw a city.

Thoughts of Misr nagged her. Should she go down now? She was ahead of news from the logging camp. But he might not be there. And she was tired. She was incapable of acting efficiently in a desperate situation. Her judgment might be clouded, too.

She settled down off the road. She would have loved a fire. The mountain nights were chilly. Gnawing dried meat, she grumbled, "I'd sell my soul for a decent meal."

Sleep brought dreams. They showed her the town, including a place where children were kept. She also saw a place where shaghûns lived, and beyond the city a tower that was an emptiness fraught with dark promise.

She wakened knowing exactly what to do. Come nightfall she would slip into the city, break into the nursery, and take Misr. Then she would flee, set an ambush down the trail and hope her shaghûn was the one who came.

Her plan died immediately. Her mount had broken its tether. Its trail led toward the city.

What would they think? Would they investigate? Of course. She'd best move elsewhere.

She trudged southward, circling the city. Time and again she went out of her way to avoid farmsteads. By nightfall she was exhausted again.

It had to be tonight, though. There was no more time.

What would she do for a mount? Her hope of escape hinged on her being able to lead the pursuit to ground of her own choosing.

She settled down near the city's edge. "Karkur, wake me when it's time."

It was a dark night. There was no moon. Clouds obscured half the stars. Narriman arose shaking. Her nerves got no better for a long time.

The streets were strange for a girl who'd never walked pavement. Her bootheels kept clicking. Echoes came back off the walls. "Too quiet," she muttered. "Where are the dogs?"

Not a howl went up. Not one dog came to investigate. Her nerves only tautened. She began to imagine something watching her, the town as a box trap waiting for her to trip its trigger. She dried her hands on her hips repeatedly. The moths in her stomach refused to lie still. She kept looking over her shoulder.

She gave the place of the shaghûns a wide berth, closed in on the nursery. Why were the youngsters segregated? Was it a place for children like Misr? The city made no sense. She didn't try to make it do so.

The only warning was a rustle of fabric. Narriman whirled,

saber spearing out. It was an automatic move, made without thought. She found herself face to face with a mortally wounded shaghûn.

He raised a gloved hand as he sank toward the pavement. His fingers wobbled. Sorcery! She hacked the offending hand, came back with a neck stroke. She cut him again and again, venting nervous energy and fear.

"What do I do with him?" she wondered. She examined him. He was no older than she. She felt a touch of remorse.

She glanced around. The street remained quiet. A convenient alleyway lay just a few steps beyond the body.

She wondered what he had been doing. Her dreams had suggested that no one wandered the streets after dark, save a night watchman with a special dispensation.

Had the horse alerted them? Were there more shaghûns to be faced? Her stomach cramped.

Maybe her father and Al Jahez were right. Maybe a woman *couldn't* do this sort of thing. "And maybe men feel as ragged as I do," she muttered. She dropped the body into shadow. "Give me an hour, Karkur." She went on to the nursery.

Anticipation partially overcame her reaction to the killing. She tried a door. It was barred from within. A second door proved as impenetrable. There was a third on the far side, but she assumed it would be sealed too.

Above, barely visible, were second-story windows, some with open shutters. If she could. . . .

She spun into shadow and balled up, blade ready. A shape loomed out of the night, headed her way. Shaghûn! Were they all on patrol?

He passed just ten feet away. Narriman held her breath. What were they doing? Looking for her? Or was her fear wholly egotistical?

There was a six-foot-wide breezeway between the nursery and building to its left. A stairway climbed the neighbor. A landing hung opposite a nursery window. Narriman secreted her possessions beneath the stair and crept upward. The stair creaked. She scarcely noticed. She could think of nothing but Misr.

The window was open. It was but a short step from the landing. She straddled the railing.

Someone opened the door to which the stair led. Light flooded the landing. A fat man asked, "Here, you. What's? . . ."

Narriman slashed at him. He grabbed her blade. Off balance, she almost fell. She clung to the railing. It creaked. She jumped for the window.

The fat man staggered, reached for her, ploughed through the railing. Narriman clung to the window's frame and looked down. The man lay twitching below. "Karkur, don't let him raise the alarm."

The room before her was dark. A child mumbled something. Behind Narriman, a woman called a question. Narriman eased into the room.

The child was not Misr.

Someone shrieked. Narriman glanced outside. A woman stood on the landing, looking down.

Narriman slipped into a hallway running past other bedrooms. Which one? Might as well start with the nearest.

She found her son in the fifth she checked. He was sleeping peacefully. His face looked angelic. He seemed healthy. She threw herself on him, weeping, and remained lost within herself till she realized he was awake.

"Mama! What're you doing here?" Misr hugged her with painful ferocity. He cried too. She was glad. Her most secret fear had been that he would have forgotten her.

"I came to take you home."

"Where's Granpa?"

"Home. Waiting for us. Come on."

"The man, Mama. The dark man. He won't let us." He started shaking. His body was hale, but they had done something to his mind.

"He won't stop us, Misr. I won't let him. Get dressed. Hurry." People were talking in the hall.

Misr did as he was told. Slowly.

Someone shoved through the doorway. "What's going on? . . . ." Narriman's saber pricked his throat. "Over there."

"A woman? Who are you?"

She pressed the sword's tip a quarter inch into his chest. "I'll ask. You answer." He shut up and moved. Small children watched from the doorway. "How many shaghûns in this town?"

He looked strange. He did not want to answer. Narriman pricked him. "Four! But one went to the lumber camp three weeks ago. He hasn't come back. You're the boy's sister?"

"Misr, will you hurry?" Four shaghûns. But one was out of town and another was dead. A third roamed the streets. Was hers the fourth?

"You can't take the boy out of here, woman."

She pricked him again. "You talk too much. Misr!"

"He belongs to the Old Ones."

Misr finished and looked at her expectantly.

Now what? Go the way she had come? She stepped behind her prisoner and hit him with her pommel. He sagged. Misr's eyes got big. She dragged him toward the fallway. He told the others, "I'm going home with my mother." He sounded proud.

She was amazed at how he had grown. He acted older, too. No time for that. "Come here." She tossed him across to the landing, jumped, hurried him downstairs. She recovered her belongings.

The fat man's woman howled all the while. "Shut up!" The woman retreated, whimpering.

Narriman looked into the street. People were gathering. "Misr. This way." She retreated into the breezeway. "A horse," she muttered. "Where do I find a horse?"

She was about to leave the breezeway when she heard someone running. "Get back, Misr. And be quiet." She crouched.

The runner turned into the breezeway. Shaghûn! He tried to stop. Narriman drove her blade into his chest. He staggered back. She struck again. This was the shaghûn who had missed her earlier.

She smiled grimly. Succeed or fail, they would remember her.

"Come on, Misr." People were shouting to her right. She headed left, though that was not the direction she preferred. Misr ran beside her. She searched her dream memories for a stable. She did not find one.

Hope of escape came out of a walking dream that hit like a fist, made her stumble.

Karkur wanted her to go eastward. There was a road through the mountains. They would not expect her to flee that way. If she reached the seacoast she could go north and recross the mountains at Sebil el Selib, where the Masters held no sway.

But this end of that road ran around the dread tower of her dreams. Who knew what the Masters would do? If their shaghûns were but shadows of themselves, how terrible might they be?

She was afraid but she did not stop moving. Karkur had not failed her yet.

And Karkur was right. It *was* the best way. She saw no one, and no one saw her. And the dark tower greeted her with an indifference she found almost disheartening. Was she that far beneath their notice? She had slain two of their shaghûns.

"Keep walking, Misr. We're going to get tired, but we have to keep walking. Otherwise the dark men will catch us."

His face puckered in determination. He stayed with her. The sun was high before she decided to rest.

## XV

"Narriman!" The voice boomed through the forest, rang off the mountains. "Narriman!" There was an edge of anger to it, like hers when she was impatient with Misr.

It was him. He had not been deceived.

Misr snuggled closer. "Don't let him take me, Mama."

"I won't," she promised, disentangling herself. "I won't." She gave Misr some dried meat. "Eat this. I'll be back in a little while."

"Don't go away, Mama."

"I have to. You stay put. Just remember what happened last time you didn't do what I said." Damn! That was unfair. He would think the whole thing was his fault. She spat, strung her bow, selected three good arrows, made sure her weapons were ready. Then she went to hunt.

"Narriman!" He was closer. Why act as if he couldn't find her?

Karkur, of course. That old lump did not dare smash things up in the Jebal. He would not want his hand seen. But he could confuse his enemies.

Brush crackled. Narriman froze. He was close. She sank into a patch of shade, arrow on bowstring.

"Narriman!" His voice boomed. More softly, he talked to himself. "Damned crazy woman. I'll use her hide to bind books." His anger was hard but controlled. Fear wriggled through Narriman's hatred.

Memories flashed. His ride down Wadi al Hamamah. Her rape. The day he had come for Misr. Her knees weakened. He was a shaghûn. He had conquered her easily. She was a fool to challenge him.

Brush crackled ever closer. She saw something white moving among the trees. His horse. That was him. Coming right to her.

There he was. Black rider. Nightmare lover. Misr's father. She pictured Mowfik and Al Jahez. "You!" she breathed. "For what you did to my father."

A twig snapped as she drew her bow. The horse's head snapped up, ears pricking. Her arrow slammed into its throat. It should have struck the shaghûn's heart.

The animal kept rising into a screaming rear, hooves pounding air. The rider went over backward. Narriman heard his breath explode when he hit ground.

Up she sprang. She let fly again. Her shaft passed through his djellaba as he rolled, pinned him for a second. In that second Narriman loosed her last arrow.

It glanced off his hip bone, leaving a bloody gash across his right buttock. He stumbled a step, fell, regained his feet with a groan.

Narriman drew her saber, stalked forward. Her mind boiled with all she wanted to say before she killed him.

He regained control, drew his own blade. A strained smile crossed his lips.

Narriman moved in carefully. I'll attack to his right, she thought. Make him put more strain on his wound. He's battered and bleeding. He'll be slow. I can wear him down.

"Little Fox. Little fool. Why did you come here? Outsiders don't come to the Jebal. Not and leave again."

There'll be a first, then, she thought. But she did not speak. Things she wanted to say rattled through her mind, but not one reached her lips. Her approach was as silent and implacable as his preceding her rapes.

She threw three hard, quick strokes. He turned them, but looked disturbed. She was not supposed to do this, was she? She was supposed to fall under his spell.

"Narriman! Look at me!"

She was caught by the command. She met his eye.

The fire ran through her. She ached for him. And to her surprise, she ignored it. She struck while his guard was loose, opened a gash on his cheek.

He went pale. His eyes grew larger. He could not believe it.

She struck again. He blocked her, thrust back, nearly reached her. He knew she was not dealing with a little girl anymore.

He beat her back, then retreated. A weird keening came from him, though his lips did not move. Leaves stirred. A cold wind rose. The tip of Narriman's saber drooped like a candle in the sun. She shifted it to her left hand, pulled her dagger and threw it. Mowfik had taught her that.

The dagger struck the shaghûn in the left shoulder, spun him. The cold wind died. Narriman moved in with her odd-looking saber. Fear filled the shaghûn's eyes.

He plucked the dagger from his wound and made those sounds again. His wounds began to close.

Surprise had been Narriman's best weapon. Fate had stolen that. She feared she had more than she could handle now.

She launched a furious attack. He retreated, stumbled, fell. She cut him several times before he rose.

But he had his confidence back. She could not kill him. He

smiled. Arrow, saber, and dagger. She had exhausted her options. She did have poison. Would he step up and take it? She had a garrotte given her by one of Al Jahez's men, half a love offering and half a well-wish. But would he hold still while she used it?

Brush crackled. She whirled. "Misr! I told you. . . ."

The shaghûn smashed into her, knocked her saber away. His fingers closed around her chin and forced her to turn toward him.

## XVI

Lost! she wailed inside. She should have listened to Al Jahez and Mowfik. The fire was in her again, and she could not stop him. He stripped her slowly, taking pleasure in her humiliation.

He pressed her down on the stones and pine needles and stood over her, smiling. He disrobed slowly. And Misr stood there watching, too terrified to move.

Tears streaming, Narriman forced her eyes shut. She had been so close! One broken twig short.

She felt him lower himself, felt him probe, felt him enter. Felt herself respond. Damn, she hated him!

She found enough hatred to shove against his chest. But only for an instant. Then he was down upon her again, forcing her hands back against her breasts. "Karkur," she wept.

The shaghûn moaned softly, stopped bucking. His body stiffened. He pulled away. The spell binding Narriman diminished.

"The Great Death!" she breathed.

It had him, but he was fighting it. Amber wriggled over him, flickering. There were few bloody veins in it. His mouth was open as though to scream, but he was gurgling a form of his earlier keening.

Narriman could not watch.

It did not occur to her that a mere shaghûn, even a shaghûn of the jebal, could overcome Karkur's Great Death. He was but stalling the inevitable. She crawled to her discarded clothing.

Misr said something. She could not look at him. Her shame was too great.

"Mama. *Do* something."

She finally looked. Misr pointed.

The shaghûn's face was twisted. The muscles of his left arm were knotted. The bone was broken. But there was just one patch of amber left, flickering toward extinction.

He had bested the Great Death!

A silent wail of fear filled her. There was no stopping him! Raging at the injustice, she seized a dead limb and clubbed him.

Misr grabbed a stick and started swinging too.

"Misr. Stop that."

"Mama, he hurt you."

"You stop. I can do it but you can't." Did that make sense? How could she explain? He's your father, Misr? I can murder him but you can't? No. Some things could not be explained. "Get away."

She swung again. The shaghûn tried to block with his injured arm. He failed. The impact sent him sprawling. The Great Death crept over him. She hit him again.

He looked at her with the eyes of the damned. He did not beg, but he did not want to die. He stared. There was no enchantment in his eyes. They contained nothing but fear, despair, and, maybe, regret. He was no shaghûn now. He was just a man dying before his time.

The club slipped from her fingers. She turned back, collected her clothes. "Misr, let's get our things." For no reason she could appreciate, she recalled Al Jahez's words about severed heads.

She collected the shaghûn's sword, considered momentarily, then gave him the mercy he had denied her.

"You killed him, Mama. You really killed him." Misr was delighted.

"Shut up!"

She could have closed her eyes to his screams, but his dying face would have haunted her forever. It might anyway.

When all else was stripped away, he had been a man. And once a mother had wept for him while a dark rider had carried him toward the rising sun.

One of the hardest things to find within the sub-genre known as Sword and Sorcery is a touch of humor. When it's found, almost every preconception about requirements goes by the board—including my original specification of "no male protagonists." In this story, the thief Clea definitely takes a subordinate part—or does she? We'll leave it to you.

Stephen Burns is, he says, thirty, and shares his house with a cat. He lives on an island in the St. Lawrence river; there are very definite seasons there, and perhaps because of that, his writing is also seasonal, coinciding with the severe winter; the rest of the year he works as handyman and jack-of-all-trades to finance his writing. This is his third sale—but the other two magazines to which he sold ceased publication before they printed his work. Defying his reputation as a Jonah, therefore, we are happy to bring you his first appearance in print—and hopefully not his last!—MZB

# TAKING HEART
## by Stephen L. Burns

The past-midnight quiet in Yuelianq Thief-Keep came to a sudden end when a knife came flashing out of the dark.

The knife buried itself point-first in the wooden crescent of stool showing between the night-jailer's legs. Jailer, stool, and his upraised wineskin went toppling over backward. He had barely hit the floor when a soft, hoarse voice came out of the same dark nowhere as the knife.

"Silence, on your life! How much are you paid, Guard?"

The jailer dared to peek fearfully over his overturned stool, past the knife. "Little," he whispered.

"Enough to be worth your life this night?"

The jailer shook his head so violently that his earrings rattled.

A piece of darkness detached itself from the unlit corridor, and became a small figure robed and hooded in black. "Up," came the voice. Within the dark hood, no face could be seen, but the blade of a knife protruded from one long sleeve, bright, sharp and ready. The jailer scrambled to his feet, eyes on the knife.

"Your keys, guard. We pay a visit to the thief Raalt." The

knife showing from one sleeve winked out of sight. The sleeve moved, and before the jailer's amazed eyes the black-handled knife embedded in the stool pulled itself free and flew past him like a darting bird. It vanished inside the sleeve hilt-first.

"Take your lamp and lead the way."

The jailer halted before one particular cell door in the dank stone corridor, and gestured toward the iron-bound door.

One black sleeve swept outward. "Open it." The nightshade visitor's voice showed no overt edge, yet it was there, as a leather sheath contains the ready steel edge of a sword. The jailer heard that silent edge and unlocked the door with a nervous rattle of keys. He picked up his greaselamp and, with an unhappy sigh, went into the cell.

The thief Raalt was a large, hard-muscled man, handsome and blond-maned. He lay sleeping on the rank straw piled at the far end of the cell. Stout chains rimed with rust ran from the shackles on his thick wrists to a massive iron ring set in the rough stone of the cell's back wall. His ankles were shackled as well, the chains just as sturdy.

He roused at the light in his eyes. "A *visitor*," the jailer husked.

Raalt looked past the jailer and saw the mysterious, part-of-the-dark form of the black-robed visitor. It stepped closer, ominously silent.

Raalt drew into a crouch, paled, but did not look away. "Are you Arrmik, come for your Heart?"

It had been the Heart of Arrmik that he had stolen, and after a long chase and fierce struggle, he had been captured. He had brought down fourteen guards and soldiers before he had been overmastered by a pike blow to the back of the head. He was still alive only because he had managed to hide the Heart before his capture. Its return was greatly desired.

The robed figure drew closer yet. Raalt's muscles began to twitch as he readied himself to battle the thing.

Then the cell suddenly filled with the sound of light chiming laughter. The sleeve-shrouded hands threw back the hood and pulled down a black veil, revealing a woman with short midnight hair and wide-set black eyes. Her elfin face was alight with mischievous delight.

"*Clea!*" Raalt groaned. His mouth twisted angrily and he slumped back to the straw with a jangle of chains.

"How would you like to be free of this awful place, dear Raalt?" She grinned at him and winked. "Can the reputation of the Great Thief Raalt bear the shame of being rescued by a woman?''

Raalt wondered what God bore him such a grudge.

"There is a price, of course! I get half of what the Heart of Arrmik brings or I leave you here." She shook her head sadly. "The torture is to begin at dawn. I hear that they can keep a man in living agony for days—*weeks* if he is really strong . . ."

Raalt groaned again. Being captured was bad enough; having to be rescued was worse yet. That it was Clea who would rescue him, and the price she demanded, was almost too bitter a turn to bear. He stared bleakly at his shackles and rattled his chains dejectedly. He thought about hooks, hammers, pincers and red-hot irons probing tender places. He shuddered. What other choice did he have?

"I agree," he said sullenly, promising himself dire retribution.

Clea's smile was like the twist of a knife. "Swear an Oath on the souls of your father and mother that you will obey me and not try to betray me until after we have gained the Heart and sold it."

"No!" Raalt shouted. "You ask too much!"

"Probably." Clea turned to go.

"Wait!" Raalt looked as if he were swallowing something that went down hard and tasted bad. He was; it was his pride. "I so swear," he grated, his teeth clenched. "—And I further swear that you will pay for this!"

Clea shrugged, her smile unchanged by his threat. "Set him free." The jailer scurried to comply. "Now I will leave a little puzzle in your name."

As Raalt stepped free from his chains, Clea went to the wall where the iron ring was fastened. Using a bit of chalk taken from her pocket, she drew a large square around the ring. It started from the floor and looked like a low door with the ring at its center. She scribed a symbol at each corner of the square, then above the square she scrawled the word BEWARE. A pinch of powder taken from a black leather pouch was then rubbed onto the stone just over the ring. Raalt's spine tingled as he sensed magic being gathered.

"Now." She moved her hand and instantly one of the black-handled knives was in it. Whispering some oddly cadenced chant under her breath, she tapped the powdered spot with the knife's hilt.

There was a long sighing sound and the whole square went black, as if that section of wall had suddenly opened on a chasm of night. The iron ring dropped to the floor with a dull *chang*, its anchoring part having disappeared along with the section of wall that held it. Raalt stared at the hole as if he expected some fell creature to come climbing out of it at any moment.

Clea grinned, obviously pleased with her work. "That should give them something to ponder." She nudged the iron ring over the dark threshold with her toe. It fell, dragging chains and shackles behind it. There was no sound of a bottom being struck.

"Now they will believe that you escaped by some power that they know not, and it will occupy them for a while." She winked at Raalt. "It will not hurt your reputation, either. They will think you a wizard now, and fear you more!"

"You thought of everything," Raalt muttered in grudging admiration. He had to admit that it was a pleasure to watch Clea's devious mind at work—when it was not working against him.

"Don't I always?"

Clea led Raalt to a place just outside the Thief-Keep's walls and halted him by a thick clump of bushes. Under the bushes three bound and gagged soldiers writhed like armored worms. She retrieved a tunic, hooded cloak, sword, sheath and belt, handing them to him silently.

Once Raalt was dressed, they put some distance between themselves and the Keep's somber stone walls. Clea set the pace, moving quietly as a hawk's shadow on the ground. Raalt stalked along beside her, already chafing under the unhappy bargain he had been forced to strike. Only his oath and the memory of experiences of other days kept him in check.

He had last clashed with Clea some two years before. She had turned up just in time to turn the tide in a pitched battle with a horde of Nariman Tribesmen who wanted to relieve Raalt and his two confederates of the spoils from the robbery of a gem merchant. Clea had joined the fighting like a demon incarnate, those inexplicable black-handled knives of hers leaving and returning to her hands like edged lightning and never missing their marks.

The skirmish was nearing an end when Raalt had broken away on horseback with the chest of gems. He had never planned to share the booty and cared little how the end of the battle went.

Clea had seen him and waded through a knot of six tribesmen, scattering them like leaves. She had run him down on foot and unhorsed him. He had tried to defend his prize with his sword, but she had evaded his every stroke and thrust. She led him away from the chest, disarmed him, then doubled back to take his sword, horse, and his share of the gems, leaving him unarmed and smarting to face his disgruntled associates. He had just barely been able to talk his way out of that with his skin intact. That had not been the first time they had clashed.

Now here she was again, and she had forced him to swear that damned oath—which made it that much harder for him to find a way to master her.

Clea interrupted his thoughts. "We should be far enough away now. Tell me where you hid the Heart."

Raalt squared his broad shoulders. First things first. Get the Heart, then figure out how to keep it from her. There *had* to be a way. "I did not have much time to hide it. The guards were hard on my heels—"

"Because you were too stupidly certain of your strength to plan your theft carefully." Clea said scornfully. "You just grabbed it and ran, didn't you?"

Raalt bristled, his hand falling to his sword-hilt. "Why do it otherwise?" he snarled. "I am not some weak woman, bent on avoiding a fight! I brought down fourteen guards, alone, and got the Heart to a safe place!"

He caught himself and took a deep breath to master his anger. Allowing her to provoke him would not bring the Heart closer. He spoke stiffly. "I flung the Heart into the fountain in the old Eastern Square." He looked grim, as if he had just told her that it was in a cave guarded by a thousand hungry Bloodwraiths.

Clea frowned, puzzled. "That is not too shabby a place."

"Thank you. But we still have to get it out somehow. . . ."

Clea shrugged. "You just wade in and dive for it—the fountain cannot be all that deep."

Raalt paled. "Into all that *water??* Never!" He shuddered, just thinking about it. He would rather face Bloodwraiths or Sandmaws. Once, on a small bet, he had climbed laughing into a cage to wrestle a gûr-rhakhar, and feared nothing with blade, teeth or claws. But he could not abide the water. He was a child of dry, barren lands and unable to change.

Clea hung her head and rubbed her forehead as if she had a headache. "Then how were you going to regain the Heart if you are afraid of the water?"

"I am *not* afraid!" Raalt snapped. "I just do not *like* the damned water! As for the Heart, I would probably threaten someone into getting it for me—I guess I had not thought about it. Not yet."

"No, it is not likely that you would have." Clea shook her head sadly. "Come on, let us get it now. You will not get wet, I promise."

\* \* \*

They approached the old Eastern Square through an unlit, trash-strewn alley. When they reached the alley's end they peered out from behind some piled bales, taking care that they were not seen.

"There are a few people about," Clea whispered. "Let us think this through and plan it out."

"Why bother?" Raalt pulled his sword partway out of its sheath. "We—you—get the Heart out of the cursed water. I cover you, and anyone daring to interfere gets a belly full of steel! How would you," he stressed the word scornfully, "do it?"

Clea regarded him bleakly. "Raalt, truly you are as strong and fast as the best of them, and you know your blade better than most. You are a good thief, but your artlessness will one day be the death of you." She turned away, leaving Raalt to decide if he had been given a compliment. She scanned torch and moonlit square carefully, her sharp black eyes missing nothing. "I do not see any guards or soldiers about, but you never can tell. . . . Exactly where did the Heart land?"

"Right in the center of the fountain. It sank quickly."

Clea nodded and pointed to an amply fleshed, kohl-eyed prostitute lounging in a doorway about a third of the way around the square from their hiding-place. "We will use her, I think." She pointed to a still-open wine stall. "—and that place. Wait here."

Before Raalt could argue or question, Clea was gone. "Damn her," he muttered, resigning himself to waiting and thinking of various ways he might wrest the spoils from the Heart out of her hands. The oath she had bound him to reduced his other options.

Clea reappeared quickly. "Everything is set up," she said, sounding very pleased. "Here is the plan. You and I pretend that we are drunk."

Raalt said nothing, wishing he was drunk—and alone.

"We wander over to that winestall and buy a skin of wine— here is some coin. Just a man and his woman out at the evening's dregs, buying some wine before we go someplace private. Got that?"

Raalt frowned, but nodded.

"We laugh often and look harmless and happy. After we buy the wine, we move toward the fountain. But before we get there, I will break away from you, laughing and teasing. When I reach the fountain I will dive in—just acting silly, it would seem. You follow behind, pick up my clothing, and go to the fountain's rim still playing your role. Got that?''

Raalt thought that Clea's plan was getting more ridiculous by the moment. But he would let her have her way—his time would come. He nodded curtly.

"The whore's cue is my leaving your side. She goes to the winestall and starts an argument over the price of a flask. I told her to be loud and crude, so that anyone watching will have to divide their attention between her and us.

"I find the Heart and you have my robe ready at the side of the fountain so that I can step right into it. I will pass the Heart so that nobody can see that I have taken something from the fountain. Then we leave, still keeping up our act—just two drunken lovers and no one the wiser!''

Raalt's impatience flared. "But why go through all that nonsense, Clea?'' He gestured toward the square. "Nobody watches, and even if someone does and tries to interfere, he will die regretting it!''

Raalt had learned his craft from the Great Thief Wegan, and he had always told Raalt that fancy plans were for those without the might or confidence to simply take what they wanted. Anyone uncomfortable with that forthright approach would be better off as a pickpocket or priest if they still wanted to steal but lacked the balls for a man's methods.

"Was anyone watching when you stole the Heart?'' Clea glared up at him.

"I didn't think so,'' he snarled, clenching his fists. "I got away!''

"But only for a while! Use your head *and* your arm! That will make you more than twice as strong! Never leave anything to chance—*never*!'' Clea checked her scorn and continued more gently. "Theft is a game and an art; always be at least ten steps ahead and make every move beautiful.''

Raalt had suffered enough of Clea's impudence. He quivered with repressed violence, and was on the verge of breaking his oath when Clea touched his arm and said, "I'm sorry.'' He felt a strange tingling sensation that spread from her touch and caught a vague whiff of some sweet spice. The anger seemed to sigh out of him all at once and on its own.

Clea linked her arm in his, her smile winsome and apologetic. "Ready partner?''

He shrugged uneasily, wondering where his anger had gone. The tingle was gone and the scent faded before he could place it.

Clea's smile turned into a comradely grin. "Let us be at it, then!"

Arm in arm they weaved out of the alley and onto the moonlit square. Clea's laugh rang out high and sweetly girlish, sounding silly from too much wine. She clung to Raalt's arm as if afraid that he would get away from her, and her hip bumped against him at every step. She seemed every inch a giddy young girl.

Though stiff and uncomfortable at first, Raalt soon began to swagger as he relaxed into his assigned role. The change that Clea had undergone helped. She scarcely resembled the ever-contrary, sharp-tongued creature come to plague his life again. Now that she was not seemingly going out of her way to rub him wrong, she seemed more attractive, more like the kind of woman he knew and could bend to his will. The way she hung on his arm made him realize how small and waif-like she really was, made him realize that she must have her own weak spots.

Then he remembered something else Wegan had taught him, a thing he himself knew to be true; that a woman's heart was her weakest part.

It was like a light dawning inside. All the signs had been there. She had sought and saved him, brought him fine clothes and a weapon. Even her constant arguing could be seen as a kind of wry courtship, as with children. As part of her plan she got to hold him and play at romance. Had she not desired that, she would have made another plan.

Raalt looked down at Clea, smiling in his new knowledge. His face took on the devilish grin that had led a hundred maids to his bed. *A woman's heart is her weakest part;* that would be a part of the way he would out-fox Clea the Fox. He tightened his arm around her and winked conspiratorily. The smile she returned was open, lovely. *Vulnerable.* Raalt laughed aloud.

They arrived at the winestall. Raalt dickered hard for the wine, falling into the spirit of the exchange. Partway through his haggling, Clea tugged at his sleeve, indicating that she wanted to whisper something to him. He bent to listen, but instead of words, he received a wet tongue in his ear, provoking a laugh from the beaky, bearded merchant. Her wet probing continued longer than he might have expected—though not as long as he would have liked—and there seemed to be nothing of play-acting in it. Again he caught that soft scent—cinnamon perhaps.

The bargaining done and wine in hand, they wandered toward the center of the square. Clea laughed often and kept rubbing against him as they walked. An occasional eye turned their way, sometimes set in a frowning face, but more often followed by an approving nod.

They were partway across the square when Clea broke away, giggling and teasing. She threw her robe off her shoulders, laughing as she let it drop to the ground. She danced back a step, her black eyes bright and merry. Her small fingers flew at the buttons of her cotton undergarment as she pranced backwards.

Just before she reached the fountain the last button came free and the cotton chemise pooled around her feet, leaving her pale and naked in the moon's lambent light. Raalt stumbled to a halt, his eyes seeing nothing but the dancing white flame of her small body.

Part of his mind had been worrying at different ways to deal Clea out of the Heart's spoils once he had captured her heart, but the dry bones of his plans turned to dust as she captured his full attention with the simple fact of her beauty. Behind him he half-heard a woman begin to curse stridently.

Clea leapt to the rim of the fountain, calling him. She blew him a kiss, then turned and dived into the fountain.

Raalt bent and picked up her robe, fear and desire grappling inside him. He had a terrible urge to run and dive in after her. Before he could steel himself for such an act of bravery, the sound of the argument reached a more fevered pitch. He heard and remembered what he was supposed to do.

He hurried to pick up her other garment, then almost ran to the side of the fountain. He stood shifting his weight from one foot to the other, staring at the water and thinking that he never could have really followed her into it. The square remained quiet. Fingering his sword, he turned back toward the water, beginning to fear that Clea had drowned—or worse. She had been under a very long time, and who knew what horrors all that water might hide?

Suddenly her head broke the moon-rimed surface before him. Her hand came out of the water and she thrust the leather pouch that the Heart had been in when he had stolen it into his hand. He closed his fingers around it in relief—he had wondered if the water would willingly give it up.

"Quick, my robe," Clea gasped, her breath short from the time she had spent submerged. Raalt held it up, still clutching the pouch, licking his lips at the sight of her as he draped the robe over her shoulders. It broke his heart to see her covered again.

When the pouch had touched his hand he had felt a powerful impulse to take the Heart and her robe and run, turning the tables. But the earlier sight of her burned in his mind like a beacon too bright to turn away from. He stayed.

Now wearing her robe, Clea stepped closer and embraced him, running her wet hands down along his spine and making him shiver. "I have some rooms for us already," she whispered. "Let us go celebrate!"

Raalt lifted her from the fountain rim and set her on the ground. Clea took his arm and held on tight. Together they left the fountain and headed across the square.

"See what we can do together, partner?" Clea breathed softly, smiling up at him.

"And the night is still young," he replied, stopping her for a kiss. She responded with considerable passion. He was certain of it—that tantalizing, elusive scent was cinnamon.

They passed the edge of the square, Raalt glowed like a lamp; the Heart was once again in hand and Clea was as good as his. He swore to himself that by morning she would be begging him to keep her half of what the Heart brought. His oath would hold; she would betray herself. The thought of seeing Clea brought low made his grin grow even wider.

Raalt could scarcely believe the luxury of the rooms Clea had arranged. They had two large rooms interconnected by an arched door hung with glittering beadwork. The main room was larger, and had a door to the street. The smaller room, containing kitchen and bath, opened onto a small garden.

The whitewashed stone walls of the main room were hung with spills of silk and dyed cotton hangings. One side of the room, on the street-door end, held a mountain of cushions and pillows, all soft and richly embroidered. On the other side there was a huge silk-curtained bed. The furniture was all of rich dark woods or carved stone. Nightingales sang from wicker cages, filling the incense-sweet air with soft music. The room was lit by fragrant beeswax tapers, and there was bread, fruit, cheese and wine already on hand.

Raalt toured the main room in wonder, the still-wet pouch momentarily forgotten in his hand. The room confirmed his estimation of Clea's motives; this was a love nest if ever there was one.

Clea was just turning from pouring them wine when she saw that he was about to open the pouch. She paled and nearly dropped their cups. *"Don't open that!"* she shouted, real fear in her voice.

Raalt halted uncertainly. "Why not?"

"Gods! That is the Heart of Arrmik!" She came only a step closer, and stood as if ready to flinch away instantly.

"So?" he said uneasily, his fingers on the thong binding the pouch shut.

"The Heart is *cursed*! Only the Priests of Arrmik can look upon it and live—that is why it is kept covered! Did you not know? Do you not bother to learn something of what you steal?"

"Well," Raalt began unhappily, feeling his control over her beginning to slip away. He did not want to admit that he did not, and had not; knowing that it was valuable was enough. He was tempted to open the pouch anyway, just to prove that her fears were unfounded, but decided against it on the off-chance that she was right. You could never be certain about curses; sometimes they were just words to frighten away the gullible, but now and again they had a power better left unprovoked.

Clea went to Raalt's side. "I am sorry, but I did not want to lose you." The smile she gave him would have made the face of a stone statue crack as it tried to smile back. "Put it in your belt for safe-keeping tonight."

She handed him his cup. "I will have to find something else for you to unwrap and enjoy."

Raalt grinned hungrily at her thinly veiled invitation and put the pouch away. Then he helped himself to his wine.

Clea watched him over the rim of her cup and spoke offhandedly. "It is a good thing that you did not try to open that pouch while you were stealing it—they would have found you dead with it still in your hand. You would have drowned on dry land!"

Raalt choked on his wine. Clea had to thump him on the back several times before he was able to get his breath back.

"I—I would have dr—dr—" He could not say it out loud.

Clea giggled and ran her fingertip down along the hinge of his jaw, down the side of his neck and to the center of his chest. "Arrmik is a God of Desert Water," she breathed. "It is told that once he drowned an entire city that turned from his worship." Her fingers played over Raalt's chest knowingly, making his breath catch, making the tide of visions of drowning recede a bit. He threw back another gulp of wine.

Clea's maddening fingers continued their work. Her tongue wet her lips and she looked at Raalt expectantly.

Raalt forced the last of the water-thoughts from his mind and put his cup aside. He gathered Clea into his arms, crushing her small body against his, enveloped in the just-reappeared cinnamon scent, reveling in the helpless way she clung to him. Their mouths met and she held on even more desperately.

Raalt broke the kiss, and when he saw the heavy-lidded look in her dark eyes he wanted to crow in triumph. The Fox was almost skinned.

As his hands were slipping down her back to cup her buttocks, she slipped out of his embrace unexpectedly. "Now wait," she said, her face elfin and mischievous. "Let us not hurry! I am going to bathe before we go any farther—the water in that fountain was *filthy*!" She wrinkled her nose to show what she meant.

"You think so, do you?" Raalt chuckled, moving toward her with his arms poised to catch her. She danced back out of his grasp, shaking her finger at him and laughing.

"You do not want to bed a woman smelling of stale water and camel lips, do you? Work on the wine and I will be done before you even miss me."

Raalt opened his mouth to protest. Clea darted forward and put her finger to his lips. "No complaining or I make *you* take one!"

Raalt gave her his most wolfish grin. "I drink. *You* hurry."

"I will," she said huskily, meeting his eyes.

Raalt let her lead him to the big drift of pillows and waited while she removed his cloak, sword, and belt for him as if she were a slave girl. He dropped to the pillows and took the mug and flask she handed him, pleased with this new Clea. She was his, and by daybreak the Heart would be his as well.

He watched her move to the other end of the room, her slim hips swaying provocatively. She flashed him a smile full of tender promise, then stepped through the beaded curtain.

Listening to her splashing, Raalt patted the pouch and drank his wine, well pleased. He had good wine, a rich room, the Heart, his freedom, and best of all the sweet knowledge that he had finally found Clea's weakness—and she was falling without a struggle. He could already see himself counting her share of the spoils from the Heart—not that she should have had one in the first place.

What delicious justice; she had tried to take his Heart, but he had captured hers instead. Clea the Fox had met her match in Raalt the Thief, and high time too.

He was working on his fifth mug of wine when he decided that she had been splashing long enough, by damn. He stood up just a bit unsteadily and stretched, every muscle standing out in sharp relief. He grinned wickedly as he shed his tunic and then dropped his clout. After a last sip of wine he headed for the beaded curtain wearing a big smile and nothing else.

Raalt passed through the clicking beads, grinning and scratching his crotch. One good look and she would be out of that tub quick enough.

When his eyes fell on the tub his grin crumbled to dust and his knees nearly buckled under him. There in the big wooden tub sat the ample-fleshed, kohl-eyed whore from the fountain square. Clea was nowhere to be seen.

The whore leered and winked. "There y'are buck! The young Missy says how you be ready for sport, an' I guess y'truly be! Ah, y'lookin' so—"

*"Where is she?"* Raalt roared, his handsome face going black with rage, his hands groping for the sword left behind in the other room. He balled his fists and advanced on the woman in the tub.

The whore cringed back, splashing. "She *gone*, Master," she cried. "She leave me as present, she did! One gold Finger to fight with wineman, twő more to hide in garden till she come f'me, then wait in tub f'you, Master!"

Raalt moaned and spun around, then ran back to his discarded clothing, searching for the pouch. When he found it he snatched it up and worried at the thong, cursing steadily, his face fearful.

At last the thong gave way. He upended the pouch and out dropped a large wet rock. He squeezed his eyes shut in denial and clenched the rock in his fist as he slumped to the pillows in defeat. Clea had beaten him yet again; led him down the garden path only to step in fresh wet dung.

He felt someone touch his shoulder, and looked up to see the wet and dripping corpulent courtesan. She spoke fearfully.

"Missy tol' me—an I near forget—to tella y'best 'member what she say 'bout bein' ten steps 'head." The poor woman looked like she expected him to strike her.

Raalt did clench his fist again, but after a moment his hand dropped limply. The rock fell from his fingers, dropped to the pillows, then rolled to the floor. He clamped his jaw to keep in another moan, and hung his head to hide his face.

The kohl-eyed whore knew what to do. She stepped closer and drew Raalt's head against her ample belly.

She cradled his head tenderly and ran her fingers through his hair. "There now," she crooned, "there, there, my baby."

Just as that tender moment was occurring, Clea was already on a fast horse and riding out of Yuelianq. She had already disposed of the Heart of Arrmik and her saddlebags were heavy with gold.

It had been easy—too easy really. But the game had been great sport, and it had been profitable. She regretted that she had not been able to stay to see the look on Raalt's face—that might have been worth half of the gold after all.

Almost as precious as the gold was the bit of rumor she had heard while in Yuelianq. It seemed that Timoor of Morn was a poor loser and had put a good price on her head. That sounded like an interesting challenge; trying to sell her own head, collecting the price herself, and keeping it on her shoulders in the bargain.

But with a bit of careful planning. . . .

Clea threw back her hood and dug her heels into the horse's side, spurring him to a run. She laughed aloud and left Yuelianq behind, riding toward the setting moon.

Early in the reading for this anthology, this story came in, and I knew at once that I wanted it. It had everything I had specified for this kind of story; strong woman protagonists, well-realized characters, and a definite feel of the magical. I knew, too, that the first story I made a definite choice would inevitably shape the stories to be chosen after it, since I would be, consciously or unconsciously, choosing stories which would work with it and balance it.

Yet there was one problem; I had definitely decided that I would use no science fiction, only fantasy of the specific sword-and-sorcery variety. And this story, while it had the fantasy feel I wanted, used some of the language of science fiction; for we see a world reduced to village life without our current techno-structures, and the story speaks of mutants.

In the end, though, I chose the story over the taboo, for two reasons. One was simple; most of the best fantasy of the forties and fifties, and virtually all of that written by Leigh Brackett and C.L. Moore, employed some of the language of science fiction to structure their fantasies when fantasy was unpopular or taboo. The other was the simple excellence of the story. It begins, as do many of its kind of story, with a journey; a swordswoman and songsmith arriving in a strange place; and goes on to explore alienation and terror, building to what was, to me, an almost unendurably poignant ending . . . or is it? Whatever the classification of this story, I felt I was pleased to have it as one of the cornerstones around which to build this anthology.

I was even more astonished to discover that a story told with such a sure hand is the work of a beginner; this is Emma Bull's first professional sale. She says of herself that she is 28 years old, lives in Minneapolis with her husband and two cats, and enjoys drawing and music. She says that she usually enjoys writing, but usually it's a compulsion, like biting her nails.—MZB

# THE RENDING DARK
## by Emma Bull

Marya tightened her reins and turned in the saddle, squinting against the snow thickening in the twilight air. She grinned at the short, cloak-muffled figure that rode up beside her. "You know, I thought I heard you swear just now."

Kit snorted. "I said, 'Mother of little pigs!' You promised me that Sallis was two days' ride from Lyle Valley. We are now two days' ride from Lyle Valley. And I am cold. And wet. And getting more of both. And I don't see a town."

Marya laughed. "Why did I ever call you Woodpecker? You scold like a jay."

"Marya, blast it, where's the town?"

"Over the next rise, oh ye of little patience. And if you'll be good, I'll buy the first round when we get there."

"And I'll buy the second and third as usual, so where does that get me?" Kit scowled.

"Oh, quite a way into a drunken carouse. Hallo, there!" Marya raised her left arm, pointing, and snow-reflected light slipped off the gleaming black of claw and tendon.

Below them, barely visible through the falling snow, gas lamps glowed like sparks in a feeble row.

"I'm never wrong," Marya said.

"I could remind you of that pack beast you bought in Hobarth."

"Everyone gets one free mistake."

"Motherlorn wretch! C'mon, let's go!"

Kit booted her mount's ribs, and surged downhill through the piling snow. But Marya hesitated. Had a shadow quaked under the boughs of the pines? She shook her head. *I'm tired. There isn't enough light to cast a shadow by.* The wind wailed behind her as she followed Kit down to Sallis town.

When she reached the gate, Kit was already there, cursing elegantly.

"So use the knocker," said Marya.

"I *have* used the knocker. Twice," Kit snapped and yanked the rope again. The iron arm boomed against the wood.

The gatekeeper's look-see slid open. "What do you want?"

"*In*, dearie," Marya replied. "What do *you* want when you knock at gates, hmmmm?"

"It's late, and the weather's poor, and—"

"And that's all the more reason to let us in out of it," Kit snapped. "This must be one fine town, if you're afraid of two riders."

"I only meant to say—"

"Here, maybe this'll make you happy." Kit rode close to the look-see and pulled her cloak back, showing the red-and-blue of the Songsmith patch on her sleeve.

"Your pardon, Songsmith, I didn't—"

"Please, just the gate," said Kit, and Marya reflected, not for the first time, how remarkably well a trained performer could make a sigh heard. Ice cracked loudly as the bar was pulled back, and Marya and Kit trotted through.

*The large, soft-spoken type*, Marya decided upon seeing the gatekeeper. *My favorite*. She pushed back her hood and smiled down at him. "Thank you. And I apologize for my companion's sharp tongue."

Kit blinked and stared at her as the gatekeeper said, "No, no, it's for me to—"

"We've been riding all day, and the weather . . ."

He looked sympathetic. "Early for this," he said, kicking his boot toe through the powder. "The wolves are down from the ridge already, and there's stories of things. . . . It'll be a bad year, I think."

"It's been a bad year for the last half-dozen of them," Kit drawled.

Marya frowned at her, and smiled again at the gatekeeper. "We'd better find an inn, before she eats one of the natives. Is there one straight on?"

"There *is* only one. Left at the green-shingled house there—" he pointed, "—and down the lane some ways. It's Amali's Halt."

"Thanks. Um, when are you through here?"

"Hour and half-a-turn." He looked up at her.

"Come by when you're through. She'll probably sing something," Marya smiled and jerked her thumb at Kit. "And Give News, of course."

His smile was shy and charming. "I wouldn't miss it."

"Come on, Marya!" Kit called. "If I sit this animal much longer, I'll freeze to the saddle!" She had turned her mount and started down the street.

"Thank you again. Oh," said Marya, "something to get warm with." She drew her left arm out of her cloak at last, holding a coin.

The gatekeeper's face went slack as he stared at her left hand. Marya looked down at it herself, and tried to see it without familiarity: lean bone and tendon and long, curving, cruel claws, all black and shining, cupping the coin like a cage of black iron. Bitterness twisted in her stomach unexpectedly. She watched his face as she flexed the fingers, and saw terror in his eyes when the tap of a talon made the coin ring. He snapped his gaze up to her face. She stared back at him, solemn and silent. After a still moment, she tossed the coin to him. He made no move to catch it. They both watched as it made a little hole in the snow; then she turned her mount and rode down the street after Kit.

"Well," said Marya as she caught up to the Songsmith, "so much for my evening."

"Huh?"

She held up her left arm and wiggled the black fingers.

"It bothered him?"

"It bothered him."

"Creeping, superstitious, Motherlorn provincials." Kit sounded as if she were warming up to something. "Unwashed, unlettered, sheep-screwing, bear-buggering, backwoods—"

"Oh, pipe down," Marya interrupted. "You're only burned because you think if I can't get laid, you shouldn't either."

"That's not true!" Kit shrieked.

Marya grinned wickedly. "If I could get fish to take bait the way you do, I could be a rich woman on the coast."

The gatekeeper's directions were good. The inn they reached was an immaculate little place, and seemed to radiate welcome like heat from an iron stove.

"Bless us all," Kit sighed contentedly.

"I'll take 'em to the stable," Marya offered, swinging out of the saddle.

"You're a dear. I'll order you a wonderful dinner."

"Don't eat it all before I get there."

Kit made a face at her and disappeared into the inn.

Marya found the stable easily. It was clean and well-lit, and the coal-burning Fireproof in the harness room kept the biting edge off the temperature. She looked on approvingly as the stable hand unsaddled their mounts and rubbed them down.

"I'll bet you don't have much to do in weather like this," she commented.

"No'm," said the boy, and flashed her a smile before he bent to brush a long-haired fetlock. He ducked under the animal's belly and stood up. "But we're lively come summer."

"What's your name?"

"Gerry, mum." He looked up and grinned. "At your service." He swept her a road-show bow, the currycomb flourishing wildly with his arm.

"Good," Marya laughed. "If you can get the burrs out of that beastie's coat, that'll be service indeed."

Gerry grinned again and turned back to his work.

She watched him out of the corner of her eye while she wiped down her saddle. She was careful to keep her cloak draped over her left arm. At last she said, "You're very good with the animals. How did you learn so well, so young?"

A wistful smile flickered at his face. "My dad taught me. My dad's Evan Tentrees, and he's the best . . . was the . . . best . . ." Suddenly he turned his face away from her.

"Did I . . . say something dumb?"

His brown hair flurried with the force of his headshake.

"You're lucky," Marya continued. "I wouldn't recognize my dad if he kicked me."

"I . . . gotta get something." He bolted into the feed room. When he came back shortly, empty-handed, Marya looked a question. "Couldn't find it," he said, too loud.

A throttling silence followed. Marya broke it at last with, "I'm sorry. I guess I did say something stupid. Want to tell me about it?"

He shook his head again, and Marya saw her mount flinch away from the force of the currycomb stroke. Then he said, "My dad was . . . killed."

"Umm." Marya felt as if she'd been holding her breath. "Recently?"

"Last week. He was up on the hills, hunting strays. They went out to look for him the next morning. He was . . . he was . . ."

She heard the quivering in his voice, and headed him off. "Was he caught in a storm?"

Gerry shook his head. "There was something . . . clawed him up, tore him. Something big."

"Wolf? Cat?"

"Bigger."

*There's something familiar about this,* Marya thought. She finished with the tack, wished Gerry a good evening, and hurried into the inn.

Kit waved furiously at her from a table by the dining room hearth. "Just wait 'til you see dinner!" she crowed, grinning.

"Food always lifts your spirits, Woodpecker. The only time you're ever civil is when dinner's imminent."

"Fingerfish in wine sauce, venison pie, baked squash and apples, new bread, greensprouts, and cider. Ah, here it comes!"

The innkeeper was a big woman, still flushed from supervising the kitchens. She set the tray down on the table and smiled at Marya. "I know what travelling in this kind of weather does to an appetite, dear, which I told your friend the Songsmith. Nobody goes hungry in Amali's Halt."

"It take it you're Amali?"

"That's me."

"Delighted to meet you."

"And your venison pie," Kit added.

Amali chuckled. "Eat it all, dears. And if you fancy it," she went on, suddenly shy, "we'd be pleased to have you in the taproom after."

Marya shot a look at Kit and found her smiling. "I think we might do that," Kit said. "And if you wouldn't mind, I might even feel like singing a bit."

"It'd be an honor!" Amali beamed. "Enjoy your dinner."

Marya waited until Amali was out of earshot before she said, "Tsk. Another year of this and you'll be spoiled rotten."

"Not with you along to keep me in my place."

"A heavy responsibility."

"Shut up and eat."

Marya obediently forked a mouthful of squash and swallowed it before she went on. "Just heard an odd thing."

Kit looked up, then put her fork down. "That's your 'I think we ought to do something' voice. Spill it."

Marya told her about Gerry's father.

"Bear?" Kit said when she was done.

"That's what I thought, at first. But aren't you Carrying News from Lyle Valley about a bear in these hills?"

"Yeah. They killed one two weeks ago."

"That's what I thought. So, two bears in the same range of hills? And both out this late in the year?"

"Unlikely."

''Very. Then what *is* out there?'' Marya stabbed a piece of pie for emphasis.

''How would I know? Look, I'm on my way to Samarty to pick up a manuscript for the Guild. On the way, I'm delivering news. I am not fighting dragons, rescuing golden-tressed idiots locked in towers, or knocking down windmills. What do you want, to organize a hunt?''

''Well . . . yes.''

Kit leaned her chin in her palms and looked at her. ''Marya Clawfinger, you're hopeless.''

''No. Hopeful. You're using your 'I can't reason with her, so I'll have to give in' voice.''

''We'll talk it over in the morning. Eat.''

The guitar's last chord clung to the air in the taproom, making the listeners reluctant to drive it off with applause. Marya smiled as Kit lifted her head and blinked, as if coming out of a trance. The subtle cue touched off a storm of clapping. *Wonderful thing,* Marya reflected, *the symbiosis between performer and audience. Is that instinct, or does the Guild teach these things?*

Then Kit set the guitar aside and stood slowly up, and the room plunged into silence. Everyone in the room had waited for this, the moment when the Songsmith would Give News. Marya leaned back to enjoy it.

''From the north and the east,'' Kit's voice reached out, enfolding the room. ''From silver-roofed Sandyn and the Firehall I come. I am the voice and the bearer of the past. What will you have of me?''

Kit's delivery warmed the traditional words. Someone in the crowd shouted, ''Lyle Valley!'' and his neighbors murmured assent.

Kit nodded slowly and closed her eyes. The whole room seemed to tip forward a little with expectation. Then, clear and bright, tuneless and tuneful all at once, Kit began to chant:

> Allysum Gredy bore a boy
> With the first snow of November.
> Ere the snow had come and gone again
> Pneumonia took old Francis Berne
> And balanced birth and drying.
>
> Etin Yama's grocery burned,
> And Etin blamed Jo Hurlisen.
> The council fined Jo three months' wage,
> And bid him quit cigars.

Protecting flocks on Canwit slope,
Rey Leyne and Winsey Wittemer
Slew a winter-colored bear,
But something still kills sheep and cows
Along the southern ridge.

Nil Sabek and Margrete Durenn
Have sworn the Binding Promise,
And Hary Lil, in his best boots
Walks daily out with Mother Pent.

"Life, death, commerce, and love: Lyle Valley is well."

The room hummed with talk when Kit finished—neighbors laughing and gossiping over the news. Marya smiled and waited for the next town to be called out, and for Kit to start again.

And the taproom door slammed open. "Hey!" somebody yelled, then stopped.

The boy in the doorway was the stablehand, Gerry; the young woman he was carrying was a blood-spattered stranger.

"Nan!" Amali cried. The tray in her hands hit the floor with a clang, and she ran to catch the woman around the waist. Marya elbowed her way to the door. Someone leaped out of a chair and pushed it toward Amali, who lowered Nan into it. "She's my daughter," Amali said wildly to Marya, who wondered why it mattered.

"Are you hurt?" Marya asked, finding the pulse in the blood-stained wrist, peering into the woman's eyes, noting evidence of shock. Nan shook her head.

"Get her closer to the stove and wrap a blanket around her," Marya ordered. "Give her mint tea or water. No alcohol."

"And then ask her what happened," said Kit, appearing out of the crowd at Marya's side.

"At the gate," Nan said, still breathing hard. "Cal. He's dead. And Jimy."

Marya heard a noise in the back of the room, a little cry.

"How?" Amali asked, her voice tight.

"Cal . . . Cal was opened up from neck to crotch. Just opened up. Jimy's throat . . . was ripped half away." Nan began to sob weakly.

Sudden motion made Marya look toward the door. Gerry had taken a pace into the room, and his lips still held a half-formed word. He clutched at the door frame, his gaze leaping around the room. Then he turned and darted out the door.

"One of you," Amali shouted, "hand me that blanket

from—oh.'' She stared down at Marya with the blank look of panic. ''Oh, no. Then someone—something—must have come through the gate.''

''What? Why?''

''Cal's the gatekeeper.''

''The . . . gatekeeper?'' Marya whispered, and looked up, wide-eyed, at Kit. Kit reached out and gripped Marya's left shoulder. The singer's fingers were warm through her shirt, and the contact seemed to trickle strength into her.

''Let's go see,'' Marya heard her own voice like a grim bell in the silence.

Outside there were two sets of tracks through the drifted snow: Nan's, floundering wildly toward the inn; and another trail, straight and certain, pointing away, toward the gate. Marya scowled and crouched down for a better look, balancing her scabbarded blade across her knees. Then she swore.

The prints were of heelless boots, ridge-soled for good traction on damp and dirty floors, boots for a farmer or stablehand. . . .

''What is it?'' Kit asked.

''Gerry,'' Marya said, dropping the name like a stone down a well. ''He's after the thing that killed his father. Come on.''

And they ran.

Marya drew her sword as she bounded through the snow. She heard Kit cursing, ''Marya! Blast you into darkness, wait for me!'' But she was afraid to slow her pace. The gate court was only a turn away. . . .

She made the turn—and stopped, her sword half-raised, dread and disbelief freezing her limbs. Gerry stood in the middle of the court. His face twisted with horror, he held a length of timber thrust out before him with both hands. He might have thought of it, moments before, as a cudgel. Now it was the only solid thing he had to keep between him and the creature before him.

The creature. . . . Black shreds of it seemed always to be stripping away, like black steam, in a wind that blew nowhere else in the street, yet nothing ever fell to the snow, and there was never less of it. It walked upright, and was tall as a bear and gaunt as a half-burnt tree. She heard Kit's voice weak beside her. ''Oh, Mother's Pigs. . . . How can I describe that at the next town?''

A dark arm-shape swept out, swift and easy, and slapped at the boy. The timber hit the snow in two splintery pieces.

''Gerry, get away!'' Marya leaped at the thing, sweeping her sword in a cut at the dark midsection.

Gerry was screaming and screaming, and suddenly not

screaming, falling out of the shadow-thing's embrace with his throat and chest blooming bright and shining red, red bubbling at his mouth where he tried still to scream.

Marya's blade sliced into shadow—and stopped, as if stone had formed around it. Stone was filling the veins of her right hand, calcifying her nerves, brittling her bones, and devouring its way into her shoulder and chest. She wanted to draw a breath, and hadn't the strength. Her sword fell to the snow as she staggered backward, fell to her knees, her human arm limp and swinging wide. She stared at it blankly.

And the shadow turned toward her. The mouth gaped, the eyes glowed with decay—she wanted to shut her eyes, kneel down, and wait for it to go away.

The black arms reached out, obscene parody of comfort, to gather her to it.

"No!" Kit shrieked behind her, and darted past, her dagger a sliver of light in her hand.

"Get back!" Marya yelled, but Kit drove the bright steel up into that thing of tattered darkness—

—and stopped. Kit's mouth opened round with shock. Around her folded the impenetrable shadow of the creature.

"Kit, move it! Get back!" Marya shouted again. Kit seemed to come awake, and flung herself backward. The black thing lashed out. Blood stained the snow where she fell.

"Kit!" Marya slid to her side.

"It's pulling my soul out through the hole in my arm," Kit mumbled.

"What?"

"I can feel it go. Not much nourishment in souls . . ." Kit's head slipped sideways.

The creature leaned like a black flame over them, seeming to swell and pulse. Marya grabbed frantically for her sword. Or tried to grab. Her human arm wouldn't obey her.

She lunged up from the snow, to the being's other side. "Here!" she screamed. "Over here, pigfeed! Short-shaft!" She scrabbled up a fistful of churned-up gravel and flung it left-handed at the dark thing. Its nightmare mouth opened in a hiss that cut into her skull, and it surged toward her. *Wish that hadn't worked quite so well*, Marya thought as she struck out with her taloned arm. Her fingers sank into shadow.

Heat rushed through Marya's bones as the hiss became a sharp and sudden snarl. *I've hurt it!* she exulted. Her skin was hot and prickling. She clenched her claws in the shadow-stuff of the thing, and it slashed wildly at her head, shrieking like steel on stone.

Her body flooded with more-than-fever. *It's burning me*—then her terror was swallowed up in awe. *No . . . I'm burning.* She was not the fuel, but the fire itself; the world lay before her as kindling and coal. Huge with strength, she flared up to scorch the stars, feeding on their power. . . .

The black thing flung backward, howling, leaving flickering darkness fading in her fist. Suddenly she was only a little cold beast kneeling in the snow, and all power had fled. She wanted to scream out for it, to rend flesh, shatter stone, in search of it.

She lunged for the writhing shadow. It swung again at her, missed, then turned and hurtled like some dark driven leaf through the gate and into the night beyond.

The power was gone from her. She looked wildly around the street, envying even the flaring of the lamps. But she had to remain human; there was something a human needed to do. . . .

Then she saw the sprawled red-haired figure in the snow. "Kit!" she cried. "Woodpecker—"

She sank to her knees, cradled the Songsmith in her dark arm, and listened for Kit's breathing. Warm air stirred against her cheek; yes, she breathed. Now the shoulder . . . She searched her clothes and Kit's for something that was neither blood- nor snow-soaked, and cursed aloud when she couldn't find anything.

"Oh, bright Mother. Here," someone said softly above her head, and a clean cloth napkin appeared in front of her face. She grabbed it and made a pad, tied it against Kit's wound with her own sash.

"I need a cloak for her, a blanket, something . . ." Marya muttered. A bright blue wool cape swung into sight. She tucked it under and around Kit. *Why isn't she conscious?* Marya wiped the hair out of her eyes. Before her the street lamps showed darkened snow, the gate closed at last, and three people she was clearly too late to help . . . Her head hurt, and her body felt too heavy to move.

"Should we take her to the inn?" she heard behind her. She turned.

"Amali!"

"I've been here for . . . a while, but you were. . . ." Amali fluttered her plump hands.

"The word you're looking for is probably 'rude.' " Marya shook off inertia and lifted Kit, letting her snow-sodden cloak swing forward to hide her left arm.

"No harm done," Amali said with a little shrug. "Medics are always odd when they're working."

"Hmm."

"But I hadn't thought a Payer of the Price could take the medics' training."

Marya's foot came down a little too suddenly, and her teeth clacked shut. "A what?" she said.

"A Payer of the Price. I saw your arm, while you tended the Songsmith."

"You did." *Surely,* she thought, *the wretched woman will shut up* . . .

"You shouldn't try to hide your mark, you know. You bear it to show us our Mother's anger at our tampering with Her holy secrets. . . ."

"That's enough!" Marya hissed. Amali's mouth opened and closed. "I'm sorry," Marya said. "I'm not . . . religious."

Amali stared at her warily. "I'll pray for you," she said at last. "Let me go ahead and get a bed ready for her."

Marya nodded, and Amali waded away through the snow.

"She means well," croaked Kit's voice near her shoulder. "Just misinformed."

"Woodpecker? How d'you feel?"

"Like I got hold . . . of the wrong end of a lightning bolt."

"There's a right end on a lightning bolt?"

Kit opened one eye and frowned. "Are you hysterical?" she said faintly. "You're not making any sense."

"You should talk."

"No, I shouldn't. I should rest. If you weren't hysterical, you'd know that."

Marya snorted. "Never try to speak rationally with someone who's lost blood."

"Not blood," Kit shook her head weakly. "More like . . . strength."

"That's what happens when you lose blood."

"No. That's what I meant about . . . about a lightning bolt."

"Huh?"

"Instead of getting a blast of something . . . that—that thing sort of took something out of me."

"Something out of you . . ." Marya repeated. Her right arm had felt that way, as if the strength had been sucked away from it.

"My shoulder hurts," said Kit, almost firmly. "And I'm cold. Don't just stand here."

"Piglets, you're fussy," Marya smiled, and took long strides in Amali's tracks.

Sunlight poured like a liquid through the door as Marya pushed it open a finger's width. "Kit? Are you awake?"

"The place is lit up like the damn Ship come to harbor, and she wants to know if I'm awake," Kit grumbled.

Marya stuck her head into the room and grinned. "Your body I can cure. Your disposition is beyond me." She settled on the end of the bed. "So otherwise, how do you feel?"

"Pretty good, actually. Much better than I ought to, considering how bad I felt out there in the snow."

"Hmmm," said Marya. "Let me look at your arm."

"It was as if. . . ." Kit paused while Marya unwound the bandages, "as if I could feel myself dying—which is ridiculous, since it isn't much of a wound."

"True. It's not. It's also clean, and doing all the things it ought to be doing."

"So I suppose it was just fear. A literal example of being scared to death."

"Maybe." Marya sat back and folded her hands, twining flesh with polished black. "Maybe not."

"Maybe not?"

Marya got up and shot the bolt on the door.

"Marya?"

"I've got something I want to show you."

"My mother warned me about women like you . . ."

"Very funny. Watch this."

Marya crouched down by the iron stove near the bed, and opened the fire-door. "It's lit, right?"

"If it hadn't been," said Kit, "I think we would have noticed."

"Yes, but you can see the flames, can't you?"

Kit sighed. "Humor her. Yes, I can see them."

"All right." Marya stretched out her left hand, through the iron doorway, and spread long clawed fingers over the fire like a black-ribbed net. She felt the heat billowing past—and nothing else. *Am I crazy?* she wondered, suddenly afraid. *Was I crazy last night, when this worked?*

Then her shoulder began to tingle. Fever-warmth swept up her left arm, fever-dizziness engulfed her. She was deafened by her own heartbeat.

Between her fingers, she saw the flames struggle, sink; the coals darkened, orange to crimson to wine, then black and ash-gray.

"Urk," Kit said behind her.

Marya sat back on her heels and rubbed her eyes. "That's what I like about you. You always know what to say at times like this."

"Mother at the Helm—"

"It isn't magic, blast it!" Marya snapped. "Calm down. It's part of the . . . the change. You know perfectly well it is."

Kit set her hands firmly on her knees and took several deep breaths. "You're right. I'm calm. Perfectly. Did you know you could do that? Before now?"

"I tried it last night, in my room. I don't think I could before last night."

"So where did it come from?"

"I have a theory . . ."

Kit closed her eyes. "I hate it when you say that."

"You want to hear it?"

"I'm sorry."

"All right. I remember an experiment my mother had me do when I was a kid, with a family of snow hare kittens. I raised half of them in pens outdoors. The other half stayed indoors. The rabbits outdoors changed coloring the way snow hares always do, brown in summer and white in winter. The rabbits raised indoors were never anything but brown."

Kit frowned. "You must have botched it. Snow hares don't do that—and what does that have to do with putting out fires, anyway?"

"I'm getting to that. Pay attention. She explained that my little project showed how living things can sometimes be born with characteristics that don't appear until they're triggered by something outside themselves." Marya flexed her dark fingers. "I think, last night, I had a characteristic triggered."

Kit shook her head impatiently. "You've been cold before. And scared. What—" Her eyes widened. "Triggered by . . . that . . . thing?"

Marya nodded.

"No."

"What's your theory—coincidence?"

"Why should it have any effect on you?"

"Because," and Marya's voice was flat, "that thing and my arm are . . . related."

"That's sheepcrap. A big, steaming—"

"I can use my arm to absorb heat, you saw that. I think the thing we went up against last night can do the same. I think that's why it tears its victims open. It sure as day isn't eating them.''

"You're wrong." Kit's face was pale and set.

Marya asked softly, "How do you know?"

"Because you're not like that thing! If you're trying to tell me you are—"

"No, no, no. I'm human—I was, I still am. Just because those rabbits never turned white didn't mean they weren't rabbits.''

"Shut up about your Motherlorn rabbits.''

Marya wanted suddenly to scream at her. She bit the inside of her mouth instead, and took a deep breath. "All right. I'm just saying—"

"I don't want to hear—"

The door bolt clacked against its socket. "Songsmith?" came Amali's voice from outside the door. "Is everything all right?"

"Oops," Marya muttered, and leaped to unlock the door.

"Is everything all right?" Amali repeated, her plump face full of cheerful concern. She carried a pair of copper-and-brass cans. "Here's hot water. Did you sleep well? Does your shoulder hurt you?"

Kit graciously acknowledged the hot water and followed Amali into the bathing room, letting all the rest of the innkeeper's speech go unanswered.

"Her shoulder's fine," Marya said when Amali came out with the empty water cans. "I looked it over. Has there been any more news?"

"News?" Amali said, straightening the covers on the bed Kit had left.

"Of that thing last night."

"It's certainly not been seen again."

"Certainly?"

Amali frowned and plumped a pillow before she said, "Such things can only walk among us at night, while the Mother sails in dream."

*A god who goes to sleep when you need her most,* Marya thought. *Wonderful.* "You're sure the Mother herself isn't re-sponsible for little treats like that?"

"The Mother does not create evil," Amali lectured mildly. "Evil comes from us. But She allows evil to walk among us to teach us our errors. When we've learned and corrected ourselves, She will rid the world of such terrible things."

"So all we have to do is be very, very good and the creature will go away."

Amali blinked. "Disrespect doesn't become a Payer of the Price, dear."

Marya clenched her teeth. "Isn't someone at least organizing a hunt for the monster?"

"Wolves come down from the hills in winter," Amali smiled. "Do you go out hunting them every time, or do you simply take sensible precautions?"

"We aren't talking about wolves."

"There are many dangers this far from the cities. We live differently here."

"And die differently, too, if that creature is any indication," Marya snapped.

Kit strolled out of the bathing room, dressed and drying her hair with a green towel. "What's this about dying?" she asked.

"Nothing to be concerned about, Songsmith," said Amali. "Will you want to travel on today? The weather is good—"

Someone tapped furtively on the door. "Amali?" came Nan's voice, very soft. "Come down quick. The whole town's down there. They're going to go out and—" She'd opened the door and slid through. At the sight of Marya and Kit, she pressed her hand to her mouth. "Oh. Oh Mother."

"I have things to do downstairs," Amali said in a rush, and turned frantically toward Nan and the door.

"And something to do up here first." Marya stretched out her arm, black and shining, and pushed the door closed. Amali turned, and Marya saw that the jolly innkeeper mask had crumbled. The woman's eyes were full of tears. "The truth, please," Marya finished gently.

Nan made a strangled noise. Amali closed her eyes and gulped air.

"Wait a minute," said Kit. "What did I miss?"

"I don't know yet, Woodpecker," Marya replied. "But something out of the ordinary is going on here—" she raised an eyebrow at Amali and Nan, "—and I think these two can tell me all about it."

Amali shook her head. "No. I'm sorry. You should have the truth; you of all people should be trusted with the truth. But not now."

"What? Why not?"

"There are people downstairs who are ready to murder what they should only pity. I may be able to keep them from finding . . . what they hunt."

"The creature," said Marya.

Amali looked away and nodded.

Marya watched her for a moment before she said, "It killed three people last night."

"It couldn't—" Amali began, then nodded again.

"We've got to go!" Nan hissed at Amali. "Downstairs—" Amali's face was set in an anguished stubbornness.

"We might be able to help," Marya said.

Amali bit her lip. "If I tell you . . . promise you'll let it live."

"If we can," said Marya.

"Now, *wait* a minute—" Kit began, but Marya gestured her quiet. Amali looked from Marya to Kit. Then her gaze turned downward.

"The . . . creature we hunt," she said at last, "is my child."

Marya was too stunned to do more than blink. *You knew it was a mutation,* she told herself. *It had to be child to something. But not to this pudgy, red-faced, normal little woman . . .*

Amali continued, "Nan was my first-born. Then I had . . . this one. He was simple, he had to be fed and cleaned—" Her voice cracked and faded, and she pressed her fingers to her lips before she spoke again. "I thought She had judged me strong enough to raise a Payer of the Price. May She help me, *I* thought I was strong enough." She turned to Marya and lifted her head, in pride, or defiance. "Nan and I cared for him for fifteen years. We kept him locked away, for fear the townfolk would do him a mischief."

*Or was it,* Marya thought, *that you didn't want Sallis to know you had a mutant in the family?*

Amali hesitated, then plunged grimly back into her story. "A few months ago—things began to happen. I was afraid. I . . . Nan and I . . . Mother forgive me, one day we locked the door of his room and went to Lyle Valley. We came back two weeks later."

Tears began to roll down Amali's cheeks. "We buried him after dark, here in the foothills. He was so . . . he must have been dead, he must have! The Mother has brought him back, to punish me for not trusting Her, for my fear, for . . . not loving him." And Amali buried her face in her hands and sobbed.

Kit reached a hand halfway out to Amali's shoulder, paused.

"Could the thing be caught, and confined?" Marya asked finally.

"What?" Kit's voice squeaked a little.

Amali replied, "I think so."

"*Why?*" Kit wailed.

"Then you have until we find it to convince me that we ought to," said Marya, and started for the door.

"Hold it right there!" Kit said in a voice that rattled the window glass. "Are you going crazy?"

"No," Marya said patiently, "I'm going with the hunting party."

Kit opened and closed her mouth. "Then so am I," she said at last.

"But your shoulder . . ." Marya and Amali said almost at once.

"Where's my cloak?" Beneath Kit's glare, Marya recognized the Last Word.

The foothills were sullen around them, red-washed in the setting sun, thickly clotted with pine groves. Marya squinted in the lash of the bitter wind, switched the reins to her clawed hand, and tucked the other into her armpit to warm it. *Somewhere in all of this,* she reflected, *there's a demon that eats souls. No, somewhere there's a pitiful mutated something that lives on pure energy. Wish I could get Amali to tell me all she knows about it.* She looked down at her black hand. It reflected sunset like a bloody knife. She concentrated on it, trying to draw heat from the winter sunlight as she had drawn from the fire, but it stayed profoundly, fiercely cold, and still.

She clenched her legs on her mount, and it trotted forward through the snow to where Amali was riding. Behind her she could hear Kit's beast surge forward to Amali's other side.

"All right," said Marya. "We've diverted the rest of the hunting party, and we've followed you from spot to spot for the last hour. What are you going to do when we find it?"

"Amali!" Nan's voice rang out. Marya looked up to see her topping the nearest ridge, around a great plume of frozen snow. "He's nearby! There are tracks here, and a dead—"

Marya flung herself out of the saddle to the ground before she quite knew why. A slight, heavy motion in the pine boughs, a shadow. . . . Her mount screamed, and the snow around her steamed with blood. "Get back!" she yelled, but Kit and Amali had already lunged away from the twisting, dying animal with the black monster on its back.

Marya drew her sword, then realized there was nothing she could do with it. *If it will only stay interested in its kill long enough that I can find a way to stop it,* she thought. But the hell-window eyes turned to her, and it rose and faced her. Her stomach wrenched. *The mind of a retarded sixteen-year-old,* she realized—*I hurt it. It understands revenge.* She raised her sinister arm before her, and thought about death.

The impact of the creature's leap drove her down to the snow. Her shoulder jarred against ice and rock, and she cried out, but her dark arm held steady against the weight, held the nightmare face at bay.

Suddenly her hand coursed with heat, and the creature hissed and struck out at her. She felt a line of freezing pain at her temple and knew it had cut her. The world seemed to be separating into fragments, which in turn began to drift apart from each other. *I'm feverish,* she realized. *My brain's going to cook.*

She heard a thud, and cold showered her face. It happened again, and the demon shadow as gone from above her.

"Marya!" she heard Kit yell. "This way!" A lump of snow whizzed past her head.

She looked wildly in the direction of the voice. "You're throwing snowballs?" she shrieked.

"Come on, will you?" Kit howled back, and grabbed another handful of snow. Amali was crouched at her feet, and seemed to be trying to force both her mittened fists into her mouth. "This won't work—no, here it comes! Move!"

Marya dived for Kit, and reached her side just as the Songsmith fired another snowball. The creature staggered back a step, then came on again.

"Snowballs?" said Marya.

"Well, they're slowing it down!"

"But why?" *The thing absorbs energy,* Marya realized. *Snowballs have energy of motion. Like my sword, and Kit's knife, when we used them last night. But snowballs don't have someone hanging onto them. . . .*

"Snow!" Marya shouted.

"Yes, so what?" Kit yelled back.

Nan was struggling up to them through the drifts. Behind her, Marya saw the towering snow-plume that topped the near ridge, arching in a heavy half-tunnel.

"This way!" She half-dragged Kit toward the ridge. Behind them, Amali and Nan floundered aside as the monster swept forward.

"Take my sword," Marya panted, and thrust it hilt-first at Kit. "You're going to drop this—" she pointed up at the curve of snow, "—on that thing. As soon as I've got it underneath, chop through the ice near the point of the ridge."

Kit looked dubious. "This'll work?"

"I don't know," said Marya. At the corner of her vision, a shadow grew quickly larger. "Go, move it!"

She dodged aside as the creature lunged at her. If she could keep her footing now, and keep moving back . . . She could see hints of humanity now in the wild visage—in the shape of temple and cheekbone, in the motion of the gaping jaws—and the terror made her want to huddle whimpering in the snow. She kept moving.

The shadow of the snow-curve cut the ground beneath her into parts of dying light and blue dusk. The black shape crouched, her only warning of its sudden spring. Marya flung herself aside barely in time. She hit the snow hard, and tasted ice and grit in her mouth.

"Kit!" she gasped. "Now!" She rolled fast and came floundering to her feet in the deep snow, ready to leap out of the path of the avalanche of snow and ice . . .

. . . that didn't fall. "Kit!" she yelled again. "Knock it down!" The creature was stalking her once more.

"It won't fall!" shrieked Kit.

Marya spared a glance toward the base of the ridge. Kit was hacking furiously. It was not enough to break down the arch of snow. Marya looked back at the nightshade face all too close to her, and heard a strangling cry she couldn't keep back.

"Jump!" shouted a voice somewhere above her.

"What? Who . . . ?" The monster crouched to spring.

"Jump clear!" she heard again. "Hurry!" Behind her she heard a wooden groan, and a sudden roar. Her mouth and eyes filled with snow.

"Marya?" Kit called wildly. "Are you all right?"

Marya sat up and shook snow out of her face. "I think so. What happened?"

Kit knelt down next to her and looked her over critically. Then she pointed back toward the ridge.

The snow-plume was gone. At the foot of the ridge was a small mountain of snow and ice. Near it lay one of the riding animals, still saddled. Nan was at its head, patting it, talking to it. It tried to rise, and failed.

"Nan saw what we were trying to do, and that it wasn't working," Kit said. "She drove the critter out onto the arch, to bring it down."

Marya nodded, and dragged herself to her feet.

"You're sure you're all right?" Kit asked.

"I hurt all over," said Marya. "A mere nothing." She trudged over to Nan.

"Its leg's broken," Nan said.

"I thought so. I'm sorry."

Nan smiled at her, though the smile was a little lopsided. "It was you or it."

"True. But I'm still sorry."

Nan shook her head, knelt by the beast's head, and took a hunting knife out of a sheath at her belt. Marya looked away quickly, out over the mound of broken snow. Was that a bent, black arm? *No*, Marya realized, *just a tree branch swept down. The creature is buried. By the time it can dig its way out, if it can, it'll be too weak to fight back. And Amali can have her mutant captive back. I wonder how long it will be before she tries to kill it again?*

As if answering her thoughts, Amali appeared at her left shoulder. "Is he dead?"

"I don't think so. It's a hard creature to kill, you know."

Amali looked away. "Even you can't understand."

"I admit, weird, coal-black children who suck the life out of things are difficult to empathize with."

"I loved him at first," Amali murmured.

Marya frowned and looked at her.

"That's so hard for you to believe? Mothers love clubfooted children, they love their simple children. My son was no different."

"No different?" Surprise added a squeak to Marya's voice. "A withered, demonic—"

"He wasn't always like that!" Amali shouted. "That's why I thought you could . . . He was simple, and his left foot was black and twisted and hard as stone. It was only last year that he began to change, and he began to kill things. Before that, he . . ."

Marya felt her eyes ache from staring. Her tongue seemed stuck in her dry mouth. She turned away from Amali, and found Kit, wide-eyed, watching her.

"Don't look at me like that," Marya rasped. "It's not true." But she remembered the wild, blood-thirsty rush of power she had felt in the courtyard at the gate, when she ripped energy away from the mutant child.

"Marya—" Kit reached toward her. But her hand stopped halfway between them.

Marya stared a moment at that hand, before a sob bruised its way out of her throat, and she turned with a wrench and ran.

Her foot caught in snow suddenly deep and uneven, and she fell forward. She stared for a moment at her arms sunk to the elbows in a slope of snow, before she remembered: the avalanche. *If it had just fallen on me, too!*

A little well appeared in the snow before her. Loose powder sifted into it. It grew larger. And suddenly the mass before her shook and shifted, and knotted black twigs, four of them, poked out of the snow.

It wasn't until they clenched that she recognized them.

She wrenched her left hand out of the drift and grabbed the mutant creature's fingers, yanked at them until the arm was clear of the snowbank. Then she scrabbled until she found the face. It seemed even more human now that weakness had shrunk it. It struggled, twisting its head and free arm. She reached down and plunged her talons around and into its throat.

The blistering heat that raced up her arm was almost familiar. Under her, the creature bucked and writhed, screaming thinly. She heard a human scream, too, behind her, before the roaring in her ears deafened her and dragged her into the dark.

She seemed, after some time, to be waking up. Something about waking struck her as inappropriate; the place, perhaps . . . Someone was sobbing drearily. Marya felt something nudging against her shoulder. "Huh?"

"Mother at the Helm. You're still alive."

"Kit? Where . . . what are we . . ."

"Doing here? Never mind, you'll remember soon enough."

And suddenly Marya did, as she recognized the weeping as Amali's. "Oh," she said. "Oh, oh, oh, oh—"

Kit's slap stung her cheek. "Quiet. It's all right. You're all right. Someone would have had to kill it eventually. Can you get up?"

"I don't know."

"Well, try. I want to get out of here."

Marya nodded. It hurt her head. Kit half-lifted her, and they stumbled to one of the remaining riding animals.

"We're just leaving?" Marya said. "Shouldn't we help—"

"Right now, neither of us is likely to be much help. Nan will get Amali home. I want to get back to the inn, pick up our stuff, and go."

"Travel at night?"

"There's a moon."

Marya shrugged and let Kit boost her up to the saddle. The Songsmith scrambled up in front and urged their mount into a fast walk.

For half an hour, Marya watched the moon-cast shadows of trees deepen and stretch blue-black across the snow.

"D'you want to talk about it?" Kit said finally.

"Well . . . no. Not really. What I want is for it to have never happened."

"Then it's a deal. It never happened."

"What if that happens to—"

"It won't happen to you," Kit said.

"You don't know that."

There was a long silence. "No, I don't. But what am I supposed to do about it? Hand you over to the peacekeepers? 'Got a dangerous mutant here, Officers,' " Kit grated. " 'Well, no, I guess she's not dangerous yet. But she might be, someday . . .' No, thank you. I'd feel stupid."

Marya looked for something else to say, and couldn't find anything. They rode half a kilometer before she murmured, "Thank you."

"Mmm," said Kit.

"For trusting me, I mean."

Kit turned in the saddle, and their mount stopped. "Are you going to keep brooding over yourself?"

"What? No."

"Good. You're a pain when you brood. I don't suppose you brought anything to eat?"

"There's dried fruit in the saddlebag," Marya said.

"Dried fruit. I ask for food, and you talk about dried fruit. The cold has addled your brain," Kit grumbled. "Hand me a Motherlorn raisin." And they rode on.

Charles Saunders, a native of Pennsylvania, has lived for the last fourteen years in Canada, where, in the intervals of teaching psychology, sociology, and "the odd creative writing seminar" he has been writing African-oriented fantasies since 1971. He has appeared in the *Best Fantasy Stories of the Year*, has appeared in the anthologies *Amazons I* and *Hecate's Cauldron*, and has written two novels for DAW: *Imaro*, and the forthcoming *Quest for Cush*. Currently he is working on the third *Imaro* novel.

I first encountered Charles Saunders in connection with another contributor to this volume; Charles de Lint, with whom he created the excellent small-press Triskell Publications. Over a period of three or four years they created *Dragonbane*, edited by Saunders, *Beyond the Fields We Know*, edited by De Lint—in which Diana Paxson and I both appeared as contributors—and combined the two magazines as *Dragonfields*.

Saunders says that he owns a kalimba, "but there is nothing magical about his playing," and adds an historical note, that the warrior women of the Dahomey were a real, not an imaginary tribe, and may have been the original Amazons.

Out of more than two hundred stories which I read for this anthology, "Gimmile's Songs" was the only one I accepted virtually by return mail. You will note that it begins in much the same way as Janet Fox's *"Gate of the Damned,"* with a warrior woman swimming in a river, and intercepted by men who have designs on her . . . but I don't think the two stories could be less alike.—MZB

# GIMMILE'S SONGS
## by Charles R. Saunders

The banks of the Kambi River were low and misty, crowded with waterbucks and wading birds and trees draped in green skeins of moss. Dossouye, once an *ahosi*—a woman soldier of the Kingdom of Abomey—rode toward the Kambi.

Slowly the *ahosi* guided her war-bull to the river bank. She knew the Kambi flowed through Mossi, a sparsely populated kingdom bordering Abomey. Between the few cities of Mossi stretched miles of uninhabited bushland speckled with clumps of low-growing trees. Dossouye watched sunlight sparkle through veils of humid mist rising from the Kambi.

"Gbo—stop," she commanded when the war bull came to the edge of the river. At the sight of the huge, horned mount, the birds fled in multicolored clouds and the waterbucks stampeded for the protection of the trees.

The war-bull halted. Dossouye gazed across the lazily flowing river.

"What do we do now, Gbo?" she murmured. "Cross the river, or continue along the bank?"

The war-bull snorted and shook its curving horns. In size and form, Dossouye's mount differed little from the wild buffalo from which its ancestors had been bred generations ago. Although the savage disposition of its forebears was controllable now, a war-bull was still as much weapon as mount. Dossouye had named hers "Gbo," meaning "protection."

With a fluid motion, the *ahosi* dismounted. Her light leather armor stuck uncomfortably to her skin. Days had passed since her last opportunity to bathe. Glancing along the banks of the Kambi, she saw no creature larger than a dragonfly. The prospect of immersing herself in the warm depths of the Kambi hastened her decision.

"We will cross the river, Gbo," she said, speaking as though the beast could understand her words. "But first, we'll enjoy ourselves!"

So saying, she peeled the leather armor from her tall, lean frame and laid it on the riverbank alongside her sword, shield, and spear. Knowing Gbo would also prefer to swim unencumbered, she removed the war-bull's saddle and bridle.

Naked, she was all sinew and bone, with only a suggestion of breast and hip. Her skin gleamed like indigo satin, black as the hide of her war-bull. When she pulled off her close-fitting helmet, her hair sprung outward in a kinky mane.

She waded into the warm water. Gbo plunged in ahead of her, sending spumes of the Kambi splashing into her face. Laughing, Dossouye dove deeper into the river. The water flowed clear enough for her to see the silvery scales of fish darting away from her sudden intrusion.

Dossouye surfaced, gulped air, and resubmerged, diving toward the weed-carpeted floor of the Kambi. When her feet touched bottom, she kicked upward to the bright surface. Suddenly she felt a nudge at her shoulder, gentle yet possessed of sufficient force to send her spinning sideways.

For a moment, Dossouye panicked, her lungs growing empty of air. Then she saw a huge, dark bulk floating at her side. *Gbo!* she realized. Shifting in the water, she hovered over the war-bull's back. Then she grasped his horns and urged him toward the surface. With an immense surge of power, Gbo shot upward, nearly tearing his horns from Dossouye's grip.

In a sun-dazzling cascade, they broke the surface. Still cling-ing to the war-bull's horns, Dossouye laughed. For the first time, she felt free of the burden of melancholy she had borne since her bitter departure from Abomey. Lazily she stretched across the length of Gbo's back as the war-bull began to wade shoreward.

Abruptly Gbo stiffened. Dossouye felt a warning tremor course through the giant muscles beneath her. Blinking water from her eyes, she looked toward the bank—and her own thews tensed as tautly as Gbo's.

There were two men in the river bank. Armed men, mounted on horses. The spears of the intruders were leveled at Dossouye and Gbo. The men were clad in flowing trousers of black silk-cotton. Turbans of the same material capped their heads. Above the waist, they wore only brass-studded baldrics to which curved Mossi swords were sheathed. Along with their swords, they carried long-bladed spears and round shields of rhinoceros hide bossed with iron.

One rider was bearded, the other smooth-chinned. In their narrow, umber faces, Dossouye discerned few other differences. Their dark eyes stared directly into hers. They sat poised in their saddles like beasts of prey regarding a victim.

Dossouye knew the horsemen for what they were: *daju*, foot-loose armsmen who sometimes served as mercenaries, though they were more often marauding thieves. The *daju* roamed like packs of wild dogs through the empty lands between the insular Mossi cities.

Through luck and skill, Dossouye had until now managed to avoid unwelcome encounters with the *daju*. Now . . . she had run out of luck. Her weapons and armor lay piled behind the horsemen.

Her face framed by Gbo's horns, Dossouye lay motionless, sunlight gemming the water beaded on her bare skin. The two *daju* smiled. . . .

Dossouye pressed her knees against Gbo's back. Slowly the war-bull waded up the incline of the riverbottom. The bearded *daju* spoke sharply, his Mossi words meaningless to Dossouye. But the eloquence of the accompanying gesture he made with his spear was compelling. His companion raised his own weapon, cocking his elbow for an instant cast.

Gbo continued to advance. Dossouye flattened on his back, tension visible in the long, smooth muscles of her back and thighs. As the war-bull drew closer, the bearded *daju* repeated his gesture. This time he spoke in slurred but recognizable Abomean, demanding that Dossouye dismount immediately.

Whispering a command, Dossouye poked a toe into Gbo's right flank. Together they moved with an explosive swiftness that bewildered even the cunning *daju*.

Hoofs churning in the mud of the bank, the war-bull shouldered between the startled horses. Then Gbo whirled to the left, horned head swinging like a giant's bludgeon and smashing full into the flank of the bearded *daju*'s mount. Shrieking in an almost human tone, the horse collapsed, blood spouting from a pair of widely spaced punctures. Though the *daju* hurled himself clear when his horse fell, he landed clumsily and lay half-stunned while Gbo gored his screaming, kicking steed.

At the beginning of Gbo's charge, Dossouye had slid downward from the war-bull's back. When Gbo hit the *daju*'s horse, she clung briefly to her mount's flank, fingers and toes her only purchase against water-slick hide. Dossouye was gambling, hoping the unexpected attack would unnerve the *daju* sufficiently long for her to reach a weapon.

When the horse crashed to the ground, Dossouye leaped free, hitting the river bank lightly like a cat pouncing from a tree. Her luck returned; the second *daju*'s horse was rearing and pawing the air uncontrollably, its rider cursing as he hauled savagely on the reins. A swift scan showed Dossouye that nothing stood between her and her weapons. As she darted toward them, she shouted another command over her shoulder to Gbo.

Hoofbeats drummed behind her. Still running, Dossouye snatched up her spear. Then she whirled to face the onrushing *daju*.

The beardless warrior charged recklessly, Mossi oaths spilling from his lips. Without hesitation, Dossouye drew back her arm and hurled her weapon full into the breast of the oncoming horse. Though the distance of the cast was not great, the power of the *ahosi*'s whiplike arm drove the spearpoint deep into the flesh of the *daju*'s steed. In the fraction of a moment she'd had to decide, Dossouye had chosen the larger target. Had she aimed at the man, he could have dodged or deflected the spear, then easily slain her.

With a shrill neigh of pain, the horse pitched to its knees. The sudden stop sent the *daju* tumbling through the air. He landed only a few paces from Dossouye. As the *ahosi* bent to retrieve her sword, she thought she saw a bright yellow flash, a spark of sunlight from something that flew from the *daju*'s body when he fell.

Dossouye's curiosity concerning that flash was only momentary. To save her life now, she must move as swiftly as ever on an Abomean battlefield. Sword hilt firmly in hand, she reached the fallen *daju* in two catlike bounds. His spear had flown from his hand; he was struggling frantically to pull his sword from its scabbard when Dossouye's point penetrated the base of his skull, killing him instantly.

Turning from the *daju*'s corpse, Dossouye surveyed the scene of sudden slaughter. The horse she'd speared had joined its rider in death. Its own fall had driven Dossouye's spearpoint into its heart. The bearded *daju*'s steed was also dead, blood still leaking from gaping horn wounds.

The bearded *daju* lay face-down in the mud. Gbo stood over him, one red-smeared horn pressing against the marauder's back. The *daju* trembled visibly, as if he realized he lived only because of the command Dossouye had earlier flung at the war-bull. Because the *daju* spoke Abomean, Dossouye wished to question him. Without the *ahosi*'s word, Gbo would have trampled the man into an unrecognizable pulp.

Like a great, lean panther, Dossouye stalked toward the prone *daju*. Anger burned hot within her; the high spirits she had allowed herself earlier were gone now, leaving her emotions as naked as her body.

Reaching Gbo, Dossouye stroked his side and murmured words of praise in his ear. Once again, the war-bull had lived up to the meaning of his name. Dossouye spoke another command, and Gbo lifted his horn from the *daju*'s back . . . but only slightly. When the man attempted to rise, his spine bumped against Gbo's horn. Instantly he dropped back into the mire. He managed to turn his head sufficiently far to gaze one-eyed at the *ahosi* standing grimly at the side of her mount.

"Spare . . . me," the *daju* croaked.

Snorting in contempt, Dossouye knelt next to the *daju*'s head. "Where are the rest of your dogs?" she demanded. "From what I've heard, you *daju* travel in packs."

"Only . . . Mahadu and me," the *daju* replied haltingly. "Please . . . where is the *moso*? Mahadu had it. . . ."

"What is a '*moso*'?"

"*Moso* is . . . small figure . . . cast from brass. Very valuable . . . will share . . . with you."

"I know exactly what you wanted to 'share' with me!" snapped Dossouye. Then she remembered the bright reflection she had spotted when the beardless *daju* fell from his horse. Valuable?

"I saw no '*moso*,' " she said. "Now, I'm going to tell my war-bull to step away from you. Then I want you to get up and run. Do not look back; do not even think about recovering your weapons. I want you out of my sight very quickly. Understand?"

The *daju* nodded vigorously. At a word from Dossouye, Gbo backed away from the prone man. Without further speech, the *daju* scrambled to his feet and fled, not looking back. Swiftly he disappeared in a copse of mist-clad trees.

Gbo strained against Dossouye's command as though it were a tether immobilizing him. Dossouye trailed her hand along his neck and ears, gentling him. She could not have explained why she spared the *daju*. In the Abomean army, she had slain on command, as well-trained as Gbo. Now, she killed only to protect herself. She felt no compunctions at having dispatched the *daju* named Mahadu from behind. Yet she had just allowed an equally dangerous foe to live. Perhaps she had grown weary of dealing death.

Impatiently she shook aside her mood. Again she recalled the fleeting reflection she had seen only moments ago. A *moso*, the *daju* had said. Valuable. . . .

It was then that she heard four sharp, clear musical notes sound behind her.

As one, Dossouye and Gbo spun to confront the latest intruder. A lone man stood near the bodies of Mahadu and his horse. But this one did not look like a *daju*. Indeed, never before had Dossouye encountered anyone quite like him. He was a composition in brown: skin the rich hue of tobacco; trousers and open robe a lighter, almost russet shade; eyes the deep color of fresh-turned loam.

His hair was plaited into numerous braides of shoulder length, each one sectioned with beads strung in colorful patterns. Beneath the braids, his oval face appeared open, friendly, dominated by warm eyes and a quick, sincere smile. A black mustache grew on his upper lip; wisps of beard clung to his chin and cheeks. His was a young face; he could not have been much older than Dossouye's twenty rains. He was as lean in build as Dossouye, though not quite as tall.

In his hands, the stranger bore the instrument that had sounded the four notes. It was a *kalimba*, a hollow wooden soundbox fitted with eight keys that resonated against a raised metal rim. Held in both hands, the small instrument's music was made by the flicking of the player's thumbs across the keys.

No weapons were evident to Dossouye's practiced gaze. More than one blade, however, could lie hidden in the folds of the stranger's robe. As if divining that thought, the stranger smiled gently.

"I did not mean to alarm you, *ahosi*," he said in a smooth, soft voice. His Abomean was heavily accented, but his speech was like music.

"I heard the sounds of fighting as I passed by," he continued. His thumb flicked one of the middle keys of the *kalimba*. A deep note arrowed across the river bank—*blood, death*.

Gbo bellowed and shook his blood-washed horns. Dossouye's hand tightened on the hilt of her carmined sword.

"Now I see the battle is over. And you certainly have nothing to fear from me."

He touched another key. A high, lilting note floated skyward like a bird—*peace, joy*. Gbo lowed softly as a steer in a pasture. Dossouye smiled and lowered her blade. Rains had passed since she had last known the serenity embodied in that single note.

But she had been deceived before.

"Who are you?" she demanded.

"I am Gimmile, a *bela*—a song-teller," he replied, still smiling. "You can put down your sword and get dressed, you know. I will not harm you. Even if I wanted to, I don't think I could. One Abomean *ahosi*, it seems, is worth at least two *daju*—and I am certainly no *daju*."

Dossouye felt his eyes appraising her unclad form. She knew she was bony, awkward . . . but that was not what Gimmile saw. He had watched her move, lithe and deadly as a great cat. He noted the strong planes of her face, the troubled depths of her eyes.

Dossouye did not trust Gimmile. Still, he had spoken truth when he said he could not harm her. Not while she had a sword in her hand and Gbo at her side.

"Watch him," she told the war-bull.

As Dossouye walked to her pile of armor, Gbo confronted the *bela*. Gimmile did not flinch at the size and ferocity of Dossouye's mount. Instead, he reached out and touched the snout of the war-bull.

Seeing the *bela*'s danger, Dossouye opened her mouth to shout the command that would spare Gimmile from the goring he unwittingly courted. But Gbo did nothing more than snort softly and allow Gimmile to stroke him.

Never in Dossouye's memory had a war-bull commanded to guard allowed itself to be touched by a stranger. She closed her mouth and began to don her armor.

"Were you about to cross the Kambi when the *daju* attacked, *ahosi*?" Gimmile asked, his hands pulling gently at Gbo's ears.

"The name is Dossouye. And the answer is 'Yes.' "

"Well, Dossouye, it seems I owe you a debt. I think those *daju* might have been a danger to me had you not come along."

"Why a danger?" Dossouye asked, looking sharply at him while she laced her leather cuirass.

"A *bela*'s songs can be . . . valuable," Gimmile replied enigmatically. "Indirectly, you may have saved my life. My dwelling is not far from here. I would like to share my songs with you. I also have food. I—I have been alone for a long time."

He plucked another key on his *kalimba* . . . a haunting, lonely sound. And Dossouye knew then that her feelings echoed Gimmile's. Her avoidance of human contact since she had left Abomey had worn a cavity of loneliness deep within her. Her soul was silent, empty.

She looked at the *bela*; watched Gbo nuzzle his palm, Gbo trusted Gimmile. But suspicion still prowled restlessly in Dossouye's mind. Why was Gimmile alone? Would not a song-teller need an audience in the same way a soldier needed battle? And what could Gimmile possess that would be of value to thieves? Surely not his songs or his *kalimba*, she told herself.

Suddenly Dossouye wanted very badly to hear Gimmile's songs, to talk with him, to touch him. Weeks had passed since she last met a person who was not a direct threat to her life. Her suspicions persisted. But she decided to pay them no heed.

"I will come with you," she decided. "But not for long."

Gimmile removed his hand from Gbo's muzzle and played a joyous chorus on the *kalimba*. He sang while Dossouye cinched the saddle about the massive girth of the war-bull. She did not understand the Mossi words of the song, but the sound of his voice soothed her as she cleaned *daju* blood from her sword and Gbo's horns.

Then she mounted her war-bull. Looking down at Gimmile, who had stopped singing, Dossouye experienced a short-lived urge to dig her heels into Gbo's flanks and rush across the river. . . .

Gimmile lifted his hand, waiting for Dossouye to help him

onto the war-bull's back. There was tranquility in his eyes and a promise of solace in his smile. Taking his hand, Dossouye pulled him upward. He settled in front of her. So lean were the two of them that there was room in the saddle for both. His touch, the pressure of his back against her breast, the way he fit in the circle of her arms as she held Gbo's reins—the *bela*'s presence was filling an emptiness of which Dossouye had forced herself to remain unaware, until now.

"Which way?" she asked.

"Along the bank toward the setting of the sun," Gimmile directed.

For all the emotions resurging within her, Dossouye remained aware that the *bela* had indicated a direction opposite the one the fleeing *daju* had taken. Yet as she urged Gbo onward, her suspicions waned. And the memory of the flashing thing the beardless *daju* had dropped faded like morning mist from her mind.

A single pinnacle of stone rose high and incongruous above the treetops. It was as though the crag had been snatched by a playful god from the rocky wastes of Axum and randomly deposited in the midst of the Mossi rain forest. Creepers and lianas festooned the granite-gray peak with traceries of green, curtaining galleries and windows hacked from living stone.

This was Gimmile's dwelling.

Dossouye sat in a cloth-padded stone chair in a chamber that had been hollowed from the center of the pinnacle. Its furnishings were cut from stone. Intricately woven hangings relieved the grayness of the walls. Earlier, Dossouye had marveled at the halls and stairwells honeycombing the rock.

As she finished the meal of boiled plantains Gimmile had prepared, Dossouye recalled stories she had heard concerning the cliff-cities of the Dogon. But Dogon was desert country; in a land of trees like Mossi, a spur of stone such as Gimmile's tower was anomalous.

Little speech had passed during the meal. Gimmile seemed to communicate best with his *kalimba*. The melodies that wafted from the eight keys had allayed her misgivings, which had been aroused again when the *bela* had insisted Gbo be penned in a stone corral at the foot of the pinnacle.

"You wouldn't want him to wander away," Gimmile had warned.

Dossouye knew it would take an elephant to dislodge Gbo once she commanded him to remain in one place. But Gimmile had sung his soothing songs and smiled his open smile, and Dossouye led Gbo into the enclosure and watched while Gimmile, displaying a wiry strength not unlike her own, wrestled the stone corral bar into place.

He played and smiled while leading Dossouye up the twisting stairwells through which thin streams of light poured from small ventilation holes. He sang to her as he boiled the plantains he had obtained from a storage pot. When she ate, he plucked the *kalimba*.

Gimmile ate nothing. Dossouye had meant to question him about that; but she did not, for she was happy and at peace.

Yet . . . she was still an *ahosi*. When Gimmile took away the wooden bowl from which she had eaten, Dossouye posed an abrupt question:

"Gimmile, how is it that you, a singer of songs, live in a fortress a king might envy?"

Gimmile's smile faded. For the first time, Dossouye saw pain in his eyes. Contrition stabbed at her, but she could not take back her question.

"I am sorry," she stammered. "You offer me food and shelter, and I ask questions that are none of my concern."

"No," the *bela* said, waving aside her apology. "You have a right to ask; you have a right to know."

"Know what?"

Gimmile sat down near her feet and looked up at her with the eyes of a child. But the story he told was no child's tale.

As a young *bela*, new to his craft, Gimmile had come to the court of Konondo, king of Dedougou, a Mossi city-state. On a whim, the king had allowed the youthful *bela* to perform for him. So great was Gimmile's talent with voice and *kalimba* that the envy of Bankassi, regular *bela* to the court, was aroused. Bankassi whispered poison into the ear of the king, and Konondo read insult and disrespect into the words of Gimmile's songs, though in fact there was none.

When Gimmile asked the king for a *kwabo*, the small gift customarily presented to *belas* by monarchs, Konondo roared:

"You mock me, then dare to ask for a *kwabo?* I'll give you a *kwabo!* Guards! Take this jackal, give him fifty lashes, and remove him from Dedougou!"

Struggling wildly, Gimmile was dragged from the throne room. Bankassi gloated, his position at Konondo's court still secure.

Another man might have died from Konondo's cruel punishment. But hatred burned deep in Gimmile. Hatred kept him alive while the blood from his lacerated back speckled his stumbling trail away from Dedougou. Hatred carried him deep into a forbidden grove in the Mossi forest, to the hidden shrine of Legba. . . .

(Dossouye's eyes widened at the mention of the accursed name of Legba, the god of apostates and defilers. His worship, his very name, had long ago been outlawed in the kingdoms bordering the Gulf of Otongi. At the sound of Legba's name, Dossouye drew away from Gimmile.)

In a single bitter, blasphemous night, Legba had granted Gimmile's entreaty. *Baraka,* a mystic power from the god's own hand, settled in Gimmile's *kalimba* . . . and invaded Gimmile's soul. Wounds miraculously healed, mind laden with vengeance, Gimmile had emerged from the shrine of evil. He was more than a *bela* now. He was a bearer of *baraka,* a man to be feared.

On a moonless night, Gimmile stood outside the walls of Dedougou. Harsh notes resounded from his *kalimba.* And he sang. . . .

> *The king of Dedougou is bald as an egg,*
> *His belly sags like an elephant's,*
> *His teeth are as few as a guinea-fowl's,*
> *And his bela has no voice. . . .*

In the court of Konondo, the people cried out in horror when every strand of the king's hair fell from his head. Konondo shrieked in pain and fear as his teeth dropped from his mouth like nuts shaken from a tree. The pain became agony when his belly distended, ripping through the cloth of his regal robes. Only the *bela* Bankassi's voice failed to echo the terror and dismay that swiftly became rampant in Dedougou. Tortured, inhuman mewlings issued from Bankassi's throat, nothing more.

Gimmile had his vengeance. Soon, however, the *bela* learned he had not been blessed by Legba's gift of *baraka.* For Legba's gifts were always accompanied by a price, and Legba's price was always a curse.

Gimmile could still sing about the great deeds of warriors of the past, or about gods and goddesses and the creation of the world, or about the secret speech of animals. But the curse that accompanied Gimmile's *baraka* was this: the songs he sang about the living, including himself, *came true!*

"And it *is* a curse, Dossouye," Gimmile said, his tale done, his fingers resting idly on the *kalimba's* keys.

"Word of what I could do spread throughout Mossi. People sought me out as vultures seek out a corpse. They wanted me to

sing them rich, sing them beautiful, sing them brave or intelligent.
I would not do that. I had wanted only to repay Konondo and
Bankassi for what they had done to me. Still, the *baraka* remained within me . . . unwanted, a curse. Men like the *daju* you
killed surrounded me like locusts, trying to force me to sing
them cities of gold. Instead, I sang myself away from them all.''

"And you—*sang* this rock, where no such rock has a right to
be?'' Dossouye asked, her voice tight with apprehension.

"Yes,'' Gimmile said. "I sing, and Legba provides.''

"Legba sent you this tower,'' Dossouye said slowly, realization dawning as Gimmile rose to his feet. Gimmile nodded.

"And Legba has also sent—''

"You,'' Gimmile confirmed. His smile remained warm and
sincere; not at all sinister as he flicked the keys of his *kalimba*
and began to sing. . . .

Dossouye's hand curled around her swordhilt. She meant to
smash the *kalimba* and silence its spell . . . but it was too late
for that. Gimmile's fingers flew rapidly across the keys. Dossouye's
fingers left her swordhilt. She unfastened the clasp of the belt
that secured the weapon to her waist. With a soft thump, the
scabbard struck the cloth-covered floor.

Gimmile placed the *kalimba* on a nearby table and spoke to it
in the same manner Dossouye spoke when issuing a command to
Gbo. As he walked toward her, the instrument continued to play,
even though Gimmile no longer touched it.

Scant heed did Dossouye pay to this latest manifestation of
Gimmile's *baraka*. Taking her hands, Gimmile raised the *ahosi*
to her feet. She did not resist him. Gimmile sang his love to her
while his fingers tugged at the laces of her cuirass.

He sang a celebration to the luster of her onyx eyes. She
stopped his questing hands and removed her armor for the second time that day. He shaped her slender body with sweet words
that showed her the true beauty of her self; the beauty she had
hidden from herself for fear others might convince her it was not
really there.

Gimmile's garments fell from him like leaves from a wind-
blown tree. Spare and rangy, his frame was a male twin of
Dossouye's. He sang her into an embrace.

While Gimmile led her to a stone bed softened by piles of
patterned cloth, the *ahosi* in Dossouye protested stridenly but
ineffectively. She had known love as an *ahosi;* but always with
other women soldiers, never a man. To accept the seed of a man
was to invite pregnancy, and a pregnant *ahosi* was a dead one.

The *ahosi* were brides of the King of Abomey. The King never touched them, and death awaited any other man who did. Such constraints meant nothing now, as Gimmile continued to sing.

Dossouye's fingers toyed with the beads in Gimmile's braids. Her mouth branded his chest and shoulders with hot, wet circles. Only when Gimmile drew her down to the bed did he pause in his singing. Then the song became theirs, not just his, and they sang it together. And when their mouths and bodies met, Gimmile had no further need for the insidious power of Legba's *baraka*. But the *kalimba* continued to play.

Abruptly, uncomfortably, Dossouye awoke. A musty odor invaded her nostrils. Something sharp prodded her throat. Her eyelids jarred open.

The light in Gimmile's chamber was dim. Dossouye lay on her back, bare flesh abrading against a rough, stony surface. Her gaze wandered upward along a length of curved, shining steel—*a sword!* Her vision and her mind snapped into clear focus then, the lingering recall of the day and night before thrust aside as she gazed into the face of the bearded *daju*, the attacker whose life she had spared.

"Where is . . . *moso?*" the *daju* demanded. "You have it . . . I know."

Dossouye did not know what he meant. She shifted her weight, reflexively moving away from the touch of the swordpoint at her throat. Something sharp dug at her left shoulderblade.

Ignoring the *daju* she turned, slid her hand beneath her shoulder, and grasped a small, sharp-edged object. She raised herself on one elbow and intently examined the thing she held in her hand.

It was a figurine cast in brass, no more than three inches high, depicting a robed *bela* playing a *kalimba*. Beaded braids of hair; open, smiling face . . . every detail had been captured perfectly by the unknown craftsman. The joy she had experienced the night before and the fear she was beginning to feel now were both secondary to the sudden pang of sadness she experienced when she recognized the tiny brass face as Gimmile's.

"That is . . . *moso!*" the *daju* shouted excitedly. Eagerly he reached for the figurine. Ignoring the *daju*'s sword, Dossouye pulled the *moso* away from the thief's grasp. Her eyes swiftly scanned the chamber. With a tremor of horror, she realized she was lying on a bare stone floor next to a broken ruin of a bed.

"Hah!" spat the *daju*. "You know how . . . to bring *moso* to life. Legba made . . . Gimmile into *moso* to pay for *baraka*. But *moso* can . . . come to life . . . and sing wishes true.

Mahadu and I . . . found *moso* near here. Could not . . . bring
to life. We were taking *moso* . . . to *baraka*-man . . . when we
saw you. Now . . . you tell . . . how to bring *moso* to life. Tell
. . . and I might . . . let you live.''

Dossouye stared up at the *daju*. Murder and greed warred on
his vulpine face. His swordpoint hovered close to her throat.
And she had not the slightest notion how Gimmile could be
made to live.

With blurring speed, she hurled the *moso* past the broken bed.
The figurine bounced once off jagged stone, then disappeared.
With a strangled curse, the *daju* stared wildly after the vanished
prize, momentarily forgetting his captive. Dossouye struck aside
the *daju*'s swordarm and drove her heel into one of his knees.
Yelping in pain, the *daju* stumbled. His sword dropped from his
hand. Dossouye scrambled to her feet.

Twisting past the *daju*, Dossouye dove for his fallen sword.
And a galaxy of crimson stars exploded before her eyes when the
booted foot of the *daju* collided with the side of her head.

Dossouye fell heavily, rolled, and lay defenseless on her back,
waves of sick pain buffeting her inside her skull. Recovering his
blade, the *daju* limped toward her, his face contorted with hate.

"I will . . . bring *moso* to life . . . without you," he grated.
"Now . . . Abomean bitch . . . *die!*"

He raised his curved blade. Dossouye lay stunned, helpless.
Without a weapon in her hand, not even her *ahosi*-trained
quickness could save her now. She tensed to accept the blow that
would slay her.

The *daju* brought his weapon down. But before it reached
Dossouye's breast, a brown-clad figure hurled itself into the path
of the blade. Metal bit flesh, a voice cried out in wrenching
agony—and Gimmile lay stretched between Dossouye and the
*daju*. Blood welled from a wound that bisected his side.

The *daju* stared down at Gimmile, mouth hanging open, eyes
white with dread and disbelief. Dossouye, consumed with almost
feral rage, leaped to her feet, tore the *daju*'s sword from his
nerveless grasp, and plunged the blade so deeply through his
midsection that the point ripped in a bloody shower through the
flesh of his back.

Without a sound, without any alteration of the expression of
shock frozen on his face, the *daju* sank to the floor. Death took
him more quickly than he deserved.

Dossouye bent to Gimmile's side. The *bela* sprawled face-
down, unmoving. Gently Dossouye turned him onto his back and
cradled his braided head in her lap. Though his life leaked in a

scarlet stream from his wound, Gimmile's face betrayed no pain. His hands clutched his *kalimba*, but the instrument was broken. It would never play again.

"I never lied to you, Dossouye," Gimmile said, his voice still like music. "But I did not tell you everything. The king of Dedougou has been dead three hundred rains. *So have I*. After I sang my vengeance against Konondo and Bankassi, after I sang this tower to escape those who wanted to use me, the truth of Legba's curse became clear. I would forever be a *moso*, an unliving thing of metal. Only great emotions—love, hate, joy, sorrow—can restore me to life. But such life never lasts long.

"It was your rage at the *daju* who stole me that brought me to life by the river. I saw you . . . wanted you, even as the *daju* did. The *baraka* of Legba gave you to me. I wish . . . I had not needed the *baraka* to gain your love. Now . . . the *kalimba* is broken; the *baraka* is gone from me. I can feel it flowing out with my blood. This time, I will not come back to life."

Dossouye bowed her head and shut her eyes. She did not want to hear more or see more; she wished never to hear or see again.

"Dossouye."

The *bela's* voice bore no sorcerous compulsion now. Still, Dossouye opened her eyes and looked into those of Gimmile. Neither deceit nor fear of death lay in those earth-brown depths. Only resignation—and peace.

"I know your thoughts, Dossouye. You bear the seed of a—ghost. There will be no child inside you. Now, please turn from me, Dossouye. I do not want you to see me die."

He closed his eyes. Dossouye touched his cheeks, his lips. Then she rose and turned away. His blood smeared her bare thighs.

Memories diverted by the fight with the *daju* returned in a rush of pain. Even as she gazed sorrowfully at the dust-laden remnants of the accouterments of Gimmile's chamber, Dossouye remembered his warmth, his kindness, the love they had shared too briefly. The memories scalded her eyes.

Dossouye and Gbo stood quietly by the bank of the Kambi. The sun had set and risen once since they last saw the heat-mist rise from the river. Dossouye stroked Gbo's side, thankful that Gimmile had penned him the day before. Formidable though the war-bull was, there was still a chance the *daju* might have brought him down with a lucky thrust of sword or spear.

In her swordhand, Dossouye held a brass figurine of a *bela* with a broken *kalimba*. Tarnish trickled like blood down the metal side of the *moso*.

"You never needed Legba, Gimmile," Dossouye murmured sadly. "You could have sung your vengeance in other cities, and all tne kings of Mossi would have laughed at Konondo's pettiness, and the laughter would have reached Dedougou. The sting of your songs would have long outlived the sting of his lash."

She closed her fist around the *moso*.

"You did not need Legba for me, either, Gimmile."

Drawing back her arm, Dossouye hurled the *moso* into the Kambi. It sank with a splash as infinitesimal as the ranting of woman and man against the gods.

Mounting Gbo, Dossouye urged him into the water. Now she would complete the crossing that had been interrupted the day before. Her road still led to nowhere. But Gimmile sang in her soul. . . .

Charles de Lint says of himself that he has spent his life hopping from country to country; born in the Netherlands, of Dutch, Spanish, French and Japanese descent, he has lived everywhere from France to Turkey, but settled down, about ten or twelve years ago, in Canada, with "a zillion books and an orange cat named Gurgi." In the introduction to another story in this anthology, I have mentioned his association with the small but highly literate and professional Triskell Press, and with Charles Saunders.

When I first read this story, of the swordswoman Aynber and her companion Thorn Hawkwood, the wizard, I was hesitant, feeling that a second character named Thorn would be confusing. In view of the Phyllis Ann Carr story earlier in this volume, where Frostflower, the sorceress, travels with swordswoman Thorn, I asked Charles de Lint if he would mind changing the name of his male character, and was told that Thorn Hawkwood had appeared in print before the swordswoman Thorn; the pair had appeared together in *Dark Fantasy*, another of those excellent and professional small-press fantasy magazines, published by Gene Day, as well as in *Sorcerer's Apprentice*, edited by Liz Danforth.

I still felt that since Karr's works have appeared in several mass-market paperbacks and would be, perhaps, more familiar to the audience, the name of de Lint's character should be altered somewhat; so this story has been edited slightly to emphasize the "Hawkwood" part of the name rather than the "Thorn."

De Lint says of his heroine and her friend that "there are a couple of other stories about this pair lying around in rough draft," and adds that he hopes to use them eventually in a novel. We hope so too; while for those who have not met the small-press editions, we are proud to present this first appearance in mass-market form. De Lint wished me to add the following note;

"*Valley of the Troll* was bought in 1978, soon after it was written, by Gene Day of Shadow Press, and set to wander loose in the world once more by his unfortunate and untimely death. I was wondering if you'd mind dedicating the story to Gene, as he bought my first Aynber story many years ago; a wonderful man who'll be missed both for his art and especially for the very human being he was." If he brought Aynber and Thorn Hawkwood into print for the first time, we're delighted to dedicate this appearance of the pair to his memory.—MZB

# THE VALLEY OF THE TROLL
### by Charles de Lint

> "And Old Troll picked o'er spoils long pawed
> and worried travellers' bones long gnawed
> and listened ever o'er the roar
> for horses hooves as they'd come before . . ."
> —J.E. COPLIN

"They've a two-hour lead on us, Hawkwood, perhaps three," said Aynber. She lifted her eyes from the trail, pushed her hat back, and mopped her brow.

"I tell you," Thorn Hawkwood replied over the dull clopping of their horses' hooves, "that it's treasure we should be seeking, not some piddling bounties."

"No more talk of treasure." She shook her head resolutely. "There's a surety of a thousand gold pieces on Guil's head, with another hundred for each of his men. Damme! The last treasure hunt you led us on near' cost me my life . . ."

"But just think of the treasure," he continued glibly. "Mounds of it, Huntress. More than we could spent in a score of lives."

Aynber sighed. Her companion's spiel had become all too familiar over the last two weeks of hard riding through this misbegotten wilderness, following the trail of the highwayman Guil and his band. She sat loosely in the saddle, fingering a thin scar on her cheek. Surely the gods would have mercy on her and Hawkwood would come down with laryngitis, or perhaps his tongue would fall out? She shot a hopeful glance in his direction.

Under the brim of her hat her hair was the color of sun-ripe corn, framing an oval face with full lips and wide-set eyes, before it fell down her back in long unbound tresses. She wore a doeskin shirt, with knee-length trousers to match, neither of which hid the gentle swell of her breasts, or the sweet curves of her figure. Overtop was a woolen tabard, while at her belt hung a dagger, a long thin sword, and a leather pouch holding a half-score *lessen-yaln*—Aelfin death-stars, small five-pointed discs wrought of star-silver.

"Jewels with which we could ransom a kingdom," Hawkwood was still saying. "Aye, and gold and silver beyond counting. . . ."

"Na, na," she said irritably, scowling.

His clothing was somber, all grays and blacks. He was dark-haired, with a thin nose, high cheekbones, and a wisp of a mustache that quivered catlike when he spoke. A dusky cloak hid the rapier sheathed at his side. From under a small peaked cap his eyes, narrow and piercing blue, glittered with an unmistakable passion for the aforementioned wealth.

"It's this endless bedamned road," she added, "through lands so uncivilized that I haven't seen a tavern, aye, or had a drink, since we left Calthoren. And as to your treasure, doesn't it seem just a *little* bit odd to you that all we've got to do is ride in and collect it?"

"Well, so said old Grimble," replied Hawkwood, "and in all the years I've known him he's never steered me wrong."

"Aye, so you say. Still, if it's such a simple matter, why hasn't he shaken his fat arse and come traipsing out here himself? Eh?"

"Aynber, Aynber . . . he's an old man, and unlike us, he's not fit to rough the wilds. Besides, in return for his map, I promised him a third share. . . ."

"You what?"

There was a definite rising anger in her voice. Knowing her temper all too well, Hawkwood ignored her, whistling tunelessly through his teeth.

"Hawkwood . . ." she began threateningly.

"A lovely countryside really, don't you think?" he replied with a grin. "Minds me of my homeland, it does, though it's a touch more wild and not nearly as cheery. Hist! What's that?"

He pointed to the shadows at the base of an old ash tree leaning precariously over the roadway. Aynber followed his finger with her eyes, one hand streaking for the hilt of her sword, when a large jack rabbit sauntered out from the shade. It took one look at the pair, ears twitching, before it bounded away. Hawkwood laughed.

"A third's not too much, really," he said.

Aynber loosened her grip on her sword's hilt and glowered at him.

"Just saying that we're searching for the treasure—which we're not—and just saying we found it—which we won't—do you think for a moment that I'd share it with that fat sniggering toad? Na, na, there'll be no fool's quest for me. Guil's bounty will be quite enough, thank you very much."

Hawkwood made no reply.

*   *   *

The next morn found them resting their horses, still on the trail of the highwaymen. Aynber leaned forward, resting her palms on the pommel of her saddle.

"They've split up," she said. "See, Guil and the one with the poorly shod mare follow the roadway, while another's cut across the field there." She pointed out the tracks as she spoke, her eyes raking the roadside. "Ah! And the other two have headed south. Well, it's Guil I want."

She shook out her reins and her mount stepped briskly forward, along the roadway. Muttering, Hawkwood followed.

Their way led through copses of pale gray beech, bordered by thick bushed hawthorns and briars, until it topped a hillock. There the road led into a small vale. At its bottom was a river that cut like a slash through the length of the valley, deep, though not wide. Crossing the water was a wooden bridge, held together with thick ropes, and by it, a rude cot of turf and stone.

"This is it!" cried Hawkwood.

Aynber turned in the saddle to see him scrabbling about in his pouch. Soon, he was busily perusing a map written on a scroll of animal hide, the corners of which kept turning up on him. He mumbled eagerly to himself as he struggled with it. Looking up at last, he said: "It matches the map, see? Well, save for the bridge. It must be newly built, or at least since the map was made."

Aynber sidled her mount up to his to look at the map herself.

"So it is," she mused. "I wonder who lives there?"

Hawkwood shaded his eyes to peer closer.

"There's such a rubble about it that I'll wager no one's been there for at least five years . . . except for . . . no!" He turned to Aynber, anguish written plainly on his face. "Do you think Guil's been there and snatched the treasure before us?"

"Well, his trail leads that way, and if he's not got it, I'm sure anybody who's come by here before us has had a crack at it."

"Without the map?" asked Hawkwood disdainfully, recovering his composure. "Come. Let's go."

He put heels to his horse and trotted ahead. Aynber shook her head, following at a slower pace. The cot might well be a sanctuary for pursued outlaws. Aye, and the brush along the roadside grew high and thick enough to hide an ambush.

"Seems a bit precarious," offered Hawkwood as she joined him by the bridge. Two thick strands of heavy rope, tied about a pair of stumps, was all that anchored the poorly made structure. "Still, I'm sure it'll take our weight. See there?" He pointed to the opposite bank where the mouth of a small opening stood out darkly against the gray granite of the cliff, just above the waterline. "That'll be the cave that's on the map."

As he started across, Aynber held back, looking about the deserted cot and its surroundings once more. There was an odd taint in the air that didn't sit right with her. An intangible essence that she couldn't quite put her finger on. Giving up, she sighed, started to follow Thorn, and saw it: a long craggy arm snaking from underneath the bridge, reaching for the leg of Hawkwood's horse.

"Hawkwood! Look out!"

He turned with a smile to see her gesturing at the side of the bridge.

"Oh, no," he called back gaily. "You'll not trick me so easily." Remembering the scare he'd thrown into her the day before with the jack rabbit, he shook his head at such an obvious attempt to get back at him. His horse squealed, cutting into his reveries. Gasping with shock, he felt it being pulled from beneath him. Falling from the back of his mount, he saw a huge grinning face leering at him; in one hand was his horse, whinnying its terror. The other was reaching for him.

"An ogre!" Scrambling back, he almost fell off the opposite side of the bridge. In a flurry of panic-swift movement, he raced back to where Aynber waited. Once there, he looked back and saw his horse being pulled from the bridge, its legs pumping madly as it strove to escape its captor.

"No, I think it's a troll," said Aynber, regarding the panting form beside her from the back of her mount.

"But my horse. . . ."

"Gone now, I should think, O great Thorn Hawkwood, mightiest of wizards, fiercest of warriors," replied Aynber with a mocking laugh. "What now? Have you a spell to lay low this monster? Or will you fare forth and slay it with one blow of your matchless sword-arm?"

"Bedamned to the troll. What of my horse?"

"Ah, but with the troll's treasure you'll be able to buy a stable of noble steeds. All you need do is waltz in and collect it."

Hawkwood was silent for a moment.

"I think we should forget about the treasure," he muttered at last. "I've heard tales about troll's gold. It's cursed, 'tis said. Gives you warts, turns into mud and. . . ."

"Na, na," broke in his companion. "It appears that there is a treasure after all, and I for one think it's time we studied on a plan to get it."

\*     \*     \*

Later, as they rested amongst a stand of birch and maple by the crest of the hill where first they entered the troll's valley, Hawkwood's enthusiasm returned, as well as his modesty. That Aynber was actually interested in the treasure now was just another feather in his cap.

"As soon as my spell takes effect—a most difficult spell, I might add, one that only the hardiest of adepts would ever attempt —you will creep down to the troll's cave, step lightly over his sleeping body, and bear away armloads of gems and gold!"

"There's a little weakness in your plan," returned Aynber, absently tracing the scar on her cheek as she spoke. "Mainly, that your spells have a tendency not to work at all, or they backfire to ill effect. Usually on me, if I'm not mistaken. Like that time in the Dead Marshes near Franwath, when you were going to turn a giant lizard into a hummingbird and my . . ."

"This is different. It's only the simplest of spells, one that even an apprentice's apprentice might try without too much difficulty."

"Ah," said Aynber with a smile. "If that's the case. . . ."

Hawkwood scowled and muttered something inaudible into his mustache.

Aynber stood on the cliff's edge, glancing from the way below to where Hawkwood sat pulling vials and small bags of strange powders from his journeysack, setting them out in a neat order before a low fire. She took a deep breath and doffed her tabard and boots. Her sword and hat she laid atop them, tying a sack to her belt, in which to store the hypothetical treasure should she find it. With a last look at Hawkwood, she slipped over the rim of the cleft. Gingerly, she made her way down to the river. At its edge, she patted her pouch of *lessen-yaln* reassuringly, checked the thong that looped her dagger in place, and dove in.

She gasped at the icy chill as her body met the cold water. The shock took her breath away, though she soon warmed with the effort of her swimming. Before the mouth of the cave, she clambered onto the rocks, her clothes dripping. She wrung the water from her hair, looking again to where Hawkwood sat brewing his spell over the fire. When he waved confidently to her, she faced the entrance once more, and stooping, entered. No sooner was she out of sight, then a great cloud of green-tinged smoke erupted from Hawkwood's fire. As it billowed about him, he slumped forward, narrowly missing the fire, to lie fast asleep on the grass.

Inside it was dark; damp and dark with a fetid troll-reek in the air that made her gag. She longed for a light, cursing herself for not having thought of it sooner. Undoing the loop about her dagger, she took a death-star from her pouch and moved on, her fingertips tracing the wet slimy surface of the tunnel. Slowly, she made her way.

*Damme!* she thought as she marched along. *It makes my skin crawl.*

Memories crowded her mind, jostling the senses she needed to warn her of the troll's presence. Yarg hunts in the dark woods above the moors of Boscawen vied with reminders of a dozen other skirmishes and battles. Aye, and that time the marsh-dwellers rose up against her foster-clan and young Kalin was slain. *Oh, Kalin. . . .*

Suddenly she stumbled over something that lay across her path. She leapt back, dagger and *lessen-yaln* ready. She stood unmoving, stilling the surge of adrenalin that shook her. Only the sound of her own raspy breathing filled her ears. Cautiously, she crept forward once more, tracing the object before her with trembling hands. It was the troll and—*Thank the Gods for miracles!*—it was asleep. For once one of Hawkwood's spells had worked.

She was still nervous as she stepped over the sleeping form, only to plant her foot into what must be the remains of Hawkwood's horse. A nauseous feeling rose from the pit of her stomach and she was sick. Shuddering, she moved forward, the foul taste of bile still in her throat, and tripped over a jumble of bones. The clatter of the bones seemed to raise a terrible din in the narrow confines of the tunnel. Aynber poised motionless until she was certain that the troll had not awakened. When no sound came from where it lay, she let her breath out and hurried on.

As her receding back disappeared around a corner, a glittering eye opened in the still face of the troll. Grinning hugely, he stood with a silent whisper to follow her.

Aynber's way sloped downward now. The footing of the tunnel became progressively muddier and so soft that her bare feet sank into it. Low plopping sounds echoed dully about her when she lifted them. She shivered as she imagined what sorts of pale leeches, or other slimy creatures, might be hiding in the mud and . . . was that the sound of someone treading through the muck behind her? She stopped to listen. Shrugging, she put it down to a reverberation of her own footsteps and went on.

Ahead, a dim yellow glow showed against the heretofore utter darkness of the tunnel. Aynber smiled to herself as the way grew brighter. Before her she could make out glitters and sparklings in the pallid light that could only be the treasure. Now here was something indeed. Not only had his spell worked to good effect, but Hawkwood's information was for once correct.

Her smile grew broader when she stepped within the chamber. Walled, floored and ceiled with mud it might be, still it was filled with such wealth that she gasped for sheer pleasure. She walked about, lovingly lifting here a gold necklace hung with saffires and jade, a tiera set with an enormous diamond, there an ornate goblet of some unfamiliar glinting metal, imbedded with precious jewels that bespoke a king's ransom. Everywhere, coins of silver, copper, gold, glinted and shone, some with markings that placed their age at least a century in the past. Here was one, even, with the visage of Lord Tanlan upon it, the founder of Calthoren in the dawn days of the Eastern Kingdoms. Aynber filled the sack at her belt as swiftly as she might. Knowing full well that it would take at least a lifetime to gather up the whole treasure, she chose only the best.

So caught up was she, that she almost missed the unobtrusive sucking sound, like a heavy foot being lifted from deep mud. When it did register, a chill ran down her spine. Slowly she turned to see the troll in the threshold of the chamber, the phosphorescent light of the treasure room outlining it against the deeper dark of the tunnel.

"Garna's got ye, pretty gold-hair," it said with a hideous chuckle, its voice low and cracked with little use.

Aynber backed away from the monstrous form that was advancing upon her. Feral red eyes glared unblinkingly, huge in its misshapen face, and yellow teeth showed through the tangle of its filthy beard.

"Garna want ye," it chuckled again.

The troll stepped forward, matched by a similar step backward by Aynber, only now her back was against the dank slimed walls of the chamber. There was no farther she could go. *Lessen-yaln* and dagger leapt into her hands from where she had lain them while she gathered the treasure. The sack was full and heavy, fastened to her belt.

*Damme you, Thorn Hawkwood!* she thought. *I'll kill you if I ever get out of here.*

"Pretty gold-hair," said the troll. "Garna wants to play wi' ye."

It advanced again.

"Aye," said Aynber through clenched teeth, "you misshapen coupling of a pig's arse and a wart! But first you'll have to catch me."

As she spoke, she loosed the death-star in her hand. Straight and true it flew to imbed with a sickening thud in the troll's broad forehead. The troll shook its head bemusedly, as though only a gnat had landed on its brow, and reached for her. Gold goblets and crowns broke 'neath its tread as it shambled toward her. Aynber stared in horror as the creature bore down on her, the *lessen-yaln* stuck in its skull to no avail.

She slipped 'neath its grasp at the last moment. As she bolted for the door, a long arm caught at her shirt and pulled her back. Desperately, she hacked at the front of her doeskin with her knife. The troll fell back, clutching her shirt. Bare-breasted, she flew up the tunnel, knife in one hand, the other steadying the treasure sack that bounced at her thigh.

"Come back, gold-hair!" bellowed the troll from behind her.

It threw a jewel the size of a man's fist after her. The gem struck her in the arm, numbing it so that she dropped her dagger. She gave no heed to the loss, though, and sped on.

Behind, the troll raged and shrieked, tearing at the rough walls of the room, until it lumbered after her. At first she made good headway, having both a headstart and the swifter limbs, but the mud bogged her down, and once moving, the troll's speed increased until it fairly shot down the tunnel after her.

The ground became more solid under her feet so that she made better time. The troll did as well. She cast a useless glance over her shoulder, for it was too dark to see her pursuer. Still, she could hear its raspy breath and pounding feet not two dozen yards behind her.

She fell asprawl again over the remains of Hawkwood's horse. Floundering in the gory remnants, her one thought was that safety was now near. In a moment, she was up, the treasure sack yet secure. Lungs gasping, sharp pains lancing her sides, she managed a last burst of speed and tumbled out of the cave's mouth, almost falling into the river. The instant before she dove in, she realized two things: one, that the treasure sack would slow her down, and two, the troll could probably swim faster than she could. In the time it took for the thoughts to flash through her mind, she spun about, scrambled for handholds on the cliffside, and clambered up.

The troll was at the cave's opening before she'd gone half the distance. Looking back, Aynber saw it shrink back from the water. The troll caught her eye, grinned horribly, and followed her up the cliff-face. As she reached the top, she threw down a heap of rock, striking the troll so that it fell heavily down to the water's edge. A sudden idea was burning in her thoughts. *It fears the water, does it?* She raced for the bridge, as the troll scaled the rocks once more, reaching the overpass just as its head topped the rim.

Across the bridge she pounded. Reaching her pile of clothes, she tore her sword from its scabbard and returned to the swaying causeway. Wildly, with heart pounding and lungs desperate for air, she cut away at the supporting ropes, while the troll loped across it toward her. She could almost feel the troll-breath upon her, when she sawed through the last strand. The whole structure fell away from where she stood. With a thunderous crash, bridge and troll thudded into the opposite cliff. The troll scrambled to its feet, shaking with fury and choking on the dust. It hesitated at the water's edge—Aynber knew it longed to plunge in just to get at her—before it raced up the rocks to roar its fury at her. She paid it no mind.

After she called her horse, she lashed the treasure sack to its saddle and slipped into her boots and tabard. She picked up her hat, glancing at Hawkwood's sleeping body as she did.

"Wizard! Bah! I should leave you here for all the help you've been."

With a sigh, she wearily lifted his still-sleeping form, laying it across the neck of her horse. One last glance she threw to where the troll stood. Laughing, she blew it a kiss, shook out her reins, and set her steed at a gallop along the homeward trail.

Behind, the troll bellowed still. When she was out of sight, it squatted on its haunches, tearing at the ground. Shards of rock and clumps of dirt sprayed about its figure, until a thought slowly entered its dim mind. Thick fingers rose the rubble to cut the air in crude cabalistic figures, and all the while it muttered to itself: "Garna no get gold-hair, gold-hair no get gold . . . Garna no get . . ."

Aynber drove her over-burdened mount as fast as she dared. Only when she felt confident that they'd put enough distance between the troll and themselves did she ease it to a slow walk. Cursing the still-sleeping Hawkwood, she mused on the where-abouts of Guil and his men. More than likely, they'd rendez-voused somewhere beyond the troll's valley, and by now, were far away.

How many miles had they ridden since Garna's valley was left behind? She puzzled over that as well, giving up when her weariness became so much that it was all she could do just to stay in the saddle. She ached all over, was still damp, and the rough wool of her tabard chaffed her skin. Ah, still the treasure was worth a few small discomforts. Coming to a halt in a small track just off the woodroad, she dropped Hawkwood to the ground, almost falling from the saddle herself.

*How long is this bedamned sleeping spell supposed to last anyway?* she asked herself.

She dismounted, rubbed down her horse and staked it out. The twilight was edging the sky with night, when she thankfully collapsed onto her blankets, not even bothering to have a look at the treasure. As her weariness washed over her, her last thought was that she was only courting danger sleeping in the open like this. Half-determined to rise and find a safer spot, she fell into a deep sleep.

"On your feet, doxy!" The harsh voice disturbed a pleasant dream of a youth with curly hair and strong lean limbs.

Aynber struggled to waken.

"What . . . ?" she began. A chorus of rough laughter and a booted foot against her side was the only answer. Someone grasped the folds of her tabard and lifted her to her feet. Her eyes flickered open and she strove to bring awareness into her sleep-fogged brain. It was night. A pale moon hovered above the trees, seeming to mock her helplessness.

"So this is the great Huntress?"

She focused on the speaker, recognizing him with a shock. It was Guil! Aye, Guil, and with him, four of his men. They swaggered before her in the dim light, gaudily clad in stolen finery—a sharp contrast against the dirt of their skin and the filth matted in their beards and hair. She twisted in the arm-breaking grip of the one that held her. Another stepped up and cuffed her savagely across the face. Sniggering, he tore the tabard from her shoulders. Her breasts heaved in the moonlight, as she struggled powerlessly. He smiled with appreciation and bent down to loosen the ties of her trousers.

"She's a woman, right enough, for all her manlike ways," he muttered.

Aynber lunged at him, dragging the man that held her forward. Her knee rose up to catch the man bending before her on the chin. He fell back, his eyes glazed. Shaking his head, he rose and struck her in the face with the full of his fist.

"Leave her be, Draln!" cried Guil. "Damme! Are you all fools? Ten thousand in gold Kesser's offered for her in one piece, unhurt. He wants to wring every last cry of pain from her for what she did to the thieves' guild in Nalbur."

Aynber stared at the bearded highwayman in shock.

"Aye," he said laughing. "Does it surprise you? A bounty offered for a bounty hunter? You'll see soon enough. Twas a pretty racket you broke up then, and Kesser's not forgotten. Thieves are thicker than water, my brave Huntress, and gold is gold. Ha! And so easy in the taking."

Aynber strained in her captor's grip, to no avail.

"Tie her up. Like the other one," said Guil with a disdainful wave of his hand. "And just remember: they're both worth money. Two thousand for her, with an extra fifty for any in her company."

She fought like a tigress, yet for all her effort, they soon had her trussed. She gnashed her teeth in helpless fury. Once bound, they let her fall, so that she lay on her stomach, her arms tied behind her. With a sudden surge of hope, she felt the pouch with her death-stars beneath her.

"What's this, then?" cried Draln, ripping the treasure sack from her saddle. Guil approached him as he tore it open.

"Damme!" muttered their leader. "The bitch had a treasure on her." He rubbed his hands with glee. "What a night, oh, what a night!"

They retreated to where they'd readied a fire; flint and steel soon had the tinder blazing. By the light of that fire, the highwaymen pored over the troll's treasure. Wineskins were taken from saddles, exclamations filled the air, and through it all, Aynber attempted to get at the knife-sharp discs in her pouch. She cast an eye to where Hawkwood lay bound, just on the edge of the firelight.

He looked up as he felt her attention upon him and smiled. Shadows that might have been bruises splotched his face. He rolled about so that she could see the ropes that bound him and her eyes went wide with wonder. Thin tendrils of smoke rose from the cords. After a moment, he pulled his hands apart. He was free. She shook her head in disbelief as he cautiously loosened the ropes about his feet and crept across the grass to her.

"How did you do that?" she asked in a whisper, when he was near.

"A simple spell," he said with a shrug. There *were* bruises on his face.

"You'll have to show me sometime," she said.

"It takes years of self-discipline," he explained and proceeded to launch into a long discourse until Aynber's sharp whisper brought him back to their surroundings.

"Damme you! Will you just set me free?"

He crouched behind her and began to work at her bonds.

"Leave me a little skin, would you?" she complained, glancing nervously to where their captors lounged by the fire, their voices getting progressively louder and more slurred as the wine seeped into their blood. Bounty or no bounty, she was sure that once the alcohol took much more effect, they'd be upon her.

"That's the last," muttered Hawkwood.

Aynber flexed her arms with a grimace. Her head still rang from the blows she'd received.

"How are we going to take them?" Hawkwood asked.

Aynber stared at him, unable to believe his words.

"Are you mad? I've but two death-stars left, and without other weapons, how long do you think we can hold them off? Na, na, their time will come soon enough. For now . . . we flee."

Silently, they crept from the boundary of the campfire's glow until the darkness of the surrounding woods swallowed them.

Draln shook the empty wineskin and threw it away with a curse. He scratched at the stubble on his cheek and rose to relieve his bladder. Pulling at the thongs that held up his trousers, he glanced over to where Aynber should have lain.

"She's gone!" he cried.

Guil stumbled to his feet.

"Bedamned to the lot of you!" he bellowed. "Who was on guard?"

"Ha!" said Draln, inspired by the vast quantities of wine he'd consumed. "You were, Guil."

"Aye," added the others, quick to take his lead, "it was you."

Guil glared at them, fury roaring in his eyes, until he broke into a wild laugh.

"Mount up," he said at last, still gasping for breath. "Gods! I'd never've thought you'd've had the wits to think of that. Come, now, if we hurry we can still catch them . . ." He caught himself, glanced at the treasure sack, and laughed again. "Ah, to hell with her. We've all the gold we'll ever need right here."

A week later, outside of The Serpent's Tongue in the small coastal town of Thistral, there were six weary steeds tied to the hitching rail, while within, an argument was ensuing.

"You can take your dung and mud, me buckos, and pawn it off elsewhere!" cried the proprieter of the inn. Behind him stood a half-score of the local men, tall brawny lads—able, willing, and more than ready for a tangle.

Guil and his men stared aghast at the treasure sack. How had it changed to this, from the gold and jewels they remembered? There was no time to look for an answer to that riddle just now, though, for the men behind the innkeeper were advancing upon them. The highwaymen beat a hasty retreat through the door, making for their horses.

Suddenly, Draln clutched at his throat. A fountain of blood poured from between his fingers and, gurgling, he fell to the ground. As his hand dropped from his throat, Guil and his remaining men saw the *lessen-yaln* imbedded there.

"I can take you dead or alive," came a familiar voice, resounding over the street.

They looked up to see the Huntress facing them, her tabard caked in mud. In her left hand was another death-star, in her right, a long thin blade. Leaning casually against a building behind her was Thorn Hawkwood, a grim smile playing on his lips, a blade in his hand. He stepped forward to stand beside her.

Four swords whipped out of their sheaths. In that time, another *lessen-yaln* sped from Aynber's hand, ripping into Guil's chest. As he fell forward, a cry dying on his lips, the others moved forward, thought better of it, and dropped their weapons. A few years in the jail in Calthoren was better than sure death.

Aynber laughed as she crossed the street.

Later, in the inn, she handed her sword to a youth.

"My thanks for the loan."

With an elbow propped on the table, Aynber threw back a mug of ale, wiped her mouth appreciably, and smiled to hear the tale of how Guil and his men had tried to buy drink and food with a sackful of dung. Yet when she thought of the treasure sack that she'd filled with her own hands, a frown furrowed her brow.

"How . . . ?"

"The curse!" cried Hawkwood, snapping his fingers. "Remember I spoke of a curse? The troll put a curse on the gold!"

Aynber raised a refilled mug to her lips. Fingering the scar on her cheek, she glanced through the inn's door to where the highwaymen were tied to their mounts.

"Well, there'll be no curse on that gold," she said nodding to them. "At least that's certain."

# IMPERATRIX
## by Deborah Wheeler

I arrived late at the For-Hire matches at Reymuth and had to elbow my way rudely into a proper vantage point. The crowd pressed at me, traders seeking bodyguards, petty lordlings looking to replace slaughtered men-at-arms, mercenaries after new recruits, and pickpockets after everyone. The dusty ring lay before me, empty.

A sigh went up as the ringkeeper raised the pennants for the next match: red and black for a novice, then a long pause while he searched in his chest for the other—purple! A grizzled soldier at my side shook his head. "A Weire, and at full moon! We're soon to see a very stupid greenie become a very dead greenie."

"These matches aren't to the death, are they?" I asked, uncertain. Reymuth was far from home and customs diverged wildly in these desperate times.

"Try telling that to an angry Weire," he snorted.

The Weire emerged from the contestant's tent and dropped its purple silkene cloak in a disdainful heap. I had only seen one before and not at such close range. Its size and vitality startled me, its utter, intrinsic alienness. The light which burned in those four black eyes could not in any way be human, nor the finger-long, needle-sharp fangs, at their apex now with the phase of the moon. It shrugged beneath its elaborate harness of leather and hoard-jewels, rumbling ominously. "Berserker!" hissed the veteran beside me.

She had already stepped from the tent and stood cloakless, deathly still in the arena. Once I had laid eyes on her I could not look away. It was not her tall, whipcord-muscled body clad in supple leather which held me, nor the eyes that glowed with fever blue behind the traditional mask. I had no time to search my feelings as the ringkeeper held up his hand for bids. The crowd rustled restively despite the low minimum.

"What's wrong? Why don't they offer?" I asked the soldier.

"Not daft, you know," he answered. "What commoner would work with a Weire that can't be blood bound to him? And as for that crazy greenie-girl, even if she isn't dead or crippled afterwards, she's just proving she has no sense."

"Maybe she's very good—"

"Or very desperate." He turned his shoulder to me in disgust and made off through the throng.

The ringkeeper still called for more bids, all well below my purse. I raised my hand. "Win or lose?" "Both," I said. My neighbors stared openly at me. All the "win" bids were for the Weire, but I wanted the option if she survived.

She turned to look at me for a fleeting moment as she took her place in the ring center. In those burning azure eyes I saw, or perhaps I only imagined I saw, such relentless will that I did not know if I wished her victory or the peace of death more.

"Weapons?" called the ringkeeper.

"Tangles," I called.

"No, bare hands!" roared the others. They surged like a many-headed, ever-hungry beast lusting for blood.

The Weire stepped to its place, dwarfing her by two heads' span. I winced, wishing I had not bid and could leave now. The ringkeeper clanged his gong and it was too late.

The Weire snarled, its huge muscles rippling beneath its pearlescent fur as it settled into a stance and raised its joint-sundering arms. I remembered the old adage, *Who rules the Weires rules the kingdom*. But who could challenge such a massive, indomitable monster?

She was instantly a blur of movement, slamming aside one heavy arm as her other hand sped upward, angling sharply toward the vulnerable base of the Weire's throat. In the blink of an eye, her boot had swept its feet from under it, her fingers digging deep into the vital reflex point. The Weire went down, coughing and spitting in outrage, rolling heavily to break her hold by its sheer mass. The crowd grew suddenly, horribly, quiet.

The Weire heaved itself to its knees, but she had already spun behind it to land an explosive kick on the side of its heavy-boned skull. Another sweeping step took her directly in back of the creature, a knee between its scapulae driving it forward to its face in the dust. On a man it would have worked, but Weires are not so easily stunned, and it caught itself with one forepaw, recovered, and leapt directly to its feet.

I saw her eyes flash grim as she circled it, looking for another opening. Enraged, it would not stop for mere pain now. She would have to disable or kill it, or she would not leave the ring alive.

The Weire closed with alarming, dazzling speed, swinging a punch like a mallet at her head, impossible to block in its utter power. She curled in a circle toward it, seizing the Weire by the neck as if they were dancing partners, and spiraling it away and downward along the arc of its own momentum. The great beast staggered, clawing at her and knocking her to her knees. It reached for her as she threw her weight on her hands, lashing out with one booted foot.

The Weire howled and fell back. She scrambled to her feet and backed off, taut and alert. Whether by luck or art, she had surely stunned it, for it lay grunting and pawing its eyes in the gray dust.

The ringkeeper came out and counted the full five which declared her a winner, while the crowd muttered, cheated of its death. I went around to the pursekeeper's stand behind the tent and put down the hiring fee.

She came, bearing the traditional long knife and a small leather pack, which she set at my feet as she put her mark on the deed of release. For a moment it seemed she was about to write her name, which of course a mercenary for hire could not do, but then she made a clumsy, ordinary bird-mark, the novice sign, and turned back to me. She was still wearing her contestant's mask. The pursekeeper motioned for it; they did not give away anything.

She untied the mask, still fixing me with her searing blue gaze. Her face resembled her body, strong, functional, hinting at a bitter, uncompromising spirit. She touched me, disturbed me in ways I could not name.

"Name?" I asked, a little too brusquely.

"Charlla. And I serve?" Her voice was of medium pitch, as pure as a bell.

"I'm Eddard and you're for my master, not me."

"Well," she said, picked up her pack and followed me to the inn. She was easily as tall as I and her easy, swinging stride more than matched mine.

I wanted to ask what had driven her to accept challenge of the masterless Weire, but custom forbade. The rules of For-Hire meant that she had sworn under truthscan that she was free and without blood-price on her head; that was all an employer was entitled to know. But where had she learned to fight like that? Not in any backwoods garrison I knew of. I had heard drinking tales of Weiremasters, but they were all of the old, old royal blood.

When we stepped through the open portal of the inn, doubt assailed me for the first time. An unknown greenie, fierce though she might be, was not what my master had had in mind. We needed dependable protection until we could reach the sanctuary of Har Ynion. Why had I even bid on such an unrealistic choice? I had been better educated than most men-at-arms and did not believe in witches, but there was something about her that caught at me, compelled me, almost gave me hope in these darkest of days.

We climbed the narrow wooden stairs back to the small private rooms. I opened the door and went in first. He lay on the rude bed, my dear lord, his eyes still eagle bright.

"Eddard," he said, motioning me forward. "What fortune?"

I stepped to his side and bowed. Charlla moved in her long, powerful stride to the bedside, her eyes darkening to mystery in the ill-lit room. Slowly she went down on one knee as was proper, but with such grace and strength that the gesture was no obeisance, but a courtesy.

"*This* is all you could get!" stormed my lord.

I trembled a little, but not from fear of him. His wounds in the last terrible siege had cost him dear, and he could not afford the luxury of unnecessary anger. "She bested a Weire," I protested.

He hauled himself up on his one good shoulder and glared at her from beneath wild, bushy brows. "Did she?"

She stirred, a flicker of quiet power beneath her smooth, unreadable surface. He lowered his eyes. "She'll do for now." She touched her fingertips to her lips and forehead in the formal gesture. "My lord Bardon."

"Eddard—"

"My lord, I swear I didn't tell her!"

She brushed my protests aside and stood. "My lord, as I am now your shield arm, I must tell you that Reymuth is not safe for you. You are a marked man, and the Imperator's troops are but a day's march away."

"Child, how came you to know who I am, and such news of the Imperator?"

She shook her head proudly, as if her hair were loose and not tightly bound beneath a tooled leather cap. "I'm no child!"

Lord Bardon's voice deepened into the kindly stern tones I had obeyed and respected all my years. "I am your master, child, and you are whatever I choose to call you. Or did you shame your bond oath when you vowed service at the For-Hire meet?"

"My lord." Charlla bit back a reply and bowed her head, trembling a little. "I have seen your—likeness before, had heard of the siege and fall of Bardon Tower. As for the rest, it is rumor, but from a source I trust."

I dropped to my knees beside him. "We dare not risk a longer stay, lord. Another day will not see you stronger, and we must not get cut off from the inner roads."

He drew in his breath, gathering the rags of his once-massive strength, and sent me down to pay our accounts and have our mounts made ready. We took the traders gate from the town, mostly deserted in the late of the day. A pair of cutpurses leapt out at us as we neared the northern forest, but Charlla beat them off with her long knife with easy competence. My lord smiled as she came trotting back to us after chasing them into a darkening copse. I drew an easier breath, knowing he was pleased.

"We will not camp tonight, but backtrack along the sun's path," he said.

I began to protest, but Charlla silenced me, saying, "You yourself said it, Eddard. There is only more peril in delay. Our mounts are still fresh, and once we find the entry point we can relax a little. Until then we must push on."

We went on through the deepening forest, Charlla leading the way with a small torch, then my lord Bardon slumping in weakness in his saddle, and I at the rear. Leaves of a thousand dead seasons muffled the hoofbeats of our mounts, and I startled more than once at the innocent sound of a wakeful night creature. Once Charlla drew us to an abrupt halt, motioning for silence and shielding the light of her torch, listening intently.

It seemed like a dream, following her through the night, keeping the brilliance of her beacon ever before my eyes, following her . . . Although I was worried for my lord and his deep, unhealed wounds, and frightened lest an errant sound signal the dreaded Imperator's troops, there was such comfort in Charlla's strength and certainty that the distance passed quickly.

She drew us to a halt and extinguished the stub of her torch. Above the choppy trees, the stars glimmered in their slow circling dance. A milky veil tinged the east. It was nearly dawn.

"We are almost there," she said quietly. "Can you smell it?"

"I thought only those—" I began.

"Hush!" said Lord Bardon. "Lead on, child. These old bones are ready for a rest."

I caught the ghost of her smile in the faint half-light. She turned her mount, doubling back the way we had come . . . And suddenly the emerald gossamer of the *inner* road surrounded us, piercing us with its brilliant light. Lord Bardon slipped from his saddle with a cry of relief, for each path through the inner world was distinct, unique and untraceable. We need fear no pursuit now, not until we arrived at Har Ynion.

I leapt from the back of my mount and went to see to him, leaving Charlla to attend the beasts. She accepted the task without complaint and soon joined us with the food bags and waterskin.

"I gave our mounts a measure of meal," she said, drawing a small knife to slice a round of hard cheese for my lord. "They'll have to wait to forage; the stuff beneath their feet looks like grass but has no sustenance."

I took the slivers of cheese and chunk of bread from her and fed him with small bites and sips until he drifted off into exhausted sleep. I looked down at his face, etched sharply in the steady green light. Gray, like a secret, silent enemy, had invaded his hair and beard since the wanton destruction of our home.

"Damn the Imperator and all his henchmen!" I muttered in sudden, protective anger.

Charlla, sitting cross-legged apart from me, looked up, her eyes glittering like some strange gemstones. "It is a tragedy when so many good men must suffer," she said.

"Tragedy!" I spat, keeping my voice low so as not to disturb him. "It's evil, all of it, from the bloodthirsty blackguard himself to his demented lust for power. He's been seizing one kingdom after another until there's no stopping his terrorist reign."

"The bloodshed is wrong, I agree. I cannot stomach it any more than you can. I condemn it, but—but not the dream of uniting the whole land. We were once one, you know, in the Golden Ages when the inner roads were built, the Weires came into our world from another, and many more marvelous things, when men could live in peace with their neighbors without constant, bickering warfare."

"It's a man's right to defend his own," I retorted.

"Through law and justice, not indiscriminate pillage that starts an endless blood-feud," she answered me, the light in her eyes flashing with inner fire.

"Who are you to mouth such highborn philosophy?" I drew back a little at her intensity. She had accepted challenge of a Weire, after all; she might be capable of anything. . . .

"I am—" She cut herself off abruptly, and the flame in her

deep blue eyes smoldered down under tight control. "I am only one who is tired of slaughter. At the hands of each petty lordling or the Imperator's warhounds, it does not matter. People die, and their dreams die, too."

"Dreams!" I cried, the vision of Bardon Tower crumbling into burning rubble rising before my mind's eye. "What could you know of lost dreams?"

"Because I too have a dream, a dream of a land united in peace, a dream of people living their lives in harmony and good will."

"Then you had best slit your own throat now and hope to see it in the next world, for you won't find such a fantasy at the hands of the Imperator," I snapped, all the bitterness of my lord's ruin and our exile of terror welling up in me. I drew my cloak around my shoulders and turned my back to her. I did not want to hear her next whispered words, although they were meant only for herself.

*"I will see it."*

She was still sitting guard duty when my lord awoke, wan but refreshed. We mounted still-hungry beasts and traveled on through the deep green light. Since I had no noble blood, I could not sense where we were through the elastic distortion of space which marked the inner roads. I only know that we went on for some time in that curious suspension of time until finally Lord Bardon signaled us to halt.

"Har Ynion," he whispered. "We are on the threshold." He looked to Charlla and she nodded.

"I should go first, my lord," she said politely.

She turned her mount, leading us again in the backtracking maneuver which opened the portals of the strange emerald pathways. Suddenly, normal yellow light flooded our senses. I raised a hand to shield my watering eyes and peer about us.

We stood at the edge of a grove of trees just outside the borders of Har Ynion. Across a gently rolling, grassy slope I could see the force-shielded walls of the sanctuary. The road before us lay open, inviting. I urged my mount forward.

Charlla raised a cautionary hand and drew her long knife. "This is the most dangerous part," she warned. "We must ride prepared."

We spurred our beasts into a ground-covering trot, scanning the surroundings for ambush cover. I heard my lord cry out as his mount stumbled and recovered, jarring him cruelly. My nerves tightened with fear and I glanced up at Charlla, riding at our head as if she were born to it.

We came down one hill and across the flat expanse at its base, seeing the rocks and bushes which had been hidden from our sight before. The shelter of the sanctuary grew ever closer, the open gates holding welcoming arms to us.

The howl of a battle-pitched Weire shattered our hopes as we drew almost within reach of our goal. My heart stilled within me as I saw them pounding toward us from around the walls themselves, a small cadre of the Imperator's personal troops and at their head, a giant Weire bearing the sash of the royal household guards. We pulled our mounts to a halt.

Charlla whipped around to face us. "I'll go first and draw them," she shouted in the oncoming din. "Eddard, take Lord Bardon around to the right to the eastern gate. Don't stop for me!"

"Are you crazy?" I shouted back. My mount began to plunge about under me with excitement. They were almost upon us. I could see the needle fangs of the Weire, the black light in its four eyes as it bore down the last slope.

"Do it!" she commanded, and the regal authority in her voice shocked both of us into obedience, swinging our mounts into a hard gallop as she had directed.

At first I could hear only the pounding of my animal's hooves above the pounding of my heart, my eyes fixed on my dear lord who clung grimly to his saddle. Suddenly I heard her voice rising like a paean above the tumult, shouting, singing, chanting wild words in some ancient, alien tongue. My head throbbed with the sound of them, my heart catching in my throat at their beauty and power.

We were almost at the gates. I slashed at the rump of my lord's mount with my riding whip, sending it frenzied across the threshold to safety, and reined my own beast to a halt. Looking back, I saw her sitting tall as a goddess on her prancing steed, one arm flung wide as the Weire danced and snarled before her. The soldiers milled in confusion, keeping their distance. I drew in my breath to call to her, but the echoes of her command held my tongue.

Slowly, incredibly, the Weire bent to its knees before her, dipping its massive, terrible head. A shock wave ripped through the soldiers and I heard their cry, "Weiremaster!"

She urged her mount to the kneeling Weire, speaking to it in a voice too low for me to hear. I saw a flicker of gentleness light her face for a moment as she laid one hand on its shaggy skull. I knew then that she had deliberately spared the Weire in the arena, for she had such power over the beasts.

I trembled on my snorting, nervous mount as Charlla came toward me, the Weire quiet and obedient at her heels. The captain of the soldiers herded his men into a semblance of order, waiting, watching.

A movement at the gates demanded my attention; my lord Bardon stood there on foot, supported by two of the kind, simple folk of Har Ynion who offered anonymity and sanctuary to all who fled there. His eyes glittered, fierce as a hawk's, as she brought her mount to a halt before us. She slipped from her saddle.

"My lord, I cannot stay," she said in a low voice. "Now he will know where I am, and I will only draw destruction to you if I remain. I beg you to release me from your service."

"Child," he said softly, and reached out to sweep her leather cap from her bowed head. The knots had loosened in our last flight and it came away easily, revealing hair which was dull, dyed black everywhere except the roots, where the pure, iridescent silver of the imperial blood shone like moonlight.

She smiled fleetingly, her gaze meeting his. "I had feared you would recognize me from your time in my father's court."

"You were younger then, my lady Charalldana, and your brother—"

"My brother is Imperator now!" she cried with sudden anger. "And in his quest for power, he is tearing this land apart, slaughtering leaders and innocent folk alike. I left his bloody court when I would no longer be party to it, I—" She paused, hands resting on the hilt of her long knife, tears luminous in her eyes. "I thought I could carve out a world for myself, for my own dreams, beginning as a mercenary. Now I see that I can only bring ruin to those who have trusted me. Even these holy walls will not stop those he will send to bring me back."

"What will you do, lady?"

"My brother is right, I must go back. But not to support his bloody throne; only to rule in his stead." The azure fire in her eyes leapt high, challenging the light from her silvery hair.

"That's suicide!" I sputtered, my tongue finally having regained its wits. "You'll never be able to wrest power from him."

"I won't need to contest him by force of arms, but by force of right," she said quietly. "It's the last thing my brother will expect me to do. He won't be prepared for such a move. Besides, he has not the Weire-gift; they follow him only from old loyalty to our father. That's why he needs me to consolidate his authority. He—"

A sudden snarl from the Weire whipped her around, the muscles of her back and shoulders coiled like a tense snake. The giant beast whimpered, an incongruous sound considering its bulk and ferocity. Charalldana spoke to it in the strange, commanding tongue she had used before and it quieted.

I drew in my breath, seeing the glitter of armor and royal pennants emerging from the scrap of forest, row after row of polished, armed soldiers. There was a frantic milling in the little cadre which had lain in ambush for us. Their leader spurred his mount toward us, reining it in so fiercely that it slid to a halt on its haunches before Charalldana.

"Lady," he gasped. "Only one who can command the Weires as we have seen you do can rule the kingdom rightly. It goes hard to defy our lord Imperator, but we are for you."

"Captain, you need shed no blood for me," she replied, swinging on her mount's back. "I shall rule by force of right, not force of arms."

"Let me go, too," I burst out.

"No," she said with sudden gentleness. "You and your dear lord have shown me another way to rule, by inspiring love instead of terror. I need you safe to remind me of that truth."

I stayed, bound by the sure command in her voice, as she made her way to meet the massing army, the Weire like a massive shadow beside the mounted men. Slowly, slowly the two groups converged, the tension in me rising until I imagined I could see the very air distorting with power.

Charalldana sat on her steed straight and tall as a bulky figure in golden armor and silver head-plumes came forward to meet her. This must be her brother, the Imperator. I strained my ears and squinted my eyes for more, but we were too far away. The royal army began to seethe restlessly.

Suddenly the Imperator gestured, arm raised high in unmistakable threat. Charalldana dropped her reins on her mount's neck and lifted her arms in the gesture she had used to tame the Weire during our mad flight. I could almost hear her singing that weird, compelling, alien song. Even soundless, it stirred my blood, made me yearn for impossible mysteries.

From the dark of the woods emerged a giant Weire, dwarfing the other by a head's span, then another and another, filing in ominous procession past the embattled pair. Each massive beast dropped its head in fealty as it passed under Charalldana's raised arms until they stood in a semicircle at her back, a mass of incorruptible power.

The Imperator dropped his arm, and I thought I saw him bow

his head. The Weires closed in, tightening into a circle. The royal troops withdrew, whether in fear or allegiance I could not tell.

"What's happening?" I exclaimed, feeling the tension in my shoulders and balled fists. My mount stirred unhappily and I eased my hold on its mouth.

"He is not one to yield lightly," muttered my lord Bardon, "yet I have never heard the man who could stand against the will of the Weires."

Again I remembered the adage, *Who rules the Weires rules the kingdom.* "He might rebel."

"He might."

And so we waited, caught between the hope of her dreams and the nightmares of the ruin of our home, watching taut and strained as a mounted soldier detached himself from the mass and galloped toward us. Hope against hope, he was smiling, panting a little as if he himself had run the little distance from the forest to the gates of Har Ynion.

"Yes, what is it?" growled my lord.

"Charalldana Imperatrix salutes you," he grinned. "She says to tell you that love is not learnt by a single example but by constant reminder, my lords, and bids you to her court when you are well enough to travel."

"What of the Imperator?" my lord Bardon asked.

"The Weires will not have him now that a true Weiremaster claims the throne, and no man dares contest their choice," replied the soldier. "His fate is for my lady's mercy." He sighed, his face relaxing as if from long years of fear and strain. "And I think at last the whole kingdom will know mercy again."

I smiled and turned to help my lord to the rest of Har Ynion, now a bastion of healing instead of refuge. In my memory her blue eyes and silver hair shone, piercing me to the core, tugging at my soul to be gone and at her side. I hoped it would be soon.

Jennifer Roberson has just sold her first novel to DAW Books, a novel entitled *The Shapechangers*, with a sequel, as yet untitled, in the same world as *Blood of Sorcery*. The Cheysuli are a race of shapechanging sorcerers, and one of the forthcoming Cheysuli novels, to be entitled *The Warrior Princess*, will have Keely, the heroine of this story, as a protagonist. I spoke in the introduction of the importance of the "rape and revenge" fantasy in sword and sorcery fiction by and about women; *Blood of Sorcery* handles this universal theme with a truly unique twist.

Jennifer says of herself that "I can't NOT write; it's a compulsion." She graduated from Northern Arizona University in 1982, but her work for a master's degree was turned down as being too commercial. "I guess it was; I sold my first novel a month later." She has worked as an investigative reporter, and as an editor of an in-house magazine for an advertising agency. She enjoys rodeo riding, training and showing obedience in dogs, and being owned by two cats; she is also an enthusiastic amateur vocalist, and competed for "Rodeo Miss America" but lost. She is "29, single, and lives in Phoenix with two dogs, two cats and a jealous typewriter."

The *Chronicles of the Cheysuli*, "starting with the female protagonist in *The Shapechangers*, is intended to take readers on a hundred-year odyssey through the dynastic struggles of a shapechanging race, hated and feared by humans." After reading *Blood of Sorcery* I think you will be as eager as I am to see what Jennifer will do with the rest of the series.—MZB


# BLOOD OF SORCERY
## by Jennifer Roberson


Her memories began coming back in bits and pieces, slowly. Carefully she hoarded each one like the rarest of gems, gathering them one by one to her breast until she could judge each one for flaws; finding none, she called it good and put it into safekeeping. Slowly her hoard grew until she had a double handful of bright stones; looking at them all, she saw the colors of the rainbow and more. Looking at them all, she saw a reflection of herself.

And then she *knew* herself again, after a timeless space and place where she did not.

She was Keely. Keely of Homana. Princess-born and raised, daughter of the Mujhar himself, who held sovereignty over the realm of Homana. But more than that she was Cheysuli. Shapechanger. The daughter of a man who became a wolf at will. *Lir*-shape, the Cheysuli called it, eschewing the Homanan word "shapechanger" with all its demon connotations, for it was an outward exhibition of the eerie and consuming bond that linked man and animal. Warrior and *lir*. Only the Cheysuli had the ability. And only the warriors; male, all of them.

Save Keely.

She knew why she, alone of them all, had the ability to take the shape of any animal she chose. Unlike the others, who were linked only to a single *lir*, she was free to summon any form. The Old Blood that was so fickle ran strongly in her veins, giving her the magic that allowed her freedom as had not been known for centuries. For too long only the warriors had held the gift, and then only in the guise of a single animal. For too long the blood had been thinned and the old magic lost. Now it was a live thing again, this magic of the gods, and it was Keely's destiny—her *tahlmorra*—to pass on the Old Blood to children of her own. That, coupled with her rank as the only princess of Homana, made her a highly desirable match. And so her father had betrothed her to the heir of a neighboring kingdom when they were both just children, before either of them knew what futures lay before them.

Keely, rebellious and defiant, had ever resented the betrothal that made her less than herself; ever resented the birth that settled her future even in the cradle. She would go to Erinn, wed her island princeling, bear him sons and then—past her usefulness— fade into the grayness of later years. It was a future that faced all women of royalty whose first duty was obedience and loyalty to the House. To be used as a gamepiece to gain land, alliances, riches. Keely loved her father well; honored her Cheysuli heritage and the magic in her blood, but she did not love and honor the fetters her sex placed on her. And so she had turned from womanish pursuits to the swordplay of men, refining her skill until it equaled that of her brothers. She was a princess but also Cheysuli; warrior-born and bred for all she was a woman, and no one dared deny her her heritage. She would follow the dictates of her *tahlmorra*, which spoke of a husband and children, but she would go to the man as herself. The spirit and arrogance that made Cheysuli warriors the finest in the land also served her well, and she would not give up her selfhood.

But her independent spirit also placed her in jeopardy even as her rank placed her in the precarious position of pawn to Strahan the Ihlini, the foreign sorcerer who practiced the dark arts learned from the gods of the netherworld. Strahan wanted only power over all men, all realms, and to achieve it he needed the blood of the Cheysuli who now ruled Homana. He needed a child, a halfling, an infant taken at birth and raised in the darkness of the Ihlini, and to get that child he needed a woman. A Cheysuli woman whose blood linked her—and therefore him—to the throne of Homana.

He had taken her prisoner in Hondarth, the port city on the shores of the Idrian Ocean. She had walked into his trap with all the blindness and trust of a child. She was not a child; she was not blind and did not trust easily, and she hated knowing she had contributed to her own capture. Nonetheless Strahan held her now, imprisoned within the old castle on the Crystal Isle, only ten leagues across the water from the docks and quays of Hondarth. In all her childhood she had known the Crystal Isle as a place of mystery and whispered secrets, the birthplace of her Cheysuli ancestors who had gone to Homana to make a realm for their descendants. No one lived on the Crystal Isle now. No one went there because the breath of the gods shrouded the island in mist and magic, and the Homanans—who still feared the shapechanging sorcery of their own royal House—also feared some form of retribution if they trespassed. The Cheysuli, who knew themselves blessed by the old gods, also did not go there. Their lives were in Homana now; the Crystal Isle was of the past.

And so Strahan had made it his place; his present. He kept her there as his guest, his prisoner, and lay with her each night so the child would be conceived. The child of darkness who would slowly, carefully, patiently work its Ihlini sorcery on the House of Homana until the Mujhar and all his kin fell, and then Homana would become the realm of the Ihlini. The realm of dark magic and demons.

The trap had been sprung easily. Keely had been called to Hondarth to meet her betrothed for the first time as he arrived from his father's island kingdom. She had gone—reluctant to wed him and lose her freedom, yet recognizing the demands of her *tahlmorra*—and walked into the trap. Strahan, masquerading as the Erinnish prince, charmed her into drinking the water that took her soul. She lost her magic; lost her past, her present, her future; lost her knowledge of self. As long as her blood bore the black taint of sorcery she was helpless, stripped of her Cheysuli gifts and unable to fend off Strahan's unwanted intimacy.

But now the knowledge was coming back. Strahan's sorcery had taken her memory for countless days; now she could count them. She knew herself again, and her predicament. She knew what enemy she faced. And she knew, with all her will and strength and determination, that somehow she would get free of him.

The open casement in her room was narrow and high, but by pulling a bench over to it and climbing up Keely managed to see what lay beyond her chambers. Her prison, albeit a comfortable one. There were heathered hills and tangled forests; curving beaches that glinted silver in the moonlight and white in the day; slate-gray oceans and endless skies. Sea-spray and mist hung over the island like a veil: the breath of the gods; thick in the mornings, heavy at night, burning golden in the sunlit days. Could she put out her hand and part the misted curtain, she would draw it back and see Homana lying beyond the Idrian Ocean.

A faint breeze came in from the sea and curled through the casement, catching her tawny hair and lifting it from her shoulders. She wore it loose now, falling unbound over her shoulders to her waist, because Strahan preferred it that way. Keely, who did not, had first responded by ripping a length of fabric from the dark blue robe she wore and tying it up in a single braid. Strahan's response had been silence, and without touching her he had caused a spectral hand to loosen the plait and stroke it back into unbound freedom. Keely, shivering each time she recalled the experience, no longer braided her hair.

She stood on the bench and hugged the stone sill of the casement like a child who longs for what he cannot have. She pressed her cold cheek against the cold stone and stared out past the beaches, past the mists, and tried to see Homana.

"A caged bird," said his quiet voice. "Perhaps a linnet, or a sparrow, but certainly not the falcon, who would not countenance it, or a Homanan hawk, who knows better than to fall into the hunter's hand."

Keely did not turn. She remained on the bench, still standing at the casement, but her fingers drove so hard into the stone she felt her nails splinter.

Strahan's hands were on her, lifting her down and turning her around. Keely looked into his beautiful, bearded face and the eerie eyes: one blue, one brown, and felt the familiar revulsion stir within her soul.

"You must not grieve," he told her in his gentle, beguiling voice. "Women who grieve do not suit the men who want them. And I want you, Keely."

She closed her eyes as his hand slid beneath her robe to caress her breasts. As always, his touch raised her skin into prickles. He seemed pleased by the reaction, as if to stir any response from her was enough for him. But then he was more than a man; he was Ihlini. Sorcerer. Child of the dark gods who gave him ageless life. The only thing that kept her from being ill before him was the knowledge he might think she had conceived, and that she would never show him. It was what he wanted.

"I will keep you as long as it takes," he whispered into her hair. "Do you age before me, I will keep you young, until you have conceived by me. Until you give me the child."

She would not look into the eerie eyes that had a power of their own. To do so admitted defeat, and that she would never do. She had learned not to fight him when he took her to his bed because to fight back gave him reason to use sorcery on her, and that she hated worse than his intimacy. She was Cheysuli; Ihlini sorcery was anathema to her. Had she her full complement of arts she could withstand such dark magic, for her blood gave her a natural protection against such things, but he had made her blood black and thick and perverted. Until it ran red and rich again, she was his.

"Keely," he said quietly, "I have brought someone to you."

She did not answer. Strahan removed his stroking hand and left her alone, and when she opened her eyes she saw the harper in her chamber.

Taliesin. The white-haired man made ageless through the gift of Strahan's Ihlini father, because his harping and magnificent voice had won him fame and fortune. But the gift of immortality brought Taliesin no peace, for Strahan himself had taken his own retribution on a man he named traitor by turning Taliesin's hands into twisted, brittle, broken things, unable to play a harp. And yet he had overcome Strahan's ultimate cruelty by becoming the very traitor Strahan called him. For Taliesin the harper was also Ihlini, and a friend to Homana. And so he, with Keely, had been taken prisoner in Hondarth.

Keely, who had seen no one else save Strahan for too long, thought it was a trick of the eye. But the harper smiled sadly and came across the room, putting out his broken hands to her. She went willingly into his arms, clinging to him as if he could save her soul.

"How do you fare?" he asked at last, when she had recovered herself.

Keely's face twisted. "Well enough. I have food and wine and excellent health. He makes certain of that."

Taliesin took her hand in his twisted ones and slowly sat down on the bench. Keely, sitting next to him, thought he had begun to look old. For a man with endless life, it seemed a strange thing.

"What of you?" she whispered. "What has he done to you?"

The harper smiled a little. "Like you, he has kept me locked away. Alone. It would be a hard thing for another man, perhaps, but I have my voice. Strahan took the magic of the harp from my hands but he cannot destroy my voice, or the memory of what I had."

"I am sorry," she said softly. "You should not be here. It was me he wanted. Had you not come with me to Hondarth—"

"It does not matter," he said gently. "I would far prefer to be with you in this than think you alone with the man. And the time will come when we can win free of this place."

Keely said nothing for a long time. Finally she begged the clasp of his leather belt. At first he only stared at her, struck by her vehemence, but he complied as she asked again. Slowly he removed his belt, pulled the bronze clasp free and held it out to her.

Keely closed her hand around it tightly. She turned her left arm over, baring her wrist, and he saw the delicate tracery of scars threading the translucent skin. For a moment the muscles stood out along her jaw, then she shifted the clasp and stabbed the prong deeply into her wrist.

Taliesin cried out and grabbed at her hand, tearing the clasp from her, Keely said nothing. She sat very still with her arm upturned, watching the blood begin.

"Do you see?" she asked. "Do you see what he has done?"

The blood welled slowly out of the gash and crept down her arm. It left a trail of glistening blackness like the slime of a demon's serpent.

The harper was trembling as he closed his hand around her wrist, shutting off the blood. His face was very pale. His eyes, blue as her own, were horrified, and Keely—looking into them and seeing his suffering—felt a measure of her own revulsion rise.

"I am tainted," she said thickly. "Unclean."

"Keely—"

"I cannot stop him. The *lir*-gift is gone, lost in this foul blackness in my blood. Each night he takes me to his bed, to get a child. A child who will throw down the House of Homana." She shuddered convulsively. "I did not recall it for a very long time. It has only been the last days that I remembered, and now it is worse than before. Did he know I have recalled I am Cheysuli, he might take it from me again."

"Keely, let me bind your wound."

She smiled sadly and pulled his hand away, showing him the

wound. Already the blood had slowed. "It will stop of its own accord. It does each time. Aye," she said to his start of surprise, "I have done this before. Not to take my own life, but to see if my blood is clear." She shrugged crookedly. "Then he learned what I did and took away anything I might cut myself with. It has been weeks since I was able to see my blood—to see if I was free. I am not."

"This is the Crystal Isle!" he said forcefully. "The very seat of Cheysuli power. You have only to call upon the old gods, and you will be free."

"I have called," she told him clearly. "I have pleaded. They do not hear." Keely touched the blackness on her arm. "They cannot answer." Abruptly she rose, pacing away from Taliesin like a supple cat. When she turned back her face was very pale. "I have conceived. I bear a child . . . *Strahan's*. . . ."

"*Keely—*"

She shivered once, violently. "I have ever said I did not want *any* child. I am afraid. I will lose myself. I will become a breeder, instead of Keely. A broodmare, serviced by the finest stud available." She smiled humorlessly, sickened as she crossed both arms over her abdomen. "Before, the stud was to be the Erinnish prince; now it is Strahan. The Ihlini! And the child I bear will be a travesty of what I am." Her hands fisted. "By the gods, harper, I am afraid! I do not want this child! Before, it was because I wanted no child. Now I *must* lose it, because it is Strahan's!"

He rose and went to her. He knew her pride and strength as he knew his own, and the reflection of what made her race the finest warriors in the land. That same pride and strength had led her to learn the knife and the sword as if she were a warrior like her brothers and father. She was a princess of Homana, a Cheysuli woman bearing the Old Blood, and as fine a fighter as any man he had ever known. For her to be trapped by Strahan, trapped by the ultimate betrayal of her own body, was a prison far worse than any dungeon.

But he could not lie to her. "You cannot *wish* away a child, Keely."

She wet her lips. "Surely there is something I can do."

"It is a life, Keely. Strahan's child, aye, but do you forget you are the mother? No child who is half yours can be totally evil."

"He will take it from me," she said. "He will pervert it. He will make it a reflection of himself." She clutched at his arms. "Taliesin—*I have to lose it!*"

He took a deep breath and released it slowly. Her control was back as she waited, and finally he told her. "There *are* ways of ridding yourself of an unwanted child. You can take herbs to loosen it. They would have some in Hondarth, if you could get there." He sighed. "I cannot condone it, but I understand your fears. They have merit. But how do you propose to do it here, when Strahan keeps you prisoner?"

Her teeth gritted. "I will find a way. I will throw myself to the floor, if I must, time and time again, and lose it that way."

He smiled, amused by her determination even as he knew the consequences of such folly. "Keely. It is not so easy to do as you might think."

Her breath hurt her chest as she sucked it in. "I will risk anything to rid myself of this demon's child. I must!" She stared at him. "It is my turn to serve my *tahlmorra*. My fate. My turn to sacrifice whatever I must to serve the gods. It is a Cheysuli thing, this *tahlmorra,* but it cannot be gainsaid. To do so angers the gods, who made a fate for all of us. I have accepted mine; I will go to my betrothed when I am free of this place and bear *him* children. But I will still be myself. No man may take that from me."

He was Ihlini. He was bound by his own endless future, his endless destiny, but he knew what it was that drove Keely. *Tahlmorra*—the will of the gods—drove her entire race, for each Cheysuli born lived to serve the gods. Keely's *tahlmorra*—and her father—had decreed she wed into Erinn to tie the bloodlines to Homana, but in order to do that she must first get free of Strahan.

"Which she will never do." said Strahan himself.

Keely spun around and saw him standing within the room that only moments before had held only herself and the harper. A violet mist hung around him almost like a shroud, cloaking his head and shoulders. Strahan could use a door as well as any man, but he knew his sorcery was as good a weapon as the knife he so rarely needed.

"Time for you to go, harper," he said gently. "Keely has come to value her solitude. And my company." He smiled within the shadow of his trimmed black beard, white teeth showing clearly against the fine darkness of his features. As a woman he would have been beautiful; as a man he was handsome indeed. "Do you weary of this life, harper?" he inquired.

Taliesin, white-haired and young-faced, merely smiled. "You will do whatever you wish, regardless of my answer. So I will give you none."

Keely, sensing Strahan tested her friend, moved to the harper's side. "You will not harm him!"

"I mean him no harm." Strahan answered. "Only an ending."
His parti-colored eyes fastened on Taliesin. "Time ends for us
all, harper. Even you."

Taliesin cradled Keely's head in his broken, twisted hands.
"Do not fear for me. Do not even fear for yourself, for you are
stronger than you know."

"Harper," Strahan said briefly, and Taliesin left her alone
once more.

"Do not harm him," she told the sorcerer evenly.

"I do what I wish." His eyes went past her to the open
casement. "I weary of this sunshine."

Keely, opening her mouth to ask what he meant, closed it as
she saw him lift his hand into the air. For a moment it hung
there, as if in benediction. Then he drew a hissing rune in the
soundless air and when it had faded into wisping violet mist, so
had he.

The storm swept in suddenly with no warning from the depths
of a night so dark Keely thought she had gone blind. She sat
upright in her bed and squinted against the flash of lightning
outside her casement. Wind swept through the opening like a
capricious demon and scattered leaves about the room.

Keely, dressed only in a thin linen nightshift, pulled the
covers up around her shoulders. In another flash of lightning she
saw the steady downpour outside her casement. The wind drove
the spray into the room and dampened her hair with a fine mist.

Thunder slammed into the castle and crashed inside her chamber.
Then she realized it was not thunder but a door instead, her own,
and it stood open to the corridor. Keely opened her mouth to yell
as the figure stepped into the room.

A flash of lightning illuminated Taliesin's face, showing his
white hair and blue eyes, and Keely caught her breath on a gasp
of relief. Taliesin beckoned with one of his twisted hands.
"Keely—come quickly! This is your chance to get free!"

"Strahan—?"

"Elsewhere," he said impatiently. "Come with me!"

Hastily she climbed out of bed and gathered up the folds of
her nightshift, then she grabbed one of his hands and ran with
him as he led her down a corridor. Her heart thudded as she
realized how close she was to escape, how close she was to
freedom. And how close to discovery, if they were not careful.

He took her down the winding corridor and out into the
high-walled outer bailey. Keely had seen nothing of the castle
save from her own chambers; she paused, stumbling, as Taliesin

tried to drag her onward. The rain flattened her hair against her scalp and crept through the thin linen nightshift to the skin beneath.

Taliesin gestured. "The gates . . . *there!* Come, Keely!"

She ran with him to the tall gates, gasping as a gust of wind hammered into them both and nearly blew her off her feet. Hastily she scrubbed an arm across her face, clearing water from her eyes, but it returned as quickly as it had gone.

Taliesin pulled her against the wall as lightning slashed out of the black sky to pour light into the bailey. Keely took the chance to ask him what had happened.

"Strahan thought I was dead. I did not dissuade him of it. When he left me he also left the door undone, thinking me with his gods of the netherworld, and I made my way to your chamber. The castle is near deserted; I thought he had more Ihlini with him, but he does not. Still, this is the Crystal Isle, and for all he uses it to his own evil purposes, he must know he is not welcome here. An Ihlini among the Cheysuli gods? No. They will take their retribution."

"Why did he think you were dead?" she asked sharply.

His face was a blur in the darkness. "He has taken his father's gift from me."

"What do you say?" she demanded, growing horribly frightened for him.

Taliesin flinched as a crack of thunder broke over their heads. "His father gave me endless life. The son has taken it from me."

"*Taken* it. . . ."

His twisted hands cradled her wet face. "I am dying, Keely. At long last. I have lived more than a hundred years, but my life is ending. Strahan took back the gift."

"No!"

"I cannot say how, precisely," he told her gently, "but he has done it. Already my bones grow brittle and my heart begins to fail. *I* will not go free of this place, but I will see that you do."

"Taliesin—"

"Go, my proud Cheysuli warrior-princess. Tarry no longer. I am buying your life with my own."

She stared into his aging, ageless face, and hung onto his hands with her own, as if she could give him her strength.

He smiled, understanding. "The gates are locked but unattended. I will lift you as high as I can, and then you will have to climb the rest of the way. Can you do it?"

Keely peered through the rain at the tall wooden gates with

their heavy iron hinges and massive crossbars. They were not made for climbing. "If only I could take *lir*-shape," she whispered. "I would go as a hawk, a falcon, flying over the walls and on to Homana herself." She sighed and shivered, pushing rain out of her eyes. "But I cannot, so I will simply have to go over them however I can."

Carefully he interlaced his gnarled fingers, locked them together and smiled at her encouragingly. Keely, looking at the weak step he offered, suddenly threw her arms around him. "Taliesin—"

He unlocked his hands and held her a long moment. Then he pulled away. "You must go before I weaken. Go, Keely."

She waited as he bent and held out his hands. Slowly she placed a bare foot in them, felt him brace himself, and reached upward as he lifted. She felt the trembling in his arms and shoulders as he lifted her higher, pushing her upward toward the top. Her fingers scrabbled against the wood, seeking a handhold, and she put one foot against the rough hinges supporting the right leaf of the huge gates. Her toes flinched from the splinters and the cold iron but she gritted her teeth and sought a niche.

The top was still far over her head. Keely scraped herself upward, grunting with the effort, blinking back the rain that ran into her eyes. The thin fabric of her nightshift tore and the wood scraped across her breasts. Keely's teeth came down on her lower lip as she strained to find a hand-hold.

One foot found the crossbar. She balanced on it carefully, wrapping one hand into the iron hinge as she dragged her weight upward. She was free of Taliesin, clinging to the gates like a spider to its web. She heard him moan below her.

Keely found the heavy iron studs with her toes. They protruded from the wood just far enough for her to hook a toe over them. Carefully she slid her foot up the line of studs, seeking one less flush, and finally felt one sticking out farther than the rest. The upper hinge was above her outstretched hand but a careful boost might put it within reach. She jammed her other foot against the stud, pushed down against the crossbar and lunged upward.

Her right hand caught the upper hinge. She clung to it with all her might, using her momentum to pull herself steadily upward. She heard herself gasping, breath wheezing in her breast. The stud cut into her foot but she ignored the pain, scraping herself upward. The crossbar was well below her; she had no more foot-hold. Keely clung to the top hinge and pulled with all her strength, clawing for the top of the gate. If she fell now. . . .

She caught it at last. For a moment she hung there by both hands, feet sliding against the slick wood, then she gritted her teeth and shoved one foot into the slot between the gate and the wall. For a moment her ankle jammed; she used it and shoved upward, grunting as she jerked herself straight up toward the top. Her chin crept over the edge. Again she lifted her foot and shoved it against the wall. She gained a few more inches. Then, with eyes closed and cheek pressed against the iron lip of the gate, she swung her left leg up as high as she could and hooked her heel over the edge.

For a moment her balance faltered. Both arms and a leg grasped the top of the gate but her right foot was still caught between the hinge and the wall. Keely set her jaw and yanked it free, ignoring the sudden pain tearing through her flesh. She jerked herself up and over and balanced precariously on the lip of the gate, her belly pressed against her backbone.

Keely looked down and saw Taliesin far below. His face was upturned, watching her progress, and she saw his glorious smile in a brief flash of lightning. When another came he was huddled against the ground, and she knew he was dead.

For a moment her chest hurt so much with grief she gasped aloud. Her breath left on a faint, muted wail; her head swam crazily. Then she hung onto the gate with all her might and told herself to let the grief go, let it pass . . . her gift to Taliesin would be to escape this place. Keely sent a heartfelt prayer to the gods and then slid over the gate to begin her descent.

It was easier; it was harder. Easier because she had only to loosen her careful grip as she worked her way down, but if she did that she would slide, falling, and smash against the ground. Harder because she must cling tightly, sliding down little by little, searching blindly for any toe-hold that might slow her descent. She used the hinges, scraping her cheek and her breasts and her knees, and her elbows were bloody shreds. The blood shone black in the lightning.

One foot found the bottom hinge, the other the crossbar. Keely clung to the gate a moment, making certain of her balance, then twisted her head around to stare down at the ground. It was wet and muddy, running with rain, but it was better than the stones of the bailey.

Keely let go of the gate and jumped.

She landed hard on her feet and fell forward to her hands and knees, then flat against the ground. For a moment she lay there, gasping in the puddles forming around her face, then dragged herself into a sitting position and pushed water from her eyes. She was alive. She was free.

Keely laughed softly, staring upward into the stormy heavens. The rain still fell and the clouds blotted the moon and the stars, but she was free. Strahan could not touch her.

The gate behind her rattled and groaned. Keely jerked around, saw the bolts being drawn and leaped to her feet. As the heavy gates creaked open she began to run.

Vines and creepers tore at her legs as she pushed her way through the thick forest. She had left the smooth grassy carpet and the beaches behind, fleeing into the depths of a strange forest. Lightning showed her the way as she ran, illuminating the path before her into an eerie greenish glow. Keely pulled her sodden nightshift up around her knees and jumped everything in her way.

She tripped several times, falling awkwardly, but each time she scrambled up and ran on. Instinct told her Strahan would be close behind her, *close,* and she had no recourse to the magic that would lend her animal shape. *Lir*-shape. If he caught her, he would keep her.

Finally she sagged against a tree, exhausted, and knew she could go no farther. Her legs shook so hard she thought she might fall and it was only because she clung to the tree that she remained on her feet. For a moment she closed her eyes, gasping painfully in the rain, then a blinding light penetrated her lids and she opened them to see a smoking purple column hiss out of the black sky.

For a moment she stared in astonishment at the coalescing column, startled by its brilliant beauty. Then she saw the form taking shape deep within it, and Strahan was with her again.

"Foolishness," he chided gently. The light slowly faded, hissing, as he put out a beckoning hand.

Keely said something incomprehensible, even to herself. Then she let go of the tree and ran again.

"You will lose the child," he called after her. She shivered as she realized he had known all along, but she also heard a note of genuine concern in his voice. If she lost the child he wanted so badly. . . .

She laughed wildly as she ran. "Good. *Good!*" The rain and foliage fell behind her like a curtain.

Lightning showed her a stone looming before her. A second flash showed it more clearly and she saw the tumbled ruins of an old chapel. Keely ducked into it and fell against the cold, wet wall, head thrown back as she tried to catch her breath. She smelled mold and age. The stone was slick beneath her hands, velveted with lichen.

Most of the roof was gone. Keely could see traces of the old beamwork; though most of it was tumbled against the ground inside the chapel walls. Timbers leaned crazily against broken stone. Part of the interior was still sheltered from the elements but most of it lay open to the wind and turbulent skies. The wet walls gleamed silver in the moonlight. Keely, realizing the storm was passing over, threw her head back and saw the moonlight and stars glowing against the black tapestry of the gods.

She moved from the crumbling doorway. A shaft of the new moonlight lay upon the remains of an altar. She crept to it slowly, half-afraid of the place. She had heard of its like before, in corners of Homana, but not on the Crystal Isle. Still, it was from the Crystal Isle the Cheysuli had come, the children of the gods, and perhaps it was her place as well.

She knelt in the wet, leaf-strewn earth before the altar. The leaning stone in front of her bore runes, shallowed and roughened by age, but runes nonetheless. She put out a hand and traced them, not noticing how muddy and bloody and scraped her fingers were. She could not read the Old Tongue but she recognized a few of the symbols, and realized she had stumbled across a chapel built by Cheysuli to honor the gods she honored herself.

A step behind her brought her upright and whirling around. Strahan stood in the doorway. She saw he wore dark leathers and a crimson velvet robe. No knife at his belt. He needed none.

He gestured with the fluid grace she despised, for it echoed that of her own race. "Pay this place homage while you may. It is the last time you will see a Cheysuli chapel. From now on I will keep you locked up like a prisoner, and you will wish you had not fled."

"I was a prisoner *before!*"

He smiled. The gentleness of his face made her shiver. "But a coddled one. And you will still be coddled—for a while. Until the child is born. And then I will put you away in the cells below the ground . . . until I need you again."

Keely felt the broken altar at the back of her knees. The walls seemed to close in on her. Strahan blocked the only exit and she could do no more climbing this night.

"I fell," she told him in discovery. "Before—as I ran. I fell, and I will lose this child." She felt an upsurge of fear as she realized the truth of her words, but also a fierce joy that he would not get what he wanted from her. "You will get no halfling of *me*, Ihlini!"

He glided forward. "You may lie. You may not. But it will

do you little good, my shapechanger princess. If you lose this child I will simply get another on you." He smiled at her grimace of revulsion. "Would you not rather have it done with this first time?"

"Perhaps I will die with losing it," she said fiercely, half-hoping it was true, if only it released her from him. "Perhaps I will die, as so many women die, and then you will have *nothing!*"

Strahan approached. Keely tried to back away, met the unforgiving altar and abruptly fell over it. She cried out with the pain of it, hands pressing against the ground. Then she felt something sharp. Instinctively she grabbed it, counting it as a weapon as the arms-master had told her so many times—*when in danger use any weapon at hand, even that which is not a weapon*—and thrust herself from the ground, slashing at Strahan. She saw the knife go home in his chest.

Keely cried out. Strahan fell to his knees unevenly, both hands clawing at the knife buried hilt-deep. His parti-colored eyes were on her, wide and wild, and his mouth opened in a horrible choking groan. He fell forward against the altar, driving the knife deeper into his chest, then slid slowly sideways and rolled onto his back.

Keely shivered. She sat among the tumbled ruins of an ancient altar and shivered so long and hard her bones ached. One hand crept to her mouth and covered it, as if she would be ill, then she clenched her teeth and closed her eyes.

*I have fought before*, she thought dazedly. *Fought before with knife or sword, but always in practice. Always against the arms-master. In all the years of my rebellion—when I sought a warrior's ways instead of a woman's—I never knew what it meant to truly seek another's life.* She swallowed heavily, fighting down the sourness of bile. *By the gods . . . it is not so simple a thing to be a warrior after all!*

Keely opened her eyes at last and looked up through the broken roof. She saw the full moon clearly. The wind was fading and the thunder of the passing storm sounded more distant. Only a faint mist from the dripping trees blew through the ruin, dampening her face. Keely brushed vaguely at the spray and then looked down at Strahan.

His eyes were open. Even in death they remained eerily lifelike: one blue, one brown; the mark of a demon. Keely, shuddering again, crept slowly closer to shut them, unable to let him look on her even in death. His skin was still warm to the touch. Blood ran from his mouth into his beard.

The knife stood out from his chest, smeared with blood, but

Keely set her jaw and grasped the hilt in both hands. Then she jerked it from its bony sheath.

It came free reluctantly but finally she had it in her hands. She lifted a fold of Strahan's crimson robe and cleaned the blade, making certain she got the Ihlini's tainted blood from it. A good weapon should never suffer the enemy's blood upon it. Then she got her first clear look at it and realized her fingers, grasping it, had recognized it even in extremity.

She saw upon the hilt the rampant lion with ruby eye. Line for line, liquid in grace and form, the image matched that on her own knife, which bore the royal crest of Homana.

"But this is not mine," she whispered in awe. "Strahan took mine from me. . . ."

She stared at the hilt, running tentative fingers over the lion. There was no doubt it was from the House of Homana; it matched those held by her father; her brothers. But what was it doing in a ruined chapel on the Crystal Isle?

A faint breeze crept down into the chapel. Keely, in damp, torn nightshift, shivered against its touch. She tried to ignore it and found she could not. Finally she stared up into the dark sky and saw the stars glitter at her, as if they sought to speak.

She flipped the knife in her hand and slid the point beneath the flesh of her left wrist, opening a shallow cut. The blood spilled freely, swift and clear, bright red in the silver moonlight.

She smiled. She looked at the blood; at the knife, and recalled the stories of a kinsman who had died on the Crystal Isle some forty years before.

*"You have only to call upon the old gods, and you will be free!"* Taliesin had said.

She had not fully believed. All her life she had been taught to honor the gods, but honoring them was a custom more than a true belief, and she understood why they had not answered her before. She had not needed them then.

"I give you my thanks," she whispered into the darkness. "My kinsman; Taliesin; the arms-master who taught me well. But most of all I thank the old gods." She huddled there a moment longer, than wet her lips. "I cannot bear this child. Perhaps I will not, now, because of the violence of this night, but however it happens, I must lose it. I cannot destroy my own House."

The shadows did not answer.

Finally Keely—knowing she could not go into Hondarth wearing a torn nightshift that showed every contour of her body—conquered her distaste and removed the crimson robe from

Strahan's body. For a moment she held the garment in her hands, fighting back her revulsion at the still-wet blood, then slipped it on over her nightshift. She chopped the bottom off with the knife, took Strahan's belt and cut it to her size, then tied it around her middle.

Keely bent and grasped one of Strahan's leather-clad arms. He was slack and heavy but she gritted her teeth and dragged his body from the ruins, so he could not profane them. She left him outside. Then she went back in and knelt once more before the altar, sliding the knife back into darkness.

"I leave this here," she said quietly. "It is not mine. I have used it, in my need, and now I leave it for the next one who may call upon the gods."

She hesitated a moment, wondering if they would speak to her. Then she rose and walked from the chapel without another word, and as she passed Strahan's body she thought she heard the laughter of the gods.

Keely stood on the white, moon-silvered beach. On the distant shore winked the lantern-lights of Hondarth. Homana. Her homeland. She had only to take *lir*-shape in the guise of a hawk or falcon, and Homana would be hers again.

She wanted to go home. She wanted to be safe and warm in her father's great palace, surrounded by her tall brothers, her kinfolk, her friends. She wanted the feel of her sword in her hand; to dance again against the arms-master; to know the freedom of spirit and soul in such work. She wanted time alone, so she could deal with the loss of a child.

She longed to fly, to feel the wind against her wings; to soar among the clouds and currents and dance among the gods. To be earthbound no more but free to drift and swoop and flirt and dive; falling, spiraling upward to fall again. To lose her cares and concerns and her eternal *tahlmorra* upon the breath of the gods who had gifted her with life, with spirit, with pride, and with the *tahlmorra* that made her what she was.

Keely smiled. She stretched out her aching arms, reaching for the endless skies, and flew. Homeward. To Homana.

Pat Murphy says of herself that she "attended the Clarion work-shop back in 1978 and managed to survive," and that she earns her living as a science writer, currently working for the Exploratorium, San Francisco's unique "hands on" Museum of Science. Despite this background of science, she writes both fantasy and science fiction, often blending the two in stories difficult to categorize. The first story she submitted to this anthology, although an excellent and well-written tale, I felt to be too strongly science fictional for this particular anthology; with regrets, I returned it to her, and was pleasantly surprised to receive, soon thereafter, this story which I felt was clearly fantasy. Pat told me, though, that the story I rejected for being too much science fiction had been rejected by a s-f market for being too much fantasy; she added "My own personal method for distinguishing between the two is this—if it sells to a fantasy market it must be fantasy; if it sells to a science fiction market, it's science fiction." By those standards most of her writing has been science fiction; she has published in *Galaxy, Amazing/Fantastic, Isaac Asimov's S-F*, and various anthologies: *Elsewhere, Universe* and the *Chrysalis* anthologies 5, 6 and 9.

Most of the stories I receive which mention "Goddesses" are amateurish attempts to deal with funny religions, or strident feminist polemic. This is a most refreshing exception; yet below the level of the well-told fantasy adventure, there is a clear message for today's world. Just the same, (which I consider the mark of a good story) you can ignore, or even fail to see, the message without detracting from the slightest from your enjoy-ment of the story.—MZB

# WITH FOUR LEAN HOUNDS
## by Pat Murphy

We start with a thief: slim, wiry girl with ash-gray hair and eyes the color of the winter sky. No one knew how old she was and no one cared. Old enough to beat; just barely old enough to bed.

Tarsia was running from an angry baker. The loaf tucked under her arm was still warm. She dodged between the stalls of the market, heading for a spot where she knew she could climb the tumble-down wall that ringed the city. From there she could run sure-footed across slate roofs, hide among the chimneys. A creature of the wind and sky, she could escape all pursuit.

She heard the whistle of the guard's warning and the pounding of his running feet. Ill luck: he was between her and the wall. Behind her, the baker shouted curses. She changed course abruptly, ducking into the mouth of an alley and—too late—realized her mistake.

The walls were slick stone. Though she climbed like a monkey, she could not scale them. The alley's far end had been blocked by a new building. A dead end.

She heard the guard's whistle echoing down the cold stone walls and remembered the feel of the shackles on her wrist. Her bones ached in memory of the cold jail.

A jumble of papers that the wind had blown against the alley's end rustled. A rat peered out at Tarsia—a grizzled old grandfather rat who watched her with an arrogant air of unconcern, then turned tail and darted into a hole that had been hidden in the shadows. It was a dark, dank hole just the width of a small thief's shoulders.

Tarsia heard the footsteps at the mouth of the alley and, like a sensible thief with a healthy concern for her skin, she squeezed into the hole. Her shoulders scraped against the damp stone. A creature of rooftops and light, she wiggled down into the darkness.

On her belly, she groped her way forward, reminding herself that rats were only bats without wings. As a child of the rooftops she knew bats. But she could hear her heart beating in the narrow stone passage and she could not lift her head without bumping it. She inched forward, telling herself that surely the drain let into a larger passage; it could not just get smaller and darker and damper. . . .

A cold blast of air fanned her face, carrying scents of still water, damp stone, and sewage. At last, she could raise her head. She felt a soft touch on her ankle—a tiny breeze rushing past—with only a hint of fur and a long tail.

She heaved herself out of the drain into a larger space, quick and clumsy in her eagerness to move. She stepped forward in the darkness, stepped into nothing and stumbled, clutching at an edge she could not see, slipping and falling into a moment she did not remember.

A thunder of wings from the pigeons wheeling overhead, the scent of a charcoal fire—damp, dismal smell in the early morning—drifting from a chimney. The slate roof was cold beneath Tarsia's bare feet and the wind from the north cut through her thin shirt. In one hand she clutched the damp shirt she had taken from a rooftop clothesline. She was listening.

She had heard a sound—not the rattle of the latch of the door to the roof. Not the pigeons. Perhaps only the wind?

There again: a rumbling like drumbeats and a wild sweet whistling like pipes in a parade. From behind a cloud swept the chariot of the Lady of the Wind. She brought the sunshine with her. She wore a silver crescent moon on her forehead and a golden sun shone on her breast. Ash-gray hair floated behind her like a cape. Four lean hounds—winds of the North, South, East, and West—ran laughing through the sky at her side.

The Lady looked down at Tarsia with wise eyes, smiled, and held out her hand. Tarsia reached out to touch her.

Tarsia's head ached and her feet were cold. She opened her eyes into darkness, leaving behind the bright dream of a memory that had never been. Tarsia had watched the caravan that carried tribute to the Lady leave the city, heading north, but she had never seen the Lady.

The hand with which Tarsia had clung to the edge was sore and stiff; when she touched it to her lips, it tasted of blood. She lay half in and half out of a cold stream that tugged at her feet as it flowed past.

She could not go back, only forward. She felt her way slowly, always keeping her hand on the wall and always sniffing the air in hopes of scenting dust and horses—city smells. She heard a rumbling sound ahead that reminded her of cartwheels on cobblestones, and she quickened her pace.

The tunnel opened into a cavern—a natural formation in the rock of the Earth. Patches of fungus on the walls glowed golden, casting a light dimmer than that of the moon.

The giant who lay in the center of the cavern was snoring with a rumbling like cartwheels. He slept in a cradle of rock, molded around him, it seemed, by the movements of his body. The air that blew past the giant, coming from the darkness beyond, carried the scents of grass and of freedom.

A giant blocked her way and she was only a small thief. She had never stolen from the house of the wizard or the stall of the herb-seller. She knew only the small spells that helped her break the protection of a household.

The giant had an enormous face—broad and earth-colored. He shifted in his sleep and Tarsia saw the chain on his ankle, bound to a bolt in the floor. The links were as thick as her leg; the rusted lock, the size of her head. She wondered who had imprisoned him and what he had done to deserve it. She tried to estimate the length of the chain and judged it long enough to allow him to catch anyone trying to sneak past.

The shifting breeze ruffled his hair and the rumbling stopped. Nostrils flared as he sampled the air. "I smell you," he said slowly. "I know your scent, witch. What do you want with me now?" He spoke as if he knew her.

Tarsia did not move. One hand rested on the rock wall; one hand uselessly clutched her knife. The giant's eyes searched the shadows and found her.

"Ah," he said. "The same eyes, the same hair, the same scent—not the witch, but the witch's daughter." He grinned and Tarsia did not like the look in his eyes. "You were a long time in coming."

"I'm no one's daughter," she said. Giants and witches—she had no place in this. Her mother? She had no mother. "I'm just a poor thief from the city. And I want to get back."

"You can't get past me unless you free me, witch's daughter," he said.

"Free you?" She shook her head in disbelief. "How? Break the chain?"

The giant scowled. "A drop of your blood on the lock will free me. You must know that." His voice was unbelieving. "How can you hope to win your mother's throne when you don't even know. . . ."

"Who is my mother?" she interrupted, her voice brittle.

"You don't know." He grinned and his voice took on the sly tone she had heard from strong men who did not often have to be clever. "Free me and I'll tell you." He pulled his legs under him into an awkward crouch, his head bumping the cavern's ceiling. "Just one drop of blood and I'll let you go past. Even if the blood does not free me, I'll let you go."

"Even if it does not free you?" she asked warily.

"You doubt yourself so much?" He shrugged. "Even so."

She stepped forward, wary and ready to dart back to the passage. With her eyes on the crouching giant she nicked the scrape on her hand so that the blood flowed fresh and a drop fell onto the rusted lock. She backed away. The giant's eyes were fixed on the lock and on the smoke that rose from the lock, swirling around the chain.

She reached the far side of the cavern while the giant watched the lock, and from that safety she called out sharply, "Who is the witch who bound you here, giant? Keep your part of the bargain. Who . . . ?''

"There!" the giant said. With a triumphant movement, the giant tugged the chain and the lock fell free.

"Who is the witch?" Tarsia called again.

"Thank you for your help, witch's daughter." He stepped past her, into the darkness where the ceiling rose higher. "I will go now to play a part in bringing the prophecies to pass."

"But who is my mother?" she shouted. "You said you would tell me."

He grinned back over his shoulder. "Who would be strong enough to chain a son of the Earth? No one but the Lady of the Wind." He stepped away into the darkness.

"What?" Tarsia shouted in disbelief, but her voice echoed back to her. She could hear the giant striding away in the darkness and her mind was filled with the thunder of wings, with the baying of four lean hounds. She ran after the giant, knowing that she could not catch him but running in spite of that knowledge. The scent of fresh air and growing things grew stronger as she ran. "Wait," she called, but the giant was gone.

The air smelled of newly turned earth. She ran toward a bright light—sunlight of late afternoon. She could see the marks left by the giant's fingers where he had torn the rock aside and pushed his way out. His feet had ripped dark holes in the soft grass and the prints led down the rolling hills to the river that sparkled in the distance. She thought that she could see a splash in the river—tiny and far away—which could have been a giant splashing as he swam.

Sometimes stumbling, sometimes sliding in the grass, she ran down the hills, following the footprints. Ran until her legs slowed without her willing it. She trudged along the river bank as the shadows grew longer. She was heading north. The mountains lay to the north, and the Lady's court was in the mountains.

The light was failing when she stopped to rest. She sat down just for a moment. No more than that. Shivering in the chill twilight, she tumbled into a darkness deeper than the tunnels beneath the city.

A scent of a charcoal fire—damp dismal scent in the early morning—but Tarsia did not stand on the cold slate of the roof. The wind that carried the scent of smoke blew back her hair and the sound of wings was all around her.

She stood at the Lady's side in the chariot and the four hounds of the wind ran beside them. Far below, she saw the gray slate rooftop and the fluttering clothes on the line. Far below, the ancient towers of the city, the crumbling walls, the booths and stalls of the marketplace.

"This is your proper place, my daughter," the Lady said, her voice as soft as the summer breeze blowing through the towers. "Above the world at my side." The Lady took Tarsia's hand and the pain faded away.

Tarsia heard a rumbling—like the sound of cartwheels on a cobbled street. Far below, she saw the towers shake and a broad, earth-colored face glared up at them. Shaking off the dust of the hole from which he had emerged, the giant climbed to the top of the city wall in a few steps. He seemed larger than he had beneath the earth. He stood on top of the old stone tower and reached toward them. Tarsia cried out—fearful that the giant would catch them and drag them back to the earth. Back down to the smoke and the dust.

The scent of smoke was real. Tarsia could feel the damp grass of the river bank beneath her, but she was warm. A cloth that smelled faintly of horse lay over her.

She forced her eyes open. A river bank in early morning—mist sparkling on the grass, a white horse grazing, smoke drifting from a small fire, a thin, brown-haired man dressed in travel-stained green watching her. "You're awake," he said. "How do you feel?"

Her head ached. She struggled to a sitting position, clutching the green cape that had served as her cover around her. Wary, used to the ways of the city, she mumbled, "I'll live."

He continued watching her. "You're a long way from anywhere in particular. Where are you going?" His accent matched that of traders from the South who had sometimes visited the city.

She twisted to look behind her at the hills. She could not see the city, and she wondered how far she had come in the winding tunnels. "I came from the city," she said. "I'm going away from the city." More alert now, Tarsia studied the white horse. It looked well-fed. The saddle that lay beside the animal was travel-worn, but she could tell that it was once of first quality. The cloak that covered her was finely woven of soft wool. A lute wrapped in similar cloth leaned against the saddle.

"I'm a minstrel," the man said. "I'm traveling north."

Tarsia nodded, thinking that when a person volunteered information it was generally false. No minstrel could afford a saddle like that one. She looked up into his brown eyes—noting in passing the gold ring on his hand. She knew she could trust him as a fellow thief. As far as she could trust a thief. She was not sure how far that was, since she had always preferred to work alone.

"I was planning to head north too," she said. "If you take me with you, I can help you out. I can build a fire that doesn't smoke. . . ." She looked at the smoldering fire and let her words trail off. She knew she looked small and helpless in the cloak and she hoped that her face was pale and smudged with dirt.

"I suppose I can't very well leave you here," he said, sounding a little annoyed. "I'll take you as far as the next town."

She got to her feet slowly, taking care to appear weak. But she made herself useful—poking the fire so that the sticks flamed. She toasted the bread that the minstrel pulled from his pack and melted cheese upon thick slices.

She helped him saddle the white horse. On a pretext of adjusting the saddlebags, she slipped her hand inside and found a money pouch. Swiftly, she palmed one, two, three coins—and slyly transferred them to her own pocket for later examination. Even if he only took her to the next town, she would profit by the association.

As they traveled alongside the river, she rode behind him on the horse. "How far north are you going?"

"To the mountains," he said and began to pick a tune on his lute.

"To the court of the Lady of the Wind," she guessed, then suppressed a smile when he frowned. Where else would a minstrel go in the mountains? She amended mentally; where else would a thief go? "Could I come with you?"

"Why?"

She shrugged as if reasons were not important. "I've never been to a court before. I've heard the Lady is very beautiful."

The minstrel shook his head. "Beautiful, but wicked."

"I can pay my way," Tarsia said, wondering if he would recognize the look of his own coins.

But he shook his head again and the tune he was playing changed, mellowing to music that she remembered from her childhood. She could not remember the words except for the refrain about the beautiful Lady and the four lean windhounds at her side. The Lady was the sister to the sun and daughter of the moon.

When the minstrel sang the refrain, it had a sneering, cynical tone. The lyrics were about how the Lady had bound the spirits of the Earth, the Water, and the Fire, how she had captured the four winds and bound them in her tower, about how the world would be unhappy until the four winds were free.

"That isn't the way that I remember the song," Tarsia said when the minstrel finished.

He shrugged. "In my country, we pay the Lady no tribute. Our lands have been dry and our crops have been poor for five long years. We do not love the Lady."

Tarsia remembered the parade that was held each year in the Lady's honor when the tribute was sent. The city was noted for its silverwork, and each year, the best that the artisans had produced was sent to the mountain court. And the winds blew through the towers and brought rain for the farmers around the city walls.

Last year, at the end of a day of picking the pockets of parade spectators, Tarsia had climbed the city wall and watched from above the gate while the caravan headed north, winding between farmer's huts and green fields. On her high perch, she had been chilled by the wind—but glad to be above the crowd. The last horse in the caravan had carried a silver statuette of the Lady gazing into the distance with one hand resting on the head of a hound. Tarsia had felt a kinship with the Lady then—alone and proud, above the world.

"Why don't you pay tribute," she asked the minstrel. "Are you too poor?"

"Too proud," he said. "Our king will not allow it."

"How foolish!"

The minstrel smiled wryly. "Maybe so. The whole family is foolish, I suppose. Idealistic and stiff-necked."

"So the people of your land will die of pride."

He shook his head. "Perhaps. Perhaps not. Maybe something will happen." He sighed. "I don't know, though—the king seems inclined to rely on luck. He seems to think the prophecy will come to pass."

Tarsia frowned. "Why are you going to the Lady's court if you don't like her?"

"A minstrel doesn't worry about magic and winds." He started to play another song, as if to avoid further discussion. The notes echoed across the slow green waters of the river and the steady beat of the horse's hooves provided the rhythm. He sang about an undine, a river nymph who took a human lover, then betrayed him to the waters, letting the river rise to drown him.

Trees with long leaves trailed their branches in the water. The path twisted among the gnarled trunks. They wandered deeper into the shade and the river seemed to take the sunlight into itself, letting it sparkle in swirling eddies but never allowing it to escape. On the far side of the river, the bank rose in a fern-covered cliff, decked with flowers.

"Pretty country," Tarsia said.

"Treacherous country," said the minstrel. "If you tried climbing the cliff you'd learn that those flowers mark loose rock, ready to give beneath your hand or tumble down on you."

At dusk, they were still in the wood and the trees all looked the same. They made camp in an inviting glen, but the tiny fire that Tarsia built seemed to cast little light. Tarsia thought she heard rustling in the trees and once, while she was toasting bread and cheese for dinner, thought she glimpsed a flicker of white in the distance over the river. She wrapped herself in the minstrel's extra cloak and curled up alone by the side of the fire.

For a moment she thought that she was in the cavern beneath the city: it was dark and cold. But the wind that beat against her face smelled of flowing water and growing things, and above her, she could see the stars. The Lady stood beside her, a proud, silent presence.

They had escaped the giant and Tarsia realized that the giant alone was no threat to the Lady. They dipped closer to the earth, and Tarsia could see the winding water of the river, glittering in the moonlight. She could see a tiny spot of light—her own fire—and she thought she could see the minstrel on the ground beside it. So far below.

She thought of him coming to the Lady's court to steal and she wished she could invite him into the chariot beside her. So cold and alone he looked, as she had felt so many times on the wall in the city of towers.

"You are above all that now," whispered the Lady at her side. "You are the daughter of the moon, sister to the sun."

The lapping of the water and the soft nickering of the horse woke her. The water sounded near, very near. She sat up and blinked at the sheen of moonlight on the water, just a few feet away from her. The horse stood at the limits of his tether, pulling away from the rising waters. Blinking again, Tarsia could see the slim figure of a woman dressed in white, standing in the water. At the sound of Tarsia's movement, the woman looked at her with mournful eyes.

She held out her hands to Tarsia and water dripped from the

tips of her long fingers. Moonlight shimmered on her, just as it shimmered on the water. From her delicate wrists, silver chains which seemed to be fashioned of moonlight extended to the water.

Tarsia drew her legs away from the water, stood up and backed away. The water nymph stretched out her hands and almost reached Tarsia. The young thief could hear words in the sound of the lapping water: "Come to me, touch me, touch the river." Tarsia laid a hand on the horse, ready to vault to its back and run.

The moonlight touched a spot of darkness in the water—the minstrel's cloak. The water was around his neck and still he slept peacefully. His cloak drifted about his shoulders, moving with the water, half tangled around the tree against which he leaned. To reach the minstrel, Tarsia would have to touch the river and approach the woman of water. But no one would know if she ran away to her mother's court.

"Let me go, daughter of the moon," whispered the water. The breeze that rustled the leaves by Tarsia's head seemed to be chuckling.

"Let him go and I'll free you," Tarsia bargained desperately. "But let him go first." She did not know how to free the nymph. The watery hands reached for her and she wanted to leap onto the horse and run.

"Free me, and I will let him go," hissed the voice of the lapping water.

"But I can't . . . I don't know how. . . ."

A whisper in the night: "Give to me of yourself, daughter of the moon."

In the moonlight, Tarsia could see the minstrel's head fall back into the water and a swirl of silver bubbles rise. She stepped forward, ready to push the water nymph aside. Tarsia's eyes were wet: tears of frustration, anger, sorrow, pain. A single tear escaped, trickled down her face and fell into the river. Just one.

Tarsia grabbed the minstrel's cloak and his arm and roughly dragged him toward the river bank. At the sound of a long sigh, she looked up to see the moonlight chains on the water woman's arms fade. The nymph raised her hands to the sky in an exultant gesture and the river sighed: "Thank you, daughter of the Lady." The slim figure melted into the river, becoming one of the sparking ripples in the current. The minstrel coughed and began to move.

Tarsia lit a fire to dry him out, draping the dry cloak over his shoulders. She did not need it for warmth. She felt strong—no longer a thief, but daughter to the Lady.

"How did you plan to get along without me to build fires?" she asked the minstrel.

He shrugged his slim shoulders beneath the cloak. "I trust to luck to get me by. Luck and destiny." His eyes were bright with reflected moonlight. "Sometimes they serve me well."

The next day's ride took them out of the river canyon into the golden foothills. A boy tending a flock of goats by the river stared at them in amazement. "No one ever comes by that path," he said.

Tarsia laughed, cheered by the sight of the mountains ahead. "We came that way."

"What about the undine?" the boy asked.

"What about the undine," she said, still laughing as they rode past. "We sent her on her way."

They walked the horse along the river's edge just past the goat herd. Ahead, they could see the buildings of a small town. The sun shone on Tarsia's face and she saw the mountains, craggy peaks where the snow never melted. "Take me with you to the Lady's court," she asked the minstrel suddenly. "I know why you're going there, and I want to come."

He looked startled. "You know? But . . ."

She laughed. "Do you think I'm half-witted? No minstrel could afford a horse like this one or a fine leather saddle. I knew you were a thief when we first met." She shook her head at the incredulous look on his face. "I know you are going to the Lady's court to steal."

"I see," he said slowly. "But if I'm a thief, why do you want to come with me?" He studied her face intently.

For a moment, she considered telling the truth. But she was city-bred, not trusting. "I want to see which of the stories about the Lady are true," she said. "Besides, I can help you." She could imagine herself at her mother's side, rewarding the minstrel with gold and jewels for bringing her there, and she smiled.

"It's a dangerous place," he said.

"If you don't take me, I will go alone," she said. "If you take me, I'll pay my way. I'll pay for tonight's lodging."

He nodded at last. "If you wish, I'll take you. But it's your choice."

The breeze whispered in the tall grass of the river bank. "The wind is encouraging us," Tarsia said.

"The wind is laughing at us," said the minstrel.

In the inn that night, Tarsia and the minstrel were the center of a group of villagers. The boy with the goats had told what path they had followed. "You came past the undine," the innkeeper said in amazement. "How did you do it?"

Tarsia told them, leaving out only the water nymph's sigh of farewell. "So the river is free of the Lady's bond," said a sour-faced farmer. "She will not be happy." And the corners of his mouth turned up in a grim smile.

"Softly, friend," advised the innkeeper. "You would not want to be overheard. . . ."

"We live in the shadow of her rule," grumbled the farmer. "But maybe that will come to an end. My boy said he saw the footprints of a giant heading toward her court. These folks say the undine is free. Maybe the Lady. . . ."

"Only one of the Lady's own blood can free the winds," interrupted the innkeeper. "And she has no children."

"They say she had a daughter once," said the minstrel quietly. "I studied the ancient stories as a student of the lute. They say that the child was captured in a battle with a neighboring city. The child was killed when the Lady would not release the winds to ransom the girl."

"And the Lady mourned for her daughter?" Tarsia added tentatively.

The crowd of villagers laughed and the minstrel raised his eyebrows. "I doubt it. But the stories don't really say."

A loose shutter banged in the rising wind outside the inn. The group of villagers that had gathered around Tarsia while she had been telling of the water nymph dispersed to other tables.

"Some say that the winds that the Lady allows to blow carry tales back to her," the minstrel told Tarsia softly. "No one knows for certain." The shutter banged again and the conversations around them stopped for a moment, then resumed in hushed tones.

"The land here was green once," said the minstrel. "The people have become bitter as the land has become dry."

The minstrel began to pick the notes of a slow, sweet tune, and Tarsia went to the bar to bargain with the innkeeper for their night's lodging. She took one of the minstrel's coins from her pocket and it flashed silver in the firelight. The innkeeper weighed it in his hand and turned it over to examine both sides.

"A coin of the south," he said, then peered more closely at the profile etched on one side.

The notes of the song that the minstrel was playing drifted across the room, over the sounds of conversation. He was picking out the sad ballad about the Lady that he had played the day before. The innkeeper glanced at him sharply, then looked back at the coin. He seemed to be listening to the sound of the wind prowling around the windows.

"You are heading into the mountains from here?" he asked.

"Yes," Tarsia said cautiously. She knew that he was no friend of the Lady.

He handed her back the coin. "Good luck," he said. "Eat supper as you like, and you may sleep in the loft above the stable."

She frowned at him without comprehension. "What do you mean? Why?"

He seemed to study the minstrel's face in the dim light. "Consider it as payment for ridding the river of the undine." He smiled at her for the first time, and took her hand to fold her fingers around the coin. "Good luck,"

She pocketed the coin and returned unhappily to the minstrel's side. She did not like bargains she did not understand. Like the giant, the innkeeper seemed to think that she knew more than she did.

"Did you make a deal?" the minstrel asked.

She sat down on the bench beside him, frowning. "We're sleeping in the stable loft. No payment—he didn't even argue."

"I see." The minstrel nodded across the room to the innkeeper and the older man waved back, a gesture that was almost a salute.

"There are things on which one does not bargain, little one," said the minstrel. "You'll have to learn that."

That night they bedded down in sweet-smelling hay. Outside, the wind bayed like a pack of hounds on the hunt, and Tarsia lay awake. She listened to the minstrel's steady breathing and thought about the mountains and the court of the Lady. But she did not want to sleep and dream.

When she turned restlessly in the hay, the minstrel blinked at her. "Lie down and go to sleep."

"I can't," she grumbled back, into the darkness that smelled of horses.

"What's wrong?" he asked.

"I'm cold," she said, and it was true—even with his extra cloak around her, she was shivering.

He raised himself on one elbow wearily, and lifted his cloak to invite her to lie beside him. She snuggled against his chest and he touched her cheek lightly. "What's worrying you?" he asked. "Do you want to turn back?"

"It used to be so simple," she said, half to herself. "I used to be just a thief in the city, climbing on the city wall and laughing at people who were foolish enough to let me pick their pockets. So simple. . . ."

"What are you now?" Though his voice was soft, the question had edges.

The winds bayed and she shivered. "No one. No one at all."

The minstrel rocked her gently in his arms and she listened to his steady breathing as he slept beside her. She slept, but not easily.

The Lady's hand was warm on Tarsia's. Far below, the small thief could see the village: toy huts set on a golden hillside. The mountains rose ahead of them: cold, grey, and forbidding.

"We don't need them," the Lady said in her soft voice. "It doesn't matter that they hate me."

The wind was in Tarsia's face and the stars wheeled about her and she was high above them all. No one could touch her here. No one could put her in shackles or chase her into the sewers. She had come home.

She was quiet when they left town the next morning. The same boy who had met them on the river path was grazing his goats on the hillside. "There are robbers in the mountains," he called to them. "They'll get you if you go up there." The boy was cheerful at the prospect. "There's a dragon, too. The Lady bound him there. If the robbers don't get you, the dragon will find you and . . ."

The minstrel urged the horse through the center of the boy's herd and the goats scattered, bleating as they ran.

The horse picked its way carefully up the dry slopes. Toward dusk, the grass gave way to rough rock and the animal began stumbling in the dying light. At Tarsia's suggestion, they dismounted and led the horse. To shake the saddle-weariness from her legs, Tarsia ran ahead, dodging around rocks and scrambling up boulders, feeling almost as if she were at home on the walls of the city. She climbed a rock face and peered over the edge at the minstrel, considering surprising him from above. She saw a movement—a flash of brown—on the trail ahead of him, movements in the brush on either side.

"Hold it there." The man who stepped from behind a boulder had an arrow pointed at the minstrel. Other men closed in from behind.

"I have nothing of value," said the minstrel casually. "Nothing at all."

"You've got a horse," said the leader of the robbers. The man had a soft, lilting accent like the minstrel's. "And I think we need it more than you do." The man lifted the minstrel's money pouch from his belt. Grinning, he hefted the pouch in his hand and gazed at the minstrel's face. "Damn, but your face looks familiar. Do I know you . . . ?" His voice trailed off.

"I'm going to the court of the Lady. I need the horse to get there," the minstrel said.

"A man of the South going to visit the Lady," the leader wondered. "Strange. Since our foolish king has refused to pay tribute to the Lady, few from the South venture into her mountains." As he spoke, he fumbled with the minstrel's pouch, pouring a stream of coins into his hand. "Nothing of value," he said then. "Just pretty gold and silver." The robber held a coin up to the light of the dying sun—just as the innkeeper had held it up—and he whistled long and low. He glanced at the minstrel's face and Tarsia could see his teeth flash in a grin. "Did I say our king was foolish? Not so foolish as his son." The leader tossed the coin to another man in the circle. "Look. We've got a prince here."

The coin was tossed from hand to hand—each man inspecting the minstrel and the coin, the coin and the minstrel. Tarsia, peering over the edge, tried to remember the profile on the coin, briefly glimpsed in a dim light. She tugged a coin from her pocket and compared the cold metal etching with the minstrel's face. They matched.

"We follow our destiny and our luck," the minstrel—or the prince?—was saying. "I am on a mission at my father's request."

The leader's grin broadened and he tossed a coin into the air so that it flashed gold as it tumbled back to his hand. "Bringing tribute," the leader said.

"No." The winds were silent and the voice of the prince— once, the minstrel—was calm. "I have come to free the winds."

Tarsia leaned against the rock and listened to the rhythm of her heart—beating faster and faster. She heard the leader laugh. "What do you expect the Lady to say to that?"

"I may have to destroy the Lady. But the winds must be free. For the sake of the land you have left behind, you must let me go."

"You appeal to the honor of a thief?" the leader said. "You are foolish indeed. And foolish to think that you alone can destroy our Lady."

The prince looked up then, just as if he had known all along where Tarsia was hidden, then looked back to the leader. But his words were echoing in Tarsia's mind: "destroy the Lady . . ." And in her mind, the winds howled. The prince was not alone: the giant had been seen climbing toward her court and the undine was free. Tarsia leaned against the rock for support and listened to the men argue about what to do with the minstrel—no, the prince. She had to remind herself he was a prince. They could hold him for ransom, deliver him to the Lady for a reward, kill him on the spot, feed him to the dragon. She followed, a little above them and a little behind them as they walked to the dragon's cave, still arguing. She heard the horse nicker softly as they stood at the cave entrance. The man who held the animal's reins was right below her hiding place, paying more attention to the argument than to the horse.

Tarsia sprang. Landed half on and half off the white horse's broad back, gripping its mane and pounding its sides with her heels. The animal leaped forward—was it by the horse's inclination or her direction? she was not sure—toward the prince. The horse reared as she strove to turn it, dancing in place and throwing its head back, startled past the capacity of even a well-trained horse to bear. Tarsia fought for control, only partly aware of the men who dodged away from the animal's hooves in the dim light of twilight. She could not see the prince.

A crackling of flame, a scent of sulfur, and the mountain was no longer dark. Small thief—she had never dabbled in magic, never met a dragon. If she had imagined anything, she had imagined a lizard breathing fire.

A lightning bolt, a fireworks blast, a bonfire—but it moved like an animal. Where it stepped, it left cinders and when it lifted its head she stared into the white glory of its eyes. A sweep of its tail left a trail of sparks. Half flame, half animal—or perhaps more than half flame.

She could see the prince, standing in its path. The child of fire opened its mouth and for a moment she could see the jagged lightning of its teeth.

"Child of fire," Tarsia called to it, "If I free you will you lead me to my mother?"

The crackling warmth assented with a burst of heat and a flare of flame.

Tarsia's heart was large within her and she was caught by confusion—burning with shame and stung by betrayal. She saw the prince through a haze of smoke and anger. The coins she had stolen from him were in her hand and she wanted to be rid of them and rid of him. "I give of myself to you, child of fire," she said, and hurled them into the flames. Three points of gold, suddenly molten.

The heat of her pain vanished with them. She burned pure and cold—like starlight, like moonlight, like a reflection from the heart of an icicle.

The dragon beat his wings and she felt a wave of heat. He circled the mountain, caught an updraft and soared higher. His flame licked out and lashed the granite slope beneath him before he rose out of sight.

In the sudden silence, Tarsia fought the horse to a standstill. The prince stood alone by the cave. The world was tinted with the transparent twilight blue of early evening in the mountains, touched with smoke and sprinkled with snow.

"You didn't tell me you wanted to free the winds," Tarsia said. Her voice still carried the power it had had when she spoke to the dragon. "You didn't tell me you were a prince."

"I could only trust you as much as you could trust me, daughter of the wind."

"Ah, you know." Her voice was proud.

"I guessed. You freed the undine," he said.

"Had you planned to use me to destroy my mother?" she asked. "That won't work, prophecy or no. I'm here to help my mother, not to destroy her." She urged the horse up the canyon, following the mark left by the dragon's fire. She did not look back.

Up the mountains, following the trail of burnt brush and cinders, kicking the horse when it stumbled, urging it to run over grassy slopes marked by flame. The moon rose and the horse stumbled less often. Alpine flowers nodded in the wind of her passing and on the snow banks, ice crystals danced in swirling patterns.

The towers of the Lady's castle rose from the center of a bowl carved into the mountain. A wall of ice rose behind the towers— glacial blue in the moonlight. The ice had been wrought with tunnels by the wind and carved into strangely shaped pillars. Tarsia rode over the crest of the ridge and started the horse down the slope toward the gates when she saw the giant by the towers.

She felt the strength within her, and did not turn.

As Tarsia drew nearer she saw the figure in the ice wall—the slim form of the undine. She smelled the reek of sulfur and the ice flickered red as the dragon circled the towers.

The gates had been torn from their hinges. The snow had drifted into the courtyard. The stones had been scorched by fire.

Tarsia pulled the horse to a stop in front of the grinning giant. "So you've come to finish the job," he said.

"I have come to see my mother," Tarsia answered, her voice cold and careful.

"I hope you know more than you did when I talked to you last," said the giant.

"I have come to talk to my mother," she repeated. "What I know or what I plan to do is none of your concern." Her voice was cold as starlight.

The giant frowned. "Your mother's men have fled. Her castle is broken. But still she holds the winds in her power. She stands there where we cannot follow." The giant gestured to the tallest tower. Tarsia noticed that the wind had scoured a bare spot in the snow at the tower's base. "Visit her if you will."

Tarsia left the white horse standing by the tower door and climbed the cold stairs alone. She could feel a breeze tickling the back of her neck and tugging at her clothes. She was cold, so cold, as cold as she had been the morning she stole the loaf of bread.

A slender figure was silhouetted in the doorway against the sky. "So you have come to destroy me," said a voice that was at the same time silky and sharp.

"No," Tarsia protested. "Not to destroy you. I came to help you."

She looked up into the gray eyes. The Lady was as beautiful as Tarsia's vision: slim, gray-eyed, ashen haired, dressed in a gown as white as a cloud. In her hand, she held on leash four hounds. They were silver in the moonlight and their bodies seemed to shimmer. Their eyes were pools of darkness and Tarsia wondered what the winds of the world thought about. Where would they wander if they were not on leash? The breeze tugged at her hair and she wondered why they needed to be bound.

Tarsia stared into the Lady's eyes and the lady laughed—a sound like icicles breaking in the wind. "I see myself in your eyes, daughter. You have come to help." She reached out and touched the girl's shoulder, pulling the young thief to her. Her hand was cold—Tarsia could feel its chill to her bones.

The wind beat in Tarsia's face as she stood beside the Lady, looking down at the giant and the snowbank, silvered by moonlight. The dragon swooped down to land nearby and the glow of his flames lent a ruddy cast to the snow.

"We are above them, daughter," said the Lady. "We don't need them."

Tarsia did not speak. Looking down, Tarsia saw the piece of chain still dangling from the giant's arm and remembered wondering why he had been bound.

"You are waiting for the coming of the one who will destroy me?" called the Lady. "You will wait forever. Here she stands. My daughter has joined me and we will be stronger together than I was alone. You will be cast back to your prisons."

The dragon raised its fiery wings in a blaze of glory. The giant stood by the gate, broad face set in a scowl. The undine flowed from one ice pillar to another—her body distorted by the strange shapes through which she passed.

"All who have risen against me will be chained," said the Lady.

"That need not be," said Tarsia, her voice small compared to her mother's. Then she called out to the three who waited, "Will you promise never to attack us again? Will you vow to. . . ."

"Daughter, there can be no bargains," said the Lady. "No deals, no vows, no promises. You must learn. Those who betray you must be punished. You have power over them; you cannot bargain with them."

The Lady's voice gained power as she spoke—the cold force of a winter wind. Not angry, it was cold, bitter cold. Like the bitter wind that had wailed around the towers of the city—alone, lonely, proud. Like the gusts that had chilled Tarsia when she slept on the city wall. Like the chill in the dungeon when she was chained and unable to escape.

Tarsia looked at the hounds at her mother's feet: shimmering sleek hounds with eyes of night. Why must they be chained? She looked at the Lady: sculpted of ivory, her hair spun silver in the moonlight.

"Go," Tarsia told the hounds. "Be free." The words left her body like a sigh. And the power that would have been hers, that had been hers for a time, left her with the breath. With her sharp knife and an ease born of a magic she did not understand, she reached out and slashed the leashes that held the hounds. Beneath her, the tower trembled.

The hounds leaped forward, laughing now, tongues lolling over flashing teeth, sleek legs hurling them into the air, smiling hounds looking less like hounds and more like ghosts, like silver sand blown by the wind. The Lady's hair whirled about her. She lifted white arms over her head, reaching out to the faraway moon. Tarsia watched and knew that she would never be so beautiful, never be so powerful, never would the winds heel to her command.

The tower trembled and the scent of sulfur was all around and crystals of snow beat at Tarsia's face. She felt herself lifted—or thrown and caught and tumbled like a coin through the air.

Somehow, someone shut out the moon and stars.

A scent of a charcoal fire—damp dismal smell in the early morning—and . . . damn, she thought. Will I never be free of this? She forced her eyes open.

"You're awake," said the prince. "How do you feel?"

She had been angry, she remembered. And she had been cold with a frozen bitterness. Now she felt only an emptiness where once the power had dwelled within her. She felt empty and light.

She looked back at her mother's castle. A ruin: scorched stones marked with the handprints of the giant, dusted with snow and tumbled by the wind. The ice had crept over the ruin, cracking some stones. Tarsia shivered.

She struggled to her feet and stepped away from the castle, toward the village. Ahead, she could see snow crystals whirling on the surface of a drift. The grass around her feet shifted restlessly in the breeze. She looked at the prince and thought of all the things that she wanted to explain or ask—but she did not speak. The wind flirted with the hem of her skirt and tickled the back of her neck.

"I'll take you with me to my land if you bring the winds along," the prince said. His gaze was steady, regarding her as an equal.

"I can't bring them," she said. "I am not their mistress."

"They will follow," said the prince. "You're their friend."

The breeze helped him wrap his cape around her and the winds made the flowers dance as the prince and the thief rode away from the ruins.

Here, for a change of pace, is a story about a different kind of sorceress; a woman devoted to the healing arts, who faces an unusual challenge to her powers. Anodea Judith has had one story previously published, in the anthology *Greyhaven*, and is a physiotherapist by profession. She is currently working on a nonfiction book.—MZB

# HOUSE IN THE FOREST
## *by Anodea Judith*

The dark shape loomed up out of nowhere. It was not, certainly, what the healer had expected to find, but there was no doubt that this was the source of the distress signal. Subana frowned to herself, shuddered against the cold wind and forced herself onward.

It wasn't as if she had a choice. Ever since taking her healer's vows, four suns ago, she was required—no, compelled—to follow any distress signal she felt. The long arduous training had heightened her sensitivity so that others' pain and sickness entered her own mind—driving her onward until it was healed.

As yet, she had never failed, though she shuddered at the thought of living with some of the ailments she had come across. But then, one could always resort to petitioning the master healers, if one failed—though very few ever did. By the time you reached the point of giving up, there usually wasn't much left of you, and a sick healer was a shame to them all.

But why dwell on negativity? It's certainly no way to approach a healing! Yet even as she forced a smile upon herself, the strange dark house gave her a sense of foreboding she could not ignore. Powerless against a pain far greater than her fear, she forced herself to the doorstep and began her ritual mind cleansing.

"All that is mine, remain behind.
All that is needed shall come unheeded.
All shall be well, all shall be well.
The sun will rise where the shadows fell.
I am but a channel, no part is unprotected,
Balance will return when the evil is rejected."

She let her tension and fear fall to the earth outside the door, visualized the healer's light within her hands and knocked upon the door.

But there was no answer! At least not that her ordinary senses could perceive, though it seemed that the forest itself swayed in answer. The wind stirred in the trees; a twig snapped sharply behind her; an owl hooted in the distance.

But that was all. The house itself remained mysteriously silent. Subana extended her senses for that pulse of life she was trained to know so well. She searched her mind-screen for the spark of fire that flowed through the veins of all living creatures and found . . . nothing. Still the distress signal continued to beckon, and the feeling of pain and helplessness clutched at her belly and shortened her breath with fear.

She entered. She could not do otherwise. She had already left her day-self behind and was now totally bound to the healing.

Slam! The door cracked with unexpected fury. Stung by a fiery tongue of anger, burning within her own mind, she fell to the floor, feeling enclosed, trapped and deeply afraid. Hastily closing her eyes, she muttered the words of the litany she knew so well:

There is no pain, there is no suffering,
There is no fear, there is no death.
There is only mind, there is only heart,
The crystal of truth is the healer's art.

The words echoed in her mind; the rhythms soothed and strengthened her until thoughts of her own peril vanished, and she had, once again, the separation needed to approach her subject—whatever it might be. She opened her eyes and looked around.

It was really too dark to see anything. Instead, the darkness heightened her other senses. In her mind she heard sobbing, moaning, and angry shouting in a strange, but dimly familiar, tongue. She felt aching, loneliness, and confusion. Anger rose within her, granting her strength, and she let her breath sink into it, forcing the strength to rise up within her, like flames of a torch, breathing as if her very life depended upon it, and perhaps it did.

She suddenly realized how dark it was and remembered to light her lantern. The room seemed to jump back as if startled —afraid.

"There, there," she said soothingly, not knowing to whom—or what—she spoke. There was still no answer.

It was a small and very dirty room. One glance told her there was no one here—at least no one that she could see. One wall, looking as if it once contained stained glass panels was smashed, leaving large gaping holes where the wind entered. *No wonder I felt a draft*, Subana said to herself, pulling out her healer's cloak. Though the night was chill, it was hardly as cold outside as it was in here.

Crumpled and torn on the floor lay pieces of cloth. The healer walked over to them, pushed them with her staff and unfolded them. Startled bugs ran in all directions, running away from the light. Subana spread one out on the floor, holding the light closer.

Tapestries! Satin and velvet tapestries! She tried to make out the patterns through the dirt and torn places. A maiden, naked, standing huge in a forest, hands outstretched. Her body was so crumpled it was barely discernible, and it seemed there were red stains on the face and breasts.

Subana's body retched with nausea, but the trembling around her quieted a little. The wailing was now dying into a soft moan, like the sound the wind makes as it dies down after a storm.

She brushed the tapestry and hung it over the broken windows, cutting off some of the cold air. She felt some small sense of relief—because it was warmer, or because the room itself was responding to her care? *Don't be silly*, she thought, but the master's voice floated in her ears: "Anything is possible—especially the unlikely."

A sudden rumbling behind her cut off her thoughts and sent her whirling, knife in hand. There was still nothing to see but a faint glow emanating from the corner of the room—with nothing there to cause it.

*It must be just the light playing tricks*, she thought, and went forward, knife held firm, to investigate.

There was a dusty board in the corner. She flicked it aside, clawing her way through old cobwebs and more startled bugs. Beneath it was a table of sorts, lying on its side, covered with broken pieces of mirror. As she bent over, one of them caught the light, creating a brilliant and startling flash—golden like the morning sun. Was this the source of the strange glow she had seen earlier?

A strange sense of power and fury began to emerge within her. It was a quiet strength, as old as time itself. It filled her and quieted her, heightening all her senses. She thought she heard the sound of breathing around her—or was it the wind? She opened her senses to the raw experience and let her conscious mind retreat. Whatever this was, it was beyond her ability to intellectualize it. She opened further.

"Mother of All Living, where am I?" Her voice reached into the shadows, and the shadows moved. A vision of her own mother came to her, with a shining and happy face as she returned triumphant from her healer's training. "Welcome, daughter," the vision said, but she pushed it away. She was to have left her day-self behind. No place for it here.

She righted the table, brushing off the leaves and dust caked upon its surface. Beneath, it was smooth and cold, and white—or was once. She felt a cry of pain as she touched it, and then within, tears of relief.

She wanted to cry—oh, how she wanted to cry. She felt anger, outrage, burning shame. She felt her sister's hatred from when she was raped. She felt her mother's pain in childbirth. She felt the forest dying, the animals crying for food, huddling in fear, as the world of stone crept ever closer. She fell to her knees, overcome by the grief around her.

*There is no pain, there is no suffering, there is no fear, there is no death.* The litany for a moment calmed her, but with less power than it had before. It was now overshadowed by a new sound.

Laughter. Deep, bitter, cackling laughter. "No death!" it echoed. She was flung flat against the floor, wrestling a monstrous invisible weight upon her chest, forcing her breathing to gasps. She heard the screams of death around her, saw battlefields of wounded, saw earthquakes and forest fires. She heard the cries of the wounded, felt the grief of bereaved parents and children. And then nothing. A nothing quieter than she had ever known. Was this death?

The vision receded. The cackling softened but continued.

"Who are you?" she called into the emptiness when she could find her voice.

Her head was filled with sound. The sound of wind and water, of ocean and flame, of children and animals, of dying and of birth.

The sound retreated. She sat up. A cup rolled to her from the corner. A dirty silver cup, long and slender, engraved with ancient symbols. The table shook, a piece of mirror fell off, and again she saw the blinding light that was sun and fire and moonlight all at once.

Who was trying to speak to her through all of this? What force was behind such unspeakable power?

And then she knew where she was. "Mother of All the Gods!" she cried, falling to her knees. Images of ancient times swam before her—of holy shrines where priestesses worshiped the Great Mother, the spirit of nature, the joyous force of life. She saw images of temples long since destroyed, buried and forgotten—but not dead. Still pulsing with the power of truth, they lay broken, trampled, and crying for help.

Suddenly she understood the language inside her head. It was the language of wind, the language of animals, and a language of great power. The voice of the Goddess enveloped her, taking hold of her mind.

"You have found me, my child. Now you must help me. Help me, for they have come and tried to destroy me. They have taken this place where my children came to worship me. They have taken my children and tortured them for their love of me. No longer do babes suckle at my breast. No longer do the rivers flow clean and clear. They have stolen the land that provides for them, and I am dying. The gods are not immortal—they do die—but slowly and with great pain, for they take all humanity with them. When they die, their children die too!" The unmistakable shriek of the crone echoed in her mind.

"Oh, my Lady, my Goddess, my Queen! I am at your service. I am your child, your daughter, your granddaughter, your servant. And I shall serve you now!"

And she began to clean. She took water from her pack and cleaned the chalice—and it seemed it held the ocean and the rains and all the rivers, and that they were all glad for the cleaning. She placed her lantern in the front, toward the south—for it seemed the right place. The lantern brightened and took on a blue-white flame. The altar glowed with the light of jewels in the moonlight. The forest stirred. The wind quickened.

She worked all through the night without tiring. She found an old twig broom and swept the floor. She brushed out the tapestries and hung them on the walls. She placed fresh fruit upon the altar and burned some cleansing herbs. She sang as she worked. She sang songs of love. She sang old ballads of gallantry and magic. She sang songs of worship for the Lady. And all the while she felt better and better. The aching ceased, the moaning stopped—until it became but a subtle undertone beneath the joy she felt, the constant reminder of the Death Crone to value life. A new joy rose within her, and with it a feeling of wholeness—of kinship with all life.

When morning came, the place had been transformed. As the sun came up, it shone upon the little altar, catching again the mirror set upon it. The light played upon the tapestries, and as she looked, she noticed the picture had changed. The Maiden's body was bulging with the promise of new life, the flesh was clean and healthy. In her hand she held the moon and the stars, and rainbows fell from her hair. And she was smiling—a deep radiant smile.

Subana smiled too, with peace and satisfaction. She felt truly healed inside, as if she had been filled in places that had been empty for lifetimes.

She went to the altar and smiled again, picked up the chalice and scattered a few drops about her. She made the sign of self-protection over the altar and drank deeply of the water.

"Lady, may you ever be whole!"

She looked at herself in the mirror. Another face looked back at her—a face of radiant beauty, everlasting patience, endless love.

"My child," she heard, "may you know that I am always with you."

A final tear slid across Subana's cheek and splashed on the altar.

"Mother, I thank you," she said softly.

She walked out the door into the morning light and birdsong.

Diana Paxson first attracted critical attention with the near-classic "Song of N'Sardi El" in the anthology *Millennial Women*. Since then she has appeared in the anthologies *Hecate's Cauldron* and *Greyhaven*, as well as publishing her first novels, *Lady of Light* and *Lady of Darkness*, with Timescape. Most writers sooner or later write about a series character; Diana has written several stories about Shanna, the warrior princess. The first was "The Dark Mother," in Andy Offutt's collection *Swords Against Darkness*.

Diana said about this story that she did not choose to write it; rather it chose her, the story of how Shanna first found her sword, and the dedication with which she was to fight. She asked herself, "How did Shanna choose to become a warrior?" and this was what happened.

I mentioned in the Introduction the three taboo subjects for the parameters of this anthology, and that each of them was broken exactly once, by a story which grabbed and held me so hard that I chose the story instead of the taboo. Stephen Burns's story "Taking Heart" overcame my reservations about male protagonists; Emma Bull's "The Rending Dark" caused me to overlook the language of science fiction; and my third taboo, explicit rape, was swept away by the power of this story.—MZB

# SWORD OF YRAINE

## by Diana L. Paxson

"What you have been is forgotten—" sang the priestesses, three dark figures formed from shadow, the feminine darkness of the soul.

"What you will be is yet unknown—" their voices echoed and re-echoed from the arching walls of the cavern that men called the Womb of Sharteyn, as if the spirits of all who had ever pledged themselves to the goddesses of the Shrine were joining them.

Shanna shivered, but not from the chill in the air. The weight of stone above her, the weight of years during which this place had been sacred to the people of Sharteyn, the weight of expectation laid on a daughter of the princely house, all oppressed her, and no holy voice spoke to set her free. She pressed her forehead against the time-worn rock of the cavern floor as if she could force it to respond to her.

"Your bodies are the vestures of the Goddess—"

Shanna pushed herself upright, the hard muscles of her fore-arms and shoulders flexing visibly, and sighed. She had built those muscles through patient, painful hours spent lifting the round shield and swinging the wooden practice sword. What goddess had such muscled arms? But even her brother, who had taught her swordplay, would have been shocked if she had asked to dedicate herself to a god.

She shook back her black hair rebelliously. She should be with him now—with him and their father, who was leading his inadequate levies against the rabble of that master of bandits, Kintashe, somewhere beyond the forests that surrounded the Shrine.

"Your spirits are Her secret shrines—" the priestesses sang.

The other girls knelt around her with demurely bowed heads. After a week among them she could catalog them like one of her father's bards—Martiella of the laughing glance who was clearly marked for the service of Ytarre, and her friend Kima, as shy as a quail; plump Talia, who had stood Shanna's friend when the other girls jeered at her lean height and strong arms; Jori, a landowner's daughter devoted to Kera by birth and character; Danilla and Alise and Sirenne. They all knew already which goddesses would claim them, why was it so hard for her?

"Open your hearts and She will surely come to you!"

The chanting faded into a rustling silence as the other girls got to their feet, but Shanna remained still, searching her inner darkness for some Sign.

"My lady Shanna, you must come now!" the sharp voice of the priestess of Kera made a mockery of the respectful words.

Shanna nodded and got smoothly to her feet, forcing herself not to slump. She was uncomfortably aware of their stares—disapproving or bored or amused, like the remote scrutiny of the goddess images enshrined in the walls. Artamise, Hiera the Queen, Hekaite and all the others were worshiped here, even Yraine, Lady of Stars, whose only image was the perpetually burning altar fire. Its fitful light struck fire from golden vessels and canopies of silver filigree, glowed in the hearts of jewels that were the fruit of centuries of tribute to the Shrine.

*And tomorrow I must dedicate my life to one of them,* she thought, *and no one will know it is all a sham but I. . . .*

Sandaled feet slapped softly against the bare stone as the girls followed the priestesses through the maze of passages up to the

House of Maidens outside. Shanna bowed her dark head and followed them, her shadow stabbing ahead of her like a sword.

Shanna was fighting Someone whose face was hidden behind the leather flanges of the practice helm. It did not matter who he was. Only the sword mattered as it blurred toward her, thundering against her little shield. She retreated, crouching so that she could spring when—yes, there was an opening! Her weapon snapped past the enemy blade and *thunk!* the impact jarred her arm as her opponent's shield met it. But already Shanna was swiveling so that her own lifted shield could take his answering blow. *Thwack! Crack!* The rhythmic beat of wood on leather, wood on wood, went on—

And then, abruptly, she was awake. Shanna was lying tangled in her blankets in the dormitory, but still she heard the thunder of wood on wood. There came a rending groan and someone shouted in hoarse triumph. The gate! The stone wall that surrounded the Temple buildings was broken by a stoutly framed gate of mountain oak. Someone must be trying to break in!

Talia stirred and groaned on the pallet next to her. From across the room came sleepy mutterings. "What is it?" called someone faintly. "Who's making all that noise?" Shanna struggled to sort out the sound of men's voices and breaking wood, and the sharp crack which must be the rest of the gate giving way.

"Kintashe!" cried Kima. "The bandits are here and they'll murder us all!"

Shanna's heart thudded painfully. Had Kintashe beaten her father, killed him? A woman screamed harshly and another began to curse. Their attackers must have found the priestesses. Despite her grief Shanna was still trying to decipher the sounds outside. It had never occurred to prince or priesthood that anyone would violate the Shrine.

In moments the invaders would be here. With bitter humor Shanna thought, *Now we will see if the Goddess can take care of Her own!*

Kima was weeping loudly now, drowning out the other sounds. "Be still!" Shanna hissed into the darkness, "Do you want them to hear us?"

The sobs were abruptly stifled, although she could still hear sniffling and an occasional gulp. From outside came coarse laughter and the sound of something heavy being dragged along.

The dormitory door crashed open and Martiella, whose pallet was nearest, tumbled backward with a snapped-off shriek like a

snared bird. Torchlight flared crazily on the whitewashed walls.
The other girls huddled against the wall, clutching their thin
blankets around them, and after a moment's thought Shanna
stifled her pride and imitated them.

*Don't draw attention to yourself—let them think you're a
ninny too!* Surely there was nothing they could do against armed
men, and yet some part of her was already scheming to find a
way—

"So this is what they were protecting!" The torch behind him
set the man's shadow lurching monstrously across the floor. "I
thought they must have the treasury of Sharteyn in here!"

"Something better, this is—" said another voice hungrily.
"Girls!"

Two more men pushed through the door, dragging the priestess of Kera between them. Her skirts were bloodied and Shanna
realized in horror that she had been hamstrung. She fell heavily
to the floor as they released her, then pushed herself up on her
arms, glaring.

"Cursed, you are cursed, and the Goddess will shrivel your
manhood if you touch them. They are noble virgins here for their
pledging, and till that is accomplished, no meat for any man!"

"Sweet meat indeed—" said the hungry voice, "and who
would waste time on an old hen when there are such tender
pullets in the yard?" He lifted his torch and its light flickered
golden across the row of pale faces and staring eyes. Martiella
gasped and pulled her blanket over her face, baring her leg
halfway up the thigh. The man's eyes lingered there a moment
before passing on.

Shanna listened carefully, but there were no more sounds from
outside. She felt a sick certainty that they had killed the other
two priestesses.

"Is this all of you?" the harsh question startled her. This man
was better armed than the others, in a leather vest studded with
plates of dull steel.

"Eight sweet virgins, Capo—" said the man with the hungry
voice. "*Noble* virgins," he mimicked cruelly.

"Our luck," said the leader, "and it's about time. The promises Kintashe made us are rotting with him, but the lords of
Sharteyn will pay well to get their daughters back again!"

Shanna sat back with a sigh. These were the rags of a defeated
army then, not the vanguard of victors. Her father had won.

"Alive, but not, ah—intact. Cap, we'll be the laughingstock
of the taverns if we let them go virgin home!"

"They'll be worth more if we leave them alone—" the man

they called Capo began, but the tall scarred fellow beside him interrupted.

"*If* we ever get the ransom. . . ."

The fourth man was shaking his head. "It doesn't make sense—they don't build walls like that just to guard women. There must be something else here!" The eyes of the others moved from the girls to his face.

Capo nodded. "You thought of that too—"

The priestess of Kera shut her lips obstinately. Suddenly the leader's sword flicked at her throat.

"No—haven't you done enough to her?" cried Talia. "Leave her alone!"

The bright sword swung toward Talia's breast. Shanna tensed to spring to her defense and forced herself to be still.

"Well?" Capo's eyes were still on the priestess. "Would you rather I used this on *her*?"

The older woman swallowed. "Take oath that you will spare the maidens—"

"We'll spare their *lives* . . ." he said agreeably, and the other men laughed. "I swear it," he smiled, "by Toyu's holy spear!"

"There's gold in the hidden Shrine," the priestess said dully. "But the caverns are forbidden to men. You will find only death if you dare enter the Womb of Sharteyn."

There was a moment's silence as the men thought of the wombs that had given them birth and the graves that would gape for them some day. *Some day soon!* thought Shanna viciously, for already they were relearning their smiles. *They will take the gold. Will the goddesses punish them for the defilement, or will they take vengeance instead on all Sharteyn?*

Talia had sagged back against the wall, shaking, and Shanna inched closer to her and took her hand.

"Well, now—" Capo said at last. "I think we have a little exploring to do. Laxo, I'll want you to scout around and make sure nobody's coming to surprise us—" The scarred man nodded. "And Merig and Ven, I want you—"

"Aw, Capo, can't we stay and guard the girls?" asked the big man.

"Wouldn't want them to sneak off and get help, would you?" The leader sighed. "I can see you'll be no use to me until you've spent your loads. Stay here then, but use them one at a time, while the one who's not busy stands guard."

"And you, Ven—" said the scarred man, pausing in the doorway. "You leave some of them unopened for me!"

The room was very silent when Capo and Laxo were gone.

Ven and Merig looked over the girls like foxes surveying a hencoop, their grins broadening. Shanna felt a sour satisfaction as their eyes passed over her, knowing that while there were girls like Martiella available they would have little interest in *her*. The priestess had collapsed into semi-consciousness. Talia and Jori bent over her, trying to bind her wounds.

"All right—*you*!" Ven bent and ripped Martiella's blanket away. The girl shrank back, shaking her head, and he swore and patted his dagger. "Don't be stupid, girl—do you want to lose your beauty as well as your maidenhead?"

Slowly, Martiella got to her feet. Ven yanked open her sleeping shift, swallowing audibly as he saw the perfection of her tilted breasts and her swelling thighs. Martiella was still numbly shaking her head, but Kima shrieked as he pulled her friend against him and began to kiss her brutally. He let her go with another oath as Kima's screaming went on.

"Can't a man do his business in peace? Look, Merig—you can manage this lot while I take the hen into the other room. Then I'll come back and you can have your turn."

There was a flutter of sobbing as the door closed behind them, and Shanna felt a remote sympathy. These girls all expected to be married soon, and most of them were realistic enough not to expect husbands who would be the romantic figures of their dreams. But they would at least have been married with honor, and who would want them now after they had been soiled by such as these?

"All right, my little birds—" Merig settled onto the bench beside the door. "It's your choice whether you get stuck by a cock or a sword, and the first will be more fun for everybody, so you sit still! Don't worry, there are enough of us to go around!" His grin displayed a row of broken teeth like the stones of a shattered tower.

The muffled pleading from the other room swelled to a scream. It was followed by another, abruptly stilled. *Poor Martiella*, thought Shanna, *but at least she is alive. For now. . . . If these bastards can loot the Shrine, why should they bother with the tricky business of ransoming us?* She supposed that was why the leader had let Ven and Merig have their way. Once the men had the gold, they might abandon the girls or carry them off, but it was more likely they would kill them as they had the priestesses, for surely the vengeance of the Temples would follow them if anyone was left alive to identify them.

*Yes, we will all die . . .* she told herself, and felt a curious quiver just beneath her ribs, like the tremor one feels at the turn of some tragic tale. *And will that be the answer to all my questioning?* And the end to all striving, the excuse for every failure. . . .

What could she do about their situation in any case? There were four armed men, and nothing that could serve as a weapon in the room. If the girls acted together they might be able to overwhelm one man, but some of them would get hurt. Shanna looked at the girls cowering in their thin blankets or staring at the man with fascinated eyes. *No help from this lot, not with this man.*

Merig was watching them with an anticipatory smile, like a trader at a fair. Picking out his pullet, thought Shanna. And afterward? Having disposed of the girls they would take the gold, and what would the despoiled goddesses do to the land that had failed to protect their Shrine? The gods were sufficiently unpredictable even when all their ceremonies were correctly performed.

For a moment Shanna seemed to see Sharteyn's barley fields blighted, carrion birds busy in her pastures, and a red tide staining the sparkling sea. A deeper kind of horror twisted in her belly then, and she remembered that she was the Daughter of Sharteyn. Perhaps there was no way to save the Shrine, but she must try at least.

The muscles in her buttocks tensed and she began to pull her feet under her.

There was a step in the corridor. The door opened and Martiella stumbled in. Ven gave her a push and she collapsed into Kima's arms. There were bloodstains on the back of her white gown. As she lay, shuddering soundlessly, Ven sat down in Merig's place, looking around him with a satiated grin.

Merig had already taken one swift step forward and grabbed Talia by one arm. The girl's normally high color was all gone, and for a moment her eyes met Shanna's, then she nodded and allowed herself to be hauled from the room.

Shanna forced herself not to hear what was going on in the other room. *I won't waste the time you are buying for us now— Ven has gone a long time sleepless, and now that he's had a woman he'll be relaxed. He's the one to go for, soon—soon. . . .*

She watched him beneath her lashes while he shifted position until he was comfortable and gradually stilled. She eased over to Jori and the other girls who were tending the priestess as if to help.

"I'm going to try to take out our guard as soon as he's a little more relaxed," she whispered. "Tie him with the cords of your robes once I've got him down."

"You're crazy!"

"Do you all want to end up like Marti and Talia, or worse? With him out of the way, we can ambush the other one and maybe get away before that Capo returns."

The girls were gazing at her wide-eyed, but the priestess murmured a blessing. Would they help her? She fought the temptation to creep back to her pallet, and taking a deep breath, eased slowly across the room. She was a body's length away from him, an arm's—Ven looked up at her, his eyes assessing her body before he thought to wonder what she was doing there. Then he wrenched his sword free and swung it toward her. She leaped backward and faced him, half-crouching.

"Well, my pretty, so you just couldn't wait? Wouldn't you rather feel my other weapon? You're a skinny wench, but you might provide some sport. That's a good girl, go on back to your blankets now— I won't make you wait too long!" He was smiling, beginning to straighten as he assumed her compliance, and Shanna felt herself flushing.

But his sword was still ready. Now that she had lost surprise, to reach him she must face its point or edge. If they all rushed him at once, perhaps—but peripheral vision showed her the other girls transfixed and staring. They had seen Martiella's shift stained with blood, but the unknown ravages of a sword scared them more.

Shanna's eyes returned to the blade, like a sword of fire in the torchlight—the steel blade of a warrior that she had never yet held in her hand. But she had seen enough swords to know that this was a good one. She wondered what great warrior's body he had taken it from. It would cut cleanly; there would be pain like a bright blossom in the mind, and then—the embrace of the Goddess, or nothing, depending on whose beliefs were true.

There was an integrity to that steel that transcended the wretchedness of the lout who bore it. *He should not have it . . . he cannot understand its soul*, thought Shanna as Ven moved and light rippled along the blade. She remembered the flicker of flame on water, and the frosty glitter of the stars. She took a deep breath, then another, willing the thudding of her heart to slow. *If he believes I am not afraid he will not know what to do . . .*

"Will you kill me?" she asked softly. "But what if that is what I want? And what will your Capo do if he finds only seven girls to ransom when he returns?" She stepped forward and he brought the sword around, but she was already moving in the other direction, advancing and retreating before him as if the sword and its prey were partners in some fatal dance. She moved smoothly, her grace disguising her increasing speed. Half-mesmerized, Van followed her movements until Shanna sensed that she had begun to control the rhythm of their interaction, not he.

*Ah, Goddess, if any goddess will hear me now—help me!* Something in the core of her being grew very still, as if from afar she heard a crystal bell.

For a moment Shanna paused, confusing the man, then she leaped toward the bright blade like a bride running to her beloved. It touched her; she turned so that its flat seared across her belly and then her momentum bore him down.

"Jori! Now!" she called to the girl who had been helping the priestess, for her weight could not hold him long. Ven grunted and started to shout. Shanna jammed her left forearm between his teeth, feeling the pressure as they clamped down, but no pain, not yet. Then Jori and Danilla were sitting on his feet, fumbling with their waistcords. They grabbed his wrists. Shanna jabbed the fingers of her free hand down on Ven's eyeballs to distract him, then tore her arm free while Jori jammed cloth into his mouth for a gag.

Shanna sat back, chest heaving. The madness of the fight still buffered her pain as she struggled with the realization that she had won, that the Goddess had indeed answered her prayer.

Ven twisted and glared at her over the gag, but the other girls were swarming over him, and he was not so much bound as swaddled in strips of cloth. *We'll need some of those strips to secure the other men—* Shanna realized that she was assuming they would be able to. So were the other girls. She met their eager glances and knew that they *expected* her to save them now.

"Hush!" she got to her feet. "That other one—that Merig—may be occupied with poor Talia now, but he'll finish his business soon enough if he hears us squawking. Pull this trash into the corner and get back to your beds—" she continued to direct them, listening for any sound from outside.

Waiting, it seemed as if Merig and his victim had been gone a long time. It would have been helpful if Talia had the presence of mind to grab the man's dagger and stab him while he was on top of her, but Shanna knew she should be grateful to her friend for keeping the fellow occupied so long. But now she heard a laugh and then suppressed sobbing. Heart pounding, Shanna gripped Ven's sword and took up her position beside the door.

It creaked open. Merig pushed Talia ahead of him into the room. The other girls burst into a cacophony of wailing; he stopped and stared, and in that moment Shanna sliced across the backs of his knees in the same stroke that had hamstrung the priestess of Kera not so long before.

He crumpled with a yell. Shanna froze, waiting for the pounding of feet in the corridor. But there was nothing. If Capo or the other man had heard they were probably laughing at the fuss some girls made over a lost maidenhead. The other girls knew their business now, and soon Merig was trussed even more effectively than his companion.

Talia stared at Shanna, wonder momentarily overcoming her pain. Then she began to tremble, and as she sank down on her pallet the other girls crowded around her, whispering eagerly.

But Shanna remained where she was. Carefully she wiped the sword on the skirts of her shift, then hefted it, brought it down and around again. Its weight and balance were not so different from her wooden practice sword, but no wooden blade ever sang so sweetly through the air, and wood did not quiver like a live thing in the hand. *Steel!* she thought exultantly. She lifted the blade into First Guard, for a moment almost forgetting where she was and how it had come to her. Her trained muscles flexed to propel her into the stylized sequence of the sword dance.

"Shanna!" Jori's cry jolted her back from that still place where she and the sword were one. "The others will come soon. What should we do now?"

Shanna glanced at the window. The stars were paling. Soon would come that threshold hour when even shadows grew dim. She thought for a moment.

"Jori—you must lead the others out by the side gate. If you can reach the forest by dawn they'll have a hard time catching you even if they do know where you have gone. Head south— there are farms that way, and they can send messengers to Sharteyn."

"But the priestess can't walk, and what about you?"

"Go on—" the older woman spoke hoarsely. "There is nothing you can do for me! The sooner you get help the sooner they can send a chirugeon to me here."

Shanna gestured impatiently. "Why do you think I want you to lead them? I must stay here and try to defend the Shrine. I'll do it better if I know you are free. . . ."

Talia was on her feet already, her high color beginning to return. She pushed Danilla toward the door and turned to Shanna. "Thank you, my sister!"

Shanna nodded abruptly, unable to reply. If only she had acted sooner and spared Talia this pain! But the other girl was a survivor. Talia would be all right in time.

She was not so sure about Martiella. She had wanted to give herself to the Lady of Love, and had been claimed by the Lord of Lust instead. Now she lay rigid in her blankets, staring at something no one else could see. Neither Jori nor Kima could move her, and after a few moments Jori shook her head.

"We'll have to leave her here—" she said unhappily.

"Yes—but go on now, there's not much time!" Shanna danced with anxiety. She followed until Jori and the others were through the door, watched the pale figures flit across the courtyard, watched until the side gate shut behind them and they were gone.

She stood still a moment, breathing the fresh damp air of early dawn and willing her thudding heartbeat to slow. Then she heard a muffled groan from the dormitory. She ran back down the corridor. Had one of the bound men gotten free?

When she reached the doorway Martiella was bending over the man Ven. Blood glistened in the torchlight. Then Martiella sat back, smiling dreadfully. In one hand she held the knife they had taken from the man's belt and in her other, a mass of flesh that dripped bloodily.

Martiella spoke for the first time since Ven had thrust her back into the room. "See. I have saved you. He won't do that to any woman ever again . . ." Nodding, she showed Shanna what was in her hand.

Shanna tasted bile and the sword twitched in her hand as if she had seen some monster in her path. In another moment she would strike. She backed away, staring. It was Martiella's right, surely— Shanna had not been raped; she could not judge the other girl. But as she reached the corridor nausea overcame her and she retched painfully. Her feet bore her away from the bloody room.

*Goddess!* she thought, *We are as bad as the men! Goddess of Sharteyn, what will I do?*

She stopped then, and saw that her steps had carried her to the door to the Shrine, and it was open.

The leader of the bandits must have found it. The great doors could be fastened only from the inside, so she could not shut him in. Her duty became painfully clear. She would have to go after him before he could finish stripping the Shrine and bear his loot away; she would have to deal with him before the fourth man, Laxo, finished his scouting outside.

Carefully, Shanna threaded her way among the passages that

led down to the caves. Originally they had been natural fissures in the rock, but through the centuries they had been smoothed and widened by women's hands. How many centuries? No one in Sharteyn now knew, though the caverns had been sacred before the Katyan Empire overshadowed the northern lands. Curiously, the thought of the Shrine's antiquity steadied her, as if the evanescence of her fears made them irrelevant.

She found the man Capo as he was about to start upward again, dragging his treasure behind him on a length of tapestry. When he saw who was facing him he grinned and lowered his sword.

"Did Ven send you after me? Is something wrong?"

Shanna stared at him, realizing he did not know she was armed. Perhaps she could surprise him after all. Her skirts flapped around her legs as she settled into a guard, and she hitched at them in annoyance—she had always practiced in a short tunic at home. But she had used her waist cord to tie up Merig, and she had no way to kilt it up now. But she could not fight anyone this way! Frantically she tugged at the drawstring until the garment slithered off her shoulders and pooled around her feet. Capo's eyes widened as she stepped free.

"They must be having quite a party up there! And they sent you down to get me?" one bushy eyebrow quirked. "You're on the skinny side, but not bad—"

Shanna wrapped the shift around her left arm with a quick swirl. As she stepped forward he saw the sword.

"Crazy hen!" he murmured, but his eyes were still smiling as he drew his own blade.

The reinforced jerkin protected Capo's upper body from anything but a really strong thrust, and he was heavily muscled, obviously a veteran of everything from pitched battles to tavern brawls. Shanna's training had covered sword-to-sword combat as well as sword and shield, but what chance did she have against such a man? She read in his face the marks of lost sleep and hard riding—perhaps fatigue would slow him down. Goddess! she would have to be swift, and sure!

Shanna bit her lip in concentration. *Pretend this is just another practice bout!* She tried to will away the disorienting awareness of her nakedness, of his eyes upon her, of the flat stares of the goddesses on the walls. *Strike quickly, while he is still laughing at you!*

She took a deep breath and leaped forward like a stooping hawk. Her blade slithered past his, slicing the skin of his neck as he hurled himself to one side. The wind of his return blow fanned her ribs as she recoiled. His eyes were narrowed in a face that was red with anger now, and she thought that he was not seeing her as a woman anymore, only as a body attached to a blade—as an enemy.

Again she lunged. The paired blades clashed and only a quick twist of her arm kept her own sword in her hand. Now Capo was attacking; Shanna gasped as her swathed arm took a glancing blow and the torn flesh where Ven had bitten her throbbed sickly. *Careful!* the thought passed in the moment before he came at her again, *That's not a shield!*

Her chest heaved as he forced her around the altar, seeking to back her into one of the grottoes where her supple speed could not be used. Firelight gleamed from her sweat-moistened skin, turned the man's harsh features into a devil-mask. Capo moved more slowly, knowing he had her on the defensive now.

"You've done well, girl, but why fight me? This isn't the weapon I want to sheathe in that white body of yours!" He waved his sword suggestively and grinned. "Come now— surrender!"

Shanna stood, trying to catch her breath, shaking her head. "Is that all you think a woman's for? I don't surrender. I'm the Daughter of Sharteyn!"

"The old fighting blood—I should have known." He nodded slowly. "Well, I've another notion then. You like to fight? Then join me—with this treasure for a start, we could carve out a kingdom! What kind of life can you expect otherwise? You are a falcon among hens! Come—" he held out his hand.

He looked younger, almost handsome, when he smiled. Could he be telling the truth? Even if she defeated him, what would they think of her in Sharteyn? She would be a female freak with a sword. She looked desperately around her, seeking an answer in the painted goddess faces that looked down at them. *Their* treasure, she thought. *If I take it, will they really care?*

A chill wind sighed through the cavern and she shivered. She blinked as the altar fire blazed high. The fire of Yraine. . . . Perhaps the other goddesses were wood and stone, but Yraine lived in the holy fire. Where could Shanna journey that the stars did not see? What tribe of men did not use fire?

"I cannot," she said aloud at last.

Capo sighed, brought up his blade and advanced on her again. The alteration in his stance told her he meant to finish this quickly now.

*Goddess!* Shanna's spirit cried, *I have kept faith with you! At least let me die well!*

That was her answer. She understood it as her own blade lifted steadily. Death was the truth of the sword; death was the bridegroom who would have her maidenhead.

The air burned her bare skin. Fire burned in her enemy's eyes. Time slowed; she could think even as her body moved, *As this is my first battle and my last let it be perfect; Goddess, may this be my sacrifice to you!*

The blades kissed and parted. As Shanna leaped past, Capo's steel seared her side. But she had space to move now. The air was luminous, the faces of the goddesses glowed. *Steady, steady,* Shanna told herself, seeking the perfect inner balance, the core of stillness from which all action must flow.

She glimpsed the overhand cut flashing down at her, but there was ample time for her to shift her own guarding blade so that his slid along it away from her; abruptly she released the pressure, momentarily unbalancing him. She swooped in; with a jerk he recovered, his sword whipped around with all his weight behind it and Shanna leaped backward again. Every nerve and muscle was at full stretch now, body and being joined in ultimate harmony.

This was the rhythm! Advance and retreat and around again as the stars circled the heavens and the fire leaped and fell. Now Shanna felt the meaning of the sword dance she had practiced so long. Her senses encompassed her enemy—he was part of her as she was part of the burning air, the fire, the stone on which she danced, her sword. . . .

The weapon's own momentum brought it up, the blades clashed; for a moment the opponents strained breast to breast, and Shanna laughed. Then in a single motion they sprang apart, but Shanna knew it when Capo began his lunge, knew the path of his blade, knew the exact adjustment her own must make to deflect his blow. This was the unity she had never known with other women, this the ecstasy she had longed for when she dreamed of love!

Now she saw neither the man's face nor the cavern around her. Eyes like two stars filled her vision, eyes whose light expanded until Shanna saw nothing at all.

From some other universe a harsh voice cried—"Capo, Capo, the girls are gone!" The other man had come back.

From deep within, words like struck crystal sounded, *"Daughter, the time is Now!"*

The end. The final movement in the Dance.

Poised, Shanna extended her blade, smiling, turning sideways, her other arm flung wide as her opponent moved into her embrace, the perfection of her balance holding her even as their bodies came together and were one.

"Capo-o-oo!"

Shanna's widened eyes barely focused on the scarred man, Laxo, who stood at the entrance to the cavern, his face twisting as he watched them.

A falling sword clanged on stone.

Shanna stared at the contorted face so close to her own, its mouth curled in a parody of a kiss. Uncomprehending, she watched the fire in his eyes dim; then his weight sagged against her, the metal plates on his jerkin scraped her breast and he slid away from her, his body pulling slowly free from the sword that had impaled it until it lay at her feet and was still.

Laxo, still hovering at the cavern-mouth, saw her standing above his leader with a bloody sword in her hand like a naked goddess of vengeance, and turned to run back up the passageway out of the Shrine.

But Shanna remained where she was, staring down at the body while her racing pulse slowed and the glory ebbed away.

"I have killed a man. . . ." She flogged her numbed brain to articulate the understanding. "I am a woman who can kill."

No good to say that women did not slay with the sword. She had done it, and she knew that if there was need she could do it again. And something more—she knew that there would be a return of the craving, not to take life, but to experience that moment of union with an enemy when life and death are one.

The Goddess had spoken to her at that moment, as She never had before. Unsteady with reaction, Shanna stumbled to the altar of Fire and carefully balanced her sword on its stone rim.

"Goddess, hear me!" Shanna laid her palms flat upon the bloody blade. "I do not know what You want with me, but You have claimed me—so You take my pledge, now!" She drew a harsh breath, her lips moved in the sword oath. She had heard her brother and others swear these words, and had never known she had memorized it until now.

"Before the Lady of Stars and by Her Holy Fire I swear—I will never be false to the Truth that is within me; I will deal justice to my enemies and keep faith with my friends! And if ever I dishonor lord or kindred or the blade I bear, may it turn against me and may my ghost forever wander without comfort in the dark!" She fought for breath. She was trembling, and it was hard to make her lips obey.

"Yraine, I pledge myself to You! Lady of Wisdom, I am Your sword to spare or to slay!" Shanna's shout rang against the arched stonework of the cavern, and the wind of some great Presence passing sighed around her and made the holy fire blaze high. Then the fire resumed its steady flickering and Shanna was alone.

But not quite alone. Carefully she wiped the sword clean on the rags of her shift and then, grasping it firmly, strode up the dark passage toward day.

Michael Ward said, when he first submitted this story, that he had no doubt I would soon be surfeited by stories of the usual Amazon taking cities and pitting her strength against men. He was right; far too many stories I received were about what I soon came to call "your generic barbarian sorceress" or even "Conan in drag." Instead, he sent me what he called a "Tall Tale."

Mike said of himself that he shares a birthday "with John Cheever, Dashiell Hammett, and, I am given to understand, Harlan Ellison." He didn't say so, but maybe there's something in astrology after all? He has sold a couple of science fiction pieces, but this is his first fantasy tale, "Not counting a surrealistic romp through an utterly literary magazine," which not only didn't pay him but made him buy his own copy of the magazine. That'll serve him right for trying to be literary, say I!

He is "divorced, childless, and trying my level best to have fun living in Baton Rouge," where he works at winning creative awards for an advertising agency.

Like all good Tall Tales, this one begins in a tavern, with our warrior woman cadging drinks by telling about the one that got away—only this time the survivor was herself. I have heard that there are some really weird types in those singles bars, and that a common name for them is "trolls"—but this is ridiculous. And wonderfully so. So here, just to tickle your funnybone. . . .—MZB


# DATON AND THE DEAD THINGS
## by Michael Ward


Legend has it that a cyclops is not a creature of great intelligence, and the one of my own acquaintance was certainly no exception.

Attend, and I'll tell the tale. But first, let me say—and you know me as a woman who loves a tale's telling as much as anyone loves the hearing—that a throat, my friends, is like a scabbard; properly oiled, it permits the blade more ease and readiness in the draw, and thus begets quicker and more incisive application to the play. . . .

Now, I say with ease and readiness, I encountered the creature, whose name I would learn was Daton, in the dead city, five days' ride west of the town called Rodent's Head. I had been stranded in Rodent's Head after what *I* had considered to be a minor controversy with my traveling companion. In the middle of the night he had abandoned me. But not, unfortunately, our funds or provisions.

Rodent's Head is in the best of times an unpleasant place, peopled with inbred cretins of crude appearance and distasteful habits. Now penniless and without the sanctuary of a like mind's company, I felt myself in danger of becoming infected by the town's flatulence of the spirit. And while I had, upon a time, experimented with this variety of degeneracy, it had proved thoroughly disagreeable. I was, therefore, of a two-fold purpose: escape from Rodent's Head, and track down the chitin-headed fool who had left me there.

A witness had seen him quitting town to the west.

To secure a pair of horses, one for mount, one for pack, was but the work of a few moments. This town, like most towns, was owned by men, and as you know, men seldom take notice of the real doings of women. My larder took longer to acquire—it did not walk under its own power.

I packed and mounted and rode west, quickly leaving low, gray Rodent's Head behind. There had not been a fresco, not a mosaic, not a bright tapestry in the entire town. To eyes that had, then, become hungry for color, the dawn's bloom behind me illuminated the scrubland before with a refreshing splendor. Glad to be a-move, I chose to break fast without breaking pace and consumed a few raw eggs and a brandy or two. I experienced an exhilarating sensation—as I often have, setting out on a journey—of riding forward into my future and my fate.

As the sun rose, however, the land's splendor and my own exhilaration diminished even faster than my shadow. I was breathing hard and beaded with sweat long before noon. And by the time I stopped to lunch and rest I was soaked. Riding into the afternoon sun, head lowered against blindness, wrapped against delirium, I watched the land change from scrubgrass to outright desert. There is, in point of fact, little but desert for hundreds of miles west of Rodent's Head, lending the impression that the town itself does not end, only the shelter, food and water.

How to summarize five days and nights in the desert? The hardship. The fantasies and illusions. Suffice it to say that I endured and in my own way prevailed. I traveled on. I found occasional traces of my former confederate's passage and followed them. After those five days, I came to the end of his journey.

The dead city sits steeped in a desolation and quietude that transcends even the surrounding desert. It evokes a sense of bleached death far beyond buzzards and flies. In their day, these huge constructions of carved stone must have stood as an awesome and magnificent emblem of human achievement; now they awesomely and magnificently emblemized something quite different.

Hoofprints led to a breach in the wall. Evidently my friend had thought to camp within. I followed.

And paused within the breach—I must confess—agape. Over the years, sand had piled against the wall, so that the vantage from which I now beheld the city's interior was at about third-story height. And the interior that I beheld was a space in which a migrating bird might have gotten lost—as my own gaze quickly became lost. It was a vertical as well as a horizontal labyrinth of towering buildings and buttresses and bridges, of suspended roads and paths, of projecting balconies.

I found the footprints again and followed them down the sandspill to the roof of a two-story building, then through an archway at one end. I left my horses on that roof, tethered to a gargoyle, and walked quietly through the arch. If my former companion was indeed still here—and I had seen no tracks leading out—then I wished to confront him with his blade and his wit still in the scabbards. Which reminds me. . . .

Well, Sword and wit at the ready, I walked down the hall on the other side of that arch quietly as a girl past her sleeping father's door. And my caution was rewarded. I caught a reek, from another arch just ahead and to my right, of a fire and roasted meat. After five days of traveler's fare, this sweet scent proved nearly the equal of revenge in incentive. I approached the arch along the wall, out of sight from within, paused at the arch's center.

The remark I had readied withered in my throat.

The first thing I saw in that room was a horse, hung up by its hind legs, throat cut, blood draining into a huge basin beneath the unfortunate beast.

The next thing I saw was a large spit, skewering a mostly eaten carcass of something big, over a nearly dead fire. I took a step toward the aroma.

And noticed my third thing: that carcass had been human.

I investigated more closely. Turning the spit to expose the face told me nothing; it was too well cooked. Turning the spit a bit more, though, did. My fated friend had affected a golden stud, in the shape of a pentacle, in his left ear. In the carcass's well-browned ear I found it.

Strange end. I would not presume to say it was deserved, but strange, yes, one may at least say that.

I recall closing my eyes for a moment, hearing the rumble of my stomach. And I realized, in that moment, that countering this rumble was nothing more substantial than argument.

My friend had never, in life, served me quite as well as I now served him.

One side of the room, in time past, had crumbled, leaving the floor to end in a precipice. As I wiped my hands on my breeches, I heard a sound from down there, as of stones crushed under an absurdly heavy step. I drew my sword and slowly went to investigate.

When I was perhaps ten paces from the lip, a creature of vaguely human association poked his head up and looked at me.

With his one eye.

Chin resting on the edge of the floor, the head's crown came up to about my knee's height. That solitary eye was not—contrary to common description—situated in the face's center. It was placed to one side—the creature's left—as common distribution would have it. And where such distribution predicted a second, and there was none, the face and side of the head was caved in and puckered, as if the face had been born expecting a second orb and had, then, collapsed in disappointment.

The creature opened his mouth, displaying some very impressive yellow-brown teeth, and spoke. "What manner of thing be you?" His voice was, to understate, large and low pitched.

"Human," I said evenly, on which I prided myself.

The creature placed a great hand on the floor's edge. And brought up another hand, on his other side, followed by a loglike forearm. Splay-fingered, the hand fell as the elbow rose. He vaulted himself up, and the floor shook.

His full height bettered mine by no less than twice—which, as you can observe, made him tall indeed. His complete nakedness made apparent his complete lack of hair. He was thin—speaking, of course, relatively—and his knotlike knees were greater in diameter than his legs, as were his elbows than his arms. His belly strained toward his spine, as did the flesh between his ribs. From a cord about his neck hung a sheathed short-sword which would have seemed a dagger in his hand. He squatted before me—the ceiling was too low for him to stand fully erect—and his genitals hung to the floor. Squatting, his height was just a bit more than mine. He said, "But what *manner* of thing be you? A dead thing? Or live?"

I had a sudden intuition that my former friend had answered this question incorrectly. I became, then, understandably cautious. "What about you?" I asked. "What manner be you?"

"A dead thing."

"As am I!" I said with great disingenuousness. All women early learn disingenuousness. Unlearning it is the problem.

"Long dead?"

"Oh, very."

"I am sad. She who weaned me said it is not good to eat long dead things. But not too sad for I have finally eaten, today, and I have a horse to eat, too, if I do not wait until it is long dead."

"I am very happy you've finally eaten," I told the creature. "And she who weaned you must have been very wise. And I have been delighted with our conversation. But now, I fear, I am engaged elsewhere and must go." I began backing toward the arch.

Without rising from his squat, and with an astounding burst of speed, the creature ran, arms, legs and genitals flailing. He brushed past me and blocked the arch, sending chips of stone flying when he carommed against the edge.

I curbed my astonishment at this display and took a deep breath, steadying myself for the fight I hoped to avoid. "Let me pass," I said.

"I must put you where I keep the other dead things."

I drew my blade.

"She who weaned me said there must be a place for everything." He reached for me. "And everything must be in its place."

I lunged, and my point glanced off a rib. I was next aware, for the briefest of moments, of a blurred and fumbling confusion of clublike limbs. My bruised awareness after that was of my entrapment: one of the creature's great, bony hands was wrapped about my own hand and sword hilt and wrist. His other hand was wrapped about my leg at the knee. After a few spasms of fruitless struggle I relaxed within his grip and awaited an opportunity for constructive action.

He flung me over his shoulders as if I were a cape—with much the same sensation, for me, as being flung onto a woodpile. He held my arm and leg in front of him. My face was pressed into his armpit, which was rank even to a woman who had just spent five days in the desert.

I turned my face away and had begun to think it would

behoove me to better know my foe, when he jumped off the broken edge of the floor, into the room below.

When the fog in my head had cleared—if not the pain in my hip and shoulder—I resolved to pursue my acquaintance of the creature. "By what name are you known?" I asked him.

"Daton," he replied as he carried me like a sack of turnips. Long dead turnips.

"A fine name: Daton. And a fine specimen of a . . . you are. How is it, Daton, that you know yourself to be a dead thing?"

"She who weaned me said I should not eat myself. If I be not good to eat, then I must be a long dead thing."

"That's very logical," I said. "Tell me, where is she who weaned you?"

"I ate her."

"I see. She was alive."

"Yes," he said.

After this he declined to respond to my questions, remarking that I spoke a great deal for a thing long dead, and I judged it best to desist. He carried me along a hallway with skylights cut at intervals into the ceiling, then down a flight of steps—an interesting experience in light of our respective postures—along a shorter hall, and finally through a doorway to outside. He dumped me on the ground and pried the sword from my hand.

As I tried to ease and limber my bruised and wrenched self, I saw that I was not truly outside, but was, rather, in a kind of large courtyard. A courtyard with but one exit. (My preoccupation, then, was understandably more with exits than entrances.) "This," said Daton, "is where I keep the dead things." His statement was evident. A great many dead things, of various types and in varying stages of mummification—a reason, finally to be grateful for that desert sun—lay piled about the doorway. Daton went back through the door.

But before he was gone from sight, I spied something of great interest.

The creature, Daton, removed from a wall niche just outside the door a container of shape cylindrical, of diameter equal to height, and of a volume, perhaps, that would hold two wineskins. Daton handled this container with great care and obvious affection. He unfastened the top with a strange gesture I can only describe as a twisting or wringing, looked within, closed the top with a similar gesture, and after a parting caress or two, returned the container to its niche. I was unable to perceive the contents, though he treated the container as if it held his testicles.

But the container itself. That, I had no doubt, was gold.

I resolved, then, that when I escaped this creature, I would do so with more than he had captured when he captured me.

I went to the doorway, peered around the edge.

The short hallway went straight to a rising flight of stairs. At the foot of those stairs lay Daton, curled up like a dog. And like a dog, he lifted his head and looked at me.

I decided to explore my prison.

Or perhaps, I thought, *ossuary* would be more apt.

I discovered other dead things living there.

They numbered half a dozen, and they made the inhabitants of Rodent's Head seem quite charming. They were as wasted and withered as Daton, himself—though, unlike him, their humanity could not be denied. They subsisted on what they could catch—an occasional reptile or insect—on a meager garden which they fertilized with their own meager excretions, watered with a hand pump which sporadically spat a brown and gritty broth, and on the few not too long dead things thrown in by Daton. Not one of the six had any idea how long he or she had been there. One of them told me, "Of what consequence is time when one is dead?"

I spoke with this one further, as she seemed—either by virtue of greater strength or simply more recent arrival—more in possession of her faculties than the rest. "How is it," I asked her, as we crouched near one another in the deepening twilight, "that you have not escaped? Granted, Daton is large. And granted, he is fast in his own furious and fumbling way. But surely he is no match for six."

"Of what consequence is escape when one is dead?" she replied.

It was then that I realized that her manner of speech was neither archness nor bitter metaphor; these people had actually come to believe their once expedient lie. They had come to love that which they had embraced.

"Later," I told her, "when we are fully in night's belly and I am sure Daton sleeps, I shall slip past him and be gone. You may come with me, or remain here awaiting putrefaction, as you choose."

She simply recommended I be quiet as a shadow. Daton's ears, she explained, apprehended anything louder.

I took this piece of information to heart and removed my boots. Using the long strip of cloth with which I had turbaned my head, I bound them tightly together, then to my back so they would be in no way an interference. This absorbed a few minutes. And left a few hours. Killing time has never been one of my defter abilities, due, I believe, to my rather keen awareness that it is actually time that kills us. I decided, therefore, to use this time as well as I could, and asked my acquaintance, first, if Daton never in the course of foraging left the passage to our courtyard unguarded. She explained that he had no need; the only passage into the city was the same breach through which I and my consumed companion had come. That passage, then, was the best place to apprehend wandering live things. I next asked what she knew of Daton's golden container.

In that container, she told me, was Daton's other eye.

Like all of his kind, it would seem, when Daton was born, his other eye was delivered separately. He had kept the eye always near him—not purely for reasons of sentiment. If one were to take a sip of water in which that eye had been steeped, said my companion of the crypt, one would develop for a brief time the ability to see that which one had previously overlooked. Of course I found this interesting indeed. Any vehicle of magical or mystical power would make its container—even gold—of a value inconsequential. Excitement filled me. Such a prize would make the whole adventure, which until now had been of a rather dull character, worthwhile and more.

Eventually I knew—as one knows, by the fit, one's own boot from another's—the time had come to move.

Near to the door—which I could see thanks to that exceptional desert starlight—something distastefully and alarmingly crackled under my bare right foot. I lifted my foot, slowly, from the mummified hand on which I'd stepped. And listened.

I heard nothing. Proceeding once more, I came to the door's edge, peered around.

Daton was nowhere in sight.

I stepped into the hall. What little light was there came from the doorway I had just passed through and from down the stair. I looked for the container in its niche and saw its faint golden gleam. That moment, standing in the dark, so very alone, discovering that rich, subtle glow, was exquisite. I took down the container with both hands, and unable to resist, took a moment to witness the contents.

After a bit of trial and error I determined the twisting, wringing method of unfastening the top. It was an ingenious system: two interlocking helices, one carved into the inside of the top, one in the outside of the container itself. The eye was within, sunk to the bottom of a container-full of water. The eye was about the size of an oxen's—of which some people are known to make soup. Brown iris at one end, short, slender curl of cable protruding from the other. I dipped a finger in that water. Of course, on superficial apprehension this was of a rather unappetizing aspect. I had, however, tasted worse—as recently as Rodent's Head—and because of a deeper appeal, my heart beat with a rumbling excitement as I licked my finger. It tasted like tears.

And I realized that not all the rumbling was excitement. From somewhere came a sound much like a distant avalanche. I replaced the container's top. The sound grew louder.

And I suddenly saw the source. Daton appeared in the light at the top of the stairs, coming toward me in his frenzied running squat, arms and legs whipping like tempest-lashed tree limbs.

Then he was coming toward me down the hall, arms outstretched and reaching.

I watched every instant of that run, and it was over just an instant too soon for me to get out of the way. Watched as those outstretched hands swept up the container and continued on, smashing me aside.

Then I was looking, with one eye, at the texture of the earth in the courtyard. I rolled onto my back and for a moment watched explosions of colored light that meant pain too great and too sudden to be experienced as pain. These lights cleared, and I was then looking at two Datons standing in two slightly overlapping doorways.

The way to deal with seeing double, as any dedicated drinker knows, is to close one eye. I did this, and watched one Daton, in one doorway, say, "No no no. Stay in here. In here." He opened his container, checked his eye, closed the container, caressed it, returned it to its niche, and was gone.

I had never noticed before how many different colors the stars are.

I looked at the six buildings that made up the walls of my prison. Looked at the rotted and broken beams, and the rusted ironwork that had once supported stairs, and the flimsy brown vines that covered both. All much too fragile for climbing. There were few shadows in the diffuse starlight. I opened my other eye to see if my vision was still doubled. It was. And I saw something else.

Something I had previously overlooked.

And had an idea.

The application of my idea required a certain amount of physical labor, and since I could rely on none of the dead community for aid, I was obliged to move. As I did so, beginning with standing up, my body sang a choral accompaniment of pain: the massed voices of accumulated bruises and abrasions formed a harmonic background for the strong leading voice of what I was sure was a cracked rib. As I set about the necessary tasks, the choir modulated in key many times and never slackened in intensity. Despite the music, I went on.

The weakness, dizziness, and double vision were more difficult to work within. But with endurance, they faded.

Also faded, I realized, was the effect of the eye's water, but the knowledge gained with it remained.

At dawn, which took place with the characteristic desert abruptness, I had completed my work. I had constructed a device out of a broken and rotted beam and a piece of rusted ironwork and flimsy brown vines. The beam stretched across the doorway, just above the height of my own head, soundly lashed to other beams on either side of the door with a great number of the vines. The piece of iron, a rod about half again the length of my arm, rusted to a rough point at one end, was lashed to my cross-beam so that it pointed into the hall outside the door. I was ready to initiate the play.

I peeked into the hall. Daton was—temporarily, I knew—out of sight. The container was in its niche. I grabbed it and stepped back in the doorway, facing out. And heard Daton's rumbling approach.

"Come along, cretin!" I shouted—not without, I might add, a certain satisfaction. "Come along, you ignorant, ugly pustule of an entity. I have your eye!" I glanced up to quickly check and then adjust my position so that I stood directly under my iron stake with about three feet of it protruding beyond me into the hall. I looked back into the hall upon realizing that the rumbling had grown significantly louder, and took a deep breath, steadying myself and renewing my trust in my plan.

A plan which was predicated on a final apprehension of the obvious: a cyclops has no depth perception.

My body's song of pain, still loud as ever, was now drowned—as was the approaching rumble—with the singing of excitement. "Come along, imbecile! I have your eye, and with the aid of this iron stake—*behind me*—I shall keep it!"

Daton appeared at the top of the stairs.

"Here I am," I called out. "And here is your eye. And here," I pointed up, "*behind* me, is the stake."

He was flying toward me in a confusion of flailing arms and legs. The arms then came out, parallel, hands at a level with the eye's container—and my ribs.

I held my ground.

"No no no no," I heard him saying.

He came straight toward me, and with a simplicity that was nearly beautiful, ran into the stake, driving it into the center of his forehead. And kept going.

Right through me. That was not beautiful.

The cross-beam snapped. Daton took the stake, skewering his head, with him. I saw this while I was still in the air.

When I landed—atop a pile of crackling, crunching corpses—everything dissolved into tingling light for an indeterminate time.

I surfaced from this luminous froth to the spectacle of Daton, fallen and convulsing. The ground shook with his tremors.

And finally he was still.

I was not in good shape, myself.

When I felt I could move, I did so. I will not attempt to describe the experience—understand, simply, that I would prefer not to repeat it. All of Daton's walking dead things were standing gapingly about. I gathered up the container from where it had fallen, then went over to Daton's body and took his short-sword.

I then told the dead things that they were free. They could choose to leave, and live, or they could remain and continue their half lives, as they preferred. I turned and walked away, feeling a curious mixture of sadness and elation. If any of them followed, it was not until I was well gone.

My faithful horses, I found, were safe where I had left them. I rode away, putting the dead city behind me.

Ah, my friends, I can sense your skepticism. Let us view, you would say were you not so mannered, this marvelous eye in its golden container.

I regretfully say you must take me at my word.

For you see, I passed back through Rodent's Head, lacking supplies enough to reach a pleasanter oasis. In my absence, they had noticed my liberties. Had not my body already been so obviously abused to the breaking point, I'm sure they would have done the job themselves. As it was, they confiscated the golden container to repay my thefts.

And the eye itself? Like you, my friends, they thought my story fabrication. They took the eye for that of an oxen and made a soup out of it.

Of course, they soon saw their mistake.

Janet Fox, formerly a teacher of English and foreign language, has been published in magazines and anthologies such as *Shadows II*, *The Twilight Zone*, *Amazons I*, and *The Year's Best Horror Stories*. Most of her work is of the horror and heroic fantasy genre. She is deeply involved in small press projects, and is currently doing the newsletter for SPWAO—the Small Press Writers and Artists Organization. She is now, she says, devoted to horseback riding and fishing, and "indulging myself in a few years of full-time writing." "Gate of the Damned," I feel, walks the tightrope between heroic fantasy and pure horror—and does it well.—MZB

# GATE OF THE DAMNED
## by Janet Fox

At moonrise Scorpia came upon a rocky pool fed by subterranean springs, a welcome sight after her day's travels. The massive war horse she rode rolled air out through his nostrils, and two nymphs poised on the opposite bank, wraith-pale against the forest's darkness, fled so quickly they seemed to disappear, their movements insectile despite their anthropomorphic forms.

She dismounted, sheathed sword slapping against her thigh, slipped the bridle to let the big horse drink. He had been bred for battle, not for travel and he showed it, dun coat gone lackluster, ribs showing in a ripple beneath the dusty hide. She set up camp quickly, but when the horse was tended and the fire lit, and a portion of the game she'd trapped earlier slowly roasting, wrapped in leaves, she stood and looked longingly at the water. Deciding, she undid her swordbelt, the straps that held spurs to her buskins.

Earlier she'd seen signs of men on the march, always off to war somewhere, but this glade was so secluded, so far from human habitation that it seemed safe. Completely disrobed except for the filet of leather and copper that bound her hair she stood on the rocky edge and tested the water. Her coloring was typical of her kind, skin a subtle bronze-gold that only turned a darker shade of gold under the hottest sun, hair lion-tawny. There was an ugly whitish mass of scar tissue on her shoulder

212

and a narrow welt on her ribs where a sword edge had come almost close enough.

The unexpected iciness of the water sent a shiver through her, but she forced herself to jump in and frog-kicked down through jewel-green depths to find bottom, then launched herself off slimy rock back toward the surface. She came up in a spray of water and lay back to let her lungs suck in air. Blackmane's sudden whinny disturbed the silence, and she listened to see if he'd be answered.

No answering call came from the dark forest, but the mood of peace had been broken, and she struck out for the shore. She hadn't yet reached it when she saw a rider appear, moonlight limning his shape and striking bright reflections from the metal of helmet and bridle. Another joined him, then two more. Since they bore no insignia on their shields, she guessed them to be mercenaries and by the small number, a scouting party.

"By Zan," said one of them without reverence and pointed toward her. "Is that a water nymph or a vision sent to tempt me?" He dismounted and bent his head to remove his helmet, running his hand through lank, sand-colored hair. One of the others swiveled in his saddle to point out her fire and the tethered war horse. "Her man must be somewhere about," he said nervously. "That's a soldier's camp."

Water fell in icy drops from wet hair onto bare flesh and she felt as if she'd been standing there for hours. She glanced over her shoulder, saw that the opposite shore was too far, the shoreline uncluttered by obstacles. They could easily ride around and intercept her.

"I mean no harm here," she said, raising her weaponless hand, palm up. That remark, teamed with the warrior's gesture, brought peals of laughter from the shore.

"Kilder, I thought that was supposed to be your line," said someone amid the laughter. The sandy-haired man divested himself of armor and began to wade toward her. She took quick note of his knife belt and turned to swim farther out, bringing another barrage of cries and whistles from the shore. She waited until he was almost near enough to touch, in too deep to wade, his swimming hampered by his soaked clothing. Swift as an otter she submerged and caught hold of his chiton, pulling him under with her weight. With his eyes and nostrils full of water and his arms flailing desperately, she made free to pluck his knife from its sheath. When he came up she clasped him with one arm and put the knife point firmly against his side. He struggled once, submerging them both; then relaxed and they floated to the surface.

Scorpia shook water from her eyes. "I'll kill him if I have to," she called, "but not if you let me go in peace."

Enraged, one of the others pulled off his armor and plunged into the water; another grabbed his arm and was pulled along, trying to stop him. Her arm tensed, ready to propel the knife, but there was a sudden sound of hoofbeats, and a rider on a long-legged chestnut pulled the beast to a sliding stop on the bank. "Name of the gods, what's going on here?" roared a voice that stopped the struggle on the bank and made Scorpia pause as well. She knew the sound of a voice that commanded in full expectation that it would be obeyed.

The two soldiers in the water clambered ashore, ashamed and bedraggled as their leader surveyed the situation. "Go join the others. Tell them we will make camp there." He pointed to the opposite side of the pool.

"But what about her," began one of them, but his voice faltered under the commander's gaze and he scrambled to join the others.

"You can let him go now. You have no further need of hostages," said the leader.

"Your word that I may depart in peace."

"What good is the word of someone you don't know? Let him go unless you intend to kill him out of pure malice. It wouldn't offend me much. He fell from my good graces when he fell into your hands."

Scorpia released her hostage, not happy with the bargain, but realizing it was the best that she could do. As she waded near shore, her feet slipped on pebbles and she would have fallen except for the hand the leader extended. He didn't turn his eyes from her as she emerged from the water. They were dark gray eyes, the gaze clear and steady. There was appreciation in it but no threat or attempt to demean her, to reduce her to component parts. Clumsily she got into her chiton, the damp cloth sticking to her skin.

"You're far from your home country," he said. "And without your hawkshead helmet it is no wonder you were mistaken for an ordinary woman."

"I am an ordinary woman."

"I saw the Amazons fight at Sea of Reeds," he said. "They rode big brutes, like that dun of yours." He shook his head slightly, remembering. "They were women, but they were hard to kill."

She reached down for the sword belt, but he set his foot upon it, then picked it up, drawing the sword from the battered leather of the sheath. It was a strangely lusterless, blue-gray weapon. "And some say their blades were demon-forged." He smiled and tossed it back to her. "After I had fought them, I found myself wondering what it would be like to ride with an Amazon, to fight beside her. Foolish, I suppose." He paced her toward her camp where she hurried to save her supper from burning.

"No more foolish than any other's dreams, I imagine," she said distractedly, pulling the scorched meat away from the flames. "But you mistake me. I'm not of that murderous tribe. I'm only a wanderer, looking for a place where no one is called upon to wear or use a sword." He sat down against a fallen log, beginning to remove helmet and armor. She watched surreptitiously, wondering despite herself what he looked like. His hair and beard were so black they seemed to absorb light, his face angular, reddened by wind. He was gaunt under the armor, large of hand and foot, appearing a little awkward in repose, though there'd been nothing clumsy about him when he'd ridden in to take charge of things by the pool.

She took the portions of meat she wanted, broke off a section of the tough traveler's loaf and came to sit at the opposite end of the log. "Eat, if you want to," she said ungraciously. He went to the fire and served himself and for a time they ate in companionable silence.

"A world without war," he said, finally. "I find that thought strange, but as you see, war's my business. I'm taking my men to join the armies of Baucis, King of Thurgia. My name is Telis."

"Scorpia," she said and regretted it. That had been her battle-name. She'd been meaning to change it.

Telis' army had been noisily setting up camp on the far side of the pool, the water bringing every clatter of gear, every angry voice, every obscenity clearly to them, but as it became full dark the noises abated. The dark enforced an uneasy intimacy inside the feeble circle of firelight.

"It was always easier in dreams," he said, rising to stand before her, his shape a long darkness against flickering light. "I find I don't know how to talk to you."

"What is there to talk of? For all I know I'm a prisoner here."

"Is that how you feel? Like a prisoner?"

"No."

He sat beside her. "I don't want anything you don't. If you tell me to go, I'll go." He leaned over and kissed her, possibly a little roughly, but there was nothing demanding or threatening in it. As her arms went round him in response, she wondered how he'd known how lonely the road had been, how tired she was of constant movement, new faces, unfriendly faces, how long it'd been since she'd lain with a man and how often she'd thought about it.

"Baucis' armies gather in a village called Under-the-Mountain," said Telis as he and Scorpia struck camp in thin gray morning light. "It lies three days ride from here."

"What if my direction is different?"

"Is it?"

"No." She didn't say that she had no direction and no idea where she might find what she was seeking. She didn't say that last night she'd almost lost the disoriented feeling that had followed her since she'd fled her own land. He thought she was strong. Let him keep that illusion.

"I suppose, being an outlander, you know nothing of the mountain pass called Abzu Rii," he said.

"Some farmers spoke of it in the last village, but it was all superstitious stuff. I discounted it."

"That the land beyond the pass is a domain of sorcery and things unclean?"

"If so, why should anyone want to go there?"

"Baucis wishes to capture the lands beyond, to make them safe for travelers and to free the inhabitants from the demonic powers that rule there."

"He means to save their souls even if all must die. And if there is treasure, it too will be liberated. How familiar that sounds. How simple it is . . . to kill demons."

Telis gave her a shocked look. "I'd never have thought to hear such talk from an— I know, you say you're not. Anyway, that's why armies march against Abzu Rii."

"Those villagers I spoke to didn't call it Abzu Rii. They called it the Gate of the Damned."

They left the forest behind and began a slow descent into a populous valley. The inhabitants sometimes brought them gifts of meat and bread or wine as they passed through, preferring to propitiate, rather than to resist the band of mercenaries. They might have traveled in comfort, but the pace that Telis set was too brisk for either men or animals to grow sleek and rested. Ahead of them, growing from a smudge of smoke-blue on the horizon to a gray solidity were the mountains the locals called the Oliads. As they traveled they met with other bands of soldiers, some well-organized troops, others mere mobs of undisciplined raiders.

Under-the-Mountain boasted a rude wine shop that Telis' men had no trouble locating. Scorpia didn't like the look of it. It was crowded with rough-dressed peasants and men-at-arms.

"Have but one drink with me," said Telis, "since you've decided to leave us here."

"I think it's for the best," she heard herself say with a tone of almost-regret. She accepted the battered chalice and sipped at the vinegary stuff that passed for wine, trying to ignore the rude stares and coarse remarks of the other patrons. "Maybe I'd better go," she said, finishing her drink with a grimace at its sourness. "I'm not much appreciated here."

A swarthy-faced lout crowded up close behind her and pinched her as he whispered an obscenity in her ear. It was all reflex, all one movement, the turn, the raised forearm and the elbow sent into the side of the man's stubbled jaw with her full weight behind it.

The others roared with drunken laughter as he lay on the filthy straw of the floor, working his jaw, his eyes slitted in pain. Someone poured wine on his head to rouse him. As Scorpia turned to make her exit, Telis grabbed her by the arm. "You're leaving just as things are getting lively?"

The heavy-jowled man rose, his dark eyes glowering beneath bushy brows. "Woman, you dare to strike Niarcas?"

"Not woman," said Telis, so that all heard. "Amazon."

A ripple of subdued comment went through the crowd. Niarcas looked a little surprised, but he wasn't backing away. Scorpia felt someone close behind her slip her sword from its sheath, press the hilt into her hand.

Niarcas drew his weapon, having little choice but to defend himself, or so he thought. The crowd melted away, giving them room, and once the battle was joined, there was little time to explain her way out. Though she had difficulty admitting it to herself, the situation worked a kind of magic. She could almost be back in Theopolis in training with Lea's troop. For a brief moment she wished she were.

Her opponent was far stronger than she was, and his first onslaught drove her back, almost to the edge of the crowd. Fortunately, he was also slow-witted and clumsy. She feinted and slipped back past him. Her agile movement confounded his slow thought-processes and he grew red in the face trying to keep up with her. The spectators' rude jeers did the rest to goad him into a blind charge that she side-stepped easily, sending her blade slicing into the back of his thick neck like a butcher's cleaver into meat. His eyes protruded; his mouth opened, but only gurgling sounds came out. There was a moment of suspense before his huge body toppled; then the arms and legs moved briefly in mindless reflex a moment and stopped moving for good.

Scorpia turned away, realizing she had done what she had sworn to Telis she didn't want to do. When she saw him smiling in encouragement, she raised the sword still red with Niarcas' blood and sprang at him. The distance between allowed him time to draw his own weapon, but when her lusterless blade struck, it shattered his shining one. Only two of his men recovering enough to pinion her arms managed to save him, for there was no mistaking her purpose.

In twos and threes the patrons left, murmuring all the strange things they'd ever heard about "that cursed tribe." Now they had some new material to add to their store.

Telis worked the swordhilt from her clenched hand and studied the dull-appearing metal of the blade. There was no way to disguise the shaken look on his face, though he was trying.

"Must we take this Harpy with us?" asked the man at her left whom she now recognized as Kilder.

"Yes, and you two will be her guards."

"Then you'd better guard me well," she said, "because if that sword comes back to my hand, and as often as I've put it from me, it *has* come back—"

"I'll admit the reality spoils the dream a bit," said Telis with an audible sigh, "but I wasn't lying when I said I wanted nothing you didn't want yourself. I saw your face when you made the kill."

Scorpia fell silent, having no answer for that.

The day they received orders to ride through the pass the air was heavy and still under a cloud-swollen sky. The superstitious among them ascribed it to demon-magic when a storm broke out just as the horses were toiling near the highest point of the climb. A gust of wet wind nearly sent Scorpia sprawling from the saddle, but she clung tenaciously. She found herself separated from her guards in the howl of wind-driven rain and was looking around to see if it would be possible to escape when she saw what looked like a wall falling toward her. Mud and debris, dislodged from the cliff's side was hurtling down. She put spurs to Blackmane's sides and drove him forward, giving a warning cry to alert the others.

All could not escape; she heard an awful groaning noise as the wall of rock and mud slid over mounted men. She clung to the saddle, looking back to see horses scrambling wildly atop a dark, roiling mass or tumbling down the slope, carrying their riders with them or falling and crushing them in the madness.

As if on a puff of wind the storm was blown away, and Scorpia with the other survivors was left standing soaked and buffeted at the highest point, looking back on the wreck of a great army. Telis rode up behind her on a lathered, exhausted horse, and for a moment she was disoriented enough to be glad to see him.

"We can't go back," she said, looking at the downslope.

"We still have enough men. We'll gather them and go on."

"You don't think, like some of these superstitious idiots, that magic caused the slide?" he asked when she looked at him doubtfully.

She shrugged. "Perhaps, but when you can't go back, it makes sense to go on."

An unlikely band of conquerors descended the Gate of the Damned (now closed) into a land they would have been wary of, even had it not been overgrown with squat gray trees with branches as intricate as spiders' webs, and clumps of dark grass that shattered dryly under the horses' hooves. A white bird swept over them, gave a raucous cry, wheeled to pass over them again as if spying for some unseen master.

They camped in the foothills of the crags, a thoroughly uncomfortable and dispirited band. Scorpia slept badly and awoke in the middle of the night in the midst of oppressive silence. She sat up, pulling her cloak around her, and strained her eyes for the enemy she felt was waiting out there in the dark. Clouds moved raggedly across the moon, splashing the landscape with sudden green-tinged clarity. By this light she thought she saw an impossibly small human figure crouch by a twisted tree, then dart behind a grassy hummock. Some animal, she told herself with weak conviction. But it had moved with almost human stealth as if it, too, was spying. She lay back down and fell into a fitful sleep.

It was morning before she woke again, but she knew where she was without opening her eyes. The air of this land had a coldness, a dampness to it, the feel of stale air trapped inside some underground place. Telis gave a shout and she struggled to untangle herself from the folds of her cloak. He was standing where they had posted one of their sentries the night before.

"Gone," he said. "And Ambers too. Did the beggars desert?"

Scorpia noticed a wet patch on the ground. Her fingers came away red when she touched it and above, the white bird launched itself from the branches of a tree with a cry that was very like demented laughter.

They had barely struck camp when they saw a line of riders and marching men, the armies of Abzu Rii. Telis gave Scorpia a thoughtful look and unslung her sword from his saddle.

"The scouts report something strange," cried out a distracted-looking young soldier. "They said that some in that army yonder don't look exactly . . . human."

"You don't think, do you, that I'd fight in your cause, after all you've done?"

"You can fight or not, as you choose, but we're going into battle and you're coming with us." With a smothered oath she reached for the sword but he drew it back. "I want some surety you won't turn the weapon on me before the battle is joined."

"What good is the word of someone you don't know?"

"A soldier's oath will do," he answered gravely.

"Then you have it, but only because I don't want to face your goblin army unarmed."

Riders along the western flank would later tell of cavalrymen with overly long arms that could fight on, even when their heads or helms were cleaved from their shoulders. Others would tell of facing strange foot-soldiers who were like two fighters, joined back to back, yet moved as one being. Scorpia would not doubt them because now she saw a mailed figure launch itself into a group of pikemen and send them scattering in all directions. Blackmane snorted and half reared at the scent of something alien as the giant figure lifted a man into the air, twisted him in two hands like a bit of cloth and sent him flying. As Scorpia drew near, she saw it was not a human face beneath the helmet, but the dark protruding muzzle of an animal. Its hands were almost human but clumsy, long claws curving from the spatulate fingers.

It was, she thought, either a bear-thing or a giant of a man disguised in the hide of a great bear. Before she could decide which, Blackmane was throwing his weight against the creature. Talons carved long gashes into the dun shoulder as the two giants clashed. Scorpia felt the horse falter, then she was driving her sword into the beast man's shoulders from above, feeling the grinding sensation as the blade tore through tough muscle and grated against bone. A gout of blood spurted, half blinding her as the war horse was driven to its knees by the weight of the falling beast-man. Scorpia felt herself flung forward and strove to remain conscious, even when she struck, but didn't quite manage it.

She awoke, she didn't know how much later, and felt a sticky wetness against her cheek. Mud. Her fingers slid in it when she attempted to rise, and she realized that night had fallen while she lay unconscious. Nearby she saw a headless, sword-hacked body. With a horror she'd never have felt on a more mundane battlefield, she recognized it by the clothing as Kilder. Blackmane cropped the brittle grass beside the lax body of the beast-man she'd slain. Putting her foot on the carcass, she pulled free her sword with some effort. Bodies littered the battleground. Here and there a badly wounded man stirred or moaned, a horse screamed and thrashed, but there was no help in this barbaric place, none for the wounded nor even burial for the dead.

Scorpia froze as she saw something move. Dark shapes reminiscent of the one she'd seen the night before were scuttling across the battlefield. They gathered about one of the wounded (Scorpia didn't know of which side) and the man shrieked once, ear-shatteringly and then fell silent. She dropped to the ground as several of the little forms began to gather about the headless body of Kilder. She shivered as she saw the movement of their sticklike arms and legs as they squabbled over possession of the corpse. It made Kilder appear to take on a new and strange life. She bit her lip to make herself lie still, but there was something so awful about the scene that she sprang up and with a cry brought down her sword on the swarming mass of bodies. A skinny, dark humanoid form sprawled, broken, but the rest scattered, their frightened voices eerily high and pure, like those in a boy's choir.

She saw their red eyes as they regathered. As they rushed at her, she cut and cut with the sword, severing skinny arms and legs. She saw their small flat faces, neither human nor animal but a combination of both. A single sharp tooth grew above and below at the front of their mouths, and as they attacked, she felt aching puncture wounds in her calves, her thighs. Tiny star-shaped hands clutched at her garments, pulling her down, but the milling mass at her feet made her fall. She saw sharp incisors click shut very near her eyes an instant before she was struck on the back of the head.

She awoke on a stone bench and sat up with a cry of horror. She was alone in a barren cell floored with filthy straw, an oil lamp guttering in a niche in the wall. She studied the livid puncture wounds on her hands and legs. She leapt up, startled, as the door opened and small, dark stick-figures crept in to hide in the shadows along the walls. A mild-appearing old man entered behind them. He had round, pale eyes swimming in rheum and since he was so plump, his grub-white skin was strangely unwrinkled, though he had the look of age.

"Don't worry, my dear. The Shadow People won't harm you. Not unless you prove troublesome," he said as she shrank back against the wall.

"Who are you?"

"One of Ylissa's counselors." He sat down beside her and patted her hand with a pale, age-spotted one. With the other he gestured as he spoke and it fluttered ineffectually as a dying moth. "The Shadow People brought you to me because they know I need certain things for my magics."

"What things?"

"Blood for one. You look healthy." He pinched her arm to test the thickness of the flesh as she licked dry lips, keeping watch on the Shadow People who still moved stealthily on the periphery of her vision.

"What sort of place is this? Are there other captives here?"

"This is the House of the Divine Ylissa, sovereign of Abzu Rii and the Enchanted Lands, possessor of the Lost Wisdoms— and my mother," this last said with some sense of pride, though upon studying him Scorpia wondered if Ylissa wasn't a mother in some ritual sense. She would be old indeed were she his mother in truth.

"And ah, other captives? I believe there were a few Ylissa fancied. They would probably be in her chambers now while she makes her final selection. Not everyone may receive the blessing of her touch, the favor of her love." He giggled as if he'd made an obscene jest, then he drew a thin dagger and an enameled bowl from the silken folds of his robe. "I think I'll take a little blood now," he said matter-of-factly. "Just lie back."

Scorpia laid hold of him and finding him exceedingly weak for all his plumpness, gave him a push that sent him staggering toward a far corner of the cell. As she'd hoped, his quavering cry for help drew the Shadow People after him. As she made for the door, she flung down the lamp, flames catching and spitting in the straw. Fear of the Shadow People made her slam the door closed on the old man's screams. She felt a stabbing pain and saw that one of the little creatures had slipped out the door. She kicked at it, got it underfoot and stamped it to death, the limbs breaking like dry sticks, a milky fluid oozing from the shattered body.

Outside the cell door someone had left a sword lying propped against the wall. She snatched it up and with little surprise saw that it was her own.

Shadows in the narrow corridors swam and writhed around her, so great was her fear of the Shadow People. She could feel their bites still throbbing as if they'd injected poison. Following the blind turnings of the dank maze, she at last saw light, streaming in around a door at the top of a set of narrow stone steps. She forced the door, breaking it outward with her foot, but by luck no one was there to see her do it.

Tall candles burned in a crownlike chandelier, but it was by no means light in the room. Tapestries interwoven with threads of gleaming gold and silver, tall mirrors set into the walls at odd angles, indistinct light from candles, made the room a place of dazzled vision, shifting illusions.

A figure entered, anonymous, yet female, in lustrous veils that hid her face yet revealed lithe arms and legs as she moved. By the roundness of her flesh, she seemed a young girl, yet in this room of visions it was hard to be certain. When she saw Scorpia, the intruder, she whirled, as if to run, giving out a half-shriek that was yet subdued, as if silence was the law in this place.

"Please," said Scorpia, lowering the point of the sword. "I mean you no harm. I want only to escape. If I had draperies and a veil, such as yours—"

As if awed by the weapon, the serving-girl nodded and went to a wooden chest, from which she pulled a costume much like her own. The girl giggled to see Scorpia's long bronzed body in the fluttering veils, yet the whole of this dwelling seemed ill-lighted, an illusory feeling of brightness given by mirrors and gilt and iridescent fabric. The disguise would do.

"I'll show you the door," quavered the girl. "Ylissa and her guard are busy with the captives now."

"Captives, where? Show me the place." So simply her course was diverted. In the pressure of the moment her past returned and it was suddenly impossible to leave in danger those with whom she'd fought, her soldier's oath so recently given. No one who had known her in her own land would have been surprised about such a decision, though she surprised herself a little.

"Ylissa will be angry."

"Take me to the door; I'll make my own way after that." She picked up a basket of flowers from a hallway, and when she entered Ylissa's chambers, she moved along the wall in a business-like way, set down the basket by a vase and began to arrange the flowers in it as if this were a part of her duties.

Two of the gigantic dark-furred warriors stood guard over the prisoners. Scorpia recognized several of Telis' men, then Telis himself sitting on a bench at one side of the room, his face in his hands. When he raised his head, she saw the raw gash across his forehead. He blinked, looking at her, moved as if he might have recognized her, looked blank again, whether by accident or design, she didn't know.

Ylissa lay on a dragonfooted couch before a screen of angled mirrors, all the attention of her dark eyes riveted on the prisoners. She was half hidden, half revealed by a gown of shining gold, but there was such a dazzle about her, whether from candlelight or sorcery, that Scorpia could not have described her. Hers was a delicate beauty, not of flesh and blood, but something ghostly, ethereal, here one moment, gone the next. By her outlines, and the quick glimpse of a white hand, a shapely calf and ankle, Scorpia could not convince herself that Ylissa was the mother of the old sorcerer. Perhaps he lied, or was not in his right mind.

Ylissa was toying with what looked at first to be a glass flute, gesturing to one of the animal-men to bring Telis nearer. Telis only stared at her, still too befuddled by his head wound to struggle or protest. Scorpia looked around the room, thinking that surely it must be daylight outside, though it was eternal twilight in here. She located two high windows behind heavy dark hangings that descended to the floor in graceful folds.

"Outlander, you have been chosen," said Ylissa, her voice scarcely more than a whisper.

"Chosen for what? Who are you?" Telis put up a hand to shade his eyes from moving reflections.

"Call me Ylissa, lady of Illusions, immortal in beauty. You do not yet know how honored you are."

"I don't understand."

Ylissa laughed, her voice eerily unresonant. "You look strong and capable, Outlander. You will love me well. Take away the others." She lifted the glass flute as if she would play it, and Scorpia saw that it wasn't a musical instrument at all but a blow-gun. A tiny feathered dart struck Telis in the forearm, though he didn't seem to feel it.

"Eros' dart will soon do its work," said Ylissa, reclining against the cushions of her couch and rearranging her veils as if to present herself in a light even more glamorous. "Am I not as beautiful as a goddess?"

"You glow. You are a goddess in my sight," said Telis, and Scorpia was sure he was ensorceled, for he'd never waxed so poetic in her presence. He knelt before the couch, took Ylissa's hand and kissed it lingeringly.

So intent was Scorpia in watching that she let fall the crystal vase onto the floor.

"What is that clumsy girl doing? How did she get in here?" Scorpia knelt on the floor, pretending to be desperately picking up the pieces of the shattered vase, but at an inopportune moment her sword protruded from her veils.

"Grulo, Gnarff, get her!"

The beast-men shuffled forward at a bent-kneed gait, opening their arms. With no time to draw steel, she back-pedaled, bumping the wall, her fingers finding the velvety cloth of the curtains. One of them grabbed her, talons tearing the cloth of her garment, penetrating skin and muscle with numbing force. With all her strength she pulled at the heavy curtains and they came cascading down, enveloping all three in their dust-laden folds. At Ylissa's thin, desperate scream, the beast let loose his hold, and Scorpia struggled to be free of the smothering cloth. When she threw it from her, she saw that light was streaming into the room.

Telis now lay beside Ylissa on the couch, cradling her in his arms. Scorpia heard cloth tear and an angry beast-man came shambling toward her. Holding him at bay, for the moment, with her sword, she grasped the drape on the second window and pulled it free. Ylissa screamed again, with more force and held her golden veils before her face, though Telis, like a man in a dream, was trying to fondle and kiss her. Now Ylissa could be seen in the light of day. Immortal she might be; young and beautiful, she was not.

Parts of her still had the glow and freshness of youth, but through the centuries a wasting disease had been at work. It had eaten away one side of her face, exposing a skeletal grin of naked teeth, cheek and jaw a webwork, yellowed bands of atrophied muscle. In the harsh light even her shining gossamer could not disguise how the disease had eaten a gaping wound in her right side, taking away a breast and a great chunk of her thigh. There might have been further damage but Scorpia did not strain to see it. The worst was that Telis continued to kiss the open wound of her face as if he were blind, or as if he were irrevocably in love.

Because Scorpia had held still a little too long, the great black claws were hurtling toward her face. The sword came up in time to hew two stubby fingers from the clawlike hand, but the thing only howled with anger, perhaps more dangerous wounded. Its companion had also managed to free itself and was lumbering across the room. Ylissa screamed again as she discovered her reflection in the oddly angled glass screen, the awful sight of her face reproduced to infinity. Her scream becoming a sob, she took something from beneath her veils, something that gave off a puff of greenish smoke, which she quickly inhaled. As Scorpia cut at a beast-man, her back against the wall, Ylissa, the ageless immortal, writhed in Telis' embrace and was still. Before Scorpia's eyes the bear soldiers began to shrink, collapsing in upon themselves until they were no more than moldering pelts, lifeless rugs upon the floor. She kicked away one helmet with a clang. The whole room now reeked overpoweringly of decay.

When Scorpia tried to pull Telis away, he resisted, cradling Ylissa's body in his arms, a relic, now mummy-dry and crumbling down to bare bone. Here and there it still retained some trace of Ylissa's frail beauty. "I can't leave her," he insisted. "I love her."

Scorpia went to find the other prisoners wandering around the decay-ridden rooms, to enlist their help in getting Telis out of the place. They would not come at first but must take time to scour the dwelling for the loot they'd come for. While they squabbled over the few precious ornaments that had been solid enough to resist decay, Scorpia went back to the cells below-ground to release prisoners who were still being held there. Her skin crawled as she retraced the labyrinth, and her imagination saw furtive movement in every shadow, heard clear high voices around every turn. She saw none of the Shadow People but felt that somehow, they had survived and would continue to haunt the underground passages.

When she returned the soldiers had taken custody of Telis and he was more himself, though dazed. The remnant of the army returned the way they had come, and after a few days, discovered that the mudslide had solidified enough to allow them safe passage. Telis spoke little on the journey back, yet when sunset cast uncertain golden light over the landscape, Scorpia saw a look of intense longing pass over his face as for something irrevocably lost almost before it was found. Ylissa's magic had outlived her a little, but Scorpia felt that with time, it would fade.

It was just dawn as she rose and began to gather her scant belongings. Now that the mountain pass was well behind them, there was nothing to prevent her leaving. Though she tried to move quietly, Telis heard her and sat up. Almost his old expression of keen-eyed rapacity had returned to him. "You're not leaving." The tone made it a command, rather than a question.

"It's long past time. You ask too much. Your dream almost devoured me and it's time I went in search of my own."

"You know you'll never find it."

She shrugged. "Perhaps not." As she untethered her horse, Telis moved toward her and she lay her hand on the hilt of her sword.

"I'm a better swordsman than you—if it weren't for that charmed blade," he began.

"If you think you can kill me, you're welcome to try," she said and when he was silent, she swung into the saddle.

From his belt he drew a thin, crystalline instrument that resembled a flute. "It was strange how I loved without reservation her that I first looked on," he said. "I still sometimes remember her loveliness when my eye is caught by some sun-dazzle. I think only her death broke the spell."

"You'd use magic against me? Make me your mindless slave?"

"If that's the only way I can have you. But you can still decide to stay with me."

"If that's what you call love, I'm better off without it." She swung Blackmane around and felt the sting of the projectile as it lodged in her shoulder. With mindless rage she awaited the outcome, then she shook her head as if to clear it.

Telis was laughing. "The magic in it died with time or her death. My men tried it on one of the serving-girls before we left. I still wish you'd stay but now I know you won't."

"By the Styx, you *are* a bastard," she said but without as much venom as she might have wished. Blackmane's powerful neck arched against the rein and she let him go.

Robin Bailey, like Leigh Brackett, C. L. Moore, and Marion Zimmer Bradley, suffers from the "handicap" of a gender-ambiguous name; and although the only "Robin" in my family is male, I bought the story "Child of Orcus" under the impression that this was a woman writing about a woman. Only after deciding to purchase it did I discover that Robin Bailey was a man; but like all really good writers, gender is unimportant to the perceptive eye he brings to the study of his heroine.

Two things are important to know before reading this story; first, that Caligula did actually sentence women to fight as gladiators in the Roman arena, so what I thought fantasy was historical fact, and second, that Bailey is married to a woman who bears his heroine's name, Diana, but she "bears only a spiritual resemblance" to the character in the story.

Robin Bailey, like many writers, has an unusual mundane occupation; he is a planetarium lecturer. He is also a martial arts instructor, which gives realism to his writing of warrior women. His first novel, a Timescape book entitled *Frost*, appeared in April 1983, and also involves a woman warrior; this is only his second professional sale. It's not safe to make predictions about writers—many promising newcomers don't have the discipline or interest to keep their chosen profession alive until they can make a living at it—but if Robin Bailey stays the course, he should become an outstanding name in the field.—MZB


# CHILD OF ORCUS
## by Robin W. Bailey


She stared down at the arena, squinting against the glare of the sun on white sand, wishing she were somewhere else. Yet, day after day she came, crowded in with all the others, quested about for the best seat. She was not like the others, she told herself. They were animals who came only to watch the butchery. She was different; she could not help herself. Her blood had mingled with that sand countless times until it and she were one, inseparable. It called to her at night with a voice of nightmares, and she could not help but return.

"Divine!" cooed a sweaty, wide-eyed matron in the highest

tier, her fat jowls engorged with grapes and honey-soaked sweet-meats she carried in a basket. Her man said nothing, just watched as below a *retiarius* stalked his prey across the blistering sand, and his hand made quick, furtive motions beneath the folds of his toga.

Pigs, she thought. A great cry went up as the *retiarius* made his kill. The matron leaped to her feet, spilling her basket, clapping her hands and screaming with delight. Then, realizing the fate of her sweetmeats, she bent quickly down, gathered them from the dirty, foot-trodden aisle with a broad sweep of her hand and returned them to her basket again. She licked her fingers and the next match began.

Two men strode toward the imperial box: a black slave and a legion deserter, neither worthy to be called gladiator. The new emperor only attended the games on holidays and special occasions. Today, only the least notable of dignitaries reclined there to acknowledge the combatants' salute.

Each bore *gladius* and *pugio*. They raised their weapons high. *Ave! Morituri te salutant!* they called in unison. We, who are about to die, salute you!

How those words haunted her. A year had passed since Caius Caligula, the first emperor to send females to the arena, granted her freedom and Roman citizenship. Yet, how she had rejoiced when two days later Caligula's own soldiers murdered him, gutted him as he had watched her gut so many in the games. His blood would wash an empire clean, she thought then.

It was another month before she met Messalina.

She gave her attention to the match. The two circled each other, bare of armor, afraid to engage. Suddenly, the legionnaire moved in, swung, leaped away. A deep cut streaked the slave's left arm. Blood ran down his hand, down the pugio's short blade, dripped to the sand.

A short match, she expected. Neither would ever make a true gladiator, but the legionnaire had at least some training.

"Mistress?"

She looked up, shielding her eyes against the near-noon sun. A messenger wearing a toga of the imperial house bowed, passed her a freshly minted coin stamped with the image of the new emperor, Claudius.

She sighed. Messalina had been near her thoughts all day, and now she was summoned. Perhaps the gods had tried to warn her. Well, there was no avoiding it. She gave the *denarius* back to the messenger for his service and sent him on his way.

A few among the crowd were beginning to jeer at the

combatants. It was a dull, unexciting match. The fighters had closed only twice, and neither was seriously wounded, yet. They danced around, avoiding each other.

She shrugged and rose to leave. The view was not half so interesting on the spectators' side of the high marble wall. She gave the fighters a final glance, shook back her long, loose hair, wiped sweat from her brow, kicked a patrician foot that blocked her path to the exit.

Some of the regulars recognized her as she passed among them. Attesting to the boredom of the match below, they set up a chant calling her name. Honor, such as it was, from Roman noblemen. She ignored them, kept her eyes straight ahead until the arena was behind her.

Though the sun threatened to bake her, the streets were muddy from a recent rain. The ooze seeped around her sandals, squished between bare toes. A passing cart splashed filth on her legs.

"You great, motherless hunk of fat!" She scooped a handful of mud, flung it after the driver, splattering his back and neck. He jerked his cart to a stop, turned, glared his fury. Then his jaw dropped, eyes widened. He rubbed his chin, licked lips and urged his horses to continue.

She looked at herself. Messalina would make her bathe before their audience. Mud everywhere, sandals, cloak, the short hem of her tunic, scabbard and legs.

She cursed again and sighed,

"Oh Diana, you look much better now." Messalina beamed, coming toward her across the broad marble floor. Her thin sandals made no sound, and the empress moved with subtle, sensuous grace. "If only you weren't so ridiculously tall."

Diana squirmed in the long, silken *stola* and *palla* the servants insisted she wear. It had been some years since she wore the heavy, draping garments of a woman. As a gladiator, she learned to prefer men's attire. But Messalina was right. Even barefoot she was taller than most men. This costume made her look immense.

The ancilla who bathed and dressed her spoke from the entrance. "She wears it to please you, Lady."

Diana laid a hand on her *pugio*. Strapped beneath the *stola* it was impossible to draw, yet she felt better with it near. "How would you like a split tongue, little snake?" She faced Messalina. "I wear it because she stole my other clothes."

The empress waved a hand, dismissing the indignant servant. "Still," she said to Diana with an appraising eye, "it doesn't look that bad. If your breasts were larger and you wore your hair . . ."

Diana interrupted. "You didn't call me here to discuss my physical assets. What are you scheming in that charnel house you call a mind?"

Messalina bristled, looked as if she had swallowed fire. "You dare a lot. . . ."

Diana shrugged. "At first, you could bully me with your threats. But I no longer fear the arena. Send me back if you think you can find another to run your errands."

Messalina put on a pout, crossed to a nearby table and picked up the small golden whip that was her favorite plaything. She cracked it testily. "You know Claudius won't let me hire a man. The fat fool's afraid I'd leap into bed with him, and he's right. I do it anyway when I can find a man brave enough to cuckold an emperor." She cracked the whip again, knocked a delicate vase from its pedestal. It crashed to the floor, shattering in tiny fragments. "But that's not the point, is it? You serve me because you like the pay and privileges; you can't bear the thought of regressing to the plebian *nobody* you once were. And where else, but in my service or the arena, could you use your formidable talents?"

Diana smiled a hidden smile. This was why she tolerated Messalina. Not pay or privilege, but the pleasure of trading naked truth with another female. If Messalina was a scheming, ruthless bitch of an empress, still she was a woman of courage and daring.

Messalina coiled her whip and braced hands on her hips. "Now, there's a rumor," she said carefully. "In the hills a new cult has sprung up. Some say they have the secret of immortality." She shook her head slowly, allowing a thin smile that showed sharp, pearlescent teeth.

Diana went to a shelf, drew down a leather bottle of wine and two earthen goblets.

She leaned forward in her saddle while the weary sun sank into a bed of vermilion clouds and purple shadows. A week of useless searching in the north country left her bone-sore and stiff. Her armor chafed in a score of places.

The road led down into a forest-filled valley. Better to make camp in the shelter of trees, she figured, than be caught in the open by highwaymen or the night's cool wind. She urged her plodding mount down the gentle slope.

She wondered if Messalina was not, after all, as mad as

Caligula. That fat worm also chased a dream of immortality, but he took an easier way—ordered the Senate to declare him a god. Messalina, at least, showed more imagination.

Trees loomed over her. Darkness fell through the thick leaves and branches. When she could glimpse it, the sky blazed with countless stars. Like all Roman roads, the one she traveled was well-cut. She had no trouble finding her way.

A week of riding, and still she found no trace of Messalina's cult. Probably, the empress' sources, no matter how patrician, were mad as she. Everyone wished for eternal life, especially the rich who had most to lose by dying. New religions were springing up like weeds after a wet spring in Rome. But she doubted the power that each of them claimed. If she found Messalina's cult, she would find some chicken-killers and chanters, no more. Still, because Messalina required it, she searched.

A sound startled her: just an owl watching her pass. She smiled, then. Little by little, the mood of the woods began to relax her: the somber shadows, the chirping of insects, the slight breeze that stirred the leaves.

She began to sing; her voice rose, clear and mellow, one of the songs the pit-whores sang when their gladiator lovers must fight the next day. She sang a song of love and longing, a song of well-wishing and promise, sad, yet hopeful.

Some of the pit-whores were men, and she had used them. But they never sang for her as the women sang for the males. She never felt love from them as some of the women loved the men. It hadn't mattered then, but lately, she had begun to feel an odd absence, a fear that the arena had beaten something out of her. She wondered if she *could* love.

She found a clearing by the roadside. An old firepit marked it as a place where other travelers had rested. A pile of dry wood stood nearby, and, tethering her horse, she wasted no time building a small flame. Soon, a meager meal of grains and hot, salted meat filled her belly, and she reclined back against her saddle with a *sextarius* of wine. She considered removing her armor, but her prudent nature won out. She had worn it this long; what was one more night?

The stars winked at her through the leaves, and the small fire slowly dwindled. She tipped the wine bottle again and closed her eyes.

But she did not sleep. Something disturbed her, a creeping feeling that she was not alone, that something watched her. When she could bear the sensation no longer she sat suddenly up, reached for her *gladius*. The short, wide blade hissed from its sheath, glowed redly in the dull light of embers. Diana peered into the gloom.

A young girl regarded her from across the clearing. Small, piquant breasts shone bare, pale as faded moonlight. Tears gleamed on bloodless cheeks, though she made no sound of crying. An ivory hand raised, pointed into the woods.

Then, the child vanished, dissolved like dew in the sun.

"Jupiter Optimus Maximus!" Diana leaped to her feet, made warding signs in the air. She hadn't batted an eyelash. Her visitor had not slipped stealthily into the night; she had vanished, faded to nothingness!

A blood-chilling war cry drove all thought of the girl from her mind. She whirled, bringing her sword up. Three men jumped from the shadows. She swung the *gladius* twice, raking the nearest attacker in mid-leap. He fell screaming on the ground, his stomach a red ruin.

The others hit her hard, fast, bearing her down with their combined weight. One managed to grasp her sword arm and pin it before the blade could drink again. Hissing, she sank teeth into a soft shoulder, tasted bile and bit harder, tearing flesh. Pain-screaming filled her ears, and someone rolled off her. She struck at the final man with her free hand, seeking the vulnerable eyes with her nails. A fist impacted on her jaw, an elbow dug into her throat. She looked into the face above hers, saw a big smile etch across thin lips. The eyes burned with a feral madness.

She spat in those eyes, and when her foe blinked, smashed his mouth with the butt of her head, feeling teeth crunch. She strained, unbalanced her opponent and rolled from beneath him. She sprang up, sword ready.

But the men fled. She heard the crack and crash of brush as they ran blindly into the woods, leaving the body of their third comrade. She nudged it with a toe. Her sword had done better work than she at first thought. The two slashes had opened him wide; he was already dead.

She bent closer as something caught her eye. Hard to tell when night colored the world with grays and blacks. But she swore that his hem was purple. A patrician then, and no common robber.

She dragged the body a little way into the woods so she would not have to stare at it through the rest of the night. The *sextarius* was still half-full. She picked it up, took a long draught and sat back by her saddle to consider it all.

That girl had warned her. She had pointed to exactly where

the attackers were hiding. But was it a girl? Or had she only *seemed* to disappear, some trick of the darkness and emberlight?

She wiped a trickle of blood from her lip, then built her fire high again, afraid to sleep now. Half the night she stared musingly into the flames; the other half she gazed toward the place where she had dropped the body.

Morning brought little sunlight. A thick fog settled over the wood in the pre-dawn hours, an obscuring mist that crept among the old trunks, concealing all but the most immediate stretch of road.

She crept into the brush to confirm certain fears. None of her attackers bore weapons. Killing a patrician, let alone an unarmed one, could send her back to the arena. Not to fight; she didn't fear that. But for public crucifixion.

She found the body, stared at the colorful hem, began tearing grass and weeds to cover her deed.

Quickly, she saddled her horse and mounted. The fog made little eddies as she followed the road. *Like Hades come to earth*, she thought, and hugged her cloak tighter.

After a while, the sun climbed and the air warmed; the mist began to dissipate. The land began to rise; she knew she was leaving the valley.

At the edge of the wood an old rutted path splintered from the main road. It snaked up the hillside toward an ancient villa that squatted against the brightening sky. At first she thought to pass it by, but at one bend of its craggy path she glimpsed a girl much like the one who had saved her during the night. When she tried to reassure herself with a second look, the girl was gone.

She reached down to scratch a place beneath her greave where the edge had chafed her skin, and she peered up the twisting, narrow way. Suddenly, the villa piqued her curiosity, and she frowned at the mystery this strange young woman presented. She started her horse up the rough course.

A low stone wall surrounded the estate; an arch of black iron spotted with rust spanned the entrance. The cobbled walkway crumbled under her mount's hooves, but the lawn was well-manicured, and bright vines made a beautiful, tangled lace on the villa's walls.

A huge wooden door waited at the walkway's end. A rusted ring invited her to knock. Dismounting, she thumped it loudly. No answer. She knocked a second, a third time.

At last, a bolt slid back; the door eased open. A servant dressed in blue silk greeted her with a deep bow and a ready cup of cool wine. Mildly surprised, she accepted the cup and thanked him. It was sweet and very tasty as she drained the last droplet.

"Is your master at home?" she asked, passing the cup back into the servant's hands.

He made no answer, but bowed again and beckoned her inside.

*Perhaps, he's mute,* she decided as she followed him inside and waited while he bolted the door shut.

The villa's interior was opulent. White marble walls gleamed. Intricately detailed tapestries lined the halls; vases, busts and sculptures filled every niche and corner. The floor was carpeted with rich eastern rugs. The servant led her through two chambers to another set of doors. He pushed them open for her.

The room beyond was bright with sunlight that spilled through tall slits in the walls. Within, her host labored over a block of fine, pink marble. As yet, the sculpture was nothing recognizable though a goodly amount of stone was chiseled away. When he noticed her, he put down his tools at once, brushed off his hands and came toward her, smiling.

"Decius Paulus Castus," he named himself.

"Diana," she returned, disdaining to bow, taking note of the purple on his hem.

"No more?" He raised his eyebrows quizzically, but his tone remained polite.

"Just Diana."

He scratched his chin. "Not Roman, I see, despite your masculine martial garb. Greek, perhaps? Macedonian?"

"I'm a free Roman citizen." She thought of her *rudis*, the short staff of freedom hanging from her saddle. Would he ask to see it? That was his right.

Decius frowned, shrugged, then smiled again. "Diana!" he clapped his hands. "Of course! The armor should have reminded me. I saw you fight two years ago. You were the talk of Rome, the greatest *Secutor* in the games. And a woman!"

Her turn to shrug. Then, realizing he meant only to honor her accomplishments, she bowed. The gesture cost her nothing, though it seemed to please him. After all, he was her host.

"My poor studio is no place of comfort," he apologized, leading her through an archway to yet another chamber. It was equally large and much better furnished, more suitable for entertaining. He indicated a couch where she might recline and took another close by. The servant returned moments later bearing wine in exquisitely carved golden goblets. It was obvious her host had a taste for art.

Decius sipped from his cup, raised on one elbow. "Tell me, Gladiator, what brings you so far from the Sparkling City?"

She sampled the potent drink, found it to her liking. "I seek immortality," she said with a grin and took another taste.

Decius sat back, regarded her over the rim of his cup. "Then, you've come to the right place." His smoky, dark eyes seemed to dance along the golden edge as he watched her.

She took a long moment to study her host: no fattened patrician, spoiled by Rome's pleasures. His face was lean and hard, and he was tall, almost her height, broad of chest and shoulder. If not for the telltale softness of his hands, he might have been a warrior. His hair and close beard were dark; his eyes were darker yet, like pits she could fall into.

"What did you say?"

He held up his goblet, turned it slowly between his fingers so that it shimmered in the sunlight. "Art is immortal," he said carefully, "and I've filled my house with art." He winked at her, and a subtle grin turned up the corners of his lips. "But I'm sure that's not what you meant."

He sipped his wine sensually, tongue lingering on the goblet's rim. His voice rolled around her, deep and rich, each word a kind of caress. It had been a long time since a man attracted her as this one did.

"What would you do with immortality," he asked, "if it was something just lying around to be found?"

"Give it to the empress, Messalina," she answered. "She sent me on this stupid quest."

"What of yourself? Would you not want to share it and live forever?"

She drained her cup. The servant, waiting unobtrusively near, hurried to fill it again. "I'm living extra life, already," she said, meeting his gaze. "The gods allowed me to survive the arena. What right have I to ask for more?" She rose from the couch, taking her cup, and wandered about the room, sampling the fine things that were scattered everywhere so casually.

"All rulers dream of living forever, do they not?" Decius called from his seat. "But why Messalina?"

A lap-harp stood neglected on a pedestal. She brushed her fingers over the strings, raising a discordant note. It was badly out of tune. "For the usual reasons," she answered. "Fear of death, fear of losing her throne, fear of losing Claudius. Seems the emperor has been making moon-eyes at the Lady Agrippina. Messalina thinks to win him back with such a gift and secure her title in the bargain."

"She told you this?"

Diana nodded. "I say just bed him; if she can't hold him that way, she can't hold him at all."

She tuned a string and struck another chord, frowned at the result. Decius came up behind her. "Ah, they're all so greedy, royalty," he sighed. "I wonder what the empress would give for such a secret?"

She turned to him, took a slow drink. "If your question is rhetorical, then I've no answer." She took another drink, watching him carefully. "But, if you're making some kind of offer, I can tell you there's five hundred *aurei* in my saddlebags, a mere down payment to this new priest and his followers."

"A sizeable sum," Decius agreed. "I gather you're having no luck finding what you seek?"

Diana set her empty cup aside. "Of course not. Never in all the history of Rome has there been a cult dedicated to the worship of Orcus."

"The Death-god?" He raised an eyebrow, pursed his lips.

"So Messalina's sources claim. Yet, I've found no trace of them, nor anyone who admits knowledge of them."

He indicated the lap-harp. "Do you play?"

She nodded. "I learned as a child. In the training pens it was all that kept me sane. Later, it just kept me from thinking too much. It wasn't good for a gladiator to think."

He gestured toward the couches, took up her empty goblet. "Play for me," he urged. "Those strings have been silent for such a long time. This house has thirsted for music."

It took little persuading. She lifted the harp and carried it back to her couch, balanced it on her knees. The strings had not mildewed; once tuned, they still had good tone.

A song rose to her lips. She sang of the arena; of men who died bleeding in the hot sand; of fantastic matches and legendary warriors; great beasts with ripping claws, incarnadined fangs; of ephemeral life and fleeting glory. Her hands flowed like water over the strings, coaxing strange, unnatural harmonies into her music.

The servant crept closer after the first few notes and leaned on a table to listen, not daring to venture nearer. Decius reclined quietly, puppet to whatever mood her music created. She sang a spritely tune; he laughed and stamped his feet. She sang a mourning song, and a tear trickled on his cheek.

When she finished, he looked up. "Your songs have born rare seed in the fallow place where my soul once resided." He shook his head; a great and heavy sadness seemed to hang on him. The servant at last braved a remark; what a complex picture she presented with harp on knee and sword suspended at her side.

"So sensitive a talent," Decius remarked. "Why did they send you to the arena?"

A part of her went cold inside. She looked to the unshuttered windows. The light was failing; she had sung the day away. Night was not far off.

"I killed a man." She struck a chord on the harp, a plaintive note. Decius' eyes were full of questions, but his face reflected a kind of paternal concern that made her suddenly angry. "You wonder who it was, don't you? My master, stinking pig-shit that he was. I gutted him, like the dozens I killed in the games." She gave the harp a push. In a wistful sigh of disharmonious chords, the instrument hit the floor, and its delicately carved throat cracked. Rising over the broken harp, she glared at Decius, finding a peculiar delight in the dismay with which he regarded her destruction. "You asked my ancestry when I entered," she thundered. "How could I know my ancestry? I was born a slave, a stinking Roman slave, sold to a monster before I ever knew my mother!" She ground fist into palm. "But no longer! I'm free now. I fought for my freedom and won it! No Roman patrician could ever say as much!"

Decius knelt down, scooped up the tangled pieces of the harp. Thick tears spilled down his cheeks. He cradled the instrument in his arms, rocked it as if it were a child. Moaning softly, he rose, crossed the room. At the archway, he looked back.

"Can you make such music and be so cold?"

Just another man, she told herself, and she had known so many. Yet, some quality in him had forced her to expose a part of herself she had thought long buried: a wound only scabbed over, never healed, now bleeding again. She covered the distance in three swift strides and slapped the harp from his hands, outraged. "It's so!" she hissed. "You Romans made it so!"

He stared numbly, his face so close to hers. Then, he gathered up the shattered instrument again, hurried away into the deepening twilight of the villa's halls. The servant hurried after him.

She rubbed her temples, stared down the hall, now empty. She listened for footsteps, voices, heard nothing. Where Decius had gone, she didn't know. She was left alone.

He had given no insult, no provocation to spark her Gaulish behavior. He had offered shelter and good drink. In return, she had smashed his cherished harp. She cursed her temper.

*Ungrateful,* her master had often called her. There was nothing to do now but leave quietly, and cause her host no further grief.

She passed through the studio where the shapeless stone sculpture cast a long, ponderous shadow across her path. Twilight was falling fast. She'd have little time to regain the main road before night closed in. She reached the old wooden doors and threw back the bolt.

Decius' servant was waiting. She saw at once the quarter staff in his hands and reached for her *gladius.* The blade hissed free of the sheath, but the lower length of the staff swept it from her grasp. She threw up her arms to protect her head, but the servant struck again, very skillfully, just below her ribs. Pain shot through her side. Then, came the blow to her head which blacked out all consciousness.

She woke slowly, the feel of cool stone penetrating her thin linen garment. Her armor was gone, but the weight of her sheathed *gladius* pressed between her breasts. Nearby, voices chanted strange poems to the accompaniment of flutes. She lay still, listening with eyes closed to learn what she might.

Then, another sound rose over the rest, a low, anguished moan.

Never in the arena had she heard the like. She sat up, snatching sheath, baring steel.

Decius stood but an arm's length away, watching a throng of bodies twisting, contorting in the light of torches. She recognized faces, patricians who had visited Messalina's court. Two men especially caught her eye—bite marks and broken teeth gave them away.

The moan sounded again, behind her. She turned.

An immense sculpture loomed, the god Orcus on his throne. Its stone musculature fairly rippled in the torchlight. The eyes, dark obsidian pits, gleamed. Each mighty hand clenched an exquisitely carved soul; each mighty foot ground another under its heal. It had no genitals; Orcus was a god of death, not life.

Grasped between the chiseled calves was a huge, spoked wheel. A pitiful thing that might once have been a man lay stretched over the hub. Cowering at what was left of its feet, the pale child she had met in the forest wept silent tears.

"Welcome to the Temple of Orcus." She turned to face a smiling Decius. He tapped his brow. "I apologize for my servant. He was unnecessarily brutal."

She rose from the stone dais where she had reclined, keeping her blade between them. "Given half a chance I'd have skewered him."

"No doubt," he sighed. He turned away from her, indicated the dancers as they moved through the grotto, spinning, whirling, always returning to the marble pool at the center, dipping fingers in the rippling black water, spinning away again.

"Worshipers," Decius explained, "seeking the same thing as your Messalina. But they've not yet proven their dedication to Orcus. Their supplications go unanswered."

She patted the stone dais, still warm with the heat of her body. "Some kind of altar, I suppose?" She thought to kill him then, yet she hesitated. Aside from knocking her in the head and bruising a couple of ribs, he'd done her no harm. He hadn't even taken her sword.

Decius grinned. "No, my dear." He pointed to the Sculpture, the wheel and its victim. "That is the altar. I sculpted it myself. Note the elegant detail, the imagination. Some claim all roads lead to Rome." He folded his arms in smug satisfaction and pride. "They're wrong, of course. All roads lead to Hades."

*The wheel is the world.* She could not but admire the symbolism. *The spokes are the roads; the hub is Hades. And Orcus rules over all.* It was horrible beauty.

The thing on the wheel whimpered, and she crept closer to see. Ropes had cut the flesh where the wrists were bound. Most of the fingers were missing, and the toes. Broken bones protruded through the skin. Two sightless pools of limpid humor stared blankly from the shaven skull. No, not shaven; the hair had been singed away. All the limbs were disjointed, and livid scars and welts made a crimson lace on every part. Despite the mutilated organs, she could tell it was once a man. The child at its feet looked up at her, streaming tears.

Diana resisted an urge to vomit. She had seen what men could do with a sword or trident, had witnessed the work of the great cats' claws, had waded through the bleeding entrails and severed limbs of luckless gladiators. She had witnessed the crucifixions and the burnings, the beheadings and impalements.

Yet Caligula, for all his cruelty, could have studied at Decius' feet.

She bit her lip, grasped her sword more firmly.

"You came seeking immortality, Diana." Her host slid past her, drawing a short *pugio* from the folds of his toga. He reached up, drew the sharp blade across the tattered genitals of his captive. "Watch well, for this is the secret." He leaned his head closer, oblivious to the whimpering and to the child who burst into fresh tears. The chanting of the worshipers grew suddenly louder as he caught the first drops of blood on his tongue.

Then, he cupped his hands, filled them with scarlet, and approached her.

"Taste immortality!" he crooned. "Drink the blood from a tortured man's organs each month as the moon renews itself, pray to the Darkest of Lords, and promise him the most precious thing you have in all the world." He pushed his hands toward her lips. "Perhaps, he'll heed you, then, as he heard me."

She knocked his hands away and backed a step, bringing her *gladius* between them.

"Drink with me, Diana." Decius licked the incarnadined fingers of one hand, extended the other to her. "You have a gift worth living for; play and sing to me for all eternity!"

She backed another step. "The gods must hate you to have driven you so far into madness."

He wiped his hands over his toga, staining the white linen. "They do not hate me! Orcus, himself, has granted me life eternal so that I may continue my art! All the sculptures and tapestries you have seen are mine; I made them! All the vases my pottery, the goblets my castings! Should I die and deprive the world of such beauty?"

The chanting and dancing stopped. With a chill, she realized all eyes were upon her now. The throng drew closer. She circled warily around Decius, putting him between the crowd and herself.

"What of him?" she said, jerking her thumb at the creature on the wheel now at her back. "What of the beauty he might have created? Is immortality worth so much that it drives you to this?"

Decius shrugged. "He vinted a very mediocre wine of no particular merit. All his suffering and agony, and even his life, are small price to pay. I have much yet to give the world. These hands have much to create!"

She whirled, drove her *gladius* straight into the heart of the man on the wheel. He drew a sharp breath, then sighed out his life. She brought her blade back down, faced her host. Blood dripped from her weapon's point. "Perhaps, you'd like to suck on this!"

She thrust the *gladius* upward beneath his ribs, twisted hard. But the blade came out clean.

"Again," Decius invited, smiling, holding his arms wide for her to strike.

She thrust again, twice more.

The throng of worshipers screamed, bore down upon her. She spun to fight them off.

But it was Decius who stopped them. "Behold the power of Orcus!" he roared and ripped away his garment. No wound showed on his flesh. He turned slowly so that even she could see. She stared at him, at her sword, at the altar.

"It's real!" he whispered to her as his followers began to chant and dance in a frenzy. They surrounded her, spinning and leaping, running to the pool, carrying back handfuls of the black water, sprinkling her, sprinkling Decius. "My pact with Orcus is real."

She fell back, thinking to protect the girl. But the child was gone. Diana looked for her among the others, but she was not there. She had only herself to defend.

"Your most precious gift, you said," she shouted at her host. "What did you give Orcus?"

"A diadem," he answered proudly, "of purest gold, glittering with perfect pearls and finely faceted gemstones; the pinnacle of my art. The world has never seen its like."

"When did you make it?" she challenged. "Keep back!"

He brushed aside her useless sword, a hand reached up, touched her shoulder, his dark eyes smoldered. "It was my finest creation!"

She backed away again, felt flesh touch her neck, the twisted knee of the man she had freed from torment. "You fool! And this sculpture to your god? Before or after your pact?"

"I made this entire grotto to please him."

She almost laughed. "Stupid, stupid fool! Don't you see? What work have you done since Orcus answered your prayer?

His eyes narrowed. "I have a new piece in my studio," he snapped.

"A shapeless lump of stone," she charged, "nearly chiseled away to nothing! That harp—you played it once, didn't you? Now, you can't!"

He stared at his hands in confusion. Again, the dancers stopped to watch. She sensed their unease and uncertainty. They were patricians, yes, Rome's nobility; but they were children waiting for Decius to lead them.

"You've paid a greater price than you know for immortality," she charged. "Your gate has rusted; the metal no longer shines with beauty. Your cobbled walkway is ruined; where is the beauty in that? You cannot play the harp. You cannot sculpt. Don't you see? Orcus has taken your most precious possession, all right. He has taken the very thing that made life so precious to you: your gift for creating beauty!''

''It's not true!'' he shouted. ''I still have the gift! I can still create!'' He shook a fist at her. ''You could have shared immortality with me! You loved me; I felt that when you sang for me. For just an instant, you loved me. Your perfect voice could have survived the ages, but you throw it away by turning against me!'' He backed away from her now, beckoning his worshipers closer.

She scanned the grotto, seeking the way out. A tall hedge surrounded all, and above that she saw the top of a stone wall. No arch or entrance could she find. Perhaps, it was hidden by the foliage.

''Your voice, Diana,'' Decius said softly. ''Your voice is precious to me.'' The others pressed around her, closer, ever closer as he spoke. ''And I must give it to Orcus. He demands precious things, Diana.'' To his followers he called. ''Let her ride the wheel.''

Hands reached for her, and she erupted in motion. Her sword sank deeply into one man's vitals; his blood spurted over her grip as she withdrew the blade. With her free fist she smashed at the nearest face, crushing lips and teeth. She kicked, struck with her elbows, cut and chopped until the earth was slick beneath her feet. She carved a pathway for herself and gained the center of the grotto.

How long since she had tasted fear? Decius' followers lacked his power, but they were many. She envisioned her body stretched on the wheel, maimed and broken as the thing that yet hung there. Who would come to grant her the red gift of release?

They came at her again, fanatics all, screaming. She retreated, hoping to gain more ground, but her foot caught; she slipped.

The last thing she saw before the water rushed over her was the look of fear and anger on Decius' face, and the forbidding cry that bubbled in his throat, a sound she never heard.

Fire filled her lungs and panic every other part. It was only a grotto pool, yet a current caught her, dragged her deeper than she knew was possible. All her strength proved useless; the cold black water swept her along, filling her nostrils. She opened her mouth to scream; her limbs thrashed.

Just as she knew she would drown, as she gave herself to her gods, the current released her. Wet darkness surrounded her, nothing to see. Which way to the surface? She chose a direction, prayed it was the right one, and kicked.

Her head and shoulders broke the water; she sucked air, gasping, coughing. The grotto pool had become a river; the bank was not far. When the pain in her lungs lessened she swam slowly toward it.

Suddenly, she stopped and treaded water to hold her place. A crowd was gathering on the shore; why hadn't she seen them or heard them before? She began to swim again, keeping a wary eye ahead of her.

Her foot touched sandy bottom; she stood, waded ashore, acutely aware that she had lost her sword. The crowd stared at her, silent, then parted to either side.

Eight porters bearing an immense throne came forward through the ranks, set their burden down and blended in among the other men and women. On the throne, a figure stirred, smiled, and waved her forward.

She had seen his face on a hundred fallen gladiators, watched as he stalked the arena, felt his breath on her neck each time she fought. How could she not know him when he greeted her?

She gazed back at the river and shivered, recalling the tales. Orpheus with his lyre dared such a journey to win his Eurydice; Odysseus to question the prophet Tiaresius; Theseus; Hercules; Aeneas with his golden bough and a witch to guide him. They made the descent from the upper world to the lower through caves or fissures or—by water.

*"Porta Libitinaria,"* she whispered, recalling the strange pool and the worshippers who danced around it, "A gate to Death."

"Welcome to Erebus, my child, flesh after my heart and spirit." The voice boomed, filling her.

She struck a pose. "Greetings yourself, Lord Carrion-Eater." She surveyed her surroundings. No sun, but a dull, gray light pervaded. No trees or grass, but barren plain stretched as far as she could see. In the distance to left and right two misty veils rose. If tales were true, she knew what lands lay beyond them. She repressed a shiver and turned back to her host. "Gnawed any good bones lately?"

Orcus' laughter shook the foundations of Hell itself. Though he remained seated on his throne of glittering onyx, his presence suddenly seemed to loom larger, more menacing. She trembled; her knees nearly buckled. With tremendous effort she kept her balance and her nerve, refusing to bend before him.

Then, he was once again a man on a throne, or at least, the semblance of one. "I admire a woman with spirit," he said.

She winced. So even Death had a sense of humor. She'd seen precious little of it in the arena.

He beckoned again. "Come share a cup of good Phalernian with me." A pale young woman stepped from behind the throne bearing a tray with *sextarius* and goblets. Orcus poured. He passed her a cup. "You realize, of course, you've not met the usual requirement for coming here?"

She looked at the men and women gathered around, pale shadows of their former selves; souls, she realized. She lifted the proffered cup to her lips, then sniffed. "Good Phalernian, my eye!" She cast the wine contemptuously aside and stared at the empty vessel. "That stuff reeks like . . . !"

"Like something dead?" the god offered, again exploding into laughter.

She clapped hands over her ears, waited for him to compose himself.

"Oh my," he said, wiping his lips, setting his own cup aside. "Well, your presence has altered all the rules, so let's call up my second guest." He snapped his fingers and thunder rolled out over the river where she had emerged. A bolt of white crackling lightning struck the water, sending a cloud of steam rising.

"Watch this," Orcus instructed her. "I've been practicing for some time and had no chance at all to show off." Another of the attendant spirits stepped forward, passed him a small, flat stone. Orcus rose slightly, cast the stone. It sailed out over the river and down, skipped twice on the waves. As it lifted for a third time, Diana noticed that something else broke the water's surface, sputtering.

"Decius!" she called.

The stone dipped a third time, ricocheted on the priest's skull and sank. Orcus roared, clapped his hands in delight. "Don't worry!" he snapped petulantly, noting her frown. "He's not hurt; dazed a bit, perhaps. See, he swims ashore!" He seemed to expect her approval, but the frown only deepened. "The simple amusements are all that make this place bearable." He pointed a finger upward. "*They* never invite me to visit anymore."

"Nobody likes a joker," she muttered.

Decius climbed out of the river, his once-white toga muddied, a swelling bruise coloring his left temple. No thin shadow of a man, she observed, no soul. This was the flesh and blood of Decius.

The priest started to speak.

"Be silent, Turnip," Orcus commanded. "Our pact is broken. A living mortal has entered my kingdom through the gate I charged you to guard."

"It was an accident!" Decius shouted. "The plebian bitch tripped . . . !"

She faced him. "He'll have my soul soon enough, but not with my flesh broken on your obscene altar!"

He strode toward her, reddening. "I'll feed you to him, myself, piece by piece!"

Orcus rose from his throne; Decius stopped in mid-step, surprise blossoming on his features, then fear. A horrible smile spread on the Death-god's lips. "That's better." He turned to Diana. "I never liked him, but he groveled so impressively."

"Let me fight him," she hissed. "Immortal he may be, but if I cut him in small enough pieces. . . ."

The Death-god shrugged. "To what purpose, child?"

"Vengeance," she returned. "Some poor creature suffered terrible torment at his hands before I released its tortured soul with a sword-stroke. And who knows how many others? There was a girl."

Orcus regarded her with a steady gaze. She saw her own face reflected in the black depths of his eyes. "What Decius did was according to my instructions."

She drove a fist into her palm. "But it was he who sought your teaching. Selfish desire compelled him, no higher motive, and for self-interest he traded the souls of others." She turned on Decius. "He is lower than the least of animals!"

Orcus scratched his chin. "And yet, he has served me."

She whirled again, brushing wet strands of hair from her eyes. "Have I not served you? Tally the scores, Corpse-Chewer. You owe me."

Orcus let go a laugh that made the sand beneath her feet ripple and tossed high waves on the river at her back. "Owe you, Little One?"

She braced her hands on her hips defiantly. "Summon the souls he has sent to you."

Orcus pursed his lips, then nodded. He crooked his finger, and three souls separated themselves from the crowd. The nearest showed a gaping wound on its chest; she knew him, then, for the man she had slain on the wheel. "There was a girl," she said, "already a ghost when we met."

Again, Orcus nodded, pointed to the soul who wore her sword-mark. "His young bride, a suicide. When her groom disappeared she took her life for grief. Her spirit wanders the earth, for no suicide may cross the River Styx."

It was the Law of the Gods. Diana pitied the poor child, never to know rest, denied even the meager comforts of the Underworld. Her life, too, weighted Decius' scale.

She spoke in a low, solemn whisper. "Now call those souls I've dispatched in fair combat."

The scales tipped far in her favor; she gazed with barely controlled passion on the many faces, men and women. Some she once called friend, if only for a day or a week, until they met in the arena where all friendships ended. Some she did not know; their faces had been concealed in visored helms.

She drew a slow breath. "You owe me," she said to Orcus. "See how well I've served you? But I killed fairly; my foes died fighting with weapons in their grasps." She stabbed a finger at Decius, but never looked from the Death-God's face. "I'll not let him return to the world of the living."

Decius walked calmly around her, stood at the foot of the onyx throne, folded his arms. But his expression and the light in his eyes belied his outward composure. "What are the lives of a few miserables compared to the beauty I can give the world?"

"The love a man bears his bride," she snapped, "that is beautiful! You destroyed that. You blind pathetic!" She shook her head, not quite understanding the tears that welled in the corners of her eyes, unable to stop them. "You use people! As my master used me! As the emperor to entertain the citizens! As Messalina uses me! But, it ends here." She extended a hand, appealing to the Dark God. "Hear my bargain."

Orcus steepled his fingers. "You may have noticed things are a trifle dull down here." A grin curled the corners of his lips. "What do you offer?"

"A combat," she answered, "a true Roman Games. If I win, then your priest remains here forever. If I lose, I stay to provide you with diversion in contest after contest until time and the Gods themselves end," she shrugged, watching his face grow suddenly impassive, "or until you get bored with that amusement, too."

"A brave wager." He rubbed his chin; the grin did not return to those dark lips. "A gamble that does you honor, win or lose. But you must know, child, that your own days on earth are ended. You will never leave my land."

A cold hand closed over her heart. She thought of the tales, of Orpheus and Aeneas. Were they lies? She stared at Decius' suddenly smiling face, at the mirthless visage of the Dread Lord above her. She found no words to speak, but her mouth fell open.

Orcus held out a hand toward her. "Do not fear me now, Daughter; you have known me for too long. As a slave, as a gladiator.'' The fingers of that hand curled, beckoning, and she moved across the sand past Decius, up the three short steps of the onyx throne until she stood eye-level with the Deity. ''Look into my eyes and see there is nothing to fear.'' His hand settled on her right shoulder. She cringed then, ashamed, relaxed. The touch did not chill as she expected, but warmed her.

The god smiled, then. ''You have accused my priest of selfishness. Will you fight for something besides yourself?''

Decius started. ''What?''

She turned her back on him. ''Was my offer not selfless?''

Orcus touched her other shoulder and shook her gently as a true father might. ''Indeed. And since you have no self to fight for now I'll offer new terms.'' He crooked a finger, and the soul of the man who had died on the wheel stepped from the crowd once more. ''You lived beyond your allotted time on earth, Diana, surviving in the arena when no woman should have. Time after time you eluded me, though I waited to welcome you after every game.'' He took his hands from her shoulders; she walked down the small steps and stood by Decius. The priest was pale, shaking.

''This is the shade of Gaius Antaeus, a vintner,'' Orcus continued. ''His time, and that of his bride, were cut short.'' The grin returned to his lips. ''Fight for them, if you will, child. And if you win, Gaius and bride will live again with a draft of Lethe's waters to wipe clean their memories. Is it a bargain?''

She nodded, finding that grin suddenly contagious.

But Decius was furious. ''Lord, I have served you well! Remember your pact to me. I am no warrior to take on one of Rome's best, even if she is a woman!''

Thunder rolled thickly, suddenly, drowning the priest's shouting. Orcus rose on his throne, towering darkly, eyes flashing. The sand swirled up about Decius, pelting, stinging him until he was blasted from his feet and lay whimpering on the ground.

''Toady, get up!'' Orcus commanded when the sands no longer swirled and the thunder stilled. ''You are my plaything, something to occupy my more prosaic moments, an amusement.'' A black fist shook, and the waves of the Styx leaped their banks. ''You dare think I would allow you the honor of combat with this woman? You are not worthy! Have no fear on that account. Another will do that work in your place.''

Diana stiffened, then forced herself to relax. Down here, she was rapidly learning, each new moment brought a dark new twist. It was true, without training Decius would be easy meat for her to carve. She should have foreseen Orcus would choose another champion. Everything was an *amusement* to him. With Decius to fight the amusement would have ended quickly.

"Bring on who you will," she called. "My wager stands."

Decius still cowered in the sand. "You stole my art," he moaned despondently. "I could make music, and you stole that. I created. . . ."

Orcus sighed, sat back in his seat, turned a paternal gaze on her. "You are a child of my spirit. Him . . ." He shrugged huge shoulders. "I stole nothing but what he gave away. His body lived, for he offered me his soul. What artist, what man or woman for that matter, can find beauty without their soul?"

She looked up at him, complex and magnificent and all trickery. So she had always known him, though for a while a veil had fallen over her eyes. "Call up your champion, Lord of Vultures. If you grow bored so easily, perhaps it's from listening to yourself."

He looked at her strangely, almost angrily, then titanic laughter burst from him. "Well then, so be it!" Orcus snapped his fingers. An unfamiliar spirit appeared beside the throne, a man tall as Diana, twice as broad in the shoulders, huge and rippling with hard muscle for all his paleness. "His name is Condorus."

She knew the name. A gladiator like herself, but years before her time. A *bestiarius*, he fought the big cats and bears until his foot slipped in the bloodied sand.

The souls of the old warriors lent them armor. On her right arm she strapped the *manica*, the metal-plated leather wrapping with a cinch around her chest to keep it in place. She added a *balteaus*, a wide band of metal plates which buckled around her waist and middle. High greaves protected her legs; but for this combat she refused a helm. She took a *gladius* for weapon and a small rectangular shield.

Her foe chose less armor, net and trident. A *pugio* hung on a belt around his waist.

*Secutor* then, against *retiarius*. She nodded approvingly. It was a contest she many times had won. She muttered the traditional salute, then grinned at the irony of it.

"I am *editor* and *lanista*," Orcus intoned ritualistically. "Condorus, win and you shall have life again upon the earth and wealth and power to go with it. You, Diana, win and this is your reward: Tartarus shall have the priest, and you the Elysian Fields." He raised a hand, traditional blessing. "You fight to my determination."

Condorus struck before she realized the battle had begun. His weighted net twined about her feet; he pulled, stretching her full-length on the ground. His trident sought the exposed flesh above her *balteaus*.

The spectators would be on their feet mad with cheering, she thought. But there was no *cavea* today, just a throng of silent spirits and Death himself who cheered for none.

She spat sand and brought her shield up barely in time, deflecting the fatal thrust. Poor timing; she cursed herself. She should have trapped the triple points beneath her shield's edge after turning it aside, then smashed the haft with her blade.

Too late for should-have-dones. Condorus thrust again. She screamed as one barb raked the fleshy muscle of her tricep.

"First blood!" Decius cried excitedly. "First blood to Condorus!"

Even as she screamed she sat quickly up, swung her sword and severed the short cord that bound the net to Condorus' wrist. So great was the tension he maintained to keep her feet entangled that, suddenly released, he pitched backward.

They came up at the same time, the net on the sand between them. Condorus drew the *pugio*. She eyed him warily and made a clumsy feint as if her wound had weakened her. He made a grab for his net, his best defense, as she hoped he would.

But trident, *pugio* and net were too much. Her sword darted, carving flesh from his shoulder, drawing a cry of pain. She stepped in then, smashing aside the trident with her shield, turning the thrust of his *pugio* on her *manica*. She shoved the *gladius* deep into his armpit, up through the muscle of his chest.

Condorus staggered, sank to one knee. Nerveless fingers dropped the trident. He looked up, eyes burning with pain, seeking mercy.

Orcus regarded him but a moment and turned thumbs down. Condorus' eyes closed; his body sagged and fell forward face down in the sand.

Only then did she see that he shed no blood. "What has happened to him?" she asked hesitantly. Somehow, it had failed to occur to her that Condorus was already dead and it was his spirit she fought. Yet, the spirit lay unmoving, its side gaping from her stroke.

"Nothing has happened to him," Oracus answered. "He awaits my command to rise, that's all. He knows his place is here." A deep sigh followed his words; he leaned his chin on one palm. "It was over so quickly. I'd hoped for more entertaining combat. Oh well, he *was* out of practice."

She gazed with mingled disbelief and loathing at the figure on the throne, at the souls clustered around him, a numberless mass, she saw now. Suddenly, she turned and flung the *gladius* far out over the Styx. It struck the water's surface and sank, leaving small, concentric waves to mark the place, ripples which soon were smooth again.

"The terms, Father Crow," she demanded. "I have won again."

Orcus slumped petulantly in his seat. "Gaius Antaeus is, at this very moment, hurrying to his bride. As for the rest. . . ." He gestured.

A new light caught her attention. Far to her right the veil of mists lifted to reveal meadows and valleys of breathtaking loveliness, fields of ghostly *asphodels*, spirits who made music with their laughter. "The Elysian Fields," Orcus said. "You have won paradise."

Far to her left the other misty veil parted, exposing a darkness that threatened even the glory of the Field. "That way lies Tartarus, prison of the Titan gods and all damned spirits. Your path lies there, priest."

Decius stared at Orcus, then Diana, at the Elysian Fields, at his own artless hands. Already, the color was gone from his cheeks. Pale as the other spirits, he cast one longing glance at paradise, then turned and walked toward darkness.

Diana watched his back, but no satisfaction filled her. She recalled his villa, the sculptures and tapestries, the harp and how he hungered for her to play and sing. *A plaything*, Orcus called him, an *amusement*. And an amusement that no longer amused was cast aside. Could she blame a fool if the gods made him such?

"Wait!" she shouted, and Decius stopped, turned. She strode to the foot of the throne and shook her fist. "I would fight another combat," she said to Death, "for the right to take him with me."

But the Dark One shook his head. "You have thrown away your weapon. Let it be. Go to your peace."

She spat, then winked at Decius. Lean and hard and beautiful she thought of him once, and he was still that. "Old Bone-chewer! There's no shortage of blades around you, I'll wager!"

Orcus leaned slowly forward, scratched his chin, rubbed his lips, steepled his fingers. "If you win, he goes with you. But what if you lose?"

She just smiled.

Dorothy Heydt says of herself, "As for my few words of biographical data, if I'm not careful they'll be longer than the story. You could describe me as the kind of idiot who tries to do it all at once; husband (one) kids (two) house (medium) garden (small) job (large; documentation editor at the University's computer center,) school (classics) and the odd bit of writing."

One could hardly characterize "Things Come in Threes" better than Dorothy does herself: "the odd bit of writing." It's a very odd bit indeed, but we thought it absolutely the right note on which to wind up an anthology of warrior women and sorceresses, because after reading it we groaned and said "Oh, this is absolutely the *end*." And so we let it be.—MZB

# THINGS COME IN THREES
## by Dorothy J. Heydt

*After the conquest of Tarentum [in 272 B.C.], Rome turned her attention to the small independent city of Margaron. . . .*

PSEUDOLUS MENDAX,
*Histories*

Cynthia crossed the street warily, and hurried into the shelter of the city wall. Ballista stones the size of her head had been arcing over the walls until a few minutes ago. Now there was an ominous silence outside the gates, and the men atop the walls were scurrying back and forth like a line of terrified ants. She slipped inside the door at the base of the gate tower, unguarded in all the confusion, and set her feet on the ladder.

She had climbed some ten or fifteen rungs when a great crash resounded through the darkness and nearly shook her loose. She clutched at the iron-bound casket wrapped in her stole, and struggled up the ladder to the top of the tower.

An old man sat on the wooden floor under the arrow slits, holding his head in his hands—an old man in a blue robe embroidered with silver, the mage Palamedes. A younger man bent over him, holding a cup; a fair-haired youth with a mere suggestion of beard creeping through the pimples. That would be his son Demetrios. They were the only unarmed men Cynthia had seen in the last five days. Margaron's Captain and two sergeants stood around them, their faces as gray as their beards. "Let me through, please."

The young man raised his head and scowled at her. "We don't need whores here this morning. Where's Euelpides the physician?"

"Dead these four days. I'm Cynthia, his daughter, and a respectable widow, so restrain your tongue. What happened to Palamedes?"

"One of those stones clipped him on the head," the youth said. "He's awake now, but he's not in his wits. And we're running out of time—" another great crash interrupted him. They peered through the arrow slits to the road below.

For three weeks the Romans had pushed steadily across the countryside toward Margaron's walls. There had been little of the usual devastation—farmhouses burnt down, cattle slaughtered or driven off—for the Romans were concerned simply with taking the city as quickly as they might. Now, at the base of the walls a hundred or more Roman soldiers defended themselves from the missiles hurled down onto their heads by the men of Margaron. Some raised overhead wicker shields covered with leather; others lifted the battering ram in its slings and carried it backward for another rush at the gates. The bronze-bound wood was already showing signs of caving in at the center. And the Romans, under the calm eyes of their captain, seemed ready to go on battering at the gates all day, or until they went down.

Cynthia turned back to the old mage. "Palamedes, can you stop them?" (Crash!)

The old man looked up at her and smiled. "Salted olives," he said.

"Hellebore," Cynthia muttered, and opened her casket. "Give me that wine."

Demetrios handed her the cup, and she poured dark liquid into it from a thumb-sized flask that had started life as an alabaster perfume bottle. With nods and smiles and soft words she got the mixture down the old man's throat. It was like feeding a child. "The Pleiades are down," he quoted sadly, "and the night is half gone." (Crash!)

"His talk is all like that," Demetrius said. "And I don't know how to work the spell."

"What spell?"

Demetrios shrugged. "The one that uses these." He pointed to what lay at Palamedes' side: a bronze sword, a crumpled-edged roll of parchment, a quartz crystal the size of a child's fist, girdled with a band of gold. And all three—she bent closer—marked with some kind of writing. "What do they say?"

"Well, this one says—" he pointed to the scroll—" 'I am Pargas, powerful among the *daemonia*; like Time itself I cover the land and wear down the sturdy rocks.' This one—" the sword—"says, 'I Chalkas am powerful beyond mere words; books of lore I cleave in two, and tear all windy words to tatters.' " (Crash!) "And the crystal says, 'I Krymos defy Ares and Zeus alike; swords and thunderbolts I shatter beneath my weight.' " He spread his hands again, as if to say, "That's all I know about it."

"They go together, don't they," Cynthia said. "The crystal says he can break swords, the sword says—" (Crash!)

"My father has had these things for years," Demetrios said. "He kept them in three chests, as far away from each other as he could. Until today."

"The raven is thirsty," Palamedes muttered, and reached for the wine cup. Demetrios refilled it for him.

"I don't even know if I should let them sit there, side by side," the youth went on. (Crash!) "They're growing warm to the touch."

"And you have no idea what they're supposed to do?"

"They're supposed to drive the Romans away," Demetrios said. "And you need all three if they're not to turn on you. Other than that—" he shrugged a third time. (Crash!)

"You need all three," Cynthia mused. "The sword, the scroll, the stone. Well, of course!" And she reached out to grasp the crystal, but Demetrios seized her wrist and hauled her to her feet.

"Old fool, are you going to meddle with what even *I* don't understand?" The dark stole slipped back from her head, and a shaft of light from the arrow-slit fell across her face. "Pardon me. Young fool, I should say." (Crash!)

"I'm twenty," she said, pulling her wrist away and rubbing it. "Old enough to know my craft; old enough to be a wife and a widow and to lose my father, who was all my kin, to these bloody Romans. But of course you're right," she went on meekly. "These things must be dangerous." She looked down. "Zeus! What's that?"

The boy bent down to look, and Cynthia hit him, hard, with the flat of her hand on the side of his neck. He went down softly, as she snatched the fragile scroll out of his way, and lay with his head in his father's lap.

She tucked the scroll in her bodice, took the crystal in one hand and the sword in the other. The boy was right, they were uncomfortably warm. (Crash!, and a splintering sound that went right through her heart.) She ran out onto the walls, past the line of nervous soldiers trying to find a target for their slings, and looked down at the Romans. They were just drawing back the ram for another stroke, and several feet of road lay bare before the gates. She hesitated for a moment. This was a terrible gamble, a desperate trick. "Hermes," she whispered, and threw the sword and the crystal to the pavement below. The scroll from her bodice fluttered down to join them.

A blue light was rising from the sword and the crystal as they lay together before the gates, a deadly glow that seared the eyes. But as the scroll fell between them, the light drew back and grew into a whirlpool of all the colors of the rainbow, twice the height of a man. The Romans fell back, leaving the ram to lie in the road.

Three figures rose out of the whirlpool, white and red and gold, neither gods nor men, with bodies like waterspouts and teeth like crocodiles'. The whirlpool died away in a scatter of dust devils along the road, but still the figures spun, each pursuing the next. Their terrible eyes spared hardly a glance for the fleeing Romans or the clay-faced men of Margaron huddled atop the wall; all their attention was for each other. White Pargas smothering golden Krymos bludgeoning red Chalkas cleaving white Pargas. The wall trembled.

Demetrios was beside her, rubbing his neck. "And now?"

"Now we take your father home. No man will touch the gates today. If Palamedes recovers his wits, he can send the *daemonia* back where they belong. If not—" she cast an uneasy eye on a crack slowly widening in the road below—"I'm afraid they'll bring the city down. We'll have time at least to leave at our leisure. There are boats in the harbor, and I've always wanted to see Syracuse." She urged Palamedes to his feet, and risked one more glance at the turmoil in the road.

"Paper covers stone, stone breaks scissors, scissors cut paper," Cynthia said. "Who says the gods haven't a sense of humor?"

*But it fell to the gods to subdue Margaron, which within two years' time had fallen into the sea, where its ruins may be seen to this day at low tide.*

PSEUDOLUS MENDAX,
*Histories*

## DAW PRESENTS MARION ZIMMER BRADLEY

### Darkover Novels

| | |
|---|---|
| DARKOVER LANDFALL | #UE1806—$2.25 |
| THE SPELL SWORD | #UE1675—$1.95 |
| THE HERITAGE OF HASTUR | #UE1744—$2.95 |
| THE SHATTERED CHAIN | #UE1840—$2.95 |
| THE FORBIDDEN TOWER | #UE1752—$2.95 |
| STORMQUEEN! | #UE1951—$3.50 |
| TWO TO CONQUER | #UE1876—$2.95 |
| SHARRA'S EXILE | #UE1836—$3.50 |
| HAWKMISTRESS! | #UE1958—$3.50 |
| THENDARA HOUSE | #UE1857—$3.50 |

### Friends of Darkover Anthologies

| | |
|---|---|
| THE KEEPER'S PRICE | #UE1931—$2.50 |
| SWORD OF CHAOS | #UE1722—$2.95 |

### Other

| | |
|---|---|
| HUNTERS OF THE RED MOON | #UE1713—$1.95 |
| THE SURVIVORS | #UE1861—$2.95 |
| GREYHAVEN | #UE1815—$2.50 |